HOPES AND DREAMS FOR THE SEASIDE GIRLS

TRACY BAINES

Boldwood

First published in Great Britain in 2022 by Boldwood Books Ltd. This paperback edition first published in 2023.

1

Cover Design: Colin Thomas

Cover Photography: Colin Thomas

Every effort has been made to obtain the necessary permissions with reference to copyright material, both illustrative and quoted. We apologise for any omissions in this respect and will be pleased to make the appropriate acknowledgements in any future edition.

A CIP catalogue record for this book is available from the British Library.

Paperback ISBN: 978-1-78513-801-0

Hardback ISBN: 978-1-80426-510-9

Ebook ISBN: 978-1-80426-507-9

Kindle ISBN: 978-1-80426-506-2

Audio CD ISBN: 978-1-80426-515-4

MP3 CD ISBN: 978-1-80426-514-7

Digital audio download ISBN: 978-1-80426-512-3

Digital audio MP3 ISBN: 978-1-80426-511-6

Large Print ISBN: 978-1-80426-508-6

Boldwood Books Ltd.

23 Bowerdean Street, London, SW6 3TN

www.boldwoodbooks.com

To Ant, Nick & Nelly
And the little stars of the show: Elsie, Huxley, Hadley and
California

1

CLEETHORPES, SUNDAY 3 SEPTEMBER 1939

Frances O'Leary lay on top of her bed in Barkhouse Lane, watching the shaft of light grow stronger through the gap in the curtains as the sun rose. She'd left them like that when she'd arrived home from the theatre with Jessie Delaney, her fellow Variety Girl, in the early hours. It had been a night of excitement followed by hours of worry and she hadn't bothered to undress, unable to sleep, her mind busy with what might happen today. German troops had marched into Poland only two days before and the prime minister, Neville Chamberlain, had been forced to issue an ultimatum. If Hitler didn't withdraw his troops they would be at war. It felt to Frances like the whole world had been holding its breath, hoping against hope that they wouldn't be at conflict again. But what did hope ever achieve?

A quiet tapping on her bedroom door interrupted her thoughts and Jessie stuck her head around it.

'Can I come in?' Her friend's eyes were puffy and red from crying, her face blotchy. How soon happiness turned to tears. Frances felt for her young friend, forgetting her own worries and fears and forcing them to the back of her mind.

'Of course.' Frances slung her legs over the bed, went over to the window and drew back the heavy blackout curtains to reveal a blue, almost cloudless sky. Down in the yard, their landlady, Geraldine, was slicing beans from the stalk with her ivory-handled penknife, dropping them into a white enamel pan on the path. As though sensing she was being watched, Geraldine turned and looked up at her, and Frances put up a hand in greeting. 'I haven't slept anyway.'

'I don't think any of us have. Mum and Geraldine have been in the back room since six.'

Frances smiled. 'Ah, but your lack of sleep will be for different reasons.' Jessie came beside her and the girls linked arms. 'Harry's proposal, a London impresario coming to hear you sing. And in Cleethorpes, of all places! What a wonderful night it was for you.'

Jessie gave her a half-hearted smile. 'It was. And it wasn't.' She let out a heavy sigh. 'Life's complicated, isn't it?'

Frances could only agree. And the older you got the more complicated it became, but she couldn't tell Jessie that. Instead she said, 'Lots to look forward to: a ring, a wedding...'

'But when?' Jessie's voice cracked. 'If the news is bad today, and we know that it will be...'

'Don't.' Frances loosened her arm; they couldn't give in to dark thoughts. It didn't help. 'You have to think of all the wonderful things that lie ahead for you and Harry. You'll need to set a date, find a dress... and that's just the start of your good fortune. Your mum must be so excited for you.' Harry and Jessie had met almost a year ago when Jessie was secretary at her uncle Norman's legal practice in Norfolk, and Harry a solicitor. He'd recently joined the RAF and Jessie was proud but afraid. Frances tugged her friend close. 'For a girl with the world at her feet, you're awfully glum.'

Jessie leaned her head on Frances's shoulder. 'I know. All my dreams coming true at once – only it's not what I thought it would be. I'm so confused.' She lifted her head and turned to Frances, the fear clear in her eyes. 'If it's war, Harry won't be safe, none of us will.'

Frances gripped her friend's shoulders and gave her a bit of a shake, hoping to dislodge the despair. 'Harry will be back before you know it.' They had to be strong, for who knew what lay before them. She changed tack. 'Enough of that. I didn't get a chance to talk to you much last night, there was so much going on, and I am desperate to know how it went with Vernon Leroy.'

Jessie smiled then. 'Oh, Frances, always turning your face to the sun, looking for the good. What would I do without you?'

'You'd manage.' Frances grinned. She couldn't have Jessie losing her spark. It was what Frances loved about her. They'd met when Jessie was the latecomer to the dancing troupe who were appearing for the three-month summer season at the Empire. She'd arrived with nowhere to stay and Frances had brought her to Barkhouse Lane, which Geraldine had taken on only a week before, having inherited it from her aunt. The terraced house had been drab and neglected but over the last two months they'd all worked together to make it a cosy home. 'Come on, tell me what the marvellous Mr Leroy said?'

'I was so excited, so nervous, that I can't remember half of it.' Jessie's green eyes began to recover their sparkle. 'Harry had just proposed, and I was walking on air. We went back to the dressing room together and Mr Leroy was there with Mum and the star of the show, Madeleine Moore.' She stopped, smiled. 'He told me I had a great voice, had a great future ahead of me. He's thinking of putting me in his next West End production.'

'That's wonderful, isn't it?'

Jessie shrugged. 'It would've been, a few weeks ago. But now that Mum and Eddie are here with me, it's different. I don't want to leave them again. Harry's in the RAF... and if it's war...' Her voice faltered as fear took hold. Frances released her arm.

'Look at it this way: you're with your family and you're doing what you love. That's everything, isn't it?' It was so much more than she had herself. It had been four years since she'd seen her own family. Four long, lonely years.

Jessie lifted her head. 'Oh, Frances, you're right. Here's me, going on like an idiot when we'll perhaps have worse things to worry about soon.' She paused. 'Harry was so glad that I was here with you and Geraldine. He said he knew we'd all look out for each other.'

'And he's right,' Frances agreed. They had become as tight-knit as any family. She hadn't realised it before but now, as they stood on the brink of war, she knew that that's what they meant to each other.

'I'm so glad to have a friend like you, someone to share all my happiness and fears with. My secrets.'

Guilt pierced Frances. Secrets. Should she tell of her own? To do so would be such a relief – to share all that brought her happiness, gave her joy. Jessie's eyes were bright with expectation. *No, not yet. This is her moment*, she told herself, *don't spoil it*. She nudged Jessie's shoulder. 'Don't be daft. What about your mum? And your brother?'

Jessie rested her hand against the window frame, thoughtful. Her mother, Grace, had been so ill when Jessie brought her to stay at Barkhouse Lane at the end of July, rescuing her from the neglect of Grace's cousin's wife, Iris, and nursing her back to health. Her younger brother, Eddie, had been set to inherit the family legal firm – not that he wanted to, for he was mad about engines – but all the same, it was lost opportunities, so Jessie had her own guilt to contend with and Frances didn't need to burden her with any more.

'I can't talk to them like I can talk to you. I can't tell them how afraid I am.' She frowned. 'Mum's thrilled to bits for me but she's still not well. And Eddie...' She smiled. 'Eddie is thriving too, isn't he?' Frances agreed and Jessie went on, 'Do you know, when I first brought them here, I thought I'd done the worst thing, that I'd been rash and made a mistake. But it all turned out right in the end. Things do, don't they, if we have courage?'

If only courage was all it took. Frances looked at the younger girl, her freshness, her innocence. At eighteen, Jessie's age, she had been innocent too. Then it all changed. She turned away, reaching past Jessie for her washbag, which lay on the chair at the bottom of the bed. When she turned back, she made sure she was smiling. 'Let's go downstairs. I need to freshen up. We have no idea what the day will bring and I want to be ready to greet whatever comes.'

* * *

In the back sitting room, Grace and Geraldine were sitting at the oak table, stripping and slicing runner beans. An old copy of the *Grimsby Telegraph* was spread over it, a growing pile of ends and strings in the middle, the sliced beans mounting in a colander. They looked up as the girls came in.

'Morning,' Frances said.

'Morning,' Grace replied, making short work of the last bean and deftly wrapping the paper around the scrapings. Geraldine got up and took it from her, along with the colander, and Frances followed her into the kitchen.

'Let me get rid of these and we'll get on with breakfast. Same as we always do, eh?' Not waiting for a reply, Geraldine put the colander on the side and went out to the dustbin. Frances picked up the kettle and the gas popped as she placed it on the stove. The pans for lunch were on the side, the potatoes scraped, carrots chopped and now the beans would sit alongside them. Everything prepared in advance. It was the same every Sunday, she presumed, for she was always up and out, no matter how late they got back from the theatre the night before.

'Are you not going to see your friend this Sunday?' Grace called through to her.

Frances wrung out a dishcloth and went back into the room. 'I thought I'd wait until after the prime minister's announcement at eleven and then go.' Grace lifted her hands as Frances wiped the table. 'As luck would have it, her husband's home from sea for a few days. She won't be on her own.'

'That's good,' Grace said. 'Bad news is more bearable shared.'

Frances leaned against the door frame. 'It is, and at least we'll know one way or another what it's to be.' She felt the draught as Geraldine entered from outside. 'It's the indecision that's wearying. Not knowing one way or another.'

'Rather the indecision than war.' Geraldine was brisk. She went back to her chair at the head of the table.

'Yes, of course.' A small voice was telling Frances to have courage. 'It's just that I can't forget the children I saw on Friday, standing in little crocodiles, being led towards the station, evacuated to heaven knows where.' The image had stayed with her. Mothers trying to be brave, children clutching teddies, labels tied to their coats. The innocence of them... and no idea of where they were going. Or when they would be coming back.

'It's good that you don't have to, Frances. I wouldn't wish it on any mother,' Grace said quietly.

'No.' Frances folded her arms, tucking them away. If she could only talk to them of her worries, her fears, it might help. Grace was kind; she would understand, wouldn't she? There was a thump from up above, then she heard Eddie, Jessie's brother, thunder down the stairs. He burst into the room, briefly stilling the conversation. He was in his pyjamas, his wavy brown hair in disarray, and he yawned, rubbing his hand over his face and grinning, his teeth white against his tanned skin. The tension in the room seemed to break as Eddie settled himself at the table and Frances knew the moment to speak had slipped away. The kettle began to whistle, and Geraldine returned to the kitchen. The smell of bacon filled the air and the fat sizzled when Geraldine cracked eggs into the frying pan. Frances's stomach felt cavernous, but she wasn't hungry. Were any of the others?

Jessie came beside her and filled the teapot; Frances sliced the bread and took it into the room along with butter, plates and cutlery. The two of them went back for the bacon and eggs and Geraldine joined them, pouring the tea as the girls sat down, side by side, at the table. Frances watched Grace as she studied her son, the worry clear in her eyes. She caught Frances looking and they exchanged a smile.

Jessie cut a slice of bread in half, scraped a little butter across it, lifted it, then put it down again. 'Surely Chamberlain will be able to resolve things peacefully? He said it was peace with honour not so long ago. Hitler must keep his word.'

'People say lots of things,' Geraldine said. 'It's what they do that counts.' Frances nodded. She had believed her lover's empty promises. If only she'd been so wise.

'But we have to hope for the best, don't we?' Jessie was almost pleading for the others to agree with her. Frances looked down at her plate. She should eat. She should tell them. She picked up her fork.

'We do, darling,' Grace said. 'And you have so much to look forward to. Before long you'll be down in London, your name in lights.'

'Not in a blackout it won't, Mum,' Eddie said. 'It won't be allowed.' Grace glowered at him and he shrugged. He reached for a cup and ladled in three spoonfuls of sugar. Grace raised an eyebrow. 'What?' He quickly stirred the tea, took a quick gulp. 'I'm caddying for my boss, Mr Coombes. It's a long walk around that golf course.'

Grace replaced her cup on the saucer. 'Surely he won't play golf, today of all days?'

Eddie nodded, hurrying to finish another mouthful of food. 'He said he would. He told me that he wasn't going to spoil a good round of golf for something he couldn't influence.'

'I agree with him,' Geraldine said. 'But we'll all have to do our bit, as we did the last time.'

Grace briefly closed her eyes. Was she remembering her husband, Davey, who had fought in the Great War? He'd returned a broken man, as so many of them had.

'Well, I'm going, Mum,' Eddie said. 'Listening to the radio won't change things.' He would be fifteen in a couple of weeks, still a boy but almost a man. Almost. If it was war and it went on and on, then Eddie would be called up. Frances shivered.

Grace leaned forward and ruffled his hair. 'Better get yourself dressed then. Unless you're thinking of going around the golf links in your pyjamas.' He grinned, pushing back the chair and getting to his feet. They heard him rumble up the stairs and Frances saw the fear return to Grace's eyes as soon as he was gone. They were all putting on a face, weren't they? She wasn't alone in that.

Frances finished her tea, and replaced her cup carefully in the saucer as worry enveloped her again. 'Life will have to go on, won't it? For us all.'

The silence was broken only when Eddie trundled down the stairs and stuck his head around the door. He was wearing his smart trousers and shirt, his hair tidy, and he kissed his mother and looked around at them all, puzzled. 'What have I done?'

Grace took his hand, rubbed at his arm. 'Nothing, my love. Off you go.'

He slipped out of the back door, calling, 'See you later!' and they heard the clatter as he took hold of his bike, the rattle of the gate as he left.

Frances glanced at the clock. Ten minutes to nine. Time was grinding away. She looked to Geraldine, then Grace. Grace knew the ways of the theatre. She clasped her hands in her lap, took a deep breath. 'Do you miss your dancing days, Grace?'

Grace sat back into her chair. 'Sometimes, but not often.'

'What did you do?' Geraldine was curious and Frances relaxed a little. There hadn't been time for them all to chat easily because Geraldine worked long hours at the dock offices in Grimsby and when she returned the girls had already left for the theatre.

'I was a classical ballerina,' she said with pride, 'and Davey was a renowned violinist. This was all before the Great War, of course.' She paused, remembering. 'The life is different, the discipline different.'

'More respectable,' Jessie offered.

Grace frowned, her dismay showing on her face. 'Not at all. I'm not saying that what you girls do is not respectable.'

'But it isn't, Mum,' Jessie countered. 'If Aunt Iris knew I wanted to dance with the corps de ballet she'd have treated me differently. You can't say she wouldn't.'

Frances wondered how Grace would answer. Iris was a condescending snob. Frances had met her only briefly but once was enough. Over the past few years, she had realised there were many people like Iris. The problem was you never knew who they were until it was too late.

Grace was reluctant to answer. 'Possibly.'

Geraldine said, 'Well, you can't entirely blame your aunt. Variety is the child of the music hall and so many of the big stars have succumbed to drink and depravity. It hasn't earned a reputation for loose morals for nothing.'

Frances was shocked. 'That's a tad unfair, Geraldine. There are plenty of people who behave like that; it's not linked only to the theatre. Or movie stars, for that matter.'

The older woman was picking at crumbs on the table and placing them on her plate with a sprinkle of her fingers. 'I agree; it's an observation, not an opinion. But it seems more prevalent. The excess, the drama. And young girls' heads are easily turned by the lure of the bright lights. Why, only last week there was the story of that young woman from Louth. Off she went to London in search of stardom and ended up dying from some botched—' she broke off abruptly, then continued, 'operation. Such a waste.'

'But that could happen to anyone.' Frances's voice was high and she could feel her neck and face reddening. 'She had dreams.' Dreams that had led to disappointment, as they had done for her. Jessie turned and looked at her, Grace too.

Geraldine remained calm. 'We've all heard stories like this. Charming young men who only have one thing on their minds. I'm sure Grace will be worried about Jessie going to London on her own. Harry too.'

'I won't end up like that,' Jessie snapped, affronted. 'Harry's not like that.'

How it irritated. Harry wasn't like that, but Jessie had almost lost him, hadn't she, flattered by the cocky comedian Billy Lane, who had been second top of the bill during the summer season.

'You have no idea how you'll end up,' Frances said sharply. 'Look how easily you fell for Billy Lane's charms.'

'I did no such thing.' Jessie was horrified.

Frances could have bitten off her tongue. Jessie hadn't deserved that; she wasn't that kind of girl – but then, neither was she. People would make up their own minds about her, whether she liked it or not. 'I'm sorry,' she said gently. 'I shouldn't have said that. I'm truly sorry. You did nothing to lead Billy on. Billy is one of life's chancers.'

'My point exactly,' Geraldine said. Frances held her gaze,

fighting to hide her disappointment. Geraldine wouldn't understand; life was too black and white for some people.

Grace reached across and pressed at Frances's arm. 'It's all right. We're all feeling jumpy today.' She leaned back in her chair again. 'If Jessie decides to go to London I'll be worried, of course I will. I only hope she finds as good a friend as you when she does.'

Oh, the bitter irony. Frances couldn't reply. If they knew... She clutched the side of her chair. It was as if the whole world had tilted and she was sliding off the edge. 'Please forgive me, Jessie?'

Jessie shook her head, reaching out to take Frances's hand, offering a sympathetic smile. 'Nothing to forgive. Like Mum said, we're all feeling rotten.'

Frances forced herself to smile, pretending that it had all been forgotten but her heart was heavy. She pushed back her chair and stood up, picking up her cigarettes and matches from the dresser. 'I'm going outside for a smoke. Leave the dishes. I'll come back in and clear up, then I'll give the kitchen a thorough clean.'

'Good idea,' Geraldine said, tapping the table with her palms. 'I was thinking these windows could do with a wash – although it will be difficult with the tape across them.'

'I'll give you a hand.' Jessie began stacking the plates.

Grace got to her feet. 'I'll be at my sewing machine if anyone wants me.'

They were all trying to act as if her outburst had never happened, but it had, and it was awkward. Frances was glad to leave the room.

* * *

By eleven, Jessie and Frances had cleaned every nook and cranny in the kitchen and swept and dusted the sitting room. Tackling the task with more vigour than necessary had helped dilute her disappointment, if nothing else, but Geraldine's words dominated her thoughts. As the clock chimed the hour, Geraldine removed her apron and hung it on the hook by the pantry door. The girls downed tools, washed and dried their hands and went into the back room where sunlight streamed through the window, catching the dust motes as they swirled and settled. The pair of them sat down and Frances was solemn as the two older women took their places at the table. The prime minister was due to speak at a quarter past. Geraldine reached out and turned the dial on the wireless.

The small room became unbearably stuffy. Geraldine got up and pushed the sash as high as it would go. The breeze was slight but welcome, the sun bright as it moved higher into the bluest of skies. Geraldine had picked up her book, but not turned a page. Grace had gone back into her room and returned with her embroidery, the light catching the steel of the needle as it moved in and out of the cloth. Frances looked at the clock and, as the hands moved around to the quarter hour, the familiar voice of the BBC announcer broke the uneasy quiet.

'*This is London.*'

Geraldine marked her page, closed the book and placed it on the table. Grace lowered her sewing into her lap.

When Neville Chamberlain spoke, he sounded the old man he was, tired and weary. She knew it was bad news. They all did. And when he said that they were indeed at war, no one moved, no one spoke, but sat in the small silence as he continued to talk. War. It was war.

Frances tried to concentrate, but her thoughts were starting to tumble in her head. Harry would have to fight. Would Eddie? She looked at Grace's face. It was rigid, as was Geraldine's. '*When I finish speaking,*' Chamberlain continued, '*certain detailed announcements will be made on behalf of the government. Give these your close attention.*'

The silence as the speech ended was followed by the peal of bells. Small tears glistened on Grace's cheeks and she reached in her sleeve for her handkerchief, rubbed briskly at her eyes and under her nose.

'How very silly of me.' Jessie reached out, but Grace pulled herself upright. 'Don't fuss, Jessie. I'm perfectly all right.' Frances admired her inner steel. Grace might be weakened by ill health but she was a strong woman. Frances would be strong too.

Geraldine stilled her with a finger to her lips as the BBC announcer spoke again.

'*This is London.*'

Geraldine leaned closer to the wireless.

'*Closing of places of entertainment.*' The announcer's voice was crisp and without emotion. Frances gasped, her hand to her throat; she turned to Jessie, who was staring at the wireless.

The announcer continued. '*All cinemas, theatres, and other places of entertainment are to be closed immediately, until further notice.*'

Jessie sprang to her feet, but Frances tugged at her arm and pulled her down again.

'Shh,' Geraldine hissed but the words went over Frances's head and out through the window. What else was there to know? She had lost her job, Jessie too, but she couldn't leave Barkhouse Lane, not yet. Her happiness depended on it.

2

At the end of the government notices there was another silence before they played the national anthem, and all four of them got to their feet. Geraldine appeared taller than she'd ever been, her shoulders back, her head erect. Jessie knew that she'd lost her brother and her fiancé in the Great War; their pictures held pride of place in her room. So many women had been left to fend for themselves after the conflict and now it would happen again. She said a silent prayer that Harry would be safe, for he would have to fight now, like so many others who had already answered the call. The thought made her shudder. Her mother was glassy-eyed and, to Jessie, suddenly small and frail, and a shiver of fear shot through her. She was still recovering and not yet returned to her old self; would this set her back again? And what of Eddie? Would she be left with photographs, like Geraldine?

When the anthem ended, they sat back down, somewhat revived because of the music, the call for king and country, but the shock was visible on everyone's face. Grace closed her eyes, turning her wedding ring on her finger, and Geraldine reached across and lowered the volume on the wireless. Jessie sighed heavily and turned to Frances. 'What are we going to do now? That's both of us out of work.' She put her elbows on the table and rested her chin in her hands. 'There's no chance of me going to London now.'

Geraldine sighed. 'There will be worse things to worry about, young Jessie.'

Jessie was close to tears. 'I know that,' she said quietly. 'I wasn't being starry-eyed. I was thinking of our immediate problem and that's paying the rent.' She turned again to Frances, who had remained motionless throughout the broadcast. Her face was pale; it made her dark eyes darker still. 'We ought to go to the theatre, don't you think? Find out what's going to happen.' They couldn't just sit here. She had to do something to distract herself from the fear that had settled in the pit of her stomach. For Harry, for them all. She was responsible for her mother now. It would be a while before Grace returned to full strength, and although Eddie was working, he was only an apprentice. It would be years before he got a full wage, and the money Uncle Norman had given to them when they left Norfolk wouldn't last forever. She got up and pushed her chair under the table.

'Nothing will happen.' Frances stared at the wireless. 'The theatres are closed—'

'Until further notice,' Geraldine interrupted. 'Take heart, girls. The announcer also said that they would open again in some areas. Possible. And probable, wouldn't you say, Grace?'

Grace gave her daughter an encouraging smile. 'Without a doubt.' So, there was already hope then. 'Remember what your father used to say. Music gives people comfort. They won't be closed for long.'

Geraldine pressed her hands on the table in front of her.

'It's important not to panic. We will deal with whatever comes our way, just as we did the last time, eh, Grace?' Grace seemed to gain strength from Geraldine's words and Jessie was so grateful to her, so glad to be here and not with Aunt Iris. 'Whatever happens, we're all going to help each other through it. Don't forget that.'

Jessie felt her shoulders soften; Geraldine was right. She held on to the back of the chair. 'I'm going to the Empire,' she said to Frances. 'Coming?'

Frances shook herself a little and got to her feet. 'Yes. We need to find out what's going on.' Her voice was weak and she seemed dazed.

'Are you all right, Frances?' Grace was concerned.

'Yes, I'm fine.' She pushed back her chair, smiled at them all, reached out and touched Jessie's arm. 'Let me do my hair and get some lipstick on first. Can't go out without my best face on, can I now?'

'That's the spirit,' Geraldine urged. 'Business as usual.'

Jessie felt cheered. She mustn't lose sight of her goals, not for war, not for anything. She had to take care of her mum, and Eddie. One day she would buy her mum the house Dad had always promised her; it just might take a little longer than she'd anticipated.

Geraldine smiled. 'The show must go on, must it not?'

'Absolutely,' Jessie said, her spirits already revived.

* * *

When they were ready, they picked up their cardigans and bags and Frances hung back while Jessie kissed her mother goodbye. 'We won't be long, Mum. I'm sure the owner, Jack Holland, will be at the theatre and we can find out where we stand.'

'And say goodbye,' Frances added. 'A lot of the cast will head for home. There was only three weeks left of the show.' She walked over to the door. 'It might take a lot longer than that for the theatres to reopen. And we might not be in the right area when they do.'

Jessie felt a flutter of panic. She'd have to find other work here to keep them all afloat – but if Frances left it wouldn't be the same. She pushed her lip forward and Frances grinned.

'Well, I'm not going anywhere, Jessie, but the others might.'

That was what she'd wanted to hear from her friend. Jessie went to stand beside her, linked her arm through hers. 'That's the best news I've heard all day.'

Geraldine came through from the kitchen. 'I'll delay dinner as long as I can. Otherwise, I'll put yours on a low heat in the oven.' She paused. 'And, girls...' Jessie tilted her head to one side. 'Gas masks.' Jessie felt a chill ripple down her spine. They had all seen the notices urging them to carry their gas masks at all times, the government fearing aerial attack. The black rubber monstrosities in their cardboard boxes had been pushed under their beds and forgotten about.

'I'll get yours.' Frances dashed upstairs and quickly returned, handing Jessie the small brown box and putting her own over her shoulder. They would have to remember to take them with them from now on.

* * *

They stepped out into the street and walked up the small incline to the top of Barkhouse Lane then rounded the corner onto Humber Street, which opened out, giving them a glimpse of the sea. The sun glistened on the water and boats moved along the horizon, just as they always did. The sky was blue, the sun warm and it was hard to believe that it wasn't like every other Sunday. Seagulls screamed overhead, swooping, diving, and Frances wanted to scream too as panic took hold. She lifted her head; she mustn't weaken. She had to be strong. She led the way across the road so that they could look down onto the promenade where life continued as normal, because, despite the news, people were out enjoying themselves. Cars trundled past as they headed down the hill, towards the Empire.

Already shopkeepers were putting boards over their windows, paper signs declaring it would be business as usual fixed on the wooden planks. Their doors remained open and people drifted in and out as they walked along. She needed to get another job as soon as she could but so many others would be out looking for work. There would be no more holidays, no more summer seasons by the seaside – and her savings were not what she had hoped. She inhaled the sea air. *Lord, let Grace be right; let the theatres reopen soon.*

Paper strips had been pasted on the glass doors of the Empire declaring they were *Closed until Further Notice*. Bad news had not come unexpected. She pulled on the brass handle, waited for Jessie to go first, then followed. The door to the box office opened and their friend, Dolly, an usherette, came dashing out to greet them, her blonde hair a halo.

'Isn't it just the worst news? I thought them in London with all their big brains would sort it out, didn't you?'

Jessie agreed. 'I've had my head in the clouds this last week. I didn't notice how close we were to war. But to close the theatres...' Frances briefly closed her eyes, wanting to shut out the words as the girls prattled on about things they couldn't control. Empty words. She was sick of them.

'What did it matter what we thought?' Frances snapped. 'It wouldn't have changed anything.' The two girls stared at her. She was only five years older than them, but twenty-three felt a lifetime away from eighteen. She tried to remember what it had been like to be so unaware of the harsh realities of life but she couldn't.

'I'm sorry, girls,' she apologised. 'I don't know what's the matter with me.'

'It's all right,' Dolly said kindly. 'It's such a blow, isn't it? Mum was crying when the news came. Dad's lost his job; so have I. It's all such a worry.'

Frances felt for them. Dolly's dad, George, was the stage doorman and his lovely wife, Olive, was always sending him to work with little treats for the girls. 'How long have you been here?' she asked, trying to smooth things over.

'Since ten. Mr Holland asked Dad to open up and bring the wireless down from his office and put it in the bar in case anyone came. A lot of the acts have already come and gone.' The doors to the stalls had been weighted open and voices drifted into the cool of the foyer. 'I'm manning the box office in case people want their money back. Such a shame when it was all going so well.'

There was a clatter of metal from inside the auditorium.

'We need to find out what's going on in there.' Frances tipped her head towards the inner doors. 'Catch up with you later, Dolly.'

'You're not leaving, then?' The girl's face brightened.

'Not for the time being,' Frances said, for where would she go? It had meant the world to her to be able to stay in Cleethorpes for so long instead of touring from town to town, a different theatre each week on the variety circuit. A long run meant stability, a chance to save.

'Me too.' Jessie smiled. 'Cleethorpes is home to us all now.'

* * *

The house lights were on in the auditorium and members of the cast and staff were trudging up and down the steps at the front of the stage with boxes and bags, packing away props and instruments.

Mary, the wardrobe mistress, small and round with tight grey curls, was standing beside two sturdy metal clothes rails. Sally, Kay and Rita, three of the dancers who comprised half of the Variety Girls, were handing over their costumes and Mary was checking them off her list. Ginny, the other member of their troupe, was nowhere to be seen.

'Hello, ducks. When you've a minute, can you bring me your bits up?' Mary sighed. 'Who'd have thought it, eh? I prayed me ruddy socks off, I did. But there you go. At least we know what's what, don't we? Instead of all this buggering around.' Mary tried to sound cheerful, but her voice was edged with sadness and Frances clasped her shoulder, gave it a gentle squeeze. She'd thought the same herself. There was strength in knowing where you stood. Even if it was alone.

'Yes, all this buggering around has done for us all,' Frances agreed. 'But they've picked on the wrong ones this time, eh?'

The woman laughed. 'Too right, lovey.' Jessie had gone on ahead and Frances watched her disappear into the wings as Mary continued with her inventory. The ending of a good run was always tinged with sadness, but she'd never felt as she did today. She hurried down the stairs, eager to help Mary finish her task, and found Jessie and Ginny in the dressing room, whispering, their heads close. They stopped when Frances came in, and looked awkward.

'Hiya, Frances.' Ginny was subdued. She adjusted the costumes that were draped over her arm. Her glorious red hair was pulled back into a bun at the back of her head and it made her look harsher than usual. The bulbs around the mirror were lit, but the many photos, greetings cards and notes had been taken down. Only Frances's mirror remained decorated with words from well-wishers.

Jessie stepped back to let Ginny escape and they heard her tread heavily on the stairs. Frances put her bag down on the dressing table, removed her cardigan and laid it over the back of her chair.

'What's the matter with Ginny?'

Jessie shrugged. 'Upset. We all are.' She quickly turned her back and hurried out of the room.

Frances began to peel away her cards from the mirror. Cards from her brothers, the words sparse; others from her two sisters, full of news and love. Love. She chewed at her lip. How she missed them! She held the one from her parents, read her mother's words, her precise hand so familiar. Dear Mammy and Daddy. She'd been fifteen when they'd waved her off at Kildare station, the day as clear to her as if it had happened yesterday. Her mother's tears, her father's fears for her; their pride. She wanted to weep for the girl she once was...

Jessie returned with her vanity case in one hand, clutching her own treasured photographs and cards to her chest with the other. Last night she'd had a dressing room of her own, to celebrate the fact that she had her own solo spot in front of Vernon Leroy. The girls had tried to make the moment special for her, but the celebrations had been brief – as was their happiness.

Frances took down the photo of Imogen with a heaviness in her heart. Jessie put her own cards down on the dressing table.

'Pretty girl, your niece. Imogen, isn't it?'

'Imogen. Yes. Yes, it is,' Frances said, her voice softening. The weight of her lies was unbearable. Jessie trusted her, looked up to her. She caught the girl's reflection in the mirror. Would she understand? Jessie leaned over her shoulder.

'Gosh, doesn't she look like you? Is she your sisters' child? Or one of your brothers'?'

Frances swallowed. 'Jessie, she's—' She stopped as the rest of the girls trudged into the room.

'Jack's going to be ages, apparently,' Rita said, settling herself in the battered armchair. 'We might as well wait in here.' Kay and Sally rummaged around the room, picking up the last remaining hairgrips and rubber bands, putting them in a pile on the dressing table. Ginny came back and sat on the chair that she'd had all summer.

'Sorry, Frances, what were you saying?' Jessie asked as the girls chatted amongst themselves.

Frances shrugged. The interruption had unsettled her. 'I can't remember.'

Rita took out her cigarettes. 'I'm gasping for a fag.' She held out a packet of Woodbines. 'Want one?' Frances declined and Rita adjusted herself in the chair, crossing her long legs.

'Are you going to hang around?' Frances asked as Rita fumbled for her matches. She'd been a good head girl and Frances would probably bump into her again, sooner or later. Rita shook her head and her blonde ponytail swung from side to side.

'Nope. Already packed most of the stuff at the flat. Going to get the first train back to Manchester. Pointless hanging about here.' She put her cigarette to her lips, lit up, tossed the spent match into a tin ashtray. 'What about you?'

Frances leaned against the dressing table. 'Not sure. Find work. Any work will do for the time being.'

Rita nodded. 'We can't sit about waiting. We've got to get out there first, before anyone else. You know what it's like.' She puffed out a long plume of smoke. Frances watched it drift upwards. 'I'm not going to be back of the queue, are you?'

'Not if I can help it.' Frances couldn't afford to dither about. The rest of the girls were young, they would perhaps go home until things changed, but she didn't have that luxury.

Kay picked up an old copy of *The Stage* newspaper and was about to drop it into the waste basket.

Frances stopped her. 'Mind if I have a look?'

'There's nothing in it,' Kay said, handing it over. 'Nothing that matters now, anyway. It'll all be cancelled.' Frances wasn't bothered; there would be news of where other friends had been working, what theatres were still doing variety and hadn't been converted to cinemas. She had to trust that the theatres would open again and, like Rita, she needed to be ready for when they did.

She turned the pages, not really taking anything in until she read a short paragraph in the variety gossip column. 'Oh,' she gasped, putting her hand to her mouth. The girls stopped what they were doing and when she looked up, they were staring at her. She flushed, embarrassed, but her heart was thumping wildly as she tried to compose herself. 'The Randolphs are back in London. They've got a show...' She corrected herself. 'They *were* going to star in a new production at the Coliseum.'

'Johnny and Ruby?' Rita asked.

'I saw that.' Kay twisted towards Rita. 'Do you know them?'

Rita shook her head. 'I thought they were making it big in the States. Wonder what they've come back for? Surely not because of the war.' She drew on her cigarette. 'They must have been over there, what? Three, four years? More.'

'Four years,' Frances said. 'It's four.' Four years this month, the fifteenth. She'd never forget.

'I'm sure it's longer than that.' Rita was staring at her and she felt pressured to say more.

'I was on the same bill, in the chorus.' Frances turned away from them, talked to them through the mirror. It felt easier not looking at them directly. 'It previewed in Manchester, then went to London. They took it to America.'

'And you didn't go with it?' Jessie frowned at her and Frances felt her neck redden with heat.

'I was supposed to.' She hesitated, not wanting to say too much. 'It didn't work out.'

'Lucky blighters,' Rita said. 'I'd love to go to America. Not much chance of that now.' She stubbed out her cigarette, and got to her feet, sweeping her hands over her skirt to smooth the creases, picked up her bag and slipped it over her arm. 'I'm off back to the digs.'

'Aren't you going to stop and find out what Jack has to say?' Frances asked, relieved that the conversation had been brought to an end. She put the paper to one side. It was bad enough that war had been declared, but to know that Johnny was back? She needed to focus on something else, something other than him.

'Write it down on the back of a fag packet and tell me later,' Rita threw over her shoulder. 'He can't do anything and I'm not hanging around on a promise. Not my style.' Jessie dipped her head, biting her lip, and Frances had to look away in case the pair of them laughed. Rita had been through the band like a dose of salts.

Kay and Sally decided to leave with Rita. Hardly surprising, since they had followed her about all summer like ducklings. The remaining three girls finished clearing the dressing room and, when they were done, took their bags upstairs, leaving them in the small office at the stage door. George was taking down the notices from the felt board outside in the corridor and his face lit up when he saw the girls. 'Eeh, you lasses are a sight for sore eyes.' He pushed his glasses to the top of his head. 'Such a shame it had to end like this.'

Jessie put her arm about him and gave him a squeeze. 'It is, George, but we're still going to be here, me and Frances.'

'And me,' Ginny added.

He smiled, his old grey eyes crinkling. 'Well, just remember, you can pop over the road anytime and see me and the missus. You're always welcome.'

* * *

Back in the auditorium, they found the owner and manager, Jack Holland, onstage. He'd been a familiar sight throughout the production, totally hands-on and well liked by his staff on both sides of the curtain. What remained of the cast and crew were scattered about the stalls, waiting for him to speak, and the girls skipped down the steps at the prompt side of the stage to join them. He'd removed his jacket and stood in his shirtsleeves; even from a distance they could see how tired he was.

'He must be devastated,' Jessie said, pushing down her seat next to Frances. 'I know it's difficult for all of us, but he's put all his money into this place.'

Frances wriggled, making herself comfortable. 'I suppose he'll lose his shirt if the theatres don't reopen sharpish.' It was a sobering thought, but one that many theatre owners would be facing. The Empire had been closed for months, the previous owners running out of money. The same had been happening elsewhere and many of the grand old theatres had been given over to cinemas. Jack hadn't settled for the easy or, it had to be said, more profitable option, but had risked his arm on a variety show.

Jack cleared his throat and conversations stilled as he began to speak.

'I've already said goodbye to a few of the cast and crew.' He paused and Frances looked about the rows to see who had stayed. Not many. Mike, the stage manager, was sitting on a wicker hamper at the side of the stage, his arms folded across his wide chest. A couple of the cleaners had seated themselves in the back row, along with Dolly and her dad, George. The door at the back of the auditorium opened and Madeleine Moore, the top of the bill, slid discreetly onto the end of the row. It would have been easy for her to wait for news to be brought to her door but that wasn't her style. Frances turned back to hear what Jack had to say.

'Thank you to those who have remained.' He was sombre as he looked out into the auditorium, the flat of his hand above his eyes. He brought it down again, slid it into his trouser pocket, stared down at the stage thoughtfully, then up again. 'Many of you will be eager to get home, back to your families, so I'll keep it brief.' He paused again. 'War has brought our happy show to a rather abrupt end, but it was good while it lasted, wasn't it? You did me and this town proud.' People shuffled in their seats, lifting themselves a little higher. It was bittersweet, to leave in the middle of success, but what was the end of a show compared to what everyone faced once they walked out of the theatre? Frances closed her eyes, trying to concentrate on what he said, her thoughts in turmoil.

'I can't ask you all to wait and see what happens, because I can't afford to pay you a retainer.' Frances opened her eyes. It was hardly Jack's fault. It was no one's fault, was it? People had done what they could, but a line had to be drawn and they had to make the best of it.

'I will, however, pay the wages you were due this week. I feel it's the very least I can do.'

'That's kind of him,' Jessie said. 'He didn't have to do anything. He's probably worse off than any of us.' Frances shushed her, directing Jessie's attention back to the stage.

'The theatres will open again; I have no doubt of that,' he continued. 'And we need to pull together if we are to get through.' He took a deep breath. 'And win this ruddy war.' He was quiet for a time and people became uneasy. He looked up again, smiling. 'What I want to say is: keep steadfast.' He clasped his hands together and shook them fiercely. 'This world will be a sadder place without song, and dance – and laughter.' His voice wavered and he paused, composed himself before he spoke again. When he did, his voice was strong. 'When the theatres open we'll be leading the charge, my friends, because I'm going to make sure that the Empire is entertaining the crowds again. Twice nightly.' There was a ripple of applause from around the theatre and Frances joined in. His words had given them hope – and things being as they were, hope was needed as never before.

3

The following day, Frances left the house early and caught the bus for the hour-long journey to Waltham, a village less than five miles inland. Monday was washday in the Dawkins' household and she knew Patsy would appreciate the help. Finding work was a priority but she told herself that one day wouldn't make much difference if it meant she could be with Imogen.

The kids were not back at school after summer term and Frances watched the children through the kitchen window. Imogen's skipping rope was around five-year-old Colly's waist and he was holding on to it, pretending to be a horse, galloping around the lawn, three-year-old Imogen jiggling the reins. The pair of them were racing around in the dappled sunlight that filtered through the fruit trees towards the bottom of the garden. The neat white cottage in Waltham was heaven, Patsy and Colin Dawkins her angels. Patsy came and stood beside her.

'And the world keeps turning.' She put her hand to Frances's shoulder. 'What they don't know can't hurt them, thank the Lord.'

It didn't comfort her. 'If only that were true.'

Patsy ran the tap and washed her hands, flicking off the excess water before drying them on the towel that hung over the range. 'Don't worry yourself needlessly, Franny. I know they'll use the airfield, but I reckon we'll be safe enough out here.'

'I wasn't thinking of the war, Patsy; I was thinking of the future, Imogen's future.' Frances turned away from the window, and leaned with her back against the sink so that she could see her friend's face and gauge her reaction. 'Johnny's in England. It was in *The Stage*. The pair of them are back.'

Patsy hung the towel over the rail, her back to Frances.

'Ah, so that's why you came in looking like you were ready to take on Hitler single-handed.'

Frances folded her arms. 'Was it that obvious?'

'Well, they were bound to come home eventually.' Patsy turned. 'So. What are you going to do?'

Frances shrugged. 'I have no idea. I didn't sleep a wink last night, going over and over it all in my head.' She gave her a wry smile. 'It caught me off guard.' It had reignited the anger, a strong flame which she had previously let die, not giving it air so that it had almost been extinguished. Angry with him, at her herself. Had she really been so stupid? But after the anger had come curiosity. Had their love been a lie?

'You must want to do something,' Patsy said, choosing her words carefully, 'or you wouldn't have said anything.'

'I need to talk about it – and I can't talk about it with anyone but you.' For that she had no one else to blame. If only she'd spoken to Geraldine when she first moved in, it could all have been so different. 'I was so ruddy angry.' She shook her head. 'How could he turn his back on me? On us?'

Patsy came and stood beside her. 'I don't know, my love.' She leaned across the windowsill and pulled the dead leaves from the begonia that was doing its best to keep blooming. She tossed the dry leaves into the bin, brushed her hands together, pressed Frances's arm, held her gaze. 'You have to write to him.'

Frances looked down at her feet. The toes of her shoes were almost worn through; they wouldn't last much longer. 'Why?' she asked, looking back up at her friend. 'What makes you think he'd reply this time?' She had sent letter after letter to America; she'd waited for the promised ticket that never came. Even when she told him she was pregnant, how frightened she was, there was no response.

'I don't, but you have to try,' Patsy urged. 'Imogen is his child. He should support you. Both of you.'

'I am not going to use Imogen like that. Never.' She was surprised by the venom in her voice and she stopped, not wanting the poison inside her to take hold again. 'I'm sorry, Patsy. I don't want to argue with you but I'm so damn tired – and it's brought everything to the surface again. All of it – good and bad.'

'It's bound to.' Patsy picked up her wicker washing basket and settled it on her hip. 'Anyway, he should be made to pay something.'

Frances stood away from the sink and walked towards Patsy. 'It's only ever the women who pay. Imogen will be paying the price for the rest of her life.' Imogen didn't deserve the shame that would follow her around. It was her mother's mistake, but she would be the one who suffered most.

Frances followed Patsy outside into the garden. The sun was high, the breeze warm and the washing they'd done earlier had dried in no time at all. Patsy removed the prop so that the line was easier to reach and the pair of them started pulling at the pegs, folding the clothes and dropping them into the basket at their feet. Patsy had been her rock. Her generosity – and Colin's – had allowed Frances to keep her child and she would never be able to repay their kindness. She looked away, blinking back tears. Over by the vegetable patch, six-year-old Bobby was on his knees, lifting leaves, searching for caterpillars and grubs. He called out and the skipping rope was abandoned as Imogen and Colly ran over to help. Any onlooker would think they were brothers and sister.

'Why didn't you say something sooner?' Patsy asked.

Frances tipped her head back. 'I don't know. If it wasn't for Imogen, I could forget about him.'

'Ha.' Patsy raised her eyebrows. 'Could you? Really?' She rested her hands on the line and looked at Frances, who was facing her, the pair of them moving along seamlessly as they had done onstage so many years ago. Patsy had been the head dancer, keeping a chorus of twelve girls in line: a big sister, a teacher, but most of all, a friend. Frances had been fresh off the boat from Ireland and had arrived in Blackpool with her head full of dreams, wanting to make her mammy and daddy proud, their sacrifices worthwhile. The two of them had stayed in touch after the summer ended, long before Patsy had said goodbye to her dancing days to settle down with Colin. Whenever Frances was out of work, Patsy's door was always open and when she found herself pregnant and alone, it was Patsy who put a roof over her head.

'What about Imogen? One day she's going to want to know who her father is,' Patsy said, her voice low.

Frances looked to her child. Imogen was crouched with her hand outstretched and Colly was gently placing an earwig on her flattened palm. She didn't want to think that far into the future. Patsy rubbed at her shoulder. 'She'll be curious. Kids are.'

Her heart felt leaden. Patsy gave her a gentle smile. 'He would fall in love with her the moment he saw her. Who wouldn't? She's such a darling.'

'Don't,' Frances begged. She bent down and picked up the basket that was piled high with the children's clothes and the two of them went back into the house. Frances pulled out a chair, put the basket on it and began sorting the clothes into piles on the table while Patsy began making drinks for the children. Dandelion and burdock fizzed into three small beakers and Patsy pushed the cork back in the bottle with the flat of her hand.

'You can't walk away from it forever.' Frances pulled a face but Patsy ignored her. 'You'll have to confront it one day, whether you like it or not. You need to write to him. Again. And if that doesn't work, find him. Confront him.'

'I don't know if I can. If I'm brave enough.'

Patsy frowned. 'Oh, darling. I don't know anyone braver. Keeping Imogen was the bravest thing you've ever done.'

'I couldn't have done it without your help.'

Patsy was quick to disagree. 'Yes, you could. You'd have found a way. It's who you are.'

She didn't argue. Patsy was right. She would have kept Imogen, no matter what it cost. Frances clasped Imogen's small blue cardigan to her chest. Each thought of Johnny disturbed her. She put the cardigan on top of Imogen's little pile of clothes. 'He would deny it. He wouldn't want anything to damage the Randolph name. His mother would turn in her grave. I don't want to be his dirty little secret and I certainly don't want to be beholden to anyone. Least of all him!'

'It's not about being beholden. It's what's right. And his mother is gone now.'

'Ruby hasn't.'

Patsy shrugged. 'He's not responsible for his sister. And life's knocks will have changed him, as they have changed you.'

Frances didn't comment. She knew she'd lost her softness, saving it only for Imogen. Everyone else she kept at a distance. It was safer that way.

Patsy shook her head. 'Good God, you're so damned stubborn, O'Leary. It was always hell trying to keep you in line and you haven't changed at all.' She took hold of Frances's hands. 'You have to try, for Imogen's sake if not your own.' She let go of her hands, picked up the beakers. 'You know, something doesn't add up. It never has. That day me and Colin met Johnny for the first time, when we came to see the show, an idiot could see he was besotted with you. If it hadn't been for his mother, I'm sure he would have taken you with him from the beginning.'

'I can't blame his mother for everything. He was a grown man; he knew what he wanted.' She thought he'd wanted her. He had proposed, asking her to keep it quiet until he found the right time to tell his mother and Ruby. She smiled ruefully. She understood that now, when she hadn't before: finding the right time wasn't as easy as she'd thought. She heard Imogen's laughter. 'Was I a fool?'

'Not at all, my lovely girl. And he's not married or engaged, that's for sure. We'd have seen it in the papers. He might be waiting for you just as much as you're still waiting for him.'

Frances gave a hollow laugh. 'I'm not waiting for him.'

Patsy didn't hide her smile and Frances hated knowing her friend was right. 'He loved you.'

'Loved? I thought he did, but perhaps he just didn't love me enough.' The pain was coming again, up into her chest, and her ribs hurt. 'I was wrong. I was wrong about so many things. I'll never trust another man.'

'I hope I'm not included in that lump of humanity.' Colin, Patsy's husband, ambled into the kitchen. He put his baccy pouch on the table and looked about him for an ashtray. Patsy directed him with a nod of her head and went outside with the drinks.

Frances laughed. 'You're the one exception, Col. Give me a minute to put the clothes away and I'll make you a cuppa.' When she returned, he was sitting down, his back to the wall, chewing on the stem of his unlit pipe. He was a big man with a large, open face that was ruddy and weather-beaten from a lifetime at sea as a trawler skipper. His hair was thick waves, his eyes dark, and it was easy to imagine him in command of his ship and his men as they fished the Icelandic waters. Frances poured a little water from the kettle and warmed the pot, swirling it around, looking out into the garden. Imogen's dress was green with grass stains and she told Colin, as she spooned the tea leaves into the pot, 'She'd be better wearing the boys' hand-me-downs. Much as I want her to have pretty things, I don't think she's interested.' The words pained her. She had thought Imogen would have wanted the dresses and ribbons that Frances worked so hard to pay for, the sort of things that she'd yearned for herself when she was a child.

'As long as she's happy, lass. That's all that matters.'

She brought the teapot and set it on the table, went back for the mugs and sat down with him. 'It's the only thing that matters.'

He reached across and patted her hand. 'Now, who's this beggar getting us men a bad name, our Franny?'

Frances told him of the Randolphs.

'Happen our Patsy's right, don't you think?'

She rubbed at a mark on the table. 'I don't know if I can put myself through it again, Col. Waiting for a reply when nothing comes of it? And if I had to take Imogen to prove my point?' The thought made her shudder. 'It's too much of a risk. I couldn't do it.'

He opened his baccy pouch, pressed strands of tobacco into his pipe. 'Sometimes we have to take a risk. It's how we make a better catch.' He looked up, grinned, tilted his head towards the open door. 'That's how I caught my mermaid. Catch of my life.'

'Well, I must admit, not everyone goes to an end-of-the-pier show and comes back with a beauty like Patsy.'

'It was worth the long wait at the stage door, especially with that north wind coming in over the Humber.' Colin chuckled. 'She took the bait in the end.'

'She did. You're a lucky man.' Frances envied them their love for each other. Patsy had fallen for Colin and given up the stage without a backward glance.

'And don't I know it.' He rummaged in his pocket for his matches, struck one and drew on his pipe. 'Anyhow, enough of us. What about you and Johnny Randolph? Mebbe he didn't get your letters.'

'One or two I could understand, but not the number I sent.' She'd been desperate when he hadn't responded. 'I wrote every day to begin with, then every week.' She looked up, anger hardening her heart again. 'If he'd really loved me, I wouldn't have had to write at all. He knew where I was.'

She leaned back in her chair. They heard Patsy talking to the children in the garden. Colin drew on his pipe and she closed her eyes, the familiar smell taking her home to her daddy sitting by the fire in Kildare. How disappointed they would all be if they knew the truth about her life. She wrote home often, telling them of the shows she was in, the auditions, the rejections. The good and the bad – or most of it. She wanted them to think she was living the life of her dreams, but they knew nothing of Imogen. What they didn't know couldn't hurt them. It wasn't that she thought they wouldn't forgive her or take Imogen to their hearts; it was the lies she would have to weave to go back. And she couldn't do it.

Colin spoke, interrupting her thoughts. 'As I see it, you have two choices. You can forget about him altogether...' She looked up at him. He studied her eyes, smiled gently, reached out for her hand and took it in his. 'I was wrong. You have one choice, lass. I can tell that you'll never forget the man, no matter how much you want to.' He squeezed her hand. 'Not knowing is eating you up inside. Patsy's right. You must write again.'

She looked away from him, unsettled. The love was still there whether she wanted it to be or not. 'I can't.' Her heart was twisting, still bruised after all this time, so full of pain and nowhere for the pain to go. He didn't comment, and they both sat with their thoughts until he asked her about the theatre.

She told him of Jack giving them a week's wages. 'When I leave here I'll go looking for something, bar work, waitressing – anything to tide me over until the Empire reopens.'

'Why don't you come and stay here until you have something firmed up? It'd save you going hither and thither.'

Frances shook her head. 'I'm not putting the boys out of their beds. Besides, it's cheap enough where I am and I've more chance of getting a job in Cleethorpes. I'm certainly not going to put on you and Patsy more than I have already.'

'It works both ways, lass.' Colin took the pipe from his mouth and checked the bowl. 'I know you're here for her and that gives me comfort when I'm at sea.' He paused, drew again on his pipe. 'Do you think you might go back to Ireland? Now that it's war?' The pair of them had obviously given Frances's situation a lot of thought; it must have been on their minds almost as much as it had been on hers.

When times had been at their bleakest, what she wouldn't have given to walk back down the old familiar lanes, to the warmth of her life. 'I couldn't go back. We'd be meat and gravy to the gossips for years to come. I'm not letting my girl suffer that.'

'I know we've said it before, but couldn't you pretend her daddy had died? That you're a widow.'

'I can't, Col. I can live my lie here, away from them. But Mammy would know. Perhaps. One day. But not yet.' She doubted she ever would. She imagined the hurt in her daddy's eyes. No, this was her punishment.

Colin eased back into his chair. 'You know what's right for the pair of you, lass.'

Frances let out a long sigh. 'I don't know if I do, but I can only do my best.'

'That's all any of us can do,' he said quietly.

* * *

After lunch, Patsy and Frances stayed in the garden with the children, picking the last fruit from the trees. Flowers were still blossoming in the beds, bees hovering, butterflies flitting among the blooms.

'It's hard to think that things are any different from what they were last week, Patsy.' War seemed a long way away.

'I suppose that's because it's not, for most of us. For the time being. Monday's still wash day, Wednesday baking day.'

'And Colin?'

The smile left Patsy's face. 'Waiting for his call-up papers. The Naval Reserve are full of fishermen manning the minesweepers.' She was quiet. 'I thought he might have been too old. Whatever happens, he'll be at sea, fishing or fighting, perhaps both.' She sat down on the garden bench and Frances sat beside her. 'I can't believe we're at war.'

'No. It doesn't seem real.' Frances took her friend's hand and the two of them leaned back and closed their eyes against the sunshine, letting it warm them, and Frances hoped the heat would melt away the fear that kept catching at her heart.

Later, when it was time to leave, she gathered her things and popped her head around the sitting room door. Colin was settled in his armchair by the window, smoking his pipe and reading the paper, the wireless on low.

'I'm off, Col. Have a good trip.' His pipe was quickly placed in the ashtray that balanced on the arm of the leather chair and he got to his feet, opened his arms. Frances gave him a squeeze, taking in the smell of tobacco. Memories of her father erupted again and she squeezed harder, treasuring the familiarity. What it was to be held, to be loved...

'Take care, my lovely.'

She pulled away. 'And you too, Colin. Be safe.'

Patsy was waiting for her in the hall. Imogen was sitting on the chair at the side of the front door, her knees green, her socks wrinkled about her ankles.

'Are you going to give Mummy a kiss goodbye?'

Imogen slipped off the chair and threw her arms around her mother, who had squatted down on her haunches to hug her. She planted a kiss on Frances's nose.

'Sorry, Imogen, Mummy has to leave early this week, but I'll be back on Sunday, the same as always. Be good for Auntie Patsy.'

Patsy smiled benignly. 'She's always good, aren't you, Imogen?'

Imogen's curls bounced as she nodded. 'Can I go back in the garden with Colly, now?'

Frances was disappointed and Patsy pressed her arm as she stood up again. 'Don't take it to heart, Franny. It's just kids, they're all the same.'

Frances forced a smile. Were they? Or was Imogen growing away from her? She reached for her bag, which she'd left in the hall, and took out her purse. Patsy put out a hand to stop her.

'I don't need the money, Frances. Please keep it.'

Frances ignored her, taking out the ten-bob notes and pressing them into Patsy's reluctant hand. 'She's my responsibility, Patsy. Not yours. It would be taking advantage.'

'But things are different now. You don't know when you'll get work again.'

Frances was dismissive. 'I can get work. Any work will do. Something will come up; it always does.' She picked up her gas mask.

Patsy put a hand to Frances's shoulder. 'It'll work out, love. Be brave. Be bold.' They shared a smile. It was what Patsy had said every night to her dance troupe before the curtain went up. Colly ran in and Imogen followed him into the sitting room. It made her feel better; that the kids were doing what they always did brought a sense of normality. It was what she wanted for Imogen, and that she couldn't be a part of it was only temporary. One day she would have a home with Imogen, but this was the best she could do for now. She stepped out onto the path; Patsy stood in the doorway and Colly and Imogen waited at the window in the sitting room, then the three of them waved until she could see them no more.

4

Johnny Randolph placed the black coffee on the low mahogany table in front of his sister. Ruby was dressed in a red satin negligee and had sunk into the generous armchair, her long legs over one arm of it, her back against the other. She was wearing a black velvet eye mask, her long brown hair hanging almost to the floor, her hands to her head.

'Sit up,' Johnny said, taking the chair opposite her. He spread his feet, interlocked his fingers and leaned forward, waiting for her to do as he'd asked. She groaned. He asked her again, frustrated, his voice sharper this time, and she slowly pulled herself around, lifted a corner of her eye mask, grinned at him and dropped it down again. At twenty-four she still behaved like a child. He was three years older and sometimes it felt like thirty.

'Ruby, for God's sake. Take that damn thing off and drink the coffee.'

She pouted, swung her legs down and pushed the eye mask to the top of her head, blinking against the light of the room. Her mascara had run and her eyes were smoky black.

She leaned forward, picked up the cup, put it down again. 'What time is it?'

He looked at his watch. 'Twenty past eleven.'

She screwed up her face. 'Far, far too early.' She got up, wobbled and sat down again. 'I should be in bed.'

'You should be working. We both should.'

'There is no work, darling brother. Thanks to you.' She smiled, sweetly sarcastic, sipped at the coffee and pulled a face. 'That's not coffee. It's horrid.'

'It's the best you're going to get. We're not in America now.' He eased back in the armchair. He wasn't going to be drawn into an argument. The small sitting room in their rented flat reeked of her cocktail cigarettes and he'd opened the window to freshen the air. The sound of traffic and people shouting drifted in, English voices, reminding him they were back in London. Had he done the right thing, not taking up the new American contract? Their agent had been furious and cast them off like dirt on his shoe when they turned down Broadway; he couldn't blame him. He looked at Ruby, the blankness in her eyes. No, he'd definitely made the right decision. Much longer and he wasn't sure he'd have a sister to bring home.

'Better?' He softened his tone. He wanted to be tender, but Ruby would take advantage. He must stay firm.

She mumbled, pulled the eye mask from her head and threw it on the table.

He crossed his legs. 'We need to rehearse, keep in shape, develop new routines.'

'What for? The show's cancelled.' She made a sweep with her arm. 'All the shows are cancelled.' She slumped back in the chair and put the flat of her hand to her head. He half wanted to laugh at her dramatics, would've done in the past, but not now.

She tucked her legs underneath her, reached forward for the

coffee, then stared into the cup.

He couldn't be too irritated with her, understanding her disappointment, her boredom, but he was doing his best to put things right. He glanced at his wristwatch. 'I've got to go out, sort a couple of things. Have a bath. Get dressed.' He stood up, looked about him. 'Perhaps tidy up a bit?' She'd been untidy since she was a small child, but this was different; she really didn't care. The expensive clothes she'd once cherished were dropped anywhere she pleased and things had been lost – jewellery, handbags. 'I won't be long. We'll go out for lunch.' She brightened a little. 'Then we'll talk about what we're going to do next. Okay?'

She ignored him. He picked up his hat, his wallet, slipped it into his pocket. When he turned, she shrank back into the chair, her back to him, the eye mask shutting out the light.

He called goodbye and she stuck her hand up, wiggling her fingers as he closed the door.

He chose the stairs over the lift, enjoyed the burst of sunlight as he came into the lobby and stepped out into the fresh autumn air. It was good to be home, to familiar streets and sounds – even if the circumstances had not been as he'd wished. America had promised so much and delivered so little. Not that they hadn't done well; it was timing, that's all. Of the worst possible kind. He checked his watch. He had an appointment in half an hour with their new agent, Bernie Blackwood.

He walked down the Strand. The Adelphi and the Vaudeville were showing closed notices. They couldn't have come back at a worse time for work, but they couldn't have stayed in America much longer. Ruby was out of control and he'd exhausted himself trying to cover up her excess of drink and drugs, of wild partying and unsuitable relationships; keeping it out of the newspapers had cost him dearly. He waited at the kerb, watching the red buses and black cabs go by, lingering for a few minutes at Trafalgar Square.

Nelson was still standing guard, lions at his feet, and he suddenly felt comforted by the permanence of things. He tilted his face to the sun. Would the sky soon be filled with planes, ours or theirs? Trucks were rumbling down towards Whitehall, the pavements patched with khaki uniforms. He would have come back anyway, work or not. He couldn't stand by and watch his country from afar, not now it was at war. It was ironic that he felt Ruby was safer here. He put his hands in his pockets, quickened his pace. As he rounded the corner, he saw the queue and hardly needed to lift his head to see the sign on the wall: *Bernie Blackwood Variety Artistes*. He squeezed past the line of people on the stairs to Bernie's office on the first floor. What little light there was filtered from the door on the small landing that was permanently open and dust motes swirled above the heads of the eternally optimistic. A woman wearing heavy-handed make-up was smoking under a sign that said *No Smoking*.

'Hey, Johnny, old thing. Good to see you back.' He didn't recognise the tall man with the sharp jaw. 'Mickey Harper. We met at the Piccadilly?'

'Good to see you,' he replied cheerfully. He had no idea who Harper was, but that was normal these days. The Randolphs were headliners. Many people knew who they were, wanted to make themselves noticed. It was how you made your way, connections, but you had to have the talent and the work ethic. He thought of Ruby again. Would she have moved from the chair yet?

Bernie's private secretary, Shirley, was manning the desk and switchboard, keeping the mass of humanity crowded into the small office at bay. She was fierce but kind – and guarded Bernie like a lioness. She beamed when she saw him, stopped typing and got up and walked towards him, opened the small gate that kept the acts the other side of the counter.

'Mr Randolph, hello. Bernie's expecting you.' She closed the gate, batting her hand as the crowd surged forward a little, pressing on the counter. 'Wait your turn. He's got a long-standing appointment.'

Johnny tried not to smile. His long-standing appointment had been made yesterday. 'Please, call me Johnny.'

Shirley inclined her head. 'I will. Johnny. Thank you.'

He still felt uncomfortable with fame. Success was partly luck, and they had been lucky. Lucky, but not happy. Perhaps you couldn't have both.

Shirley knocked on the half-glazed door that bore the legend *Bernie Blackwood, Agent* in bold black letters edged in gold. 'Johnny Randolph is here for you, Mr Blackwood.' She opened the door wider, and stepped back to let him in.

Bernie was seated behind his broad desk, publicity photos and contracts spread across it. He got to his feet, placing his oversized Cuban cigar in the silver ashtray. He was shorter than Johnny, his thick, silver-grey hair combed back from his face. Unlike many of the theatrical agents, Bernie had a good reputation and their deal had been done by telegram followed by lunch at the Ivy. He was a kind man and fair – but woe betide anyone that crossed him.

He gripped Johnny's hand and shook it vigorously, slapping him on the back and showing him to the chair opposite his desk.

'Si' down, my boy. Si' down.' He stretched out his hand towards a chair. Johnny did as he was asked, removed his hat and placed it on his lap.

'Tea? Coffee? Something stronger?'

Johnny put up a hand. 'Not at this time of the morning, Bernie.'

'Glad to hear it, glad to hear it.'

Shirley left them to it and Bernie went over to a small table, on which was a carafe of water and glasses. He held up the carafe and Johnny assented. As Bernie poured the drinks, Johnny looked about him. The dark blue walls were covered with bills from variety shows at the Empires, Palaces and Hippodromes; with photos of Bernie with the king and queen at a variety performance; with The Crazy Gang, Gracie Fields, George Formby... Bernie was well liked and Johnny could tell from the photos that the stars were genuinely smiling and not forcing it for the camera. It was all in the eyes. Always the eyes.

Bernie set a glass down in front of him and went back to his own seat. He shuffled the papers on his desk into an untidy pile and pushed them to one side. A silver-framed photo of his wife and another of his children took pride of place. Bernie adjusted them, smiling as he did so, then gave Johnny his full attention.

'No news from Whitehall about the theatres reopening, Johnny, my boy.' He took a swig of his water; Johnny did likewise. Car horns and police bells drifted in through the open window. Johnny ran his finger around his collar. It was already stifling in the small room.

'Something's in the pipeline but nothing confirmed.' He sipped again and put his glass down. 'Not sure if they'll still go ahead with the show at the Coliseum. If the investors lose their nerve...' He leaned back in his leather chair, interlaced his fingers and rested them on his stomach. 'If they reopen, there'll be restrictions.' He splayed his hands. 'It's all down to bums on seats.'

Johnny acknowledged the fact. 'I didn't come to you about that, Bernie. I don't expect many of the shows will reopen anytime soon.'

Bernie agreed, waiting for Johnny to go on. Something in his gut told the younger man he could trust Bernie. Johnny had been reckless, turning down the Broadway contract. Their old agent, Cookie Porter, had called him a madman and maybe he was. He wasn't used to handling that side of the business. Their mother, Alice, had taken care of everything: contracts, where they performed and who with. He and Ruby had been small children when their father was killed and Alice had poured every ounce of her energy into making sure the Randolph name would headline theatres again. It felt as though he was going against everything his mother had wanted for them – but Ruby had been different, then. Johnny drew a deep breath, then exhaled. 'I was wondering if you could get us something out of town?'

'The provinces?' Bernie frowned.

Johnny rubbed his jaw. 'I know the money won't be great, and your percentage of the take will be less, so we'd be happy to pay more. Fifteen?' Bernie must think him an idiot. Perhaps Cookie was right; he was a madman.

Bernie wafted the suggestion away with a wave of his hand and leaned forward, his hands flat on the desk. 'For you. Or for Ruby?'

Johnny grasped the arms of his chair. 'The two of us. The Randolphs come as a pair – always have done, always will.' Bernie smiled and Johnny had a feeling that he wouldn't have to explain. 'You know why?'

'I had heard.'

Johnny sank in the chair. 'Already. And from America?' It was what he'd been afraid of.

Bernie was sympathetic. 'Don't worry too much, son. The time to worry is when they're not talking about you.'

Johnny clasped his hands. 'Even so, a spell somewhere quieter would take the pressure off somewhat.' Bernie opened an expensive inlaid box and offered a cigar to Johnny. 'No thanks, Bernie. I don't smoke cigars.'

'Very wise. Although I have to say I don't smoke much either – mostly it burns away in an ashtray.' He smiled. 'An expensive habit.' He picked up the cigar from the ashtray, lit it and blew out a long plume of smoke. It reminded Johnny of New York, the parties and bars, the long lunches.

He tried to relax.

'What if the show goes ahead at the Coliseum?'

'Are we tied into the contract?' It had been the first thing to cross his mind when the rumblings of war had grown louder. He had booked their passage in July and they had travelled home on the *Mauretania*, arriving the first week in August.

Bernie shrugged. 'Hard to say in these circumstances. Does war make all contracts null and void?' He leaned back in his chair. 'I don't know.'

'Bloody contracts. I hate being tied to them.'

'It gives you security, my boy. A long contract is a good thing.'

'Not when you're thousands of miles away and your mother's dying, it isn't.' Ruby had been hysterical. Not that they'd found out from Alice; she hadn't wanted them to know and had returned to England on the excuse of tying up some legal business. Their aunt Hetty had sent a telegram, against her sister's wishes, telling them of their mother's cancer. If only she'd sent it sooner. The ink was barely dry on a contract that would send them coast to coast when they got the news. Ruby had started drinking when she had barely touched alcohol before and it had been a slippery downward slope ever since.

Bernie puffed on his cigar. 'It must have been hard.'

Johnny stared out of the window at the buildings opposite. Pigeons clung to the sills, shuffling along, making room. 'I doubt Ruby will get over it. We couldn't afford to buy ourselves out of the contract and they held us to it.'

He looked back at Bernie, who moved his head from side to side.

'These things happen, my boy. If you'd been in Liverpool or London, you still might not have got back in time.'

'We would have been able to do something.' Johnny got up and went to the window, his hand resting on the wall above him. How they'd ever managed to finish the tour, he had no idea. The strain had been terrible. Ruby wasn't fit to perform some days, but he'd pushed her through it and she'd hated him for it. They'd had their differences before, but never as they had those last few months. The relief when they'd got on the boat to come home had been enormous. He turned back to Bernie. 'We'll take anything.'

'And Ruby?'

'Don't worry about it; I can handle Ruby.' Even as he said it, he doubted he could. He was in charge of their career now, their lives – and he needed to start making a better job of it. He was aware that time was against him. He might be able to defer his call-up for a while, but if not he'd have to get Ruby to Aunt Hetty in Dorset. The only problem would be making her stay there.

Bernie got to his feet, walked over and put his arm on Johnny's shoulder. 'I'll do what I can, son. Leave it to me.'

He couldn't recall the last time he'd been able to trust anyone. He drew himself more upright. 'Thanks, Bernie. I appreciate it.'

'That's what you pay me for.'

Johnny grinned. 'We haven't paid you anything yet.'

'I can wait,' Bernie said. 'I believe in you.'

Johnny nodded, not having the words, feeling that at least he'd done something right. Maybe he wasn't so mad after all.

Bernie walked with him to the door, his hand resting on Johnny's back.

'Next time we must do lunch, my boy.'

Johnny put his hat on. 'We will.' He found himself looking forward to it.

People were still queuing on the stairs and he hurried down, anxious to get back to Ruby. He felt someone grasp his shoulder and turned. The same man – Mick Parker? Harper, was it?

'See ya around, Johnny.'

Johnny stopped. 'Yes, see you around.' He hurried out into the street, blinking at the brightness of the sun. He still had no idea if he was doing the right thing; he only knew that he had to go forward and take Ruby with him.

5

On Saturday, Frances and Jessie walked along the Kingsway; the boarding houses that overlooked the promenade and beaches were all showing vacancy signs and the promenade was virtually deserted, just a handful of dog walkers and kids running along the pathways. The flower beds were still in their glory and it seemed such a waste without the crowds to enjoy them. Only a week ago they would have been getting ready for what was to become their final appearance at the Empire. Jessie had managed to get a part-time job in a solicitor's office on St Peter's Avenue and Frances had found work in a pub. It was her first proper shift later that day.

'So much has changed, hasn't it, Frances? And yet nothing has really.'

It was odd, living in such strange limbo. Places had closed, people had left, but there had been no threat, no attack as had been expected.

They strolled along the promenade, heading towards the pier. The tide was coming in and the rush and suck of the waves was soothing. All but one of the shops along the walkway were boarded up, save for a small cabin that had opened its front and was selling hot and cold drinks and snacks. A couple of old blokes sat outside, each with a mug of tea beside him on the wooden table, and they removed their flat caps in unison as the girls passed by. The one on the left was smoking a pipe and it reminded Frances of Colin. She stared across to the horizon and the boats going in and out of the Humber Estuary. Was he at sea? Had he been called up? She would find out tomorrow when she went to see Imogen. The wind blew her hair across her face and she pulled it away with her hand, losing a fighting battle. They would all be fighting soon. She turned to Jessie.

'Have you heard from Harry?'

Jessie's face shone at the mention of his name. 'A letter in the first post. He has exams again. He's busy, but he found time to write.' Jessie ran her hand along the metal railings, lifting her hand over the bumps where the posts linked to the rail as they went along.

Frances stared back at the sea. Loving Johnny had made her feel that way. Once... She closed her eyes, felt the cool wind on her face. In her dreams he'd come back to her, told her that he loved her. A happy ending. She opened her eyes and turned to Jessie.

'When did you know you loved Harry? I mean, really loved him?'

'I suppose when I thought I'd lost him forever.' She wrapped her hand over Frances's and leaned closer. 'I loved him, but I wasn't sure I was *in* love with him. I was desperate to escape from living with my aunt and uncle. Uncle Norman wasn't too bad; he gave me a job at his office and he paid for my secretarial training, so I could have stuck it, I suppose, but Aunt Iris was such a witch.' She thought for a moment. 'But if I hadn't been there I would never have met Harry, would I?' She paused. 'I was confused. My heart ached for my dad. I missed him so much, and I so wanted to make him proud of me. I thought I loved the theatre as much as I loved Harry, but it's not the same.' She looked at Frances, their eyes meeting, understanding passing between them and Frances wanted to be in love again, to have her eyes shine as Jessie's did when she talked of Harry.

'No, it's not the same at all.'

They crossed at Brighton Street, down towards the pier that stretched way out into the sea. It was odd, walking so freely, when normally they had to weave their way among the crowds that flocked to the seaside, all wanting to breathe the fresh, clean air.

'I suppose the pavilion is closed too.' Jessie was glum.

'Everywhere will be shut. Anywhere that crowds gather to enjoy themselves. It's not just the theatres but the sports grounds too. No football season, no cricket come next summer.'

'What if the theatres don't reopen?' Jessie said. 'I'm not talking about work; I'm thinking of morale. An escape. We all need it, don't we?'

'We do,' Frances agreed. The theatre had been her escape as it had been for others. You didn't have to be in the audience to want to forget your troubles. She checked her watch. 'Let's call in at the Empire and see if there's anyone about. We've time before we meet Dolly and Ginny at the café.'

They were delighted to find the entrance doors to the Empire unlocked. Frances pulled on the brass handles and they went inside. The photographs of the summer show were still in the glass cases by the box office, even though boards had been placed in front of the arched eyes of the pay desk. Frances opened the doors to the stalls and they discovered Jack sitting in the back row with Mike, the stage manager. The two men stopped talking when they saw them.

'Morning, girls. How are you getting on?'

'Fine thanks, Jack.' Jessie was cheered already. 'We only popped in to see if there was any news?'

'A little here and there. Nothing solid, but I'm optimistic. I can't say any more than that at this stage.' Jack got to his feet. He looked tired, the bags evident under his eyes. He leaned against the back of the seat in front of him.

'We understand,' Jessie said, her voice bright. 'We just wanted to let you know that we're still here should anything change. And Ginny's here too.' Jack smiled and, encouraged, Jessie went on, 'We're willing to do anything.' She turned to Frances. 'Aren't we, Frances?'

'Well, not quite,' Frances said and grinned.

Jack laughed and Mike got to his feet. He'd had a haircut and his red hair was almost stubble on his head. 'I'll be out back if you need me, Jack.'

Jack lifted a hand, gave him a short nod.

'See you later, girls.' Mike strode down the aisle and his feet were heavy as he walked up the steps at the front of the stage. There was no rush about anything these days.

'Are you still at Barkhouse Lane if I need to get in touch?'

'We are,' Jessie said quickly. 'And we can get hold of Ginny.'

Frances raised her eyebrows, puzzled by Jessie's sudden concern for Ginny. It wasn't as if the two of them had been close, more that they had tolerated each other. Six girls squashed in a dressing room had to rub along as best they could and Ginny had taken up with Billy Lane although he still had Jessie in his sights. It had caused friction between the two girls that hadn't been there before.

'I'll make sure I get a message to you as soon as I know things are starting to move. I can't promise anything.' Jack stood away from the seat. 'There might be restrictions if we do open, but...' He smiled at them both. 'When I need my Variety Girls, I'll know where you are.'

* * *

The two of them walked around the corner to Joyce's café, where there was always a warm welcome, a mug of tea and Joyce's generosity waiting for them. The café was on the corner of Dolphin Street, which ran along the back of the theatre and the gift shops, and it had become their regular haunt since they'd started at the Empire at the end of June. Ginny and Dolly were already waiting at their usual table by the window and they waved when they saw Frances and Jessie. Jessie hurried forward and held the door open; Frances caught it and stood back while a couple walked out into the street and linked arms.

Behind the counter, Joyce, the owner, called out to them as they came in. 'Hello, you lasses. Good to see you.' Dolly moved round a chair and Jessie sat down.

'Tea, Jessie? Milk?' Frances asked. She turned to Dolly and Ginny. 'Can I get either of you anything?' The girls shook their heads, pointing to the cups in front of them. Jessie took out her purse. 'Put it away,' Frances said. 'You can get the next one.'

Jessie returned her purse to her bag. 'In that case I'll have a glass of milk.'

Frances leaned on the marble counter, watching Joyce flip bacon in a pan thick with hot fat. She pressed it with a metal slice, then turned to the counter, wiping her hands on her apron. 'Tea for two?' She smoothed her black hair away from her forehead with the back of her hand, sniffed and smiled broadly, her brown, pencilled eyebrows moving alarmingly high as she did so.

'One. Jessie will have a glass of milk. I'll wait to save you bringing them over.'

'Bless ya.' Joyce took a saucer from the pile at the side of the metal urn and placed a cup on top, then drew a glass from under the counter and poured Jessie's milk. 'Did you manage to get any work, ducky? I know the other lasses have found themselves bits and bobs, and Jessie was in here the other day, telling me her news that she'd got a job at a solicitor's. She didn't look too thrilled about that, neither, but work's work, now, isn't it?' She twisted, gave the bacon a cursory glance, and turned back to Frances. 'And Ginny's got a job at the Little Laundry down by you, Barkhouse Lane way.' She wrinkled her nose. 'Not ideal – ruddy awful in hot weather, but nice in the winter, I should think.' Joyce turned back to the bacon, jiggled it onto the metal slice, slipped it onto the thick bread, stuck another round of bread on top and cut it in half. She put the plate on the counter, leaned forward and bellowed, 'Ernie, your sarnie's ready.'

Ernie shuffled up to the counter and took it. He gave Frances a gappy smile. 'Best bacon butties for miles.'

Frances agreed, watching him shuffle back, wondering how he would eat it with so few teeth. Joyce placed the milk and tea on the counter.

'There you are, ducky.' She switched her attention to the man standing next in the queue. 'Yes, flower, what can I get ya?'

Frances took the glass and mug and headed back to the table. Jessie was grumbling about her work at the solicitor's. 'Honestly, with all the hassle it took me to get here and now I'm almost back where I started. I suppose I should be grateful for Uncle Norman, really; at least I've got some work and the pay's not too bad – although Miss Beaky Bird is a miserable old so and so. Not a patch on my old boss, Miss Symonds.'

'Is she really Beaky Bird?' Ginny asked, holding her cup halfway to her mouth, looking at Jessie.

'Not really. She is Miss Bird, though. We call her Beaky because she has her nose in everything.'

Dolly laughed. Frances handed Jessie her milk and took a seat.

'Well, now I've spoken to Joyce I don't need to ask you what you've all been doing this week. I got the full rundown while she served me and everyone else.'

Dolly grinned. 'You don't need to buy a paper, that's for sure.'

'How are you finding it at the laundry, Ginny? I didn't know you'd started there.'

Ginny pushed her cup away. 'It's hard work but it's simple enough.'

'I said she should call in to see us – we're only down the street,' Jessie said. 'If I'm not there, Frances is, or Mum. You're always welcome, isn't she, Frances?'

'Of course. We Variety Girls have to stick together.' Ginny seemed encouraged and Frances felt for her. Rita, Kay and Sally, the other Variety Girls, had left the day after war had been declared, leaving Ginny alone in the flat they'd all shared, so she would be lonely, but at least her rent had been paid to the end of the month. It would give her time to look for something else.

'I wish I was a Variety Girl.' Dolly was wistful. 'It sounds so glamorous.'

'It might sound like it, but it isn't, you know that,' Frances said, laughing. 'But you're welcome to be an out-of-work Variety Girl. Or "resting" as we say in the business.'

Jessie winked at Dolly. 'You can be an honorary Variety Girl.'

'I always think of you as one of us anyway,' Frances said, because it was true. Since they'd first come together for the summer season, Dolly had been part of their lives, just as much as her lovely dad, George, was when he greeted them at the stage door each evening. 'Have you found work, Dolly?'

'With my sister. Her boarding house is now an official billet. She's already full of people from the army and I help with the breakfasts and then the evening meal, making the beds, doing the laundry.' She looked across at Ginny. 'Proper little Widow Twankeys, aren't we?'

Jessie started to sing 'Chinese Laundry Blues', playing an imaginary ukulele, grinning and tilting her head in an impression of George Formby.

'Sing up, Jessie love,' Joyce called from behind the counter. Customers at the other tables called their encouragement and it was all Jessie needed. She got to her feet and went to the front of the table. The bell over the door rang out and a sailor in uniform came in. Jessie waited while he squeezed past and then started from the beginning. Ginny and Frances got up beside her, dancing and stepping in what little space there was, joining in the chorus with Jessie, along with everyone else. When they came to the end of the song, everyone applauded.

'Eeh, that perked us all up good an' proper, you lasses.' Joyce came out from behind the counter. 'We'll have a bit of that every day, won't we, folks.' She turned to the customers, who voiced their agreement. 'Nowt like a bit of George Formby to make you smile, eh?'

'Oh, it's a crying shame that you aren't doing what you've worked so hard for,' Dolly said, as the girls sat down again. 'How quickly everyone changed when you started to entertain them. I know it's only a café, but it's almost like magic, isn't it?'

'That's exactly how I feel,' Jessie said. 'And now I've done that, I feel I can suggest something.' She grinned. 'It was what we were talking about the other night, Frances. About keeping up with our dancing.'

'Shall we get another drink first?' Frances offered. 'I feel like this might take a long time.' She got to her feet, but Jessie pushed her back down with a light touch.

'My turn this time, remember?' She took their drinks orders and went to the counter.

'What's Jessie up to?' Dolly asked.

'You'll find out soon enough,' Frances said. 'I don't want to step on her toes and it was her idea. I don't think she's willing to accept that the show is over.'

'You can't blame her,' Ginny said quietly. 'Everything was looking so good for her. I wonder if she'll go to London now?'

'I doubt it,' Frances said. 'If they start a bombing campaign, London will be top of the list. I know nothing's happened yet but it's on the cards. It's what they did in Spain. And every day we pass the Baptist chapel where the zeppelin dropped a bomb in 1916.' It was a sobering thought and a reminder to them all that war would come to their doorstep eventually. 'I don't think her mum would be happy about her going, either. Grace is in much better health, but I don't believe Jessie's ready to leave her yet.'

'Leave who?' Jessie said, setting a tray down and handing over the drinks. Dolly slipped the tray against the wall behind her.

'Your mum, Eddie, Cleethorpes. Us,' Frances said, stirring in a spoonful of sugar. Ginny sipped at the hot tea, coughed and spluttered.

Jessie was all concern. 'Are you all right, Ginny?'

The girl nodded, putting out her hand to keep Jessie back. 'My own stupid fault. Too hot.'

Frances stared at Jessie, who looked away from her. Jessie was a warm, affectionate girl who was quick to her emotions, but this concern for Ginny? What was it about? The pair of them had been at daggers drawn for most of the season, Billy Lane the cause of it, as he was of so many things. Frances wasn't the only one who was glad that he'd left when he did, before he did any more damage. The agent Bernie Blackwood had come to see Jack Holland, and Jessie too. He'd been her father's agent and had seemed a kindly sort. Billy had lingered around him like a bad smell when he discovered Bernie had contacts in the BBC. He hadn't cared one jot about any of them, leaving the show before the end of his contract and haring off to London. Well, good riddance.

'Please don't fuss, Jessie.' Ginny caught Frances's eye and flushed with embarrassment. She stared down into her cup, fiddling with the handle, and in that instant, Frances understood. The girl was pregnant. And Jessie knew. It explained everything: the whispering, the sudden closeness.

The three of them were quiet until Dolly said, seemingly oblivious, 'So, Jessie. What's your plan?' She leaned across the table, eager to join in.

Jessie was hesitant. 'I was thinking, you know. Well, when I was younger, my dad played in social clubs and pubs and I sometimes I worked with him. I haven't ever done it on my own. I thought we could do something together and share the money? Our weekends are free.'

'Not for all of us.' Frances stopped her. 'I'm working in the Fisherman's Arms and the landlady said she might need me the odd Saturday. I said I'd help when I could.'

'I thought you were working at Noble's sweet shop?'

'I'm doing both. I couldn't get anything full time. We don't know how long we're going to be out of work – theatrical work anyway. I want to save as much as I can.'

'Okay, but most Saturdays. Evenings?' Frances nodded and Jessie carried on, gaining confidence. 'And some places have entertainment on a Sunday lunchtime.'

'Not for me, Jessie,' Frances interrupted again. 'Sunday evenings, but not lunchtime.'

'Not ever?' Jessie's mouth turned down at the corners.

'Not at the moment. I'm sorry.' If she could tell them about

Imogen, they might understand. She looked again at Ginny. God, life was full of secrets – and pain.

Jessie was deflated. 'I thought we could make some extra cash and do what we're good at.' Her shoulders sagged. 'It was a daft idea.'

Frances reached out and touched Jessie's arm. 'It's a great idea. It needs more thought, that's all. Perhaps we need to find places that will take a booking first? We won't know what we'll need until we know what's available.'

'Frances is right,' Ginny agreed. 'It's okay to stand up and sing in the café and get a great response, but we need to put more effort into it if we want to make it a success. I'm all for that. Any extra money will be welcome indeed.'

Frances smiled; Ginny smiled too and she could only guess at what turmoil she must be in. The girls continued to talk but Frances's thoughts were in the past: the terror of finding out, of it being too late to tell Johnny because he'd left for America. And when he'd not replied to her letters... the pain was still raw. In her distress she'd turned to Patsy, and she and Colin had welcomed her into their home with open arms. They were family as much as anyone else ever could be. Who would Ginny turn to? One thing was for sure: she wouldn't be able to manage alone. Jessie's insistent voice broke into her thoughts.

'Can we do that, Frances?'

'Do what?'

Jessie was impatient and Frances couldn't blame her. It wasn't that she didn't want to support her – heavens, the money was bound to be helpful to all of them, but they needed to be professional in their approach.

'Rehearse, today. Jack might let us use the piano. It's not as if we'll be in the way.'

Frances bucked up. She needed to get rid of some energy and to have the whole stage to dance as she wished would be such a treat, for when she danced she could let go of her jumbled thoughts and her worries, and that could only be a good thing.

'I'm sure he would; shall we go and ask? He might still be there.'

Jessie beamed. 'Drink up,' she urged. 'The Variety Girls are going back to work. That means you too, Dolly.'

6

To Jessie's delight, the front doors were still unlocked and the girls hurried into the auditorium to find Jack sitting alone. He was leaning forward, his head in his hands as though he was praying. *As well he might be*, thought Jessie. She'd been praying too, for so many things.

He lifted his head and sat back, somewhat uncomfortable, as if he hadn't wanted anyone to see him despondent. Jessie thought he looked drained, his earlier enthusiasm having deserted him. His shirt collar was undone, his tie loose about his neck. For a moment she was wrong-footed, knowing that they had intruded, but he smiled, and she felt her confidence returning.

'Could we use the stage to rehearse, Jack? It's okay if not, you only have to say.'

Jack put up a hand. 'Careful, Jessie, you'll be talking me out of it before I've given it any thought.'

She grinned. 'We wanted to try a few things. Work on a routine, or an act we can use when the Empire opens again.'

He stood up, and punched his fist across his body. 'That's the attitude. I'm glad you're optimistic, Jessie, girls. Let's hope it's not too long, eh?' He made a sweeping arc with his arm. 'The stage is yours. Do you know where the working lights are?' He picked up his jacket, laying it across his arm.

'I do,' Frances said.

'Good, that's good.' He was forcing himself to be cheerful, but it wasn't working and Jessie wondered if he'd already had bad news regarding the theatre. If the Empire didn't reopen, she would have to go elsewhere, leave Barkhouse Lane and start again. Jack wouldn't give in so easily, would he? 'I'll be up in my office for a while yet. Mike's already gone, so if you need to stay longer I only have the one key.'

Dolly leaned forward. 'I can ask Dad. He still has one for the stage door.'

'Perfect,' Jack said. 'I'll lock up the front when I leave. If you get the key, Dolly, you girls can come and go as you please.'

They watched him walk away, the doors banging behind him, echoing throughout the auditorium.

'I'll put the lights on,' Frances said, making her way down the aisle and up the steps onto the stage. She disappeared into the darkness of the wings and suddenly Jessie felt deflated, all the energy from the fun she'd had in the café deserting her.

Ginny noticed and rubbed at Jessie's back. 'Don't lose heart now, Jessie. It's still a good idea.'

'It is,' Dolly encouraged. 'And starting anything is always the hardest part.'

They heard the thump of the lever as Frances threw the switch for the lights and the stage was illuminated. She walked out onto the stage, her fists on her hips.

'What are you waiting for, Delaney? Get your backside up here.'

The three girls grinned and dashed up the steps to join her.

'Give me a shove to get the piano onstage,' Jessie called over her shoulder, racing up the steps. Dolly and Ginny followed her into the wings, but Frances stepped between them.

'I'll do that, Ginny.'

Jessie froze, looked quickly at Ginny and then to Frances. Had she given the game away? Ginny reddened again. Frances didn't appear to have noticed. She stood one end of the piano, ready to push, and Jessie hurried to the other side.

'You bring the chair,' Frances said. 'The maestro needs to put her big bottom somewhere.' Dolly giggled and it broke the tension.

When the piano was where they wanted it, Jessie sat down and made a performance of wiggling her fingers, cracking her knuckles.

'Save it for the paying punters, Jessie,' Frances said. 'We have work to do.'

Jessie began to play anything that came into her head, songs from the summer show, songs her father had played. How she longed to feel his arms about her once more, to feel safe. She was trying not to be fearful, to keep chipper for her mother's sake if not for her own. Dolly leaned on the piano facing Jessie and rested her chin on her hands. Occasionally Jessie glimpsed the girls moving about the stage and when they stopped and came to lean on the piano alongside Dolly, she stopped too.

'Enough of enjoying ourselves. We need to get to work.' Frances stepped back and walked across the stage.

'We should have brought our practice shoes, Ginny. It would've made it easier.'

Jessie twisted on the chair. 'Well, it was all a bit spur-of-the-moment. We'll be more organised in future.'

The door at the back of the auditorium opened, letting in a shaft of light from the foyer. As it closed, a tall, slender woman came sashaying down in the aisle. She was dressed in an expensive navy suit and matching hat, a gold and navy clutch bag tucked under her arm. Jessie sprang from the chair as if she'd been electrocuted.

'Good afternoon, Mrs Holland.' Frances smiled and Jessie blushed, feeling as though she'd been caught out at school.

Jack Holland's wife looked along the empty seats. 'Where's my husband?'

Jessie stepped forward. 'He's in his office on the first floor.'

'I know quite well where his office is,' she snapped. 'Has he asked you to rehearse?'

'We asked. Ja— Mr Holland said we could use the stage,' Jessie explained. 'We're putting an act together. For when the theatre reopens.'

The woman raised one perfectly shaped eyebrow and Jessie felt like a small child. 'If it reopens.' She looked the girls up and down. 'I hope you won't be too long. Those lights are expensive. I needn't remind you of the cost of the electricity.' She spun on her heel and they watched her walk back down the aisle and out of the door.

'Cow!' spat Frances.

Dolly sighed. 'He's such a lovely man. I can't imagine how he came to marry her.' Audrey Holland had been the topic of back-stage conversation more than once.

'Once she dug her claws into him, I doubt he could escape,' Frances said.

'Perhaps we should turn off the lights, go home.' Jessie's enthusiasm had waned.

'Don't you dare,' Frances replied. 'Jack was delighted when you asked. Poor bugger looked like he'd got the world on his shoulders until you walked in. We need to support him too. If we have an act, that'll help. And we'll be cheap.'

'But not that cheap,' Jessie countered.

'That's the spirit.' Frances rubbed her hands together. 'Right, what are we going to do first?'

They found chairs backstage and brought them into the light. Dolly went off in search of some paper and pencil, came back and sat herself down facing the girls, pencil poised. Frances said, 'You can be the producer, Dolly.'

Dolly's eyes sparkled. 'Ooh, I do feel important. Does this mean I'm in show business at last?'

Frances winked at her. 'You're an honorary Variety Girl, remember? You're already in show business.'

They spent a happy couple of hours selecting songs and working out routines, and the fact that the country was at war and the theatres closed seemed to fade into the distance. They put their heads together and worked amicably, selecting first the songs and then the harmonies.

'You have a lovely voice, Frances,' Jessie said. 'Really lovely. You should sing more.'

Frances smiled. 'Thanks, Jessie. It's nothing like yours but I can hold a tune well enough. I used to sing a lot.'

'When?' Dolly asked.

'I suppose the nearest I came to success of any kind was as understudy for Ruby Randolph in *Lavender Lane*.' She paused, wondering whether she'd said too much. It was odd talking about her past; she usually avoided any conversation that might lead there. The girls were giving her their full attention, waiting for her to go on. She didn't have to tell them everything. 'When Ruby was ill, I took the lead for a while.'

'Wow, that's amazing,' Dolly gushed. 'That was a huge success. Wasn't it a record-breaking run?'

'It was.'

'And you worked with the Randolphs?' Dolly hadn't been there when she'd spoken of them last week. She didn't want to keep talking, but you could never mention working with the Randolphs and hope to keep the conversation short. Everyone was fascinated by them.

'What were they like, Frances? I've heard she's fun.'

Frances considered her answer. 'She is, most of the time.' It didn't hurt to blur the lines a little. How best to describe Ruby? One word would never do. She could be enormously generous one minute, mean-spirited the next. 'There's a huge amount of pressure being that famous. It makes her a bit volatile.' There was no need to go into details. 'Their mother was very ambitious. She was the driving force.' That was a nice way of putting it. 'But it worked. They did get to the top.'

'You're such a dark horse, Frances. You never speak of what you've done in the past.' Jessie leaned forward. 'You must tell us more, mustn't she, girls?'

Frances was torn. Talking usually helped her marshal her thoughts, helped unknot the mess of her head. But not now. They were kind, sweet girls but they had no idea of what could happen to a woman. And that was the difference. She was a woman and they were still girls. Except for Ginny, who had a hard and difficult path to walk. She was putting on a brave face but Frances could see through it, just as Patsy had seen through hers.

'Enough,' she said, getting to her feet. 'We've plenty of time to talk and the lights are burning money. We can't make Mrs Holland more sour than she already is.' She pushed her chair back. 'Jack has been generous. Let's make the most of the time we have and talk later.'

* * *

At four thirty, Frances stopped them working. 'I've got to go. I have to be at the pub for five and I need to have a quick wash and freshen up beforehand, grab something to eat. See you at home,

Jessie.' She sprang down the steps and headed outside, glad to be in the fresh air, albeit for a short time.

Jessie turned to the other two. 'At least we've got some songs, some routines. We can work more on the harmonies. We don't need the theatre for that.'

'I'll pop and get the key from Dad,' Dolly said.

Jessie and Ginny put the chairs back into the wings, leaving the piano where it was.

'I think Frances knows,' Ginny said, her voice hardly more than a whisper. Jessie was quick to reply.

'I haven't said anything. I promised – and I wouldn't dream of breaking it.'

Ginny threw the switch to kill the stage lights. They stood in the pale shadows and walked towards to stage door to wait for Dolly. 'I know you haven't. I just got a funny feeling in the café. And she wouldn't let me move the piano.'

Jessie looked down at her hands. 'Maybe you should tell her.' It would make it easier for both of them. She hated keeping secrets. 'Frances is older. She'll... Well, you know, she might know things.' Jessie was frightened for Ginny. Since the girl had confided in her, she'd been anxious, wanting to help and not knowing where to start.

'Please, don't say anything,' Ginny pleaded. 'It might be a false alarm. It's been so unsettling. War. The show ending. And worst still, Billy going without a backward glance. I already feel used and stupid, and I know Frances disapproved of him.'

'Of him. Not you. You haven't done anything wrong.'

Ginny sighed. 'Not many people will see it like that. They'll think I got what I deserve.'

'You're just one of the unlucky ones, Ginny.' She rubbed at the girl's shoulder. She was painfully thin, her soft features made sharp with fear, and Jessie wished she could do more. 'I want you to know you're not alone.'

'Thanks. But I shouldn't think your mum will be too pleased, you keeping my company.'

Jessie pulled her close, hoping to give her some comfort. 'My mum has been in show business for almost all of her life in some way or another. She's much tougher than you think.'

The door opened and Dolly breezed in, all smiles. 'The key to the kingdom,' she said, dangling it in front of her.

'Or queendom,' Jessie said, letting Ginny go in front of her. The two of them stood to one side as Dolly locked the door and tugged at it. She slipped the key into her pocket.

'Tomorrow?' she said encouragingly.

Jessie agreed. It wasn't as if they had anything else to do. 'I don't see why not. Frances is too good not to pick it up later.' She looked down the street. 'Who'd have thought it – the Randolphs. That girl's full of surprises.'

7

At five o'clock, Frances opened the back door of the Fisherman's Arms, pulled the blackout curtain aside and went in. It wouldn't be dark for at least another couple of hours, but Lil, the landlady, had taken to leaving it permanently across. She'd told Frances she had enough to do without fannying around with curtains. The back door was rarely used and it seemed sensible. Lil ran the pub on her own and it was long hours, seven days a week, so Frances imagined any shortcuts would be welcome.

'Is that you, Frances?'

Frances stepped into the private sitting room at the back of the bar where Lil was having a last cigarette before opening up. 'No, Lil. You've got it wrong. You have to say, "Is it yourself?"' She accentuated her Irish accent to make Lil laugh.

Lil took a drag, then twisted her ciggie in the ashtray on the mantelpiece behind her.

'I haven't got the voice for it, flower. Or the charm.' She adjusted her bra straps and her bosom welcomed the lift. Lil was a well-upholstered woman and went out as much at the front as she did at the back. She was in perfect proportion and had plenty of padding.

Frances draped her coat over the back of one of the two easy chairs that faced the gas fire. The room was cosy but chaotic. A small table was up against one wall, one of the flaps permanently out; old copies of the *Grimsby Telegraph* were piled high, and a stack of buff envelopes and letters had accumulated beside them, while a tin can held numerous pencils that Lil used for her crosswords. The furnishings were old and heavy, too big for the room, but Frances reflected that it was like Lil herself: warm and welcoming and built for comfort, not beauty.

'I see your filing system is under control,' Frances said, grinning at the chaos on the table.

'It works for me.' Lil turned to the mirror over the fireplace and checked her appearance. 'Eeh, them chaps out there don't know how lucky they are. I look like Mae West tonight.' She patted her bleached blonde hair that was set in large curls about her broad face. 'Come up and see me sometime.' She turned to Frances. 'Do you think I can carry it off?'

Frances grinned. 'If anyone can, you can.'

The older woman smiled. 'You're a good lass, Frances, I like you. I reckon him upstairs sent you my way in this darkness.'

'Him upstairs?'

Lil pointed to the ceiling.

Frances was puzzled. 'Do you have a lodger?'

Lil roared with laughter. 'I meant God, lovey. Upstairs. Hell, if I had a man upstairs, I wouldn't be down here with you.' She rubbed her hands briskly. 'Let's let that rum lot in, shall we?' She led the way like Boadicea and opened the door that led to the back of the bar. The tea towels were quickly removed from the pumps, the drawer to the till put in place. Frances lifted the flap of the bar, quickly checking that every table had an ashtray and a selection of beermats. When that was done, she pulled aside the curtain that covered the front door, twisting her head to look at Lil, her hand reaching up to the top bolt.

'Shall I let them in?'

Lil bent her neck and looked up at the clock over the bar that told customers when they could drink and when they could not. The woman stood rigid as the second hand clicked round and finally fell on the hour.

'Right, let's 'ave 'em.' She turned back to the bar, one hand on the bitter pump, the other on the counter. Frances unfastened the top and bottom bolts and unlocked the door.

A tall, thin man was waiting on the doorstep, newspaper under his arm, his Jack Russell terrier, Fudge, at his side. He let the dog go before him, and Fudge immediately took his regular place on the seat by the fire. As the dog's owner came up to the bar, Lil placed a pint of bitter in front of him. 'Evening, Artie.' He handed over his coins, took his pint and sat in the corner next to Fudge. Frances took her place beside Lil.

'Does he ever speak?' she whispered.

'Never. Probably be nowt but tripe if he did. Still, he comes in here, regular as clockwork, has two pints, reads the paper and off he trots. I could do with a few more like him.'

People started to drift in, haphazardly, mostly elderly regulars who were not going to let Hitler dictate their habits. Frances was busy serving one of them when there was a rustle of the curtain and a man appeared, who almost filled the front doorway. He was over six feet tall, smartly dressed, his thick, sandy hair brushed back off his square forehead. He looked about him, tipping his head in a slight nod to the other men in the room, then came to the bar, pulled out the stool by the corner and took a seat.

'Pint of the usual, Malc?'

'Aye, if you please, Lil.' He gave Frances a half-smile. 'Hullo, lass.'

'Evening,' Frances replied.

Lil took a tankard from the back shelf. 'Watch,' she said to Frances. She poured a pint of bitter, tilting the glass then slowly bringing it upright as the tankard filled, leaving a foamy head about half an inch thick. She placed it in front of the man, who put his hand around it but didn't lift it straight away. 'This is Big Malc,' she said. 'That's his tankard and that's how he likes his pint pulled. Got it?' Frances wondered what Big Malc would do if she didn't. Lil threw back her head and laughed, her generous bosom wobbling. 'Only teasing.' Big Malc grinned. 'This is Franny, Malc. She's like an angel from heaven, come just at the right time.'

Malc put his hand across the bar and Frances took it. His hand was big, his grip firm but warm. Up close he had a kind face, but Frances wondered how many people ever got that close.

'Glad to hear it, Lil. Sorry that Ted left you in the lurch, but I suppose it's the same for everyone. Some 'as got their call-up papers already.'

Lil put one hand on the bar, leaning forward, the other on her hip. 'I know. I hope it don't last as long as last time. Can't be doing with that, can we?'

Malc shook his head, supped his beer.

Customers came in a steady stream after that and there was no time to chat. The bar curved round and a partition divided the snug from the smoke room. It seemed pointless to Frances, for the noise as the place filled up was unavoidable and smoke from pipes and cigarettes created a hazy fug, which rose slowly towards the mustard-coloured ceiling.

When the rush died off, Frances refreshed the sink with hot water and the two women dealt with the glasses that had accumulated at the end of the counter, Frances washing, Lil drying. She stuck a tea towel in the glass and rubbed with efficiency born of years of practice, twisting and replacing the glasses on the shelves with economy. Some of the men were the worse for drink, their laughter louder, their smiles broader. Women with heavy lipstick and large cleavages leaned in, talking close to the men, and Frances looked on impassively, glad she didn't have to do that.

'Don't judge 'em, Franny,' Lil said, looking in the same direction. 'Some of them get knocked about a bit but they don't know no better.'

'I wasn't judging,' Frances said, disappointed that Lil thought that of her. And as she thought it, she realised that Lil was right; she had been judging, glad she wasn't one of them. Lil began wiping the bar down with a damp cloth.

'Lots of people judge harshly, Lil.' She'd had to contend with enough people passing judgement on her these last few years. Bad enough that she was Irish, that held enough problems in some quarters, and she'd only added to her difficulties.

'Born out of ignorance, flower.'

A young lad, who looked barely old enough to be served, squeezed himself to the front of the bar.

Lil stepped forward. 'What can I get ya, sonny?'

'Can the dark-haired one serve me?'

Lil winked at her. 'He wants the pretty 'un to serve him. No taste.' She moved further up the bar and got busy with another order.

Through the mirror that ran along the back of the bar, Frances could see him watching her as she rang his order in the till.

Lil stood next to her. 'He'll be in every night now, looking out for you.'

'He doesn't look old enough to be in here.'

'Probably isn't.'

The pair of them leaned against the back of the bar, watching the show before them. Big Malc was still on his seat at the corner of the bar – he'd only moved to go to the lavatory. He chatted briefly to other customers but mostly watched the goings-on, nursing a pint, which he drank at a slow, steady pace.

They had another sprint of washing glasses.

'That lad hasn't moved all night.'

'You'll see a lot like him, Franny, young and old. They're lonely. You're here to cheer 'em up.'

'Not too far from what I usually do.' Frances drained the dirty water. 'That's what Jack calls it.'

'What?' Lil hung a damp tea towel over the open bar flap.

'The theatre. He calls it the cheer-up business.'

'Well, he's right. They don't come here to hear your troubles; they come to get away from everything for an hour or two.'

Frances picked up a cloth to give Lil a hand with drying and stared out across the bar. 'I'm glad they never shut the pubs.'

'Shut the pubs!' Lil spluttered. 'There'd be a ruddy riot and no mistake.'

Lil stepped back, looked up at the clock and rang the brass bell underneath it, shouting, 'Last orders!' There was a rush for drinks and then Lil called time. Frances went out and collected glasses as people drifted out, calling night to Lil, holding up a hand and making sure Frances was included. Some of them walked perfectly well; others swayed and staggered. Lil called, 'Do be nice!' and the last couple of drinkers supped up and left.

'Will I see you here tomorrow?' the lad asked Frances.

Lil interrupted. 'Not on a Sunday, but she'll be here Monday. She'll be here most days.' She pressed Frances's arm. 'That all right with you, Franny?'

Frances's shoulders dropped with the relief, knowing she had met with Lil's approval. Lil hadn't made any promises other than to take it shift by shift to see how it went. It had been hard work, but Lil was fun, she paid cash in hand and the tips had been good. A half-pint glass that Lil had told her to put by the till had filled with coppers and thrupenny bits. It would all help.

Big Malc got to his feet. 'See you tomorrow, Lil.'

'Aye, thanks, Malc.'

He said goodnight to them both. 'Lock up after me, Lil.'

She put up a hand. 'Right behind ya.' Frances heard the bolts slide into place as she cleared the remaining glasses.

The two of them went around emptying the ashtrays and wiping them with a damp cloth.

'Have you got time for a nightcap before you go?'

'A quick one.' She was tired but her brain was fizzing. She finished washing the glasses and Lil wiped the counter. When she'd done, she took the money drawer from the till and passed it to Frances.

'Take that in the back room for me, will ya, love? While I turn off the lights.'

Frances went through, pushed aside a few papers and put the till drawer on the table. Lil followed soon after, carrying a bottle of whisky and two glasses that she squeezed onto the table, shoving the drawer aside with her elbow. 'Want a bit of water in yours?'

'That would be grand.'

Lil fetched a small jug of water from the kitchen and placed it on the table, putting the papers on one of the dining chairs.

'Move that coat and sit yourself down; you can help me tot up.' Frances picked up the red coat and placed it on the easy chair, alongside her own, while Lil poured the drinks. Lil took the back of an envelope and a pencil from the tin. She scooped the shillings from the tray, pushing them across the table. 'Add that up and tell me how much.' They worked their way through the coins, the half-crowns and the coppers. Lil licked the pencil nib and wrote the total, then picked up her glass. 'Not a bad night at all.' She took a small sip of her whisky. 'So, what d'ya think, then? Reckon you can stick it out with me?'

'If you want me, I'm here.'

Lil counted the change out of the takings and pressed it into Frances's hand. 'And don't forget your tips behind the bar.' She eased back in her chair. 'I don't know how long I'll need you. I'd thought I might be a bit light this week, but it's not been much different. Most of the regulars are too old for service. Although they're doing their bit with the ARP.'

Frances took a sip of her whisky, added more water. 'What about Big Malc?' As the words came out, she wished they hadn't. Lil would think she was being nosy. If she'd minded, she didn't say.

'Malc used to be a friend of my hubby, mates since they were lads. I think he feels he needs to watch over me, since Jimmy died, like.' Lil put her hand on the table, looked at her wedding ring. 'Keeps asking me to marry him.'

'Would you?'

Lil shook her head. 'No, lovey. Three's enough for any woman.' Frances raised her eyebrows. 'Oh, aye. I've never been short of admirers but I can manage on my own. I can't go through the heartache again.' She took another swig from her glass. 'Bend down and put that gas fire on, lovey. It's got a bit chill now we've stopped.' Frances did as she was asked. 'Have you got to rush off?'

Frances sat back down. 'No. No one to rush home for.'

'Pretty lass like you? You do surprise me.' She felt as if Lil could see right through her, that the woman knew all her secrets. For once it didn't bother her.

'There was once,' was all she willing to offer. Lil didn't press her.

'My first husband, Kenny, was killed at Ypres. Lovely lad. I was full of hopes and dreams when we wed. He was a dear man.' Lil closed her eyes, a smile playing on her face. Frances thought how tired she looked now that it was just the two of them. It was like coming down from the high after a show and Lil certainly gave a performance while she was out front. She opened her eyes. 'I wasn't the only one, though, so it helped. Lots of us women in the same boat.' She drank again. 'Then Bob, he was a good 'un. Laugh! He made me roar with his stories.'

'What happened?' She was nervous to ask.

'Accident. He worked down the docks. Looked up one day and a sack hit him in the wrong place. Killed outright. A blessing when you see how some people suffer.' She added a splash of water to her glass. 'Jimmy suffered. He'd been in the trenches too. Never got over it. Filled his pockets with rocks and walked into the water last summer. I don't think he could cope with another war. He was such a gentle man.' She stared at Frances, who didn't want to look away from Lil's pain. 'I reckon he sent you along, lass. He was like that. Help anyone except himself.' She stared into her empty glass. 'The damage of war goes on and on.'

The clock on the mantelpiece chimed midnight. 'I'd better go. I have to be up early tomorrow.'

'I've kept you too long. Will you be all right walking home? Do you want me to walk with you?'

Frances put on her coat then picked up her gas mask and flung it over her shoulder. 'I'll be fine. It's only a five-minute walk. I'm getting used to it now and the moon's still quite bright.'

Lil got to her feet. 'It's been nice talking to you, Frances. I think you and me will get along fine.'

Frances grinned, pulled aside the curtain over the back door, and repeated Big Malc's words: 'Lock up after me, Lil.'

Lil grinned too. 'Aye, I will.'

8

The vans were already lined up, steam pouring out from the chimney of the Little Laundry on Barkhouse Lane. The air smelled of soap and coal from the hopper that heated the boiler and a steady stream of women spilled into the entrance doors. Ginny hurried to join them. One of the drivers was leaning against the back wall, having a last drag on his fag, and he lifted his hand in greeting, knocking the ash away with his finger at the same time.

'Here's our lovely dancing girl, bright as the morning.' It made her smile, even though she didn't feel much like it. He took another drag, flicked his fag end to the floor, ground it with his heel. It was only Tuesday and already there was a tidy pile in the corner. 'Better get in there before ol' droopy drawers gets stroppy.' He stood back to let her pass and Phyl came running up beside her.

'Made it!' she called, following Ginny inside. The overwhelming smell of soap made Ginny nauseous and she stepped to one side, wishing she'd eaten something. Phyl clocked in and Ginny took her card from the slot, waiting for her turn.

The supervisor, Edna Bowers, was walking about, looking as if she'd sucked on a lemon, pristine in her white overalls and turban.

'Get your backside in sharpish, Thompson. We don't have time for prima donnas here.'

Phyl stuck up for her. 'Poor lass has barely set foot in the place and you're on her back.'

Edna sneered. 'As well I might. I haven't got time for slackers.' She disappeared into the laundry, the double doors banging behind her.

Phyl winked at her. 'Take no notice of her. Her bark's worse than her bite.'

They hung up their coats and left their bags in the cloakroom and quickly pulled on their blue overalls, tucking their hair inside the matching hats, and hurried to their workstation.

The room was beginning to hum with the sound of the washers, the whoosh of water and clatter of the wicker baskets being pushed along the floor. This was only her second week and Ginny had been grateful to be taken on the Tuesday after war had been declared. She was beginning to get used to the overwhelming smell of soda that had burned her nostrils on the first day. At first it had seemed fresh and she'd associated it with cleanliness and her mother, but over time, as the building grew hot with toil, it only added to her sense of sickness and detachment. Over by the machines, two women were sifting through the linen and clothing that was piled high into wicker baskets, before being loaded into the machines. They would be moved into the dryers then on to the steam rolling irons. In the far corner was a row of ironing boards, where six girls stood pressing shirts and fine silk blouses.

Phyl and Ginny went to the flat steam roller and picked up a sheet, grabbing the four corners, folding it in half then half again before feeding it through the machine.

'By, my mum would've loved to have one of these years ago,' she called to Phyl. 'The hours she spent ironing, breaking her back.'

Her mum been almost permanently bent over an iron, a pile of clothing behind her.

'Aye, must be ruddy lovely to have the luxury of having your laundry done for ya. How the other 'alf live, eh.' She reached down for another sheet, waited while Ginny found the corners. 'I keep worrying about me two brothers, gone off in the army,' Phyl said. 'I wish they hadn't gone so soon.'

Ginny tugged at the sheets and Phyl did the same. It made her think of her own brothers. All three of them had escaped, one by one, as soon as they could, taking whatever work that would get them away from their dad's fists. Would they have joined up too? There was nothing to go home to Leeds for, not since her mother had died.

'It's early days,' Ginny said, trying to concentrate as sounds in the laundry grew louder, raising her voice. 'I expect you'll hear from them before long.'

Phyl tilted her chin upwards. 'Aye.'

The two of them fell quiet as the noise in the room grew and made conversation nigh on impossible. They worked quietly, using mime to communicate. The room became much hotter as the steam presses worked their magic, the dryers and washers rumbling along in the background. It was lit by long lights high in the ceiling which added to the heat and stuffiness and she felt herself stumble forward as she leaned into the wicker basket for another sheet.

Phyl caught her hand and steadied her. 'You don't look well; are you sure you can manage?'

Ginny rested one hand on the basket, pressing her lips together as she felt bile rising again.

'I drank some milk this morning.' She looked up, smiled broadly. 'I think it was off.' She took up another sheet but felt light-headed and leaned again on the basket, gripping the side to steady herself.

Edna strutted over. 'What's going on? You'll hold everyone up if you don't keep it moving along the line.'

Ginny pulled herself upright but the sudden movement made her head swim.

'She's not well!' Phyl shouted above the noise.

'If she can't do the job...' Edna folded her arms across her chest.

'It won't happen again. I drank some iffy milk. It's upset my stomach.'

Edna scoffed. 'Your own stupidity then. I was—'

'Edna!' The manager was leaning over the rail on the upper floor. She looked up. 'Could I have you for a moment?'

Edna went off and Phyl pulled a face. 'Take no notice of misery guts.'

Ginny took up the sheet, ready to start again. 'I'll try not to.'

The machines tumbled and turned and the sound was like thunder in her head as it grew hotter. She looked up again, back to the press, leaned down into the basket, tugged at a sheet with Phyl, and stood up again. Her head spun, the windows seemed to tilt on the wall, and she heard Phyl call out, 'Catch her!' as she fell backwards onto the floor.

Her vision was blurry when she opened her eyes; someone was hauling her to sit upright, supporting her back. Phyl held a glass out and put it under her lips.

'Try and sip it.' She tried to focus but Phyl's face looked odd and misshapen. She did as she was urged and sipped. The water was cool and she wanted to gulp it down, but Phyl kept drawing the glass away. Ginny shuffled more upright.

'I'm absolutely fine. It's the heat. It's taking a bit of getting used to.' She couldn't lose this job, for where would she find another? And she still had to find somewhere to stay at the end of the month.

Edna came back as Ginny got to her feet.

'I knew it was a mistake taking you on. Not used to a hard day's work like the rest of us. Only fit for prancing about the stage, showing what you've got to all and sundry.'

'That's unfair, Edna.'

'You can keep your trap shut an' all.'

Phyl glanced at the clock. 'Time for our break anyway.' She flipped the switch that stopped the rollers and turned her back on the woman and leaned in close to whisper in Ginny's ear, 'Old sod.' She put her hand under Ginny's elbow. 'Come on. Let's get some fresh air.'

The girls sat or leaned along the low wall outside. Being out in the fresh air was bliss and a cool breeze blew, reviving Ginny a little.

Phyl held out one of her potted beef sandwiches. 'Get that down ya. Ya need something nourishing.'

Ginny put her hand up, shook her head. 'I'm fine. I must have caught a sickness bug – or it's something I've eaten.' She hadn't eaten much for days, mostly from worry, partly to save money.

'Yeah, course you 'ave,' one of the other women chipped in. 'If you need any help with that sickness bug,' she said pointedly, 'I know someone who can help.'

Ginny felt her face burn. Phyl flicked her cigarette end over the wall and slipped onto her feet, brushing down the back of her overall.

'Take no notice of her, neither.'

* * *

It was a difficult afternoon; her back was aching like the very devil but at least the sickness had gone and for that she was grateful. She carried on with Phyl, bending, tugging and turning, folding and threading the sheets through the press. Her mam would weep if she could see her now.

'When did you start dancing, Ginny?'

'When I was a kid – three, four. My mam took in washing from the theatre folks to bring in extra money. She took me with her, whether I wanted to go or not.'

Phyl smiled and she carried on folding the sheets, feeding the machine.

'She got me free dance lessons, acting, singing – whatever she could barter. She didn't want me to be stuck doing laundry like her.' She blushed. 'Oh, that sounds awful I didn't mean—'

Phyl laughed. 'Don't apologise. Christ, if I could do summat else I'd be off like a shot. I'd be sticking two fingers up to Edna and singing as I went.' She looked over to the other girls. 'Some of us have already been talking about signing up. A ruddy regimental sergeant major will be a doddle after Edna.' They looked over at her. 'Atten-shun!' Phyl saluted and the woman turned away.

They carried on and Ginny thought of her mother, pushing her forward, setting her on a path that she would never have for herself. She couldn't stay here much longer. It would be as if her mother's life had been worthless. She had to get back on the stage; she owed it to Mam, and nothing was going to stop her, not women like Edna, or men like Billy Lane.

'You've got a bit o' colour in your cheeks now,' Phyl shouted over the noise. 'Feelin' better?'

'Tons.'

Phyl was not convinced. 'You still look iffy. Perhaps you should switch to sorting for a bit. It's not so hot and you'll get more of a rest while they wait for delivery.'

When the whistle blew at four, they hurried off to the cloakroom and collected their things. Phyl pulled on her coat and scarf, checked herself in the mirror.

'Why don't you come back with us for a bite to eat? Me mam won't mind.'

It was kind but Ginny felt too vulnerable. They would ask questions and she was tired; she might slip up.

'Thanks, Phyl, but I'd best get back. I think I need an early night.'

Phyl rubbed at Ginny's shoulder. 'Another time, then? When you're feeling better?'

Ginny buttoned her coat, pulled her beret from the pocket and put it on. 'I'd like that.'

She walked out of the yard and onto Barkhouse Lane, lingering on the pavement as the other women streamed past her, back to their homes, their families. She looked down towards the house that Jessie and Frances shared. Jessie had invited her for tea on the Monday the other dancers had left and they'd all been so warm and welcoming... oh, she longed to go there now, walk in and be part of their home. She shivered, wrapped her arms about herself and made her way to the end of the street, started to walk home, then stopped, turned and looked down towards the sea. What was the point in rushing back? She headed for the Empire, knowing it would be locked but wanting to feel attached to something. She hurried past the shops, all shuttered, and arrived at the theatre. The photos of summer were still there, and she wished for a moment that she could roll back the days and start again.

There was a picture of the star Madeleine Moore, photos of the girls in their various costumes. She moved to the showcase at the other side of the door. The comedian Billy Lane was smiling out at her. How easily she'd fallen for his charms, eager to be loved. She touched the glass. Her fingertips were grubby with dirt and she spat on them, wiped them on her skirt. If only everything could be cleaned away so easily.

The sky was overcast, the clouds thick, and she made her way down towards the pier, the wind on her face. The tide was out, the edge of the water so far away that it looked as if it would never come in again. How long would it take to walk out that far? More than the energy she had. She leaned on the railings and watched seagulls waddle about on the ridges that had been left as the tide receded, drilling down with their beaks for worms. Hunger was tearing at her stomach but she mustn't eat. It wasn't a baby, just a seed – and seeds needed nourishment.

She began walking again, enjoying the feel of the salt air on her skin, tightening, tightening, and crossed the deserted road, then started walking up the commemoration steps below the Cliff Hotel. The treads were wide and broad. Auntie Beryl had lost her baby when she fell down the stairs. She stopped, her hand on the rough concrete of the wall, turned and looked again at the tide, so far, far away. She moved up the steps again, her footsteps heavy. At most she might break her ankle. She would need enough to live on while it mended, but it wouldn't take too long to heal. Yes, yes, there were things she could do...

She focused on each wide tread until she reached the top then stopped, turned back to look at the sea, lowered her eyes and slid one foot forward. It would look like an accident. She put her hand to her face, longing to feel her mother's hand there, gentle, protecting. How Mam had loved to watch her dance. She leaned forward a little further, closed her eyes, wanting to let go of everything, the rail, the world...

She felt a hand on her shoulder and staggered forward, but the hand gripped her firmly, another at her elbow. The shock of it made her scream and the hands clung tighter, pulling her back. When she opened her eyes, she saw that it was Frances, her dark hair flying in the wind, her red lips so vivid, everything about her so sharp and wild – alive. She moved her hands to either side of Ginny's shoulders.

'I'm sorry, so, so, sorry, Ginny. I called but you didn't hear me.' Frances held on to her, slowly releasing her grip as Ginny moved away from the top of the steps, guiding her onto the pavement. Her heart was pounding so loudly she couldn't make sense of what Frances was saying.

'How stupid of me! I shouldn't have startled you like that. I've given you a fright.' She led her over to the shelter by the ornamental gardens and made her sit down on the bench inside it. Ginny put her hand to her throat. She could have fallen, so easily. But she knew now that she didn't want to. Cars went past, people on bicycles – the world seemed louder that it had before. And there was Frances, beside her, talking to her. She forced herself to concentrate although she was trembling now and couldn't stop.

Frances was still fussing about her, her words a jumble. Blood was coursing through Ginny's ears, a thunderous waterfall, making it difficult to hear.

'Oh, Ginny, you're as white as a sheet.'

She must stop this. She must get home.

'You took me by surprise. I-I'll be fine in a minute or two.' She tried to smile but her teeth were chattering. 'I'm okay, truly I am.'

Frances shook her head. 'You are not okay and it's my fault. I saw your red hair and your green beret and I knew it was you. I should have waited for you to turn but I didn't want to make you fall.' She took Ginny's hand in hers. Her fingers were long, her nails perfect ovals, painted red to match her lips. Frances was always so put together. Her hands and arms were expressive when she danced; Ginny had noticed how deeply she felt the music. But it wasn't like that for her. She could dance, but she didn't love dancing. Not like Rita, not like Frances. It was just something she could do, something she'd worked so hard at to please her mother. She swallowed, pressing hard on her lower lip, holding back the tears. She must not think of her mother.

'I'm fine.' Ginny got up, sat down again, stared at the pavement. She was cold, her trembling more violent.

Frances pulled at her arm, gently this time, and patted her hand.

'You're coming with me. You're in shock.' Frances took Ginny's hand in hers, her voice softer now. 'Come and meet Lil and I'll get you some hot sweet tea. It's the very least I can do.'

9

It was three minutes past six when Frances led Ginny through the front doors of the Fisherman's Arms. Artie was sitting in his usual place, reading the *Telegraph*, Fudge the dog at his side. It raised its eyes when it saw Frances, its wagging tail beating against the leather seat. Lil was pouring a drink and looked up when they came in, her eyes flicking over Frances, then Ginny.

'Sorry, Lil. I'll make the time up.' She pulled one of the empty stools up to the bar flap and made Ginny sit down. 'This is my friend, Ginny. I gave her a fright, nearly knocked her down the stairs, so I did.'

'And you call ya'self a friend.' Lil passed the half-filled glass and bottle to the customer, took his money and held it in her hand. 'Friends like that, who needs enemies?' She winked at Ginny. 'Get a drink, Franny, and I'll have one with ya.'

Satisfied that Ginny was not going to move, Frances lifted the flap and went behind the bar and into Lil's sitting room. She hung her coat and gave her hair a quick brush. Ginny wasn't the only one who'd been frightened. A second later and Ginny would have stepped out and thrown herself down the steps. She'd considered it herself not so long ago – and all the alternatives. If it hadn't been for another girl dying from the effects of a backstreet abortion, she might have gone the same way. It had happened that first season in Blackpool and she'd been terrified. The girl had collapsed in the dressing room, blood running down her bare legs. Patsy had taken charge and done her best, but it was all too late. And it had been Patsy who comforted the girls. No wonder she was glad to leave it all behind for Colin; her life was settled now, no longer the dramas, onstage or off. Frances slipped back behind the bar. Lil was already gassing to Ginny and the girl appeared calmer, her cheeks a little flushed. She was nursing a small glass of brandy.

Lil said, 'I reckon Ginny here could do with a hot sweet tea. I'll have one too. And bring a pie, there's one in the larder. Looks like she needs feeding up.' Ginny protested but Lil was having none of it and Frances was so grateful to the woman for just being her kind-hearted, generous self. 'It's left over from lunchtime and I'll not sell it now. Nice to see Franny's friends, lass. I hope we see a lot more of ya.'

Frances went into the back room, leaving the door from the bar open so that she could hear Lil chatting to Ginny. Poor girl. Frances didn't have to imagine how she'd be feeling – she knew only too well – but what was the best way to help her? She stirred sugar into the tea, took out the pie that Lil had probably saved for her own supper, put it on a tray and went back into the bar. There were a few more customers but not many. Big Malc had arrived and Lil was introducing him to Ginny.

'So, Malc, I reckon my luck's in with these Variety Girls, don't you? I'll have the fellas beating the door down when they see I've got these beauties here.'

Big Malc agreed. 'They're no competition for you, though, Lil.'

'Ah, go on with you.' Lil batted her hand at him. Frances shared out the tea, pushed the pie in front of Ginny and placed a fork beside it.

'I couldn't,' Ginny said.

Lil insisted, 'Course ya can. You look like you could put away a few more an' all. But that'll do ya for now.'

Frances sipped at her tea in between serving but it was quieter on Tuesdays, too far away from payday, and the nights were darker, the moon less full, keeping people at home. Ginny still looked like a frightened rabbit, but a bit more at ease, and Big Malc was being kind to her. At half past seven, she slipped from the stool and took out her purse but Lil waved a hand at her.

'Ya can put that away for a start.'

Ginny became agitated. 'I must pay my way.'

Lil placed her hand on Ginny's. 'Next time you're in, ya can buy me a small one.' Lil smiled and Ginny did too.

Frances lifted the flap of the bar. 'Will you be okay going home, Ginny? You still don't look well.'

'I'm fine, now.' Ginny pulled on her coat, looking considerably better than she'd been when Frances had found her.

Big Malc put down his pint. 'Would you like me to walk with you, lass?'

Ginny shook her head vigorously and raised her hand. 'No, please. You've all been kindness itself. There's still enough light if I go now.' She was smiling, but she looked so small and delicate and Frances wondered whether she should let her go home alone, to that big empty flat. She walked with her to the door.

'Why don't you stay a little longer, Ginny? You could come home with me.'

Ginny wrapped her coat tight around herself, kept her arms across her chest. 'I'm tired. I just want to go home to bed. To sleep.'

Frances tried not to show her alarm. Should she force her? But then Ginny would understand that she knew of her predicament.

She had to be careful not to embarrass the girl; she'd already fright-ened her witless. Frances watched her walk down Sea View Street then went back into the pub. Lil was wiping down the bar that was already clean. There wasn't really enough work for the two of them, but Lil had insisted she come in. Back behind the bar, she ran some hot water and started washing the few glasses that had accu-mulated.

Lil picked up a tea towel. 'Your little friend is troubled.'

Frances stared down into the water. Troubled enough to want to end it all?

'Man trouble?' Lil put the glass on the bar; it had little specks of lint on it from the tea towel.

'You could say that.' Frances didn't look up.

'Good job you brought her back. Looks like she needs a friend.' She fixed her eyes on Frances. 'Only one reason a girl looks that troubled. Only one.'

* * *

Ginny walked down the streets, tears coursing down her face. She had a feeling Frances knew what she'd been about to do and had stopped her in the nick of time. Now she didn't know whether she was glad she'd been saved. It had been warm in the pub, the people kind; they hadn't asked questions and Lil looked a cheery sort. Big Malc had been gentle; they all had. She pulled her coat tighter and started to cry, a quiet keening that she couldn't hold back. She wanted her mum, to hold her hand, to tell her it would all be okay. As she walked down Mill Road, curtains were being drawn and she caught small glimpses of families reading newspapers, settled for the evening. She'd never known that softness of life. Nothing had been cosy, save for the times she was at her mother's side, folding washing. She put her hand in her pocket and counted her change.

The man in the off-licence was surprised to see her.

'Didn't know you girls were still here. Having another party?'

He'd got to know all four of them since they'd taken the flat. He wouldn't know that the others had left last week. It gave her a little confidence. 'Sort of,' she said, not wanting to invite conversation.

'Gin again, is it?' he said, reaching behind him, his hand hovering over the Beefeater gin on the shelf. 'Or d'ya fancy a bit of something else?'

'Gin will be fine.' She placed her coins on the counter.

'You lasses drank the last lot, already? I suppose you're waiting for the show to open again?'

'Yes,' she said and handed over her money. What did the truth matter when all was said and done?

10

Ruby heard whistling outside the door to their flat, a key turn in the lock, and Johnny came in looking surprisingly cheerful. That alone made her hackles rise.

'You sound happy.' She caught the bitterness in her voice but she couldn't help herself. She thought he might bite back but he didn't; that wasn't Johnny's way. More was the pity. He put his keys down on the small table in their hallway, and placed his hat on the chair to the side of it.

'I met up with Bernie. We took a stroll over to Drury Lane to find out what's going on up there. The Entertainments National Service Association's taken it over for the duration of the war; it's going to be their headquarters. We saw Basil Dean and Leslie Henson as it happened. What an operation they've got going on there. You wouldn't believe it. They plan to have shows touring all over the country and wherever our troops are they'll not be short of entertainment to boost morale. Isn't that great?' His enthusiasm irritated her. 'I met up with people we haven't seen for years. Bob and Betty Sharp are still going strong. They sent their kind regards to you. And their condolences.'

'More pity.'

'Don't, Ruby,' he said. 'They're a great couple. They knew Mother. And Father. They were being kind.'

'Do we need their kindness?' She couldn't remember them. It was Johnny who took notice, paid attention to the details, just as their mother had done. Mother had given Ruby other things to do. She looked away from him, guilt suddenly rearing its ugly head. She looked at her reflection in the mirror, tugged at the wispy tendrils of hair by her ears, twisted them into a curl.

'Everyone needs kindness, Ruby.'

Even me, she wanted to say but she held her tongue. Instead she said, 'What made you go there?'

'Curiosity. Knowledge. Bernie wanted to see it for himself and I thought you might want to get involved when I'm called up.'

She couldn't bear it, to think of them apart. She didn't know anything else but being with Johnny and had no idea how to live a life where he wasn't a part of it.

'I've heard they pay a pittance.'

'It's a living wage.' He loosened his tie, undid the top button of his shirt.

'Not our living,' she sneered. 'To think we could be in New York, earning thousands of dollars.'

'I agree. You waiting in an apartment for your married lover... alone on your birthday, Christmas. New Year.'

'He was going to leave his wife.' She bristled. Edgar wasn't like that. He wasn't like all the other men. He truly loved her. 'He was just waiting for the right time.'

Johnny shook his head. 'He wouldn't have found it. You trust too easily. You would have wasted your life waiting.' He put out a hand to touch her shoulder and she shrugged him off, picked up her lipstick and stroked it across her lips, pouted at her reflection.

'I found us somewhere to rehearse,' he called over his shoulder as he went into the sitting room.

'That's a bit pointless, isn't it? No show, no rehearsal.'

He put his head around the door. 'We need to keep in shape. It's all too easy to let things slide.'

'There are other ways to stay in shape.' She pulled on her coat and picked up her bag.

'Where are you going?' He came back into the narrow hallway.

'Out. To keep in shape.'

He sighed, patted the door, searching for the right words to stop her from leaving. He was wasting his time. 'Ruby—'

'Oh, don't, dear brother. Don't go all pious on me. I can't bear it.'

'Lord only knows what Mother would think.'

'She's not here to think anything, is she? And we weren't here for her when she needed us – thanks to you.' It wasn't his fault but she couldn't be angry at their mother; she wasn't here to be angry at.

He didn't answer her. It would be easier if he did. He had coped by throwing himself into his work, rehearsing long hours, perfecting steps, over and over. It was all he had left in his life – and she had nothing at all left in hers.

She left as she always did – angry with him. What had they come back to? Nothing. No show, no lights anywhere, only darkness. The blackout. New York would still be glittering brightly; it would be full of music and laughter and dancing. She hurried down the streets as dusk was falling to find a taxi, in search of colour and light. It had to be out there somewhere.

11

It had been quiet on Wednesday lunchtime and Frances pondered on why Lil employed her, for any profit must be going on her wages. Lil was at the other end of the bar, checking the shelves for stock. She sighed, scanning her list. 'It's all right working out what I need, it's whether I can get it. The brewery wagons have been requisitioned and can I get a delivery?' She blew out her cheeks. 'What a caper. Right, I'm going to call the brewery and see what they can give me.' Lil went through to the back room.

Frances started taking glasses from the shelves and polishing the mirrors behind them. In the corner, four old boys had the domino board out and were playing a game of fives and threes. The silence of the bar was punctuated with the rattle of the tiles on the wooden board. She'd climbed up on the small stool to tackle the shelf with the bottles of liqueurs when the door was pushed ajar. She watched through the mirror, her hand on a bottle of Drambuie as a familiar face appeared around it. Jessie beckoned with her finger and Frances beckoned back. Jessie pushed the door wider and crept forward, blushing a deep crimson.

Frances put the bottle back and came down the steps.

Jessie had a newspaper in her hand and she tapped the front page, holding it out towards Frances.

'Have you seen the *Telegraph*?' Her voice was high with excitement.

'I have now,' said Frances, taking the paper and reading the headlines.

'Not there,' Jessie said, leaning forward and whispering. Frances bit her lip, trying not to laugh at Jessie's discomfort. 'Page four, in the middle.'

Frances reached out and squeezed her hand. 'Sorry, Jessie. It's your face. You look so – uncomfortable.'

'That's because I am.'

Lil walked back behind the bar. 'What am I missing?'

Frances stepped out and put her arm about Jessie's shoulder. 'This is my friend Jessie. She's a Variety Girl too.'

'Another one?' Lil said, putting out her hand in greeting. 'Got me a ruddy hat trick. Three gorgeous girls.'

Frances grinned, pulling Jessie tighter. 'Jessie came to tell me something; it's on page four but I haven't had chance to read it.'

'It's the theatres!' Jessie said, her eyes alight. 'They can reopen. All the places of entertainment will be opening again.'

'Oh. Really?' Frances took the paper and found the notice. There it was in black and white.

Jessie grinned. 'It changes everything.'

'It does.' It didn't really change everything, but it was a definite step in the right direction. If the theatres reopened, she could save instead of simply managing and her plan to get Imogen and herself stable was back on track. They had hope at last.

* * *

Jessie saw the piano against the wall and Frances caught her looking. 'Have a go. It's all right, isn't it, Lil? If Jessie plays the piano?'

'Could I?' Jessie felt her fingers flex involuntarily, ready to touch the keys.

'Course it is.'

Jessie moved quickly to the piano. She lifted the lid, played a few notes. It was in tune and, delighted, she pulled out the stool and started to play. She started with 'Roll Out the Barrel', which seemed appropriate given the setting, and moved on to 'On Mother Kelly's Doorstep'. Lil came out from behind the bar, lifted her dress as if it were a crinoline and danced about the floor. The four old boys carried on with their dominoes, oblivious. Lil encouraged Jessie to go on, not that Jessie needed it. The theatres were opening again and she would take up where she left off, war or not.

When Jessie finally stopped, the customers applauded.

Lil placed her hands on Jessie's shoulders.

'Oh, that were grand. What a boon to have someone who can play that ol' Joanna properly.' She pulled out a stool and sat beside Jessie. Her cheeks were flushed and her grey-green eyes were shining with happiness. 'Perhaps you could come back tonight and play for half an hour?'

Jessie wasn't sure her mum would approve. She hadn't liked her dad playing the pubs, but as his health had failed it was the only avenue open to him. It was a far cry from the grand concert halls he'd played in when he was a young man, before the Great War damaged him forever.

'I can't pay you, lass,' Lil said. 'But you can put a glass on the piano for tips. Will that do ya?' Frances was smiling, her eyes almost pleading for Jessie to agree. 'It'll help my business no end, having you girls here. And that other beauty with the red hair.'

'Ginny!' Jessie jumped up from the seat. 'We need to tell her too.' She turned to Lil. 'Yes, yes, I will, Lil. I'll come back later, but we need to tell Ginny.' She'd meant to come in and tell Frances and then find Ginny at the laundry on her way home. It had been her half-day at the solicitor's and she'd bought the early edition of the newspaper to take home to her mum.

Lil placed her hand on Jessie's arm. 'Thank you, lovey. We need cheering up in these dark days and any little we can do to add a little lightness to proceedings will be a blessing. So get off, the pair of you. It's almost time for last orders anyway.'

'Are you sure, Lil? Don't you want me to help clean up?'

'Nope. Off you pop. I'll see ya at teatime.'

Jessie waited while Frances grabbed her jacket and bag and the two of them left by the front door.

'Did you call in at the Empire, Jessie?'

'Not yet. I thought it would be better if all three of us went. Ginny will be so pleased. She hates working in that laundry.'

* * *

They hurried into the laundry yard. Vans were arriving and linen was being taken in through a loading bay. Jessie opened the door and a few girls turned when they saw them but kept working. An older woman hurried across.

'We haven't got any vacancies – although we might have one. Someone didn't turn up today and if it happens again, I'll have a slot – but not for both of you.'

Jessie looked about her, seeking her friend but finding only unfamiliar faces. 'We came to get a message to our friend Ginny Thompson.'

The woman folded her arms. 'Well, she's the one who's not here. And when you see her, you can tell her that if it happens again she'll be getting her cards.'

Jessie was shocked. 'She's probably ill. She wouldn't let anyone down on purpose.'

'We're wasting time.' Frances was pulling Jessie's sleeve, almost dragging her towards the door. Jessie scowled at Frances, tugged back her arm, rubbed at it. 'She wouldn't be able to get a message to you,' she said to Edna. 'She's not a magician.'

'And neither am I, Miss Clever Clogs.' She turned her back on them. 'Stop gawping!' she shouted to the girls who were smiling at Jessie and Frances.

They fumbled their way out of the laundry, Jessie furious. 'What the hell are you playing at, Frances?'

Frances strode ahead. 'I'm worried about Ginny.'

Jessie dashed to her side. 'I'm sure there's no need to rush. It's probably just a stomach upset.' She stopped and Frances turned back.

'I haven't had chance to tell you.' She grabbed Jessie's arm again, started hurrying down the street. 'Ginny was about to throw herself off the steps last night.'

'What?'

'I took her to the pub and Lil gave her something to eat.' She bit on her lip. 'I should have taken her home with me.'

Jessie felt her stomach tighten and the two of them tore down Cambridge Street, and onto Mill Road. They pushed on the gate and hurried up the path, praying the door was open. It was, and they pounded up the stairs, two at a time. 'I should have stayed here with her,' Jessie said and Frances raised an eyebrow. Frances knew, Jessie thought. She knew – and she knew that Jessie knew too. Would she still want to be friends? Did friends keep secrets from one another? Frances hammered on the door, shouting Ginny's name. A door opened and the landlady appeared at the bottom of the stairs. Her dark-grey hair was in curlers, a floral overall covering her dress.

'She's in,' she called up, holding on to the newel post. 'I heard her walking about, up and down all night, she was. Although it's been quiet the last few hours. But she hasn't gone out. I'd have heard the door.'

Jessie leaned over the banister. 'Have you got a spare key?' The woman disappeared and Jessie could feel the blood pummelling in her ears. This was her fault. She knew Ginny was vulnerable. If only she'd let her stay.

They heard a jangle of keys and the landlady hauled herself up the stairs. Jessie wanted to tell her to move her ruddy arse but she bit her tongue, willing the woman to move faster. She ambled up, her round body rocking from side to side as she sorted through the keys. Time seemed to be slowing and galloping at the same time, and with every second she felt more knots grow in her stomach. *Please, please let Ginny be safe.* Frances moved away from the door and Jessie walked two steps up to the next floor to give the woman access.

'I can't say as I like doing this,' the woman was muttering as she put the key in the lock and clicked it over. 'It's not right, opening the door when she's in. Invading her privacy.'

Jessie blustered forward. 'But she's our friend and we're worried about her.' The woman stepped back and Frances swiftly pushed herself into the gap and took hold of the handle, blocking the way.

'Don't worry, we'll take the blame,' Frances said as she closed the door.

* * *

Jessie dashed in and Frances followed her into the sitting room. Everything was neat and tidy, apart from a pillow and blanket on the sofa and a bottle of gin on the floor. Frances picked it up.

'Full.' It was a relief.

'The landlady swore she hadn't gone out.' Jessie was trying not to panic, looking into the empty bedrooms. Perhaps they were both mistaken. Ginny hadn't really been going to throw herself down the steps. Frances had got it wrong.

'The bathroom?'

Jessie paled and Frances led the way. The door wouldn't open. It wasn't locked but the door wouldn't give. Frances leaned against it with her full weight and it shifted a little. She could see Ginny's red hair and she barged at the door again. The smell of vomit and worse filled her nostrils and she pressed her lips together, trying not to inhale. 'Ginny, it's Frances – are you all right?'

The girl moaned and Frances pushed herself around the door and managed to climb over Ginny, who was curled into a foetal ball. Frances squatted over her, straddling the toilet pan that reeked of illness. Jessie was pushing her head and shoulders around the door.

'Is she…?'

'She's alive, if that's what you mean.' Jessie let out a long sigh as Ginny moaned again. Frances moved behind her and pulled her up, propping her against the bath panel. 'Have you taken anything?' The girl was a leaden lump and there wasn't space to manoeuvre gently so Frances pulled her as best she could until Jessie could open the door wider. Together they dragged Ginny into the narrow hall and once she was safely out, Frances pushed open the small window in the bathroom and flushed the lavatory. The sink had remnants of vomit. She soaked a clean flannel and went back into the hall, wiping Ginny's face and hands, trying to remove the residue from her hair. Ginny's eyes rolled back in her head and Frances said again, 'Ginny, what have you taken?'

Ginny mumbled incoherently. 'P-p-p…'

'What?' Frances leaned closer.

'P-p…' Ginny started moving, trying to revive herself.

'Poison?' Jessie gasped. 'Oh, no, no. She's taken poison.' Ginny shook her head; it was only slight, but it was definitely in disagreement.

The two girls looked at each other. 'Help me get her onto to the settee,' Frances said, taking her arms.

'She looks awful.' Jessie clasped her hands round Ginny's ankles. Frances agreed but at least they weren't too late.

They managed to get Ginny onto the settee and Jessie found a bowl and ran some hot water into it while Frances fetched soap, and refreshed the flannel and towel. Ginny was still wearing the clothes she had on yesterday and the two of them undressed her to her slip. As Jessie gently ran the flannel around her neck, Ginny started to respond and they talked to her, quiet, soothing words until she was able to tell them what had happened.

'Food poisoning.'

Frances bit down on her lip. Surely the girl wasn't going to carry on with the pretence?

'The pie...' She closed her eyes, put her hand to her mouth. Let it drop again. 'At the pub. I think it was off.' She opened her eyes as Jessie adjusted the pillow behind her and dropped back onto it, half smiling at Frances. Jessie tucked the blanket under Ginny's armpits and laid a cool flannel on her head.

'Better?' Jessie asked.

'Much. Thank you.' Ginny was more alert. 'I think it was the food and—' she paused, trying not to gag '—the br... the drink Lil gave to me. And the hot sweet tea. Such a mixture.' She shuddered. 'I thought I was going to die.'

Jessie said briskly, 'Well, you didn't. And you're not going to. We're here to look after you.'

Ginny gave her a wan smile but didn't say anything. Frances yearned to offer Ginny the freedom that truth would give her, the openness of sharing her burden, but how could she? What a hypocrite she'd be, forcing Ginny to air her dirty linen and keep her own locked away. But Imogen was not dirty, was she? She was pure and innocent. She mustn't think of herself; she must think of Ginny. If the girl was trying to get rid of the baby, what would she attempt next? If she wandered further down the path it would lead her to the backstreets – and whatever way you looked at it, that would never end well. She took hold of Ginny's hand. 'You're not alone in this.'

Jessie was shaking her head. She mouthed, 'Don't', but Frances felt she had to. The next thing she tried might kill her. Jessie was squirming and Ginny looked at her, then her eyes flashed with fear.

'I know,' Frances said. Jessie let out a squeak and Ginny struggled to sit up, but Frances made her lie down again. 'Jessie didn't betray your confidence. I guessed.' She leaned in closer, passing Ginny a handkerchief from her pocket as the girl began to cry.

Ginny had looked frail and weak before the sickness and now she was more gaunt than ever. Her eyes were dark and her breath stank. How long since she'd eaten anything before the pie was anyone's guess. The pie might very well have been off but even if it hadn't, Ginny was right: the combination of alcohol, sweet tea and the pie would have upset her stomach and she might have hoped that it would do the trick.

'Whatever happens, we're here for you,' she said.

Jessie pressed her hand on Ginny's shoulder, removed the flannel and dropped it onto the windowsill. Frances wished with all her heart that she could make this easier. Jessie was kind-hearted and determined but she was naïve. Being kind wouldn't help Ginny; the girl needed to have some practical advice – and she could give it. But could she tell her everything?

'I prayed to God, night and day,' Ginny sobbed. 'I prayed and prayed and still nothing came.' Frances clasped her hand in both of hers. Ginny's fingers were thin, like the rest of her. She was a beautiful girl, but the shine had gone from her.

'And the gin?'

'For if the prayers didn't work.' Frances squeezed her hand. 'I tried to fall down the steps.' She looked at Frances from beneath her lashes. 'I know you pulled me back – but I wouldn't have done it anyway. I'm a coward.'

'You're not,' Jessie butted in. She opened her mouth to say something else, but Frances glanced at her and she stopped, perhaps knowing platitudes would be of no comfort. Frances rested the back of her hand on Ginny's forehead. It was still clammy.

'I don't think you should be on your own,' Frances said. 'You don't look at all well.' A small exaggeration given the circumstances.

'I'm fine,' Ginny said, her voice feeble. 'A good night's sleep and I'll be back at work tomorrow. If I still have a job.'

'Oh,' Jessie gasped, her voice taking on a brighter tone, 'that's what we came to tell you.' Ginny looked at her blankly. 'The theatres and cinemas can reopen. We can work again.'

Ginny sank back into the pillow. Frances got up and brought a fresh glass of water and she held the bottom of it while Ginny put her hands around it and sipped.

'I suppose that will be all right for a while, but who will want to give me a job later? I won't be able to dance.'

'You will.'

Ginny sighed. 'Don't keep trying to make me feel better, Jessie. I have to be realistic.'

Jessie sank a little, but Frances was firm. 'Ginny's quite right, Jessie, as are you. The three of us need to stick together and work something out.' If they could help Ginny, then perhaps the two of them would help her in return. The very thought prompted a twist of guilt. It was something to consider, but for the time being, Ginny's situation was the most pressing. Imogen was safe; Ginny's problems were just beginning.

Ginny looked down at her hands. 'It's not your responsibility. I was the stupid one.'

Frances rubbed at her shoulder. 'Nothing stupid about it. You were unlucky, that's all.' She considered for a moment before speaking again. Could she give Ginny hope without revealing too much of her own situation? 'I knew a girl who danced until the week before her baby was born. The head girl put her at the back of the chorus.'

'She must have looked like an elephant.' Ginny tried to smile.

'She was neat and the baby, when it came, was small.' Imogen had been a little over six pounds, so tiny in her arms...

'See, it's possible.' Jessie got up and drew the curtains. 'I'll go back and get my work clothes. I'll stay with you tonight.'

Ginny pushed herself up on her elbows. 'There's no need.'

'Jessie's right,' Frances said. 'You're very weak. We'd take you home with us, but I don't think you'd make it to the bottom of the stairs, let alone the bottom of the street.'

They would brook no argument and Jessie went off to get her clothes while Frances ran Ginny a cool bath. 'It will all seem so much better in the morning.'

'Really?' Ginny said sadly.

'Really,' Frances said, hoping she sounded convincing.

12

When Jessie returned, Ginny was resting on the settee. Frances had found her some fresh clothing then helped her dress. When she heard the front door, she came out of the bathroom, the smell of disinfectant in her nose infinitely better than what it had smelled of before. Frances was wearing a headscarf tied at the back of her neck, her sleeves rolled up to the elbows, a small tablecloth fastened about her waist for an apron, her face almost as red as the gingham squares.

Jessie put her bag down on a chair and took out a packet of arrowroot biscuits. She opened it and offered them to Ginny. 'Mum sent them. Said it's the best thing for an upset stomach.' Ginny took one, her eyes cast down. 'Don't worry,' Jessie said, sitting down beside her, 'I said that you were sick. No one needs to know anything other than that.'

'Not yet.' Frances leaned on the door jamb. 'Although you won't be able to hide it forever.' She flinched at her own hypocrisy.

'Frances!' Jessie was shocked.

Ginny shook her head. 'Frances is right. I'm not so stupid as to think I could get away with it forever.'

'That's if you are pregnant,' Frances said, bustling over to the kitchen. 'It's still early days. Billy Lane only left three weeks ago.' She took off the apron and headscarf and dropped them on top of the pile of dirty sheets that included Ginny's clothes and towels. They could drop them at the laundry. How ironic it all was. She washed her hands and went back into the sitting area. 'Hopefully, this is just down to shock from him dumping you like he did, the bastard!'

'Frances!' Jessie exclaimed again.

'Well, it's the truth. He was. Is.' She took a deep breath, let it out with a sigh. 'Then the theatre closed and you were left on your own, here. It could all be a false alarm.'

Ginny released her hands from Jessie's. 'And if it's not?' She paused.

Frances sighed.

'Let's hope for the best,' Jessie encouraged.

'But plan for the worst.' She twisted to face Jessie. 'I can't exist on wishful thinking.' Her lip trembled. 'I've been terrified. I've no idea what to do. How I'll be able to work. And what then? After...' A tear dropped onto her cheek. Frances was glad that she was talking about it. Talking helped; she knew that. Patsy had made her talk and it had saved her on more than one occasion – but only because she trusted Patsy.

'It's early days. We'll help,' she said firmly.

'Yes, we will.' Jessie was enthusiastic, her voice eager, but Ginny looked at Frances, the weight of her worry clear.

Frances looked about her. 'How long have you got left on the flat?'

'Until the thirtieth.'

'Have you asked if you can get anything back if you leave earlier?'

Ginny shook her head. 'I can't think straight. All I can think about is this.' She pointed at her stomach, which showed no signs of her problems. Not yet, at least. Perhaps she would be neat and get away with it. Some girls did.

Frances tried to be encouraging. 'Should we ask?'

Ginny shrugged. 'I don't see the point. I'll have to find something else and I'd need another deposit.'

Jessie was about to say something but looked at Frances and closed her mouth.

'What?'

Jessie reddened. Ginny looked at her. 'I was thinking...' Frances half knew what was coming next. It would be typical of Jessie, trying to solve everyone's problems without considering the consequences.

'Yes?'

'That Ginny should come and stay with us. I could share with you and Ginny could have my room.'

'Oh, no. What would your mum and Geraldine think? And Eddie. How embarrassing for him. For them all. No. No!' Ginny became quite agitated.

'They wouldn't think anything.'

Ginny was tearful. 'You have no idea, Jessie. No idea at all.' Jessie was offended. 'I'm sorry, but people will judge me by the mess I've got myself into.'

Frances leaned forward. 'And Billy will go on living life his own sweet way.' It made her sick to think of it.

'But if he knew? What if we contact him?' Jessie got up. 'My agent, Bernie, will know where he is. He was going to get him a job on the wireless.'

Ginny reached up and tugged at her sleeve, pulled her back onto the settee. 'It's a nice thought, but it's not going to happen. It's my own stupid fault. I should've said no.' She wiped her nose on her sleeve. 'I just wanted to be loved...'

Frances was quiet. She had loved Johnny and he her, or at least, she'd believed he had. She hadn't felt soiled or abused. Not then. She closed her eyes, remembering stolen kisses in the darkness of the wings, away from the ever-watchful eye of his mother and sister. What had gone wrong? She'd known what she was doing and had wanted to be a part of him, and he her. They had belonged together. It was different. She considered Ginny and how best to offer solace, knowing it wouldn't make things better.

'Perhaps Lil will know of lodgings. I'll ask her.' Frances checked her watch, stood up. 'I need to get back. I have to be at the Fisherman's before six.'

Jessie sighed. 'I'd forgotten. Tell her I won't be able to play the piano tonight but I'll come another night instead. And we still need to find out if Jack's going to open the Empire. Will you call in and check if you have time?'

Frances said she would. She picked up her jacket and Ginny shuffled to the end of the settee. Frances put out her arm. 'Stay where you are. Hopefully you'll be back to work tomorrow.'

'I will. Thanks, Frances. For everything. Cleaning, everything.'

Frances put on her jacket and flicked her hair from under the collar. 'It was nothing. Rest. It will help.' She gave her a small smile and walked towards the door.

Jessie got up. 'I'll come out with you.'

* * *

Jessie followed Frances down into the hall. They heard the click of the landlady's door.

'All right, is she? Your friend?'

'She is, thank you,' Frances said, her smile false. 'Eaten bad food.' The two girls stepped out into the street.

'I couldn't tell you before, Frances. I promised Ginny I wouldn't say anything.'

Frances adjusted her jacket. She smelled of sickness and sweat and needed to get freshened up before she went to work.

'No need to apologise; it was for the right reason. Keeping secrets isn't easy.' Her duplicity made her squirm. Jessie was a good kid, and kind, but most of all she was loyal. Would she ever forgive Frances for holding back?

'I'll say,' Jessie said, her shoulders sagging with the relief. 'I hated not telling you, but a promise is a promise. And it wasn't mine to tell.'

'Exactly.' Frances looked up at the window of the flat. 'Poor Ginny. What a state she was in.'

'But it will be better now that we can help her. We can make sure she eats properly. That's if she is... y'know...' Jessie said, struggling for the words. 'A trouble shared and all that?'

Frances smiled. 'Let's hope so.'

13

Jack Holland often questioned the choices he'd made in life, but buying the Empire had never been one of them. It had given him a sense of purpose and direction that had otherwise been lacking. If his wife could only see it from his point of view.

'Please, come with me, Audrey? It will be good for the staff to see us as a united front.'

She was leaning into the ornate mirror over the fireplace, running her index finger over her brows, smoothing them into place.

'But we're not a united front, Jack. I loathe the place. It will be the ruin of us. What will be left for our children? For us?'

She turned away from the mirror, picked up a magazine from the coffee table and sat down. 'Of all the places to invest! A damn theatre.' She flicked the pages, looking at them but not seeing. 'I tried to stop you, but would you listen?' She glared at him. 'When everything was uncertain, when the threat of war was the world's waking thought, you knew best.'

'It was a risk, Audrey – and it paid off. We've had a successful summer, the profits of which will keep us going for a while yet. And there are other opportunities already presenting themselves. It's the beginning of things, not the end.'

She sneered, but he'd become immune to her disappointment; she'd been proud of him once, in his officer's uniform, but he'd returned a different man and he knew it was a man she didn't care for. He didn't blame her. War had changed him.

He turned his back and looked out of the window. Brooklands Avenue had been a good choice, a quiet enclave of private homes, and only a short walk to the promenade. He'd thought to delight her, but nothing seemed to work.

'Why couldn't you invest in clothing, as my father did? We could be churning out uniforms.' She sighed. 'In God's name, why the theatre?'

They'd had this argument so many times. He couldn't invest in the tools of war, in armaments or uniforms – he would fight for his country another way.

'Because morale is important. Happiness is important.'

'Yours, perhaps. But not mine.' She slapped the magazine back on the low table and reached for the cigarette box, took out a cigarette. He picked up the silver table lighter and held the flame. She leaned into it and he tried to catch her eye but she wouldn't look at him. He could see the fear behind the bitterness. He'd learned a lot in the trenches, survival mostly, but about people too: how they reacted when they thought all was lost. How could he make her understand how important it was? 'I know I've asked a lot of you, Audrey, but trust me. Please.'

She blew out her smoke, licked the corner of her lips. 'Do I have an option?'

'Come with me?' he asked again.

'I don't think so, Jack. They don't need my bitterness at a time like this.'

He wasn't going to push her; Audrey would have to come

around in her own time. He leaned forward and kissed her cheek but she didn't respond.

Stepping out into the avenue, he turned right and walked down towards the sea. Despite his words to Audrey, a small part of him knew she was right. It was a huge risk. He'd had no experience of theatre before he bought the Empire, but he loved it and believed in it with a passion that he no longer felt for anything else. The looming approach of another war had left him morose, his thoughts returning frequently to the Western Front, the horror of it. He'd survived when many of his friends had not, and those that did... He sighed heavily. Audrey would never understand. She was an only child and although loss was all around her, it hadn't touched her as it had so many families. He wouldn't be called to arms this time; his injured leg had seen to that. He was too old anyway, his sight not so sharp, but his mind was, and he intended to use it.

* * *

Jessie sat in the front row of the stalls, waiting for Jack to make his appearance. Dolly was on one side of her, Frances and Ginny on the other. All three had rushed to the theatre straight from work on Thursday as Jack had sent word about the Empire. The door to the auditorium had been wedged open and cleaners, usherettes and anyone else who remained had gathered to hear what the boss had to say. Everyone had kept to their small groups, but they were all in it together. They all wanted the Empire to open its doors again. Jessie tried not to dwell on the fact that she would have been travelling to the West End at the end of the season if all had gone to plan. She thought how Aunt Iris would gloat over her failures, her inadequacies. Was she being selfish? Her mother might be safer in Norfolk, and Uncle

Norman would be delighted to have Eddie back. She balled her fists. She mustn't let doubts fill her head, not now. The theatres were opening.

'Oh, gosh, Frances. I keep praying Jack'll put a show on. I don't think I can stick another week in the office.'

'He wouldn't have called us if he didn't have some sort of plan,' Frances said, her long legs stretched out in front of her.

Ginny pouted. 'God forbid I have to stay in that laundry.' She looked at her hands, chapped and raw. 'Much longer and I'll have hands like my mother. She'd be so upset.'

Frances nudged her. 'You're doing what you need to do. She'd be proud of you.'

Ginny shrugged. 'Perhaps.'

There was a shift in energy and everyone turned to see Jack striding down the aisle, his assistant, Annie, with her ever-present clipboard, following close behind. Mike came out of the wings and sat down near what remained of his crew.

Annie stood to Jack's left, pen poised over her clipboard.

Jack cleared his throat. 'Evening, everyone. I must say, it's good to see so many of you.' He made sure he looked along the rows, making eye contact with them all, smiling encouragingly. 'The good news is that the Empire *will* be opening again. But...' He smiled wryly. 'There's always a but, isn't there?' A few nodded; a few groaned. 'I don't have an exact date.' He put his hands out in front of him. 'Many of our young men who worked backstage have already signed up. Mike here, like me, is a bit past his best so we need to stay and make sure those men have something to come back to.'

There was a call of 'hear! hear!' from some of the older members assembled.

'Those young men are already filling billets and camps in Cleethorpes and Grimsby and they'll want to be entertained.'

'Cheeky,' Doris, one of the cleaners, called out. 'I'll not be doing no entertaining, not with my bunions.'

Everyone laughed and Jack stretched out his arm, holding out his hand towards Doris.

'Thank you, Doris. That illustrates my point perfectly.' He looked along the rows, making sure they all felt included. 'Morale is important. Laughter is important. Sticking together is important.'

'By, it is, love,' Doris called out again, 'it is.'

Jack grinned. 'Those of us who are older will no doubt have memories of the hardships of the Great War.' Again, there was a general rumble of agreement and Jessie clasped her hands and twisted them. She recalled her dad calling out into the night, the sudden screams, her mum comforting him. She looked up at Jack. Could it make a difference, laughter and song? Dad had believed it could.

'I intend to do the very best I can to provide entertainment for the people of this town, the soldiers and sailors, the airmen who may come to be with us in the coming months. But...' He paused. 'I need to make money too or we'll have to close, regardless.' He thrust his hands into his pockets, suddenly uncomfortable. 'So, even though I am fighting to keep variety live in this theatre, until I can get something more solid, I will be showing films.' There was a general groan and Jessie sank into her seat. There would be little chance to perform. She tried to keep positive, but it had been a blow. A quick glance at Ginny and Frances told her that they felt the same. Dolly would have work, but even her mouth was turned down. She loved live entertainment as much as the girls loved performing.

Jack paced the stage. 'I know, I know it's disappointing, but I can compromise. We'll do cine-variety. We'll have a film then an act. A singer.' He took one hand from his pocket. 'Dancers.' He smiled at the girls. 'It will give me peace of mind to know that I'm halfway there. My man has checked the projection equipment left by the last owners and he should be able to get it all shipshape. Films are booked and on their way. That means we need to get the theatre up and running. Front of house staff?' They sat up. 'Let's get things in place as soon as we can. Annie?' She stepped forward and he touched her shoulder. 'If you take our wonderful team into the foyer, you can give them the information they need to get the Empire open on Monday the twenty-fifth.'

There were gasps of delight and Jessie clapped her hands. Something was happening at last, something good. Annie stepped down into the auditorium and there was a clatter of seats as people got up and followed her. Dolly wiggled her fingers at the girls. 'That's me,' she said in a loud whisper. 'See you all later.'

As the door banged shut, Jack came down into the stalls and walked in front of the girls. 'I can't give any dates yet, but I hope you'll be willing to take part and I'll be putting on a Christmas pantomime as planned. The scenery is already on hire, acts being contacted, bookings made. I'd like to give you girls something. Could we work together? I'm thinking especially of you, Jessie.'

His words warmed her. He'd kept his promise. When the acrobatic act had had to leave suddenly in the summer, Jessie had been given a solo singing spot. She had thought it the first step up the showbiz ladder until Jack had cut her solo with as much speed as he'd allowed it. She'd blamed the star Madeleine Moore. She'd been wrong. That was down to Billy Lane too. To smooth things over, Jack had promised her something in his next production and here it was.

Jack continued, 'We need to fill in the gaps until the beginning of December. We're looking at a couple of months' cine-variety. We can work it on minimal staff and that will give Mike time to find more crew. Okay with you, Mike?'

'Aye, Jack. I already have a couple of youngsters I can call on.'

'And George will keep us all in order, won't you, George?'

George pushed his glasses up the bridge of his nose and jiggled the arms of them over his ears. 'That's what I'm here for.'

They laughed. 'Any more of that and we'll be putting you on the stage,' Jack said.

George put up his hands. 'No, not me. I'm happy where I am.'

'We are too, George.' Jessie said. 'You're the first happy face we see when we come to the theatre and the last one when we leave. It wouldn't be the same without you.' Jessie was glad she'd spoken up. George had been almost like a father to her. She would never forget his kindness, nor Olive, his wife's, for when she'd arrived in Cleethorpes with nowhere to stay they'd taken her in without a second thought. Such kindness had been overwhelming, especially after Aunt Iris's meanness.

'It wouldn't be the same without any of you,' Jack continued. 'I feel we're more than a team; we're a family, now.' There were nods of agreement because that was exactly what Jessie felt too.

'Girls, it's good to have you here. You have my word that there'll be something for you each week, even if it's only a couple of days. We'll have to see how it goes.'

It was a small consolation for having to keep their day jobs for a while yet.

'Do you know the subject of the panto, Jack?' Jessie asked, wondering if she'd be Cinderella or Dick Whittington, certain Jack would make sure she got a good part.

'Yes, we decided on *Aladdin*. All those colourful silks and jewels will look good, don't you think? Bright baubles, a lamp to light the darkness.'

'We all need one of them,' Mike chipped in.

Jack leaned against the rail of the orchestra pit, his hands behind him. 'Keep rehearsing, girls. That way, if we can't stay open, you'll at least have something for the future.'

* * *

The girls met up with Dolly in the foyer. Ginny was still pale and gaunt, and she tugged her cardigan about her, hunching her thin shoulders forward. Jessie had been staying with her, afraid to leave her on her own.

'It's good news, isn't it?' Dolly said as the other members of staff stepped out onto the street, calling cheerio as they left. 'I know Jack will make it a success.'

'Let's hope so,' Ginny said flatly.

Jessie didn't want to be despondent. This was good news for them all; she wanted to grasp at anything that gave her the feeling that things were moving again. She grinned at Dolly. 'He will. And we have the panto to look forward to.' It was months away, but it meant that Jack hadn't given up.

'Do you know which one it will be?' Jessie was grateful for Dolly's enthusiasm. It must be difficult for Ginny to look forward to anything in the circumstances, but she mustn't let it drag them all down.

'*Aladdin*.' Hopefully they'd play to full houses again as they had in the summer, and the thought of this lifted her again. Things were getting better slowly but surely, and she had to hold on to it for there would be darker days ahead and people would need to escape them – if only for two hours in the red velvet seats of the Empire.

'Oh, my favourite.' Dolly was delighted.

'Not mine,' Ginny said. 'Seems I can't escape the laundry.'

Jessie nudged her. 'But this is better than the Little Laundry.'

'Will you stay, Jessie?' Dolly asked. 'I mean, if the Empire is ready to open again, Mr Leroy might go ahead with his show in London.'

'I don't know.' That excitement had long lost its shine. 'Things have changed so much – and I'm nearer to Harry here.' It sounded ridiculous. So near and yet so far. He could've been a thousand miles away, for letters were slow, his leave brief.

'When will you see him again?'

Jessie shrugged. 'It'll be a while yet. He has lots of exams and then he has to put in his flying hours.' She tried not to think about it too much, rereading his old letters until the new ones came just to keep him close – her longing for him a dull ache that never left her.

Frances pulled on her coat. 'Well, we can't just sit about waiting for someone else to tell us what to do. Jack said to think of the future. We need to work out when we can rehearse.'

Mention of London had brought back thoughts of Johnny – not that he had been far from her mind. And Patsy wouldn't let the subject drop, nagging at her to make contact. It would be easier now they were back in the country. Their appearances would be noted in *The Stage* so she would know where to find him. 'I'm free early on Saturday morning. I can do a couple of hours before I start my shift at the Fisherman's.'

'What about Sunday? We could get a full day in before they start putting the films on.'

'I can't do Sunday, Jessie.' It irritated. How many times would she have to repeat herself?

'You did the other week.'

Frances felt her skin prickle. 'That was different. We were waiting for news of war.' The events of that day erupted in her head. The interminable waiting, the ticking of the clock, Geraldine's condemnation of the girl from Louth. Of girls like her. 'I needed to know where I stood. We all did.' She looked at her watch. 'I have to dash. I need to be at the pub.' Anything could happen between now and December: the panto might get cancelled, she might have to find work elsewhere, leave Imogen with Patsy for longer. If the bombs fell... No, it was out of the question.

'But...' Jessie said softly.

'No buts.' It was awful not being to explain further but this was neither the time nor the place.

* * *

When Frances left, Jessie was sulky. 'I wonder why she has to go to her friends' every Sunday. It's a bit odd, if you ask me.'

'Have you ever met her friends?' Dolly asked.

Jessie shook her head. 'No. But she goes there every Sunday, religiously.'

'Maybe it is religious,' Ginny said idly. 'Perhaps she goes to church all day and is too embarrassed to say anything.'

Jessie laughed. 'Embarrassed? Frances? No, there's something she isn't telling us.'

Ginny was quiet. 'We all have secrets. If Frances wanted to talk about it, she would.' Was she talking about herself or Frances? Dolly was oblivious to what she meant and Jessie bit at the inside of her cheek. They were supposed to be friends but they were all keeping secrets.

14

Johnny leaned over the balcony of the Café de Paris, searching among the crowds. The band was playing and Joey Miller was crooning into the microphone. Waiters glided among the tables with bottles of champagne and fine wine and people ran up and down the stairs on either side of stage, or squeezed themselves into the throng dancing to 'Jeepers Creepers'. Cigarette smoke drifted up and caught in this throat. He heard a loud burst of laughter from underneath the balcony and moved further around the circle, peering underneath. Someone slapped him on the back and he turned, confused.

'We meet again, Johnny.' It was the man from Bernie's office, Mickey Harper; his brown hair was oiled back and he was wearing an evening suit that had seen better days. Johnny wanted to turn back and dash downstairs but he mustn't be rude. One wrong word and something would find its way to the gossip columns.

'Good to see you, Mickey. It's getting to be a regular occurrence.' He seemed to be everywhere his sister happened to be of late but there was no time to chat; he could miss Ruby and she would move on, leave with God knows who. He looked over the man's shoulder.

'Looking for Ruby?'

Johnny brought his attention back to him, trying to sound relaxed, as if his only intention was to buy her a drink, not drag her away from it. 'Have you seen her?'

The man smiled, or was he smirking? 'Everyone's seen Ruby. She's the star of every party since you came back to England.'

Johnny couldn't make the man out. Was he being offensive? He asked again. 'Have you seen her?'

Mickey took a drag on his cigarette, tilted his head back and blew out smoke. 'Downstairs. She's with Alex Pardoe's party. What circles your little sister moves in, Johnny. But then, everyone wants to be with Ruby. She's quite a gal.'

He *was* being offensive; Johnny clenched his jaw. 'Nice catching up with you again, Mickey.'

Mickey put up a hand. 'You too. Bound to bump into each other again.'

They wouldn't if he saw him first, Johnny thought. He pushed himself into the crowd and made for the stairs. The band had switched to a softer tempo and the crooner was taking a break, sipping an amber-coloured drink as he chatted to a couple of older women who were staring at him with dreamy eyes. Johnny weaved between the dancers, following the sound of laughter to Ruby. Her eyes were glittering brightly – too brightly – and he knew he had to handle this carefully, seeing her sway from side to side. How could he get her out without any fuss?

'Ruby!'

She glowered, then her face brightened and she threw her arms about him, excitedly introducing him to her friends. He shook hands, exchanged what pleasantries he could above the noise.

Joey Miller came back to the microphone and started talking. 'Ladies and gentlemen, we have those huge stars the Randolphs here tonight. We all know Ruby, but Johnny is here too. Where are you, Johnny?'

The spotlight searched among the crowds and Ruby stepped onto a chair, waving. There was a burst of applause and Johnny bowed, then took her hand, turning his back to the light. 'Get down,' he said, his jaw tensing. 'If you break your ankle you won't dance for weeks.'

She leaned down to him, smiling sweetly, aware all eyes were upon them.

'But it won't matter, darling brother, will it? Nothing matters any more.' She stood tall again, smiling, waving, enjoying the attention.

He took hold of her upper arm, her hand, and guided her as she stepped down onto the floor. She twirled out and away from him as she had done so many times before, sweeping a low curtsey, and he stood back to let her take the applause. The people around them cleared away to give them the spotlight and, before Johnny could do anything, Ruby dragged him onto the dance floor.

'Dance for us, Ruby,' someone called from the balcony. The pair of them looked up. He saw Mickey waving. Ruby blew him a kiss. There were more calls, louder now. Johnny stared at Mickey, who was holding on to the gold balustrade, grinning back at him. What was his game?

Ruby twisted and called to the band, '"Anything Goes".'

Johnny gripped her hand. 'No, Ruby. You're drunk.'

Ruby leaned into him as the band started to play. 'Only a teensy-weensy bit. I can do this in my sleep and you know it.'

There was nothing he could do but follow the music and dance to the routine they knew so well. Ruby was right, she could dance this in her sleep, but she faltered, wobbled and hammed it up, making her mistakes appear intended. The crowd loved her for it. When they'd finished, the applause was deafening and Johnny saw his chance. He swept her up into his arms and carried her up the stairs, knowing how much Ruby would enjoy the spectacle of it. She waved and blew kisses and he managed to smile as they made their way through the club towards the entrance. He stopped a waiter and asked him to fetch her bag and bring it to them at the door.

'I'm not going home, Johnny. It's far too early to leave.' She tried to wriggle free but he gripped her tighter. The doorman hailed a taxi and Johnny bundled Ruby into it, leaning back to avoid her flailing arms. The waiter arrived with her coat and bag, and he tipped him, then got into the car beside her.

'You spoil all my fun!' She slapped at his arm.

'That was so damned unprofessional.' He could barely speak. He'd spent half the night wandering in and out of her usual haunts in search of her. It seemed there were plenty of people who were going to party the war away – and Ruby was always able to find them.

'It was wonderful! We're meant to dance, aren't we? Entertain. It's all we have left.' She brushed at her cheeks with the back of her hand and he took the handkerchief from his breast pocket and held it out to her. She snatched it from him, leaned into the window, sulking, and he stared ahead as the taxi drove slowly down the darkened streets, the emptiness of life gnawing at his insides. Ruby was right. If they didn't have dance, they had nothing at all.

* * *

In the morning, he left her sleeping and went out to meet the eleven fifteen at Waterloo. He needed to take a trip with Bernie to sort out a little business investment he was putting together. He couldn't take Ruby – it might come to nothing – but he couldn't leave her alone either and so he had called Aunt Hetty, who, to his great relief, had agreed to travel up to London. The station was a sea of khaki as men poured down the concourse, kitbags on their shoulders. He ought to be in uniform too. The quicker he got Ruby settled, the better. Porters weaved through the crowds, shouting, calling, their trolleys stacked with cases. He searched the board for the B train and hurried down the platform, slipping between the swarming masses as they surged forward. He craned his neck this way and that over people's heads, peering into carriages until he saw a blue velvet hat with an extravagant peacock's feather fastened in the band. The eye of the feather shimmered and glistened as it caught the light. A young airman was helping the wearer of the hat with a voluminous carpet bag. As he moved aside, Johnny caught sight of Aunt Hetty giving profuse thanks and further instruction to the airman. Johnny grinned. What a charmer the old girl was! He watched her, talking the whole time, the boy's face animated as he responded, smiling broadly. Johnny walked towards them and her face glowed when she saw him.

'Aunt Hetty.' He kissed her cheek. The airman placed her bag at her feet.

'Lovely to meet you, young man.'

'You too,' he called, hurrying down the platform to join his comrades.

Aunt Hetty brushed at the shoulders of her dark blue suit. 'Johnny, my sweet boy. How tired you look.'

'That wasn't the welcome I was expecting.' He took her bag.

'Come now.' She smiled. 'You haven't asked me here to pay compliments, have you? For you'll get none.'

He laughed. She bent her arm at the elbow and he linked his through it. 'You must tell me all about America.' She paused. 'After you have told me about Ruby.'

He offered to hail a taxi but she opted to walk. 'I'd rather walk and talk. Ruby will be all ears and I want to know what the little minx has been up to.'

Johnny suddenly felt able to breathe. Aunt Hetty wouldn't

pander to Ruby; she was the nearest thing to Mother they would ever have, and still possessed the softness their mother had lost when their father died. He had forgotten.

They strolled over Waterloo Bridge in the sunshine, Aunt Hetty stopping as they went, leaning over, watching the boats slide underneath them. 'Good to see familiar sights,' she said. 'Like old friends. You can see so much from the bridge. On the streets it's all hustle and bustle, but here you have a bit of clarity.' They started walking again and he felt less troubled, enjoying the slower pace as they talked.

'I'm so glad you agreed to come, Aunt Hetty. I'm at a loss how best to help Ruby. She was distraught when Mother died. I didn't handle it very well.'

'Well, she would be, wouldn't she? A girl away from her mother, so far from home? But that's not your fault. I doubt anything you might have done would have helped.'

He pulled her closer, adjusted the bag in his other hand. That was exactly how it had felt. 'I tried sympathy, cajoling, anger, threats. Nothing seemed to help.' He could do it, so why couldn't she? He had compartmentalised it, put it to one side to do the work, but it didn't mean that he felt the loss any less. 'It's not that I didn't care.'

She stopped. People hurried around them and the traffic spat out fumes. 'You don't have to explain to me.' She rubbed at his arm and it was comforting. How lonely he'd been these last few years... They started walking again.

'We were so excited to get the chance. America! The big time. Mother was thrilled. When we sailed across the Atlantic, I thought it was the beginning of everything. But it was mostly a disappointment.'

Hetty gave a slight nod of her head. 'Dream fulfilment is a disappointment, I find. Nothing ever matches up to the dream.'

They turned onto the Strand and as they walked along, he told his aunt of the night at the Café de Paris. 'I'm not sure it's the dancing that she lives for, more the attention.' It was awful talking about his sister like this, but he knew Aunt Hetty would understand.

'It's all she's ever known. And it's a way of proving to herself that she exists.' She moved her head to indicate the Lyons Corner House. 'Shall we go in? You can treat me to a bite to eat and we can talk some more. Will Ruby be all right on her own a little longer?' She was smiling as she said it, and he knew that she was well aware that Ruby would still be sleeping off the effects of the night before.

'I have to get her away, Aunt Hetty, before she...'

'Before she what? Gets worse? Causes a scandal? Gets pregnant? Kills herself?' He looked at her and she raised an eyebrow. 'Perhaps you have things you don't feel able to tell me. Well, I can guess. Ruby will tell me if she wants to.'

He stepped ahead, opened the door into the tea rooms and found a table. He pulled out a chair for Aunt Hetty to sit down and she put her bag on another. The Nippies, as the waitresses were called, weren't called so for nothing and a petite blonde took their order and soon returned with a tray bearing tea and scones. Aunt Hetty picked up the teapot and reached out for his cup.

'Now, America. Start at the beginning.'

He told her how they had arrived, wide-eyed. It was hard to tell who was more excited – Ruby or their mother. Ruby was twenty, the world was opening up for her, but to Alice it was the culmination of her plans. Although their father, Bruce Randolph, had been a head-liner in England, he'd never been able to conquer America. Alice was determined that Johnny and Ruby would. They'd travelled from state to state: small theatres, large ones, half-empty houses and standing-room only. Alice had set up newspaper and radio interviews wherever they went, wangled invitations to the house parties of the great and good, haggled for spots further up the bill, more pay, a percentage of the box office. There had been no time to think, no time for romance, no time for anything but what their mother laid out for them. Day after day, life was a blur of rehearsals, performances and meetings.

'No time to play?' Aunt Hetty spread a generous amount of butter on her scone and took a bite.

He splashed a little milk in his tea. 'Never has been. Not much, anyway.' He thought of Frances, the dancer he had fallen in love with in the last London show they'd appeared in before they sailed for America. They'd kept their love a secret, knowing Alice would disapprove because it wasn't part of her plan. He wondered where Frances was now.

'Your mother was a strong woman. Determined,' Aunt Hetty said, interrupting his thoughts. 'But she didn't start out that way. She was much like Ruby until she met your father.' She touched at the corner of her mouth with her napkin. 'She loved the glamour of his life, the travelling, mixing with people of power and influence.' She was quiet for a moment. 'He left her in a parlous state when he died.'

Johnny nodded, remembering. He'd found her once, sprawled out on the bed, crying, her empty purse open in her hand, a few coins on the counterpane. It must have been frightening, a woman alone with two children.

'She did her best,' he said. 'She wanted a better life for us. What mother wouldn't?'

'I agree.' She finished her scone. 'Personally, I think she went too far, but who am I to judge?'

He wanted to agree with his aunt, but it felt disloyal. 'She should have told us she was ill,' he offered. 'That she was dying.'

'She should.' Aunt Hetty was thoughtful. 'More tea?'

He shook his head. 'I wouldn't have signed the contract if I'd known. We would have come home.'

Aunt Hetty gave him a sad smile. 'That's exactly why she didn't tell you. She died knowing she had done her best by you. You were her life.'

'Her entire life,' Johnny agreed. 'It's not a good thing, though, is it? To set your sights on success to the point where there's nothing else.' The emptiness of his life gnawed at him again.

'It's not, darling boy. Indeed, it is not.'

By the time they arrived at the flat, he'd given Aunt Hetty a full description of Ruby's behaviour both in America and since they'd arrived back home at the beginning of August. Only it wasn't home, was it? He didn't feel they belonged anywhere.

Johnny opened the door and stood back to let Aunt Hetty enter. She strode into the middle of the sitting room, looking about her as she did so, taking in the furniture, the lighting, the oak fire surround, the gas fire. She walked over to the window, rubbed at the cloth of the curtains, peered down into the street.

He placed her bag on the chair by the door, waiting for her verdict.

'Very nice.' She kept looking about her. 'Pleasant.' She drew the pin from her hat, which she took off and placed on the small table at the side of the easy chair. 'You rented it furnished?'

'For a year. I got an agency to sort it for us before we arrived back in England so that we didn't have to live out of a suitcase. We've done enough of that. It's close to the theatres, for rehearsals...' It had been the perfect find, but now he only saw the downsides: it was too close to the Savoy, to the clubs. Now that there was nothing to keep Ruby busy, what had seemed like heaven was now a hell. He slipped off his jacket and draped it over the back of the chintz armchair. 'Can I get you a drink?'

She shook her head. Her long grey hair was curled into a neat bun and he was fleetingly reminded of his mother. The bedroom door opened and Ruby shuffled out, rubbing at her face with her hand. Her hair was a complete mess and she padded forward, oblivious of her surroundings. Last night so glamorous, today this. That was show business for you.

She yawned, opening her mouth wide.

'Hand to mouth, Ruby. You weren't born on a farm. Manners.'

Ruby froze and looked across to where Aunt Hetty was standing beside the fireplace.

'Aunt Hetty!' Her face crumpled. Aunt Hetty opened her arms wide and Ruby ran into them. Their aunt enfolded her, her bosom a cushion for Ruby's head. When she deemed that Ruby had been comforted enough, she grasped her niece's hands and held her away from her, her eyes reflecting sadness, not disappointment.

'My dear girl, what have you been doing to yourself?' She touched Ruby's cheek. 'Dull eyes, dull skin. This will never do. We need to take you in hand.'

Ruby started to cry, little sobs that were the beginnings of a torrent. Aunt Hetty consoled her, leading her to the small sofa that faced the fire, peeled her off and sat her down. She lifted Ruby's legs and made her lie on the sofa, plumping the cushions. 'Now then, madam. You're going to behave yourself while I'm here, aren't you?'

'You're going to stay?' Ruby flashed Johnny a grateful smile.

'For a few days. Yes.' Aunt Hetty rolled up her sleeves. 'I'm going to make you something nourishing for—' She broke off and pursed her lips. 'Your breakfast, although it's well after lunch.' Ruby was about to protest but Aunt Hetty stopped her. 'Now, now! I know the ways of the theatre as well as you do, young lady, but you're not working in the theatre at the moment, and this is no time to be getting out of bed.'

Johnny stretched his neck from side to side, releasing a little of the tension that had built up these past months. Ruby would be safe with Aunt Hetty. He could leave her for a few days, knowing that she would still be in one piece when he got back.

Aunt Hetty bustled into the kitchen and he followed her. She began opening cupboards and drawers, familiarising herself with the contents, took eggs from the pantry, then milk, sniffed it, rummaged for butter. 'Scrambled eggs on toast. Can you get some bread, Johnny boy?'

He leaned over and kissed her cheek. 'I will get you anything your heart desires.' He jangled his hand in his pocket for change.

She cracked an egg into a bowl, reached for another. 'Off with you.'

Ruby had gone into the bedroom and pulled on her silk dressing gown before brushing her hair and wiping her face with cold cream. She came into the sitting room as Johnny came out of the kitchen. Aunt Hetty was right, he thought. Ruby's skin and her eyes were dull – and so was Ruby herself, inside and out. Oh, she was good at faking her smile. They'd been doing it most of their life, after all, but Aunt Hetty had sliced through to the truth like a knife and Ruby was the better for it. His sister wouldn't take it from him, they were too close, and he felt he couldn't save her without making a huge change. Aunt Hetty would give him the time he needed. Bernie had suggested he come and look at an investment and possible venue for a show, way out on the east coast at the end of the train line. Ruby wouldn't like it – but then she never liked what was good for her.

If it all worked out as he hoped, they would have a good income because he planned to put on a revue and rehearse an understudy to take his place. Ruby would have work; she would have focus and she would get well. Eventually. It wasn't fair to burden Aunt Hetty for more than a few days. He made for the door and Ruby hurried to him, standing on tiptoes to kiss his cheek.

'Thank you.'

He smiled. 'For what?'

'Aunt Hetty. It's like having a little piece of mother with us.' Her voice was soft, sad, and the bittersweetness of their aunt's being there lay heavy in her words. He pressed her shoulder, gave it a squeeze.

'I'll be back in two ticks. Behave yourself.'

'I daren't not.' It was the first time in weeks they'd shared a civil word and he closed the door behind him, a spring in his step, raced down the stairs and out into the street.

He could smell the food cooking as he dashed back upstairs, the loaf balanced on top of a white box tied with a black and cream ribbon. He'd picked up a couple of cakes from the patisserie as a treat. Ruby was setting the table, the bathroom door was open and he could hear the bath running, the smell of perfumed oil mingling with the smell of eggs. She turned, smiled and it all seemed so normal that he hoped he wasn't being too optimistic. Aunt Hetty could only stay a few days before she had to return to Uncle Jim and her work with the WVS. Would Ruby then resort to her earlier habits? He had to hope she wouldn't. And with any luck they would be away from temptation before she could do more damage to herself.

15

Johnny yawned and stretched his arms out as wide as he could. The journey to Lincolnshire seemed endless, the hours ticking by as they headed north, and he leaned back in his seat, staring out of the window. They were almost there but still a few miles yet to go.

'Had a snooze, young fella?' Bernie had the window open, his elbow resting on it, his hand on the wheel.

'I must have nodded off. It was that fry-up we had at the service station on the Great North Road. Made me drowsy.'

'It'll put a good lining on your stomach, my boy.' Bernie tooted his horn at a passing army truck and waved to the boys. Johnny yawned again, wound down his window and leaned his shoulder towards it.

'It's good to be home, Bernie. I was thinking of all the miles we travelled in the States. Wide open spaces that stretched for miles, mountains, dust bowls, trees that seemed to touch the sky. Bigger than you could imagine, if you hadn't seen it for yourself.'

'Bigger and better?' Bernie looked away from the road briefly and at him.

'No, just different.' They'd loved America in the beginning, feeling as if something wonderful was within touching distance. And it was. They'd worked hard to make it so. But it had soured and there was nothing he could do about it. Johnny folded his arms and adjusted his legs. Bernie's car was luxurious but after a hundred miles even the luxury of a Daimler waned. They'd stopped once or twice but Bernie was eager to get to Grimsby in daylight. He didn't want to be driving along unfamiliar roads in the blackout and he wanted Johnny to see the place in good light.

'Well, at least you get to see it in its autumn glory. It's a good job you could join me. When petrol rationing comes in on Monday, we won't have the luxury – or the freedom.'

Johnny looked back out of the window. Troop trucks were rattling by in the other direction, heading down south to the coast. They had passed so many of them.

Bernie pulled a cigar from his top pocket and stuck it in his mouth but made no attempt to light it.

'Thinking of joining up at any time, Johnny?'

'As soon as we get this bit of business sorted. It would keep things ticking along for Ruby until it's all over. It'll be good for her, to have a purpose. And I think she'll be better out of London – and safer.'

'From the bombs? Or the parties?'

'Both.'

Ruby was out of control and they had their reputation to think of. Yes, she'd had her dalliances, a polite way of putting her scandalous behaviour. There had been many inappropriate liaisons on her part but her relationship with a high-profile married man had nearly cost them their career – and the two admissions to private clinics, well, he didn't want to think about them. The silence of the press could be bought; everyone, it seemed, could be bought.

'What happened? She was always such a sweetie. I mean, she

still is. Don't mind a fumbling idiot with his words, my boy. I didn't mean to insult your sister.'

'Don't worry, Bernie; I know what you mean.' Bernie was being kind. Ruby was not the girl she was when they'd left for America, but he couldn't tell Bernie everything; they'd only known each other a couple of months. Johnny trusted him as much as he trusted anyone, but the work could dry up. The theatres were able to reopen but many of them were being cautious. There were more people fighting for fewer jobs. If Ruby got a reputation for letting people down, it would affect them both.

'Didn't she want to go?'

He smiled, remembering her enthusiasm. 'Couldn't wait to get on the boat at Southampton. Mother came out with us for the first couple of years and everything was great; we got a terrific reception from all the towns we played.' It was exciting but exhausting, travelling state to state: checking into lodgings then out again; brief stops when their days were empty, their nights full. They had been lonely but had jollied each other along and he'd kept Ruby busy working, rehearsing. It hadn't been as glamorous as it was made out to be.

'So I heard. The reports in *The Stage* followed your journey. Quite a name you were making for yourselves.'

'We were. But it's not home, is it? And then Mother died. And, well, I've told you all this before.'

Bernie took the cigar from his mouth and returned it to his pocket. 'Sounds to me like Ruby's still grieving and partying her way out of it.'

Johnny sighed. 'She is, Bernie, but that's not the way to do it, is it?'

Bernie shrugged. 'We all grieve in our different ways.'

Johnny looked out of the window. At least Aunt Hetty was with her and perhaps a few days of them being alone would help.

The landscape changed as they drew nearer to Grimsby, past

fine houses, a church, then along the main shopping
with jewellers and department stores. It wouldn't impress
it might pique her interest. He felt a pang of guilt. Per
should have enlarged on his plans, but would she have listene He
decided not. After all, he might not like it himself. Grimsby, what
was he thinking? It had been a suggestion from Bernie, that's all. It
was up to him to work out whether it would be suitable.

'Damn good job I've been here before,' Bernie muttered. 'I'd
have no ruddy idea where I was, otherwise.' The shops became
warehouses. Johnny took in the high, smoke-covered walls and
different smells that emanated from the dock area: coal, hemp, fish.
Mostly fish. He grimaced. It was grubby, industrial but the variety
and number of shops indicated there was money to spend. They
passed the bus station and neared the docks on which Grimsby had
built its empire. Bernie pulled the car onto the opposite side of the
road and pointed to a building slightly ahead so that Johnny had
the better view. 'There she is. The Palace Theatre.'

Johnny leaned forward and peered through the windscreen. It
was ornate, over the top, with pointed roofs, domes and cupolas. A
statue presided over the centre entrance and a long canopy covered
the frontage. It seemed that the architect had taken his favourite
features and given them all to the Palace. There was a warehouse to
the right and rear of it, a pub to the left. A large iron bridge went
over the river. Oh, Ruby would hate it. He didn't care for it much
himself.

'That's the Palace Buffet on the corner – see it? Does good business. All part of the deal.' Bernie drove slowly down the road,
pointing out the other theatres that had gone to cinema.

'Lot of competition, Bernie.'

'It's a big town, Johnny, my boy. Prosperous. Smell that money.'

Johnny laughed. 'I can smell fish.'

'Like I said. Money.' He drove into the dock area. Even though it was late in the day, there were still signs of activity; people came and went, wagons passed, and trawlers were lined side by side in the docks, packed in like sardines. 'Lots of 'em have gone, converted to minesweepers,' Bernie explained. 'But they'll be back. And boats are out there still, catching fish. We'll always need food, whether it's from the sea itself, or cargoes from other places.' They paused at the crossing while a train with numerous wagons rattled past. The gates were swung back and Bernie drove on. They came to a crossroads that had a large pub on one corner.

'We're in Cleethorpes now,' Bernie said as he changed gear and picked up a little speed. The road was long, filled on one side with small shops such as fishmongers and greengrocers, with houses along the other; nice houses they were too, with small front gardens, trees and hedges. Bernie drove up a small hill, lined on either side with boarding houses. The road curved around, showing the sea to the left and leading on to a long road that had ornate gardens to one side, a fancy hotel and a parade with shops on the other. It was much like many other seaside towns they'd worked in as youngsters – a different one each year. He smiled, remembering the fun of them, being in one place for weeks on end, making friends, relaxing. It had been the best of times, he realised now. Perhaps that was what Ruby needed.

'Your little sister will prefer this,' Bernie said as he stopped the car opposite a theatre, the Empire, and left the engine running. Johnny looked down towards the sea and the pier. It was lovely little place. He liked it.

'My good friend Jack Holland is the proud owner of that little beauty. We'll call and see him tomorrow. He's going to be putting on a bit of cine-variety to get going, testing the waters.' He started driving again and Johnny looked at the resort as Bernie gave him a rundown. 'It's all going to be a bit of a risk but I wanted you to see it for yourself. See what you think. It's all about the gut, my boy. All about the gut.'

He pulled up outside an open-air bathing pool and they got out. Johnny stretched and bent, trying to ease the discomfort of the last few hours.

Bernie stood on the pavement, took out his cigar and turned his back to the wind to light it. He puffed and blew out the smoke. 'Far enough away for you? And Ruby?'

Johnny put his hands in his pockets. The wind was sharp. What would it be like when winter came?

'It could be. I don't know, Bernie.' He didn't want to commit himself to anything that would tie them up long-term. Although, now that they were committed to war, everything was liable to change at any time and he sensed that what Ruby needed was stability. Would this offer it to her? He wasn't convinced. 'Could we look about the theatre?'

Bernie put his hand on his back as they returned to the car. 'Sure.' They stood in the fresh air for a few more seconds and Bernie said, 'I don't mind what you choose. And I mean that, Johnny.' He opened his door. 'Let's go back to the Palace and you can have a good look around. I wanted you to see what was on offer, that was all.'

They drove back down the long road, leaving Cleethorpes behind them, and Bernie parked his car outside the Palace. He checked his watch.

'Stan Simms should be here. He's the manager. I asked him to open up.' They walked to the front of the theatre and Bernie pushed on the door and walked in. A light was on in a small office to the right of the foyer and a tall man with neat white hair came out. His posture indicated a military past and he had a tidy moustache and black eyes.

'Mr Blackwood. Good to see you again.' He put out his hand

and Bernie gripped it, pumping it vigorously. He let go of Simms's hand and turned to Johnny.

'Johnny Randolph, Stan Simms.'

Johnny reached forward and shook the man's hand.

'Good to meet you, Johnny.' Stan stretched out his arm. 'Let me show you around?'

'That would be great. I'd like Johnny to get an idea of the place, inside and out – the clientele we can expect.'

Stan opened the door into the stalls. 'Follow me.' He led them down the aisle and up onto the stage. The safety curtain had been flown out and the three men stood looking out into the rows of empty seats. 'Room for one and half thousand when we're capacity,' Stan informed them.

Johnny moved about the stage while Bernie and Stan remained where they were, talking quietly. He had to get a feel for this. Bernie had already spoken of his ideas for the theatre. He knew he needed to get Ruby away from London, but not on a whim and certainly not to the first opportunity that presented itself. Bernie had been as good as his word, finding something that was mutually beneficial, but Johnny needed to see more before he made a commitment. He wandered into the wings.

'The lights are on everywhere. Take your time,' Stan called out.

He went backstage and checked the dressing rooms, the back access, the stage door. A rat scuttled into a hole. That was nothing new. He made his way up into the gods and looked down onto the stage. He could put up with anything – it didn't matter to him, but he owed it to Ruby to take care of her. Would this be too brutal? He walked back down and joined Bernie and Stan, who were sitting at the back of the stalls.

'Seen enough?'

'I have. Thanks, Stan.'

The two men stood up.

Bernie put out his hand and Stan shook it. 'Thank you. I appreciate you staying on for us. I'll be in contact from my office when I'm back in town.'

'Right you are, Bernie,' Stan said.

Bernie led the way into the light of the foyer, Johnny and Stan bringing up the rear. It was hard to tell what time of day it was inside with all the windows blackened in the foyer and as Bernie and Johnny stepped out into the street, daylight was fading. 'The hotel beckons.' Bernie slapped his back and the two of them crossed the road to the car. Three kids were running their hands over the bodywork, peering into the windows and admiring the motor. They leaped away when Bernie got to the door.

'A beauty, isn't it, boys?'

'It is, sir.'

They stood back while Johnny got into his seat and raced after the car as it moved off down the road. Johnny could see them in the wing mirror, their faces bright with nothing more than admiration. What it was to be happy with the simple things.

* * *

The dining room of the Royal Hotel on the outskirts of Grimsby docks was quiet. Staff were attentive and there were a few looks and quiet comments as Bernie and Johnny were shown to a table. Bernie picked up the menu. 'Has to be fish, doesn't it? Can't come to Grimsby and not have the fish.' He leaned back in his seat to get nearer the waiter. 'What do you recommend, old chap?'

The elderly man leaned forward, his hands behind his back, and directed them towards the plaice and they were happy to go with his recommendation. Wine was brought over to Bernie to taste and approve while they waited for the meal to arrive. Bernie touched the ends of the silver cutlery. His hands were big, practical.

'I suppose I should give you more details, now that you've seen the theatres, and there's a third one we need to look at on our way home. We'll do the Empire in the morning and see the Royal on the way back through Lincoln.' He took his glass and quaffed a little of his wine. 'Jack Holland owns the Empire outright and he's stepping up to purchase the Palace and the Royal. I'll be looking to find other theatres to add to his stable.'

Johnny frowned. 'Isn't that madness? When the theatres have been closed and no one knows if they'll change their minds and shut them again?'

'They won't. Jack and I saw action in the Great War. He's younger than I am but we played our part, although I remained in England. They shut the theatres then. You would have been far too young to notice, but it was a big mistake. Look at what Basil's doing with ENSA.' He eased himself forward. 'This is the time to buy. People are nervous; they want out and they'll lower their price to do it. Now is the time to hold your nerve.'

He thought of Ruby. He had to hold his nerve too.

Bernie continued, leaning as close as he could, lowering his voice. 'We'll all need a break from the horrors to come, because come they will and people will be looking for lightness and laughter and a chance to leave it all behind, to fall into someone else's story and have a happy ending. We all want a happy ending, don't we, my boy?'

Johnny smiled ruefully. He had lost all hope of a happy ending for himself.

'Jack's looking for investors to join him. He wants to build an empire to rival that of the Stoll-Moss chain and I want to help him do it. We wondered if you'd be interested in joining the two of us, if you worked for a percentage of the take at the Palace and shares in the company. With a name like the Randolphs, we could guarantee packed houses. It would get us off to a good start. If you would be open to something like that?'

'I might well be.' It was definitely worth consideration. It would give them an income and that's what he was looking for long term. Security for both of them. He'd be called up sooner or later and if Ruby carried on as she was, she'd have no career left.

Bernie interlaced his fingers over his stomach. 'We'd be looking at putting shows on at the beginning of December, subject to the paperwork being right. This is a reconnaissance exercise, nothing more. I wouldn't want to offer you something you knew nothing about. It's not my way.'

'I know that, Bernie; I appreciate it.'

Bernie shook out his napkin, draped it over his lap. 'Any ladies in your life other than Ruby?'

Johnny leaned back as the fish arrived and the plates were placed in front of them. 'There was, once.'

Bernie cut into his fish and put it into his mouth. 'Fabulous. Good choice.' The waiter smiled and left. 'Only once?'

Johnny started to eat. 'Only one that meant anything.'

'The one that got away?' Bernie drank more wine. 'Not like this fish, eh?'

Johnny agreed.

'What happened?'

He shook his head. 'I have no idea.' He gave an empty laugh. 'No idea at all.' Where was she now? he wondered. Was she happy? He hoped she was. If only he'd stood firm – his mother would've come around in the end because they couldn't be children forever. At the time he hadn't realised the extent of her control over them. She'd loved them – but to the exclusion of all else and it wasn't healthy. No wonder Ruby was rootless. She'd never had to think of anything but the theatre, and their mother had kept it that way.

Ruby's recklessness was grief – and it was also bewilderment; neither of them knew how to live.

* * *

He woke on Saturday morning feeling refreshed and more alert than he had in weeks. The bed was soft and he'd sunk into the feather mattress, relaxing because he didn't have to worry about Ruby. He dressed and met Bernie in the dining room where they ate a hearty breakfast before heading for the Empire in neighbouring Cleethorpes.

Bernie parked opposite the theatre. Above them the sky was thick with clouds that rolled quickly by, showing patches of blue here and there. Bernie put his homburg on and tugged at his cuffs as they crossed the road. Inside the theatre, a young girl with a mass of soft blonde curls smiled at them from the box office.

'Can I help, gentlemen?'

Bernie went to the arched window. 'Is Mr Holland here? Bernie Blackwood for him.' The girl was looking past him and straight at Johnny, her eyes growing rounder by the second. In the end he had to smile, even laugh a little, and she blushed.

'Mr Randolph, Johnny Randolph?'

'That's me,' he said as she came out of the box office. He could see that she was nervous and he felt bad.

'I'll let Mr Holland know you're here.' She almost curtseyed as she passed them and they heard her run upstairs.

'Quite a powerful effect you have on women, my boy.'

Johnny smiled. 'It's not me. It's who they think I am that has the effect.' He looked at the photos in the display cases and recognised the top of the bill. 'Madeleine Moore was here? Headlining?'

Bernie stood beside him. 'She was. Very successful summer season.'

'What was she doing here? She could top the bill anywhere.'

'Much the same as you and Ruby. Taking a step back, letting go of the pressure for a while. I believe she enjoyed it. It was successful enough for Vernon Leroy to come out of his way to see it.'

Johnny whistled through his teeth.

Bernie slapped him on the back. 'It was a special season. There's a certain magic about the place. And here's another little girl of mine, Jessie Delaney.' He tapped the photograph. 'She's going to be a big star. A big star.' Johnny saw a girl with long brown hair, attractive, but not a beauty by any means. They were about to look in the other display case when they heard footsteps on the stairs and turned to see a man with black hair, peppered with grey. He came forward, the girl from the box office close behind him. He stopped in front of them while the girl went back to her position, watching them from behind the glass front of the ticket desk.

'Jack,' Bernie said, pushing Johnny gently by the back towards the man. 'My good friend, Jack Holland. Johnny Randolph.'

'Good to meet you.' Holland looked a nice chap. There was an immediate warmth about him and he had a firm handshake. As he moved, Johnny noticed his slight limp and when he smiled Johnny could see the scar to the side of his face. Bernie had said they'd been through the Great War. At least they'd both survived, although he was well aware that scars on the outside were only a glimpse of the scars on the inside.

'Glad you could make it. Do you want to join me in my office?' They followed him upstairs to the first floor and he led them to a room where a woman with short brown hair was on the phone. 'Annie, my secretary.' Annie put one hand over the mouthpiece and said a quiet hello then returned her attention to her caller. 'She's much more than that. I couldn't do without her.' He led them into his office and the three of them sat down.

'Can I get you a drink?'

Bernie put a hand up. 'Not for me, Jack. We had rather a substantial breakfast.' Johnny shook his head.

Jack clasped his hands in front of him and rested them on the blotter on his desk. 'Glad you could make the journey. I expect Bernie has talked over what we're proposing to do?'

Johnny sat back, crossed his legs. 'He has. It's given me plenty to think about.' They chatted about shows Johnny had been in and Jack was eager to hear of their experience of America.

'Have you ever been?' Johnny asked.

'Never. I'd like to go someday. I know my wife would and I think the lifestyle would suit her.'

'It doesn't suit everyone.' Johnny got up and walked to the window, rested his arm on the frame. Seagulls gathered along the rooftops. 'What do you have planned for the winter, Jack? Would we be better suited here, at the Empire? If we decided to go ahead?'

Jack picked up a pencil, twisted it in his hands. 'We don't have the capacity to make it work. Much as I'd love to have you and your sister appear here. The Palace is more than three times our size and, in the end, it's all down to the numbers.'

Johnny sighed. 'It's always down to the numbers.' Numbers had trapped them. Numbers in their bank account that, although handsome, were not enough to free them from their contract. Not then – and what did it matter now? He turned his back to the window, leaned against the sill.

'When do I have to let you know by?'

Jack glanced at Bernie, who turned in his seat to look at Johnny. He squinted against the light from the windows, and moved so that he could see Johnny eye to eye. Johnny liked that about him. Bernie never looked away.

'Next week. Like everyone else, we put all our plans to one side when war was declared, but now we're taking back the reins with a vengeance. Christmas will be here before we know it and I want to make an extra effort this year. I feel we'll all be in need of it.'

'We will, Jack. Dark days ahead of us.'

Jack dropped the pencil into a leather tray. 'It should all be ship-shape by the end of the week. I'd then like to put our energies into the Palace and the Royal.'

Bernie got to his feet. 'Okay with you, my boy?'

Johnny came away from the window and shook hands with Jack. 'I'll let you know by Friday at the very latest.'

'I appreciate it, Johnny. I'm sure we can make it work. But it's what you feel comfortable with. Would you like to look around the place?'

He didn't see the point. 'No, I'm fine. It's a theatre, beautiful as she is. But as we won't be appearing here, I don't want to spoil myself wishing I was.' It would make him long for the days when life was simpler. They had reached the top, but it hadn't brought them happiness. The top was a lonely place if you didn't have anyone to share it with. If he'd known that, would he still have worked so hard? Johnny sucked his cheek. It was a huge risk and he wasn't sure he wanted to take any more. Not with Ruby as she was. Jack led the way downstairs. The doors to the stalls were open and a piano was being played, a girl singing.

Bernie turned to Jack, who was behind him on the stairs. He took his cigar from the breast pocket of his camel coat. 'Is that little Miss Delaney?'

Jack smiled. 'It is. She's rehearsing with two of her friends. A couple of the dancers stayed over from the summer and I'm going to be putting on live entertainment between films, just to keep something going.'

'Admirable. Admirable,' Bernie said. Johnny was intrigued. He left Bernie and wandered down the aisle, sitting in the back row. It was dark, the house lights off, and the girls were onstage in the brutal glare of the working lights that bleached the colour from everything. The girl he assumed was Jessie Delaney was playing the piano and singing, and a stunning redhead with a great figure was working on a dance routine instructed by a girl with long black hair who had his back to him. He leaned back in his seat, watching them rehearse, envying the fun they were having. When had he and Ruby last had fun? When had it not been work? Bernie and Jack stood in the doorway and he twisted to them and gave a nod of approval, then turned back to watch the girls. The girl singer was good. Very good. When she stopped playing, the three men applauded and Johnny got to his feet. As he did so, the girl with black hair turned around. He froze. The three girls leaned forward, peering out into the darkness at them. Frances? He walked down the aisle. My God, it was her.

'Frances. Frances O'Leary!'

16

The girls remained where they were as Johnny came towards them. He stopped by the orchestra pit, uncertain of how Frances would react. She hadn't replied to any of his letters and he'd never understood why. He gripped the brass rail, the metal cool beneath his fingers, and looked up at her. Her skin was milky white and she wore the same red lipstick that only made the darkness of her hair and eyes more so. Those eyes – those dark, dark eyes. He smiled but it was not returned. She had grown more lovely over the years they'd been apart; there was something about the way she held herself that was tougher, harder, but he could see beyond that. She was still the same inside; he didn't know why he knew, he just did.

'Frances. It's been a long time.' He glanced briefly at her hands, the merest flicker – and there was no ring. He felt a surge of hope. He took a chance, skipped up the stairs and onto the stage.

'Frances,' he said again and as he walked towards her he couldn't stop smiling, even though her face was set against him. He went to embrace her, but she stepped away and he let his hands drop. The two girls came closer; were they protecting her? 'Forgive my manners, ladies. Johnny Randolph.' He bowed his head slightly, put out his hand and they took it in turn, Frances reluctantly. He gripped warmly, wrapping both hands around hers, all the time wanting to take her into his arms. Her hand was limp in his and he couldn't for the life of him work out what he'd done to receive such a cool reception, so he held back, even though he longed to take her away, to talk, find out what had made her change her mind. Had she met someone else? He was certain she'd loved him. Did she love him still?

'I won't keep you.' He tried to look at the other two girls, but his gaze stayed on Frances. 'It was great, what you did was great.' The red-haired girl smiled. The one he knew was Jessie grinned as if her face would split in two, but Frances looked past him. He stood back. 'Good to see you, Frances.' She didn't respond and he turned and walked back down the stairs and into the aisle, feeling awkward, yet the blood was pumping about his body as if he'd danced for hours. Bernie and Jack were still by the door.

'All right, my boy?' Bernie tilted his chin.

Johnny put a hand on the man's back as they followed Jack out of the auditorium. 'Fine. Just fine.'

The blonde girl in the box office gave them a small wave as they came back into the foyer. He waved back. It all felt rather odd, standing here in the little theatre, the likes of which he and Ruby had not appeared in for years – and yet for the first time in ages he felt as if he was standing on solid ground. He had found her. Part of him wanted to rush back into the theatre, pull Frances into his arms and kiss her like a corny B movie, but common sense told him to be cautious. He turned to Jack and Bernie.

'About your proposition. I've made up my mind. I'm on board for the shares. The Randolphs will appear at the Palace for the winter season. You have my word on it.' He held out his hand. Jack was taken aback, as was Bernie. The two men looked at each other.

'Are you quite certain?' Bernie removed the cigar from between his teeth.

'Absolutely. We can discuss the finer details over the telephone.'

Jack shook his hand with vigour, clasping his other over the top. 'You won't regret it. I'll make sure of that.'

'I know you will. We'll be in touch, won't we, Bernie?'

Bernie's eyebrows were still at the top of his head and he pushed his homburg back onto it.

'You can be assured of it.'

* * *

Johnny crossed the road to where the car was parked. He sat on the low wall, looking up at the Empire. Bernie sat beside him.

'What was all that about?'

'That, Bernie, was about the one that got away.'

'Seriously? Which one?'

Johnny nudged him. 'Do you have to ask?' Of all the places to find her. 'The one who didn't react, the one who didn't speak.'

'The tall, dark-haired girl?'

'Frances O'Leary.' Just to say her name again was heaven itself.

'So, let me get this straight. You made a business decision based purely on seeing a girl. A girl who didn't speak. A girl who didn't react.'

He laughed, patting Bernie on the shoulder. 'I did. And I reckon it will turn out to be the best decision I ever made.'

The older man shook his head. 'I'm not going to disagree, my boy.' He paused, looking back at the theatre. 'She must be some girl.'

'She is.' He could hardly believe it. A second chance. What were the odds of finding her again? He longed to stay, to talk to her, find out what had happened, but it was enough to know she was here and the quicker he got things finalised with Bernie, the sooner he would be back.

Bernie got up and went to the car. Johnny did likewise, taking one last look at the theatre before he opened the door. He'd found her. All he had to do now was find out why she'd stopped all contact, why she'd never used the ticket he'd sent. He didn't need to write and have nothing come in return. Not any more.

Bernie started the engine. 'What about Ruby?'

Johnny settled himself in his seat as Bernie made a U-turn in the road. 'Leave Ruby to me.' She wouldn't like it one bit, but this would suit both of them. He had to help her break away from the downward spiral she was in – and he would get a chance to rekindle the love of his life. He took one last look at the theatre as they passed it. There was a chance they could find happiness after all.

* * *

Frances couldn't move. She could only watch as Johnny walked away from her.

'Did that really happen?' Jessie was shaking her head. 'Did Johnny Randolph really walk into this theatre and tell us we were good? And he remembered you, Frances, after all this time. Not everyone does. People can be flakes.'

'He's not everyone,' Ginny said. Jessie twisted to look at her and Frances turned away, moving back towards the piano. It felt as though her legs would go from under her and she needed something to lean onto. 'I've never had anyone look at me that way.' Frances sat down on the piano stool. 'You were more than an understudy, Frances, it's obvious from the way he looked at you.' Ginny leaned on the piano.

'Never!' Jessie was incredulous. 'You said you worked with the

Randolphs. You never said anything about the two of you being together.'

'There's nothing to say.' Frances didn't want to remember because it would bring back happier times and that would lead her to sadness and pain, and she hadn't time for it. 'We should be rehearsing. Time's running out and I have to go to work.' She got up, sat down again.

Jessie sat next to her, held her hand. 'You're white as a sheet.' Ginny hurried over to her bag at the side of the stage and brought back a bottle of water, pulled out the stopper and handed it to Frances, who took a sip, and then another. She'd never expected Johnny to turn up. Never. She'd thought that she would have to go looking, that he would avoid her. But he hadn't.

'What happened, Frances?' Jessie's face was etched with concern. Frances took another swig of water, and rested the bottle on her legs.

'We were in the show. Johnny asked me out and I liked him.'

'Who wouldn't?' Ginny said and Frances looked across at her and smiled.

'Yes, he's good-looking, and yes, he's a wonderful dancer – but he's also very kind and quiet, really.' She thought back to that year, a year of perfect happiness. 'I was chosen to understudy Ruby and so we got to rehearse more. He asked me out to dinner and, well, you know...' She forced herself to stand. 'His mother didn't like me. I didn't take it personally; she didn't like anyone who came close to Johnny – or Ruby, for that matter. It was sad, really, how she controlled them both.' Would he come back? What would she do if he did? And Imogen? She shook her head to try and stop the thoughts. 'I need to go to work. Lil needs me.' She picked up her bag.

'We'll walk with you,' Jessie said. 'You look a bit wobbly.'

'I'm all right.' She pulled herself more erect. 'Honestly, I am. I'm tired. We all are. It's hard juggling jobs and rehearsing as well. Please, don't fuss.' Her voice was firm now and the girls knew her well enough not to press the matter. 'I'll see you at home after I've finished at the pub.' She walked down the steps, feeling their eyes on her, glad to get out into the natural light of the foyer. Dolly rushed out of the box office, her face glowing with excitement.

'Did you see Johnny Randolph?'

She nodded, pulling on her jacket, and Dolly leaned in close. 'Don't tell anyone – well, you can tell Jessie, of course, or I will. But I overheard them talking. You'll never guess!'

'Never guess what?'

'The Randolphs are going to do the winter season at the Palace. Can you imagine?'

She gripped Dolly's arm. 'Are you sure?'

'I saw them shake on it.' She clapped her hands with delight. 'We'll have to go and see the show.'

Frances bit down on her lip. She wanted to smile for Dolly's sake, but she couldn't find it within her. 'We will,' she managed to say, letting go of her arm and striding towards the door. She needed light; she needed air.

* * *

Lil was outside the Fisherman's Arms when Frances arrived. The draymen had delivered the barrels and were closing the hatch that led to the cellar. The older of the two men got up onto the front of the wagon, the younger lad on the back, his legs dangling as the horse moved forward. Lil turned to wave them off, caught sight of Frances and rushed towards her. 'Good grief, lass, what's happened to ya? Ya look like you've seen a ghost.'

'I have.' She pushed open the door to the main room and Lil bustled behind her.

'Sit yourself down and I'll get you a drink.'

'I'd rather have a tea.' She got up. 'I'll make it.'

'You'll do no such thing. Let me put the kettle on.' Lil disappeared through the door behind the bar and came back quickly. 'I'll leave the door open till I hear it whistle. Now then. What's upset you?'

Frances wrung her hands in her lap. 'Nothing. Everything.' She looked up, gave Lil a rueful smile. 'I don't know where to start.'

'Beginning is as good as anywhere, Franny.'

But where was the beginning? She glanced at the clock. Almost eleven. Lil saw her. 'Aye, I know. My bottle man let me down this morning an' all. Still got me shelves to fill.'

Frances got to her feet. 'Let me help. That's what you pay me for.'

Lil sighed. 'If you must. We can talk while I bottle up.' The two of them went behind the bar. Crates were already upended behind it, set in front of the shelves. 'I'll make a start on the pale ale.' Lil picked up a cloth, sat astride the crate and pulled the bottles out one by one from the gap between her knees. Each one was given a quick wipe before being placed in neat rows along the wooden shelves, the labels facing forward. 'There's a satisfaction in bringing order to chaos. Suits my simple mind.'

'Taking pride in your work is what sets people apart, Lil.' Frances began laying out the bar cloths on the counter, smoothing them out with her hands.

'Now then,' Lil said, 'what's upset you this morning?'

It was somehow easier to talk with Lil's back turned to her. She was a clever old thing; she was sure Lil knew that. Frances told her of Johnny Randolph turning up out of the blue.

Lil turned. 'Johnny Randolph? Of the Randolphs?' She turned back to the shelf. 'Ruddy hell. What's he doing in Cleethorpes?'

'I don't know. But...'

'It's the "buts" that get ya every time, isn't it, lovey? But?'

She told Lil of their relationship.

'What? And he left without another word?'

Frances nodded even though Lil still had her back to her. 'Before he left, he said he would send me a ticket, my passage to America, but it never came.'

Lil got up, moved the crate and went to the next one. Fran picked up the empty and took it through the back way and returned with two mugs of tea. Lil got off the crate and bent her knees a few times.

'By, I'm ready for that.' She wrapped her hand around the mug. 'Didn't he let you know why?'

Frances sipped, the warmth of the drink making her feel less shaky.

'I wrote letters, cards, telegrams. Not one reply.'

'Ever?' Lil's face was contorted. Frances shook her head. 'How long?'

'Four years. I wrote so many times in the first few months, every week to begin with. When he didn't reply I realised he wasn't interested and I gave up. I suppose America was more exciting.' The girls were probably more exciting too.

Lil blew into her mug. 'Well, I know America's a long way, but hell, letters get through eventually.' Lil looked piercingly at Frances over her mug and Frances felt her neck redden. 'And what else? Listen, Franny. I've been around the block a few times. And I know man trouble when I see it. Like your little friend, Ginny whatsit. You're not like her, so...' She patted the counter with her hand. 'What's the "but"?'

Could she tell Lil about Imogen? Lil wasn't a gossip, she knew that, and she had a good heart. Lil held her gaze, her grey eyes soft and kind and it gave her courage.

'I have a child. A daughter. Imogen.' There, it was out, the words seeming suspended in the ether. The door opened and Artie walked in with Fudge.

Lil said, 'I'll get this.' She poured the pint and as always Artie took it wordlessly, handed over his cash and sat down, the dog at his side. Lil lowered her voice. 'His child?'

Frances nodded.

'Does he know?'

'No one does.'

'Where is she?'

'With friends.'

Lil came and stood close to her, rubbed her back. 'How have you managed?'

Frances shrugged, her throat thickening so quickly she felt she would suffocate. 'I had one good friend, Patsy. She's been every-thing to me.' She put her hand to her neck. 'It's been tough, really tough, but somehow I've survived. Imogen is my world.' Was she so different to Alice Randolph after all? Her children had been her world too – but not to let them have a life of their own? Not find love?

Lil picked up her mug. 'Well...'

'Not what you were thinking of me?'

'Now don't you start that, madam. I'll have none of you telling me what I'm thinking.'

'Sorry, Lil. I didn't mean to insult you.'

She flapped a hand. 'It'll take more than that to insult me.' Lil leaned on the bar, the bottles forgotten. 'You poor little bugger.' She was thoughtful for a moment, then stood up sharply, put her hands on her hips. 'So, what's he ruddy doing, coming here, lording it about? The rat.'

Frances looked to Artie but he was oblivious, his nose in his paper, the dog sleeping.

'That's just it. He didn't. If he'd have breezed in as if nothing had happened, I'd have been furious, but it wasn't like that.'

'Well, what was it like?' Lil was angry on her behalf.

'I think that's what upset me the most. He looked puzzled. As if...' She paused, seeing his face in her mind's eye. 'As if it was me who had let him down.'

Lil leaned back on the counter. 'Hm, did you ask him?'

'I didn't get a chance. Not this time.'

Lil raised an eyebrow. 'You think you'll get another?'

Frances lowered her voice again. 'They're set to come to the Palace for the winter season. A friend overheard him talking to the owner of the Empire.' No matter how many times she'd imagined confronting him over the years, it hadn't been like this. She'd expected anger, denial, or plain rejection. His reaction had left her confused. She sipped her tea and Lil slapped her hands together, then brushed them side to side.

'Well, when they do, you'll have to tell him.' She made a start on another crate. 'So, do you get to see your little lass?'

Frances's mind was racing with what might happen in the future. 'I see her Sundays and, if I get time, in the week.'

'Where is she? Close?'

'Waltham.'

Lil paused, a cloth in one hand. 'And that's why you can't work Sundays?'

Frances nodded.

'Why haven't you got her with you?'

'I couldn't manage. I've got to work to keep the both of us. Sometimes that's meant travelling away for weeks at a time, rehearsing all day and working all night. I can't drag her around with me, relying on strangers.' She didn't want to. Not everyone was kind or could be trusted. 'She's in a good place. Patsy has two boys and is wonderful with her.' She smiled, thinking of how well they all got on. 'More importantly, there's no one asking questions, no one judging. As far as anyone's concerned, she's staying with her aunt Patsy and that's all people need to know.' Artie rustled the newspaper as he turned the pages and the two women watched him, then turned back to each other. 'I was so thrilled to get this summer season and tie it in with the panto. It meant I could be with her more.'

Lil rubbed at her arm and Frances reached across and held her hand. 'She's safe, Lil, she's with a family.'

Lil looked at her from under her eyebrows. 'But not her mother.'

'I want what's best for her.'

'And it's breaking your heart.'

Frances looked away. It was less painful if she didn't think too deeply about it. The door to the bar opened and Big Malc walked in. She tapped the pump and picked up his tankard.

'Aye, you've got it, Frances. But just a half if you will.'

She put the tankard back and picked up a glass. Her heart had been broken long ago.

17

Ruby sat among the bubbles, breathing in the heavy rose perfume, and sank down into the warmth of the water. The room was cloudy with steam, the windows heavy with condensation. She should have opened them but she hated the sounds of the city spoiling her bath, preferring to imagine that she was somewhere else, anywhere else. The door was ajar and through it she could hear Aunt Hetty bustling about the flat as she brought it all to order. She closed her eyes. It had been heavenly to have Aunt Hetty here and not have to share her with Johnny. A wonderful two days when she'd been almost able to forget the misery of everything. Of losing her mother, of being back in England with its greyness and drabness, and war. But Aunt Hetty wouldn't stay... no one stayed. They all left in the end.

She sank deeper still, her chin in the water, her ears, her mouth, her nose, and closed her eyes, submerging herself, opening her eyes. If she stopped breathing...

The soap suds stung and she burst out of the water, blinking and gasping for air and Aunt Hetty, hearing the noise, dashed in.

'Ruby! Are you all right?' Aunt Hetty was holding Ruby's fur cape.

Ruby grinned, pushing strands of wet hair from her face, rubbing at her eyes. 'Perfectly.'

'I heard a commotion and thought you'd fallen in.' Ruby knew it was nothing of the sort; it was the reason her aunt insisted she leave the door open.

'Sorry, couldn't find the soap.' She felt around the bottom of the bath and held it up. It was clear Aunt Hetty didn't believe her.

'Isn't it about time you got out and got dressed?' She held out Ruby's cape, brushing it with her hands. 'And it's about time you sorted the mess in your room. All your lovely things just left where you've dropped them.'

Ruby pouted.

'All that eye-flashing and fluttering your lashes won't wash with me, Ruby Randolph.' She handed Ruby a towel from the rail and Ruby reluctantly took hold of it. Aunt Hetty pulled out the plug.

'Such a shame to waste the water.'

'Such a shame to waste the day, my girl.' She put Ruby's cape over her arm and pushed up the sash window, tutting as she did so. 'Out you come.' She waited for Ruby to step out of the bath before leaving the room, and Ruby wrapped the towel about herself.

Aunt Hetty had flung open the large mahogany wardrobe in Ruby's room and was unpacking one of her two trunks. Ruby sat down on the bed, rubbing her hair with a small towel.

'You should have done this yourself. You can't go living out of a trunk.'

'Why not? We've done it for years.' She let the hair towel drop to her shoulders.

Aunt Hetty slipped a black cocktail dress onto a hanger, smoothing the shoulders so that it hung correctly. Ruby pushed out her lip. Henry Longman had bought it for her in Illinois. Nice boy. Too nice. Boring…

'It's not good for you, Ruby. You need structure. Roots.' She bent down and picked up a long chiffon dress in baby blue. Eye-wateringly expensive, bought for a party at the Hollywood Roosevelt.

'Stick that one at the back. It's hideous.'

Aunt Hetty held the gown higher so that the fabric draped as had been intended. 'Why, it's beautiful.' She looked at Ruby, puzzled. 'It must have cost a fortune.'

Ruby pouted. 'It did.'

'Ah, the dress is beautiful – the memory hideous. Is that it?'

Ruby looked away. 'Something like that.'

Aunt Hetty pushed it to the back of the wardrobe. 'Come on, darling girl. Buck up.' She sat on the bed next to her niece, clasped her hand and Ruby leaned on her shoulder. Hetty smelled like Mother, the same powder, the same comforting shoulders. Tears brimmed in her eyes and she let them fall. Aunt Hetty rubbed at her hand.

'It will get easier.'

Ruby brushed the tears away. How lovely to be able to believe it, but she couldn't ever imagine that the pain would go. And she didn't want it to, for while she felt it the memory of her mother was as vivid as it would ever be.

'Sometimes it's just too much effort to breathe.'

Aunt Hetty moved her arm and put it about Ruby's shoulder and Ruby sank into the peace and comfort offered.

'I know. But time will heal. One day, you'll find that you're able to think of your mother with happiness, instead of the heaviness you carry with you now.'

They sat quietly until Ruby's tears stopped and Aunt Hetty got up and found her a handkerchief. Ruby wiped her face, blew her nose. Her aunt put her hand under her chin and tilted her face up towards her. Ruby tried to look away, but she couldn't, Aunt Hetty wouldn't let her, moving her chin until she looked into the old woman's eyes. 'Your mother was so proud of you, Ruby. It's what she lived for.'

Ruby swallowed. Her throat hurt, her eyes stung and she felt ugly. 'But we can't make her proud any more. It all seems pointless.'

'What does?'

'Everything. Dancing… Living…'

Aunt Hetty put her hands on either side of Ruby's shoulders and shook her gently. 'Now, we'll have no more of that. My goodness, action, no matter how small, is the key. Even if it's something as simple as hanging up your clothes, it will bring a sense of order to your thoughts. It all helps.' Ruby hung her head. Aunt Hetty took hold of her hands and pulled her to her feet. 'Chop, chop,' she said, briskly but not unkindly. 'Get dressed in something sensible and help me sort out this jumble.' She bent over the trunk again, scooping out a heap of clothes. 'All these lovely things!' She could see Aunt Hetty was trying not to look disappointed. How many girls would love to have what she had? She just couldn't summon the pleasure of them any more.

'Discipline, Ruby. Discipline gets you through the bad times, you know that.'

Ruby pulled on khaki pants and a sweater, tying back her hair with a silk scarf. It was a style she admired in Katharine Hepburn, that preppy casual wear that looked so effortless if you had the figure – and could afford good tailoring.

Aunt Hetty beamed. 'What a beauty you are without all that muck on your face.' She pinched her cheek.

Ruby gently batted her hand away. 'That "muck" is the finest muck a girl can buy.'

'And you don't need a drop of it, Ruby. It's what's on the inside that counts. You'll appreciate that when you get old, like me. I look like Ginger Rogers on the inside.' The pair of them laughed. 'That's better. A real smile is better than any make-up.'

Ruby started to tackle the cotton sweaters and silk blouses, folding them carefully, Aunt Hetty placing them in the chest of drawers at the side of the window. Aunt Hetty leaned again into the trunk. 'Almost done. Only your shoes. Do you want me to take them out of the boxes?'

Ruby dropped the sweater she had been folding and dashed forward. The boxes! She'd forgotten. 'No!' she exclaimed. Then, seeing her aunt's reaction, said again, softer, 'No. It's perfectly fine. I can finish the rest.' She squeezed her aunt's arm. 'Thank you, Aunt Hetty. It doesn't seem so overwhelming now.' She forced a smile. 'Shall we go out?' She glanced towards the window. 'The forecast is for showers later. We could pop along to Fortnum's, get something lovely for supper to welcome Johnny home.'

'He'll want more than a cake after that drive.' Hetty folded her arms. 'I'm not leaving a job half done. Will you finish this? Or will I have to come back with a big stick?'

Ruby smiled. 'I'll do it. It's my wardrobe and I shouldn't have left it to you to sort out. You're right. I do need to buck up. And I will.'

Her aunt raised her eyebrows. She made a move towards the bedroom door and Ruby followed her. 'I'll be back to check,' she said firmly, then softened her tone. 'You'll feel so much better if you keep yourself busy.'

Ruby closed the door as her aunt left and leaned on it. It would have been difficult explaining things if she'd opened the lid on the wrong one. She hurriedly put the boxes into the bottom of the wardrobe, leaving one until last. She held on to it and sat on the floor, her back to the bed, concealing the box's contents in case Aunt Hetty should return. She removed the lid, rifled through the envelopes, her brother's long, elegant handwriting on each one, and beneath them the ones from Frances O'Leary. At the very bottom was the ticket for Frances's passage to America. Unused. Her mother had asked her to take care of the box before she left for England, impressing upon her the importance of her task. Her mother's words were so clear, as if she were in the room.

'Frances O'Leary is nothing but a cheap gold digger, Ruby. She has bewitched Johnny and he can't see it. We need to make sure that Johnny never gets her letters.' Her mother had placed her fingers under Ruby's chin, tilting her face to hers. 'She won't be satisfied until she has taken your place, darling. She wants Johnny all to herself and we can't have that.'

Ruby touched her chin, wanting her mother's touch once more. To feel something, anything. It was such a relief when the letters had stopped coming. An overwhelming sense of her own badness swept over her. She hadn't opened them. Not one. She was protecting her brother. Fear gripped her again. What if someone else came along and took Johnny away? What would she do then?

* * *

The last part of the journey home had been hairy. With only a slice of moon that night, Bernie had crawled along the last few miles. It would have been quicker to walk. They had swerved to avoid a man wearing dark clothes and for a moment Johnny had thought they were all done for. It had shaken them and Johnny had stopped for a quick drink with Bernie, then chosen to walk the last couple of miles back home. How bleak it all seemed, to come from the bright lights of New York and be plunged back into darkness. Yet, weirdly, he felt happy, more so than he'd felt in years, and it seemed to override the weariness. He had found her.

He adjusted his overnight bag to his other hand. The lift opened and he stepped out, rummaged in his pocket for his key and let himself into the flat. The lamp was on in the small hallway and he placed his bag on the floor, slipped off his coat and hung it in the small closet, left his hat on the chair. In the sitting room, Aunt Hetty was sitting in her dressing gown and slippers, reading a book by the light of the standard lamp behind her. She smiled, removing her glasses. The room felt calmer, and he wished that Aunt Hetty could stay. She placed her book down quietly on the side table, her spectacles on top of it, and got to her feet.

'Bad journey?'

He nodded, removed his jacket and draped it over the back of the sofa. She kissed his cheek.

'Whisky?'

He sank into the easy chair.

'That would be wonderful.' They kept their voices low, Aunt Hetty taking great care not to chink the glass of the decanter as she returned it to the silver tray on the long table behind the sofa.

'How did it go?'

'Good. Better than I'd thought.'

'Not a wasted journey?'

'Not at all.'

She handed him the glass and he sipped. It warmed his throat and for a moment he closed his eyes, glad his journey was over. He opened them again. 'How has she been?'

Aunt Hetty bent down and turned up the gas fire; the ceramic radiant began to glow and she watched for a moment before returning to her seat. 'A little brighter. Still very brittle. But I don't have to tell you that.'

He leaned forward, nursing the glass in his hands.

'Oh, God, Aunt Hetty, I hope I've done the right thing.'

'Of course you have. Whatever you've done, you've done for the best. Ruby's not a child.'

* * *

Ruby stuck her head around the door. 'The wanderer returns.' She was wearing her cream sateen pyjamas and had pulled his black dressing gown over them, the sleeves rolled back. It made her appear tiny and vulnerable and for a fraction he doubted his decision. 'I thought I heard voices.' He rested his glass on the arm of the chair and got up and hugged her. When she pulled away, he rested his hands on her shoulders.

'You look much better.'

'Do I?' She smiled at him, but it didn't reach her eyes. She was still playing the game and it saddened him. He sat back in his chair and Ruby sank onto the sofa, curling her legs beneath her. When she saw his whisky, she got up and was about to pour herself one when she caught Aunt Hetty's eye, put the decanter down and instead filled the glass with water. She sat down next to Aunt Hetty.

'How did it all go?' He could tell she wasn't interested, merely going through the motions for Aunt Hetty's sake. He sipped his whisky. How much should he tell her? There would be a row, but at least Aunt Hetty was here. It would neuter her reaction to an extent.

'The Randolphs are back in business.'

'We have a show?'

Johnny took a deep breath. 'We do.'

'Which one is it? Let me guess. The Adelphi? The Vaudeville? Cabaret at the Savoy?'

'It's not in town, Ruby. I can't get anything in London, not yet.'

'Where, then?' She drank the water and placed the glass on top of her aunt's book. Aunt Hetty leaned forward and moved the glass onto a coaster, then sat back. Johnny rubbed at his lip.

'Bournemouth? No, it wouldn't be Bournemouth, not near the coast. I hadn't thought. Will you be safe down there, Aunt Hetty?' She didn't wait for her to answer. He could tell by the high pitch of her voice that she had an inkling it wouldn't be to her liking. It didn't really matter where they went, did it? Not in the long run, so why shouldn't he be with Frances? 'Bath? Bristol? Manchester?' She rattled places off the top of her head and he tried to stop her. Aunt Hetty clasped her hands together, placing them in her lap, her cheeks red. The room had become hotter and she got up and went to the fire and turned it down.

'It's not any of those, Ruby.'

She peered at him, trying to read his expression, something she'd done since they were children, trying to guess what he was feeling. Aunt Hetty sucked at her cheeks. It was best to get it over with.

'It's a beautiful theatre, the Palace. You know that I've been working on something with Bernie Blackwood? Well, he had a business proposition and that's where I've been, to check it out.' He didn't want to plead; he must be firm. 'So many theatres have closed; many of the London ones might never reopen. Lots of acts have been called up and you can't put on a show without professionals.' He waited for what he had said to sink in. 'I'm going to join the army, once this show's bedded in. You should think about contributing too.' He glanced at Aunt Hetty.

'Don't!' Ruby put her hands over her ears. Aunt Hetty pulled them gently away, glared at Johnny to get on with it.

'We're at war, Ruby. We will all need to play our part in keeping this country going.'

She sulked, picked at her nails. 'Manchester it is, then. That's not too bad. I like Manchester, plenty of shops.'

Good God, she was selfish. Didn't she realise the gravity of the situation? So many people, people just like them, had already answered the call. Was she going to ignore it, as she did everything else that didn't meet her liking? She was still such a child in so many ways.

Aunt Hetty glowered at him. 'It's not Manchester.'

She twisted to her aunt and then back to Johnny. 'Where?'

He rubbed at his forehead. How many times had he gone over how he was going to break it to her on the long drive home? Whichever way he cut it, she would hate him for it.

'It's Grimsby.' He moved to the edge of his seat. 'We'll have part of the profits, and shares. There's two other theatres and—'

'Grimsby!' Her face twisted as reality sank in, then she sprang to her feet. 'Grims. By.'

He got up, moved towards her. 'The future's uncertain, Ruby. We have to make different decisions.'

'You've done this to punish me, haven't you? Why you dirty, rotten—' She lifted her hand to strike him and he caught it. 'I won't go, you bastard! I won't go!'

'Ruby!' Their aunt was on her feet. Ruby's eyes were black with hatred and she clenched her fists, then, taut with frustration, ran to her room, slamming the door so hard that the glasses rattled and the lampshade swayed above them, the crystal droplets tinkling laughter. He made to go after her but Aunt Hetty pressed his arm. 'Leave her. She needs to cry about it.' He sank back in his chair and she fetched the decanter, topped up his glass and poured herself one. 'It wouldn't have mattered where you were going.'

'I have to get her away from temptation, and it seemed the perfect solution, so far away.' He should tell her about Frances, but what difference would it make?

'There will be temptation everywhere,' Hetty said. 'She's looking to fill the hole your mother left in her life.'

'But—'

Aunt Hetty held up her hand to stop him. 'You lost your mother too, don't forget that.'

He stared into his glass. 'It wasn't just Mother, Aunt Hetty. America changed her – and not for the better. It should have been the making of us both. Professionally, success was there for the taking. Privately?' He shook his head. 'It was a disaster.'

18

On a Saturday afternoon in early October, the girls were onstage going over what they would do as hostesses of the talent show on the twenty-first, when Dolly came down the aisle carrying a large bouquet of yellow roses. Jessie grinned.

'Another one. Who on earth they can they be from?' Frances stomped down the steps at the front of the stage.

'Ha-jolly-ha.' Dolly held the roses out to her and Frances peered inside for the envelope, read the card, and pushed it into her pocket.

'Do you want them, Dolly?'

'Oh, Frances, you can't keep giving them away.' She sniffed the flowers. 'They smell gorgeous.'

Frances took them from her and marched back onstage. 'Ginny?'

Ginny waved a hand. 'I don't have the space, do I?' At the end of September, Ginny had found new lodgings, a small room in a house off Bowling Lane. Frances had offered to see if Lil would take in a lodger but Ginny wanted to be away from prying eyes. Dolly was certain her parents would let Ginny stay with them, but she wouldn't hear of it for the same reason, not that she could tell Dolly what that reason was. Both Frances and Jessie were keeping an eye on her, making sure she was taking better care of herself, and she was beginning to get a little colour to her cheeks. As the days had passed and there was no sign of Ginny's monthlies, she had resigned herself to being pregnant. The baby would arrive in April, which gave them time to plan how best to help her. *If* they were all still around.

Jessie reached out to Frances, touching her wrist. 'I think you have to face facts. Johnny isn't going to stop, and we've all had our turn at being on the other side of your generosity.' Jessie held a blossom, admiring it. Flowers had arrived regularly since Johnny had visited the Empire in the middle of September, letters too, although Frances was reluctant to share what was in them. Patsy was her only confidante. She'd urged Frances to reply but Frances was reluctant.

'He doesn't mention anything, my pregnancy, Imogen – nothing.' It had left her more confused than ever.

'Then he didn't get the letters,' Patsy said.

'But that's ridiculous.'

Patsy shrugged. 'His mother? His sister? Perhaps they made sure he didn't get them.' It was the only thing they could think of – but if they had that much sway over him, did she really want him back in her life? 'You should write to him and find out. His mother's gone now.'

'Ah, but not Ruby, and she's her mother's daughter.'

'And you have your daughter to think about – as does he.'

The thought of losing control, of letting someone else in, had left her in turmoil. If he didn't know, she couldn't just spring Imogen on him, and at the end of the day Imogen came first. She would protect her at all costs. Nevertheless, perhaps she should write back.

'I think it's so romantic,' Dolly said now, bringing Frances back into the present. 'A long-lost admirer showering you with flowers.'

'Don't forget the letters, Dolly, or the cards.' Jessie grinned. 'I wrote to Harry; he's intrigued. As are we all. He wondered whether we'd be in for a double wedding.'

Frances was irritated. It all looked wonderful on the outside but if they knew— She tried not to snap; the girls were only doing what she would do, if she didn't know the truth. She smelled the roses and the scent soothed her. Jessie was right, they were beautiful.

'I might as well leave them in the dressing room this week,' she said. 'At least it will brighten it up a bit.'

'It'll take more than the roses to do that.' Jessie sank down onto the piano stool.

Jack had booked the Variety Girls for three evenings a week to begin with, just to see how things went. It had been hard work after the ease of the summer when being part of a bigger show had a different energy that gave them all a lift. They had to work harder to get a response. It had been worse when the moon was slight because people were nervous to venture out in the blackout and road accidents were on the increase.

'Why don't we go down there now?' Ginny suggested. 'You can put your flowers in water, and I can make some tea.'

* * *

Frances laid the flowers on the dressing table. 'Turn the lights on, Ginny, it'll warm it up a bit. It's going to be ruddy freezing in here, come the panto.' She pulled her cardigan about her.

Dolly lingered by the door. 'I'll go and find a vase.'

Frances sat on the table and eased out her chair, using it to rest her feet. Ginny settled herself in front of her mirror and Jessie slumped down in the easy chair. 'I'm glad we've got the flowers. It feels really depressing in here sometimes.' Jessie pulled at the stuffing escaping from a hole in the arm of the chair. 'It was so much better in the summer. There was energy and life about the place – and now it's flat.'

'It wasn't all good.' Ginny turned and looked at her through the mirror. The lights made her cheeks look sunken and she pulled at her hair, using her fingers as a comb.

'I wasn't thinking...' Jessie apologised.

Ginny shrugged. 'I know what you meant. When I came here I didn't count on being, well, you know.'

'Do you think you ought to write to Billy Lane?' Jessie ventured.

'And tell him what?' Ginny shook her head. 'Do you think he'd reply?'

'You won't know if you don't try.'

Frances didn't comment. Ginny wouldn't want her bitter advice.

* * *

Dolly came back with a vase of water, set it on the dressing table and unwrapped the bouquet, began to arrange the flowers.

There was a muffled rap on their door and they stopped talking. Dolly stepped forward and opened it and Grace came in carrying a bolt of red satin fabric. Jessie sprang to her feet and took it from her mother, laying it down on the dressing table. Grace smoothed her hand over the cloth and gave it a pat. 'Look at this, girls. What do you think?' Frances got down off the table and stood next to Grace; the girls crowded round.

'Lovely! What's it for?' Frances pulled out her chair, brushed her hand over the seat and made gestures for Grace to sit down, which she did.

'Thank you, Frances.' Her cheeks were pink and Jessie was gladdened to see her looking so revived. Mary, the wardrobe mistress, hadn't wanted to come back to the Empire and Jack had offered Grace the position for the pantomime. It had given Grace a much-needed boost and the extra money was welcome. 'Jack let me have a rummage around upstairs in Wardrobe. I was looking for some odds and ends so that I could make something for you three girls. This was more than I'd hoped for. It was hidden under some old curtains.' She smiled at them. 'What do you think?'

Jessie got up and hugged her. 'Oh, Mum. That will be wonderful. Red's such a jolly colour and we can use it for any Christmas shows we might get before the panto.'

'Just the lift we needed,' Frances agreed. 'Your timing is perfect.'

'I think we all need to cheer ourselves up as much as we can. It's going to be a difficult winter.' At the beginning of the month, all the twenty and twenty-one-year-old men had been told to register with the military authorities, and they all knew it was a matter of time before the age limit was expanded. The fishermen of Grimsby and other ports around the country had signed up with the Royal Naval Patrol Service and were already suffering losses at sea, the German submarines causing havoc.

Ginny looked down at her feet and Jessie reached out and discreetly pressed her arm, hoping to imbue her with a sense of hope. Frances put her arm about Grace's shoulders.

'Thanks for thinking of us.'

Grace beamed. 'Don't mention it. I'm only happy that I'm feeling up to it and able to be creative again. We led such a dull existence at my cousin's. I hadn't realised how much I missed the theatre.' She smiled at Jessie, at Frances.

'I can measure you two later. Perhaps you'd like to come along and join us for tea sometime, Ginny, so I can measure you up? You too, Dolly.'

Dolly was quizzical. 'I don't need a costume.'

Grace flapped her hand. 'I meant for tea. And why not? The costume, I mean. You'd look lovely in red.'

'I'll pass on that, but I can perhaps help with the sewing and cutting out.' She stood by Grace and smoothed her hand over the fabric, nodding appreciatively. 'Have you got a pattern?'

'I'll make one. Thank you, Dolly. It will be much easier with two of us.'

Ginny was noticeably quiet.

'Are you all right, Ginny? You look very pale, my dear. Are you eating enough? How are your new digs? Where did you go in the end?'

Ginny pleaded to the girls using her eyes and Jessie obliged.

'Mum! Too many questions.'

'Oh, forgive me, Ginny. I haven't seen you for a while.'

Ginny tried to smile. 'It's fine, Grace. My digs are... adequate.'

Jessie stepped in, sensing Ginny was floundering. 'And Joyce is very generous at the café, isn't she, girls.'

'Oh, she's a diamond,' Frances said. 'We gave her tickets to the talent show.' Jessie was relieved that, once again, Frances had swiftly diverted the conversation. Poor Ginny. Dolly was valiantly pretending that she wasn't aware of the silent signals between the three of them, but her expression told Jessie otherwise. It felt so unfair that she should be excluded especially when, over the past weeks, they had all become so close. Grace got up.

'Leave the cloth here, Mum. Frances and I will carry it home to save you.'

'Thank you, sweetheart.' Her mother's relief was obvious. 'It's dire weather outside. The rain came in and the streets are awash. It can't run down the gutters fast enough.'

Frances sighed. 'Perhaps we'll leave it until tomorrow, then. There's no rush and it will save spoiling the fabric.'

'Exactly, plenty to be getting on with before then. I'll work out a pattern first. Do come for tea, Dolly, Ginny. You'll be most welcome.'

Grace kissed Jessie on the cheek and Dolly picked up the bolt of fabric. 'I'll put this in one of the other rooms so it's out of the way. Dad will have some paper somewhere that we can cover it with, so it doesn't get marked.' She followed Grace out into the corridor.

Ginny dashed to Jessie's side as soon as they were gone. 'Oh, Jessie. I can't have your mum measuring me. She'll be able to tell straight away.'

'She won't,' Frances said, looking to Ginny's midriff. 'There's nothing there.'

'But my waist, my stomach!' Ginny ran her hands over her slightly extended belly, then rested them at her waist, looking down at herself.

'Looks like wind, or bloating,' Frances said. 'Honestly, you'll have to get tougher, darling. It's going to get a lot worse than this.'

'Frances!' Jessie was appalled. 'No need to be so harsh.'

'I wasn't being harsh.' She softened her voice. 'I'm being practical. Ginny knows that, or she wouldn't have mentioned it.'

Ginny's shoulders sagged. 'Frances is right. I don't care what most people think. Not really.' She swallowed away her fear and Jessie knew she was being brave. 'But your mum has been very kind to me and so has Geraldine. You all have. I don't want them to think I'm...' She searched for the word. 'Cheap,' she said sadly.

'They wouldn't think that.' Jessie went and stood beside her, put her hands on her shoulders. 'You might be worrying too much.'

'Or not enough.' Frances lowered her head. 'Not everyone is as kind as your ma, Jessie. There are some spiteful people about.'

Jessie was reminded of her aunt Iris. This was exactly the sort of thing she associated with the theatre, as if nice girls from middle-class backgrounds would never dream of doing such a thing.

'I know that, Frances. I'm not simple-minded.'

'I never suggested you were, but this isn't the movies.'

Jessie winced. What on earth was the matter with Frances? Sometimes she couldn't work her out. Since the moment war had been declared, she'd been angry and had remained so. While everyone else adjusted, Frances had held on to her rage and let it fester.

Ginny was getting agitated. 'Please don't fall out over me, you two. I don't want to spoil your friendship.'

'You won't do that, Ginny.' She checked the door. 'Do you think we should tell Dolly about... y'know... Ginny?'

'Jessie!' Frances was sharp. 'It's not for us to tell. It's for Ginny to decide who knows, and who doesn't.'

Jessie's cheeks burned.

'It's all right.' Ginny stepped in to defend her. 'I know you didn't mean anything by it.'

Jessie was barely able to contain her frustration. 'I don't know what on earth's wrong with you, Frances. I was thinking that Dolly could measure Ginny and leave excess for letting the seams out. No one else needs to know. Not until Ginny's ready to tell. And we might have thought of something else to help by then.'

Frances sighed, shaking her head. 'I don't know what ruddy miracle you think's going to happen.'

'I think telling Dolly—'

'Telling me what?' Dolly said, coming through the door, and Frances glared at Jessie. Jessie felt sweat prickle on her skin, even though the room was chill; she clenched her fists.

'Not tell you, ask you,' Jessie said, thinking on her feet. Frances turned her back, scowling at her through the mirror. 'If you would mind measuring Ginny here, save her having to keep coming along to Barkhouse Lane.' She began searching for a tape measure, anything to avoid looking at Frances.

'Of course.' Dolly acted as if everything was perfectly normal when it was clear it was anything but. Ginny went over to her and took her hand, drawing her into the room.

'It wasn't just that, Dolly. Although I would like you to measure me and fit my costumes. I should have told you earlier.'

'You don't have to tell me anything you don't want to.' Dolly's smile had disappeared.

'I know,' Ginny said kindly, 'but we're all of us friends, aren't we? And you'll find out sooner or later.' Ginny took a deep breath. 'I got caught. With Billy.' She looked at Dolly under her eyelashes. 'I'm in the – the family way.'

Dolly stared at her friend, then leaned forward and hugged Ginny.

'Oh, Ginny! I'm so sorry. That's so unfair.' She drew back but held on to Ginny's hands. 'Of course. I'll do whatever I can to help.'

Jessie glanced towards Frances, who shook her head and looked away.

Ginny sat back in the easy chair, and the room prickled with tension until Dolly said, 'I know it won't be any comfort, but my sister got caught out. She married the bloke and she's very unhappy. At least you'll be able to have the baby adopted. If that's what you want, of course,' she said quickly, her neck reddening. 'Oh, I hope I haven't put my foot in it.'

Ginny reassured her. 'Don't worry. Who knows what's best to say? Or best to do.' She stared down at the floor and picked at the stuffing of the arm as Jessie had done earlier. 'I will be having it adopted. I can't manage on my own and Billy won't want to know.' She let out a long sigh, then looked up at them all, smiling sadly. 'I'd rather give the baby away to have a better life than I could provide. I don't want to struggle like my mam did. She wanted so much better for me.'

Frances pushed back her chair and picked up her bag. 'I've had enough for today. We might as well go home.'

Jessie was still mad at Frances, madder still at herself. It wasn't her secret to tell – but she hadn't told it, had she? And she'd managed to save the situation. It was Ginny who'd decided otherwise.

'I'm sorry, Ginny. I was only thinking to save your embarrassment. I didn't mean to make things worse.'

'You didn't, Jessie. I feel much better now that Dolly knows. To tell the truth, I was terrified of anyone finding out, but you're such good friends and somehow it makes this horrid situation feel less daunting.'

Jessie was uncomfortable. She wouldn't fall out with Frances; their friendship was too important to her. She put out her arm. 'Let's walk the long way home. We can walk with Ginny to her lodgings.'

They left by the stage door, Dolly crossing over the road for the short walk to her house, the girls turning down into Market Street with Ginny. The rain had stopped but large puddles had collected around the gutters and, as they passed the trees, the wind gusted, showering them with raindrops that had gathered on the leaves.

When they arrived at the bottom of Bowling Lane, Ginny bade them stop. 'I'll be fine from here.'

'Are you sure? We don't mind going with you to your door.'

'Thanks, Jessie,' Ginny said, 'but honestly, I'm fine. I don't need protecting.'

'Too late for that, eh,' Frances said. Jessie turned on her heel, only to discover Frances looking kindly at Ginny. 'Some of us learn the hard way.' It was a truth that couldn't be argued with and the two girls exchanged glances. Ginny turned and walked away and they watched her for a while before moving on again. Jessie stuffed her hands in her pockets, pulled them out again, smoothing the flaps down, her mother's words in her head, telling her it would spoil the line of her coat. Frances was silent as they walked down St Peter's Avenue.

'Aren't you going to speak to me?' Jessie said when she could stand it no longer.

Frances stopped and turned to look at her. Her dark eyes showed sadness more than anger.

'You put Ginny in an awkward position. Dolly too.'

Jessie bit at her cheek. 'I know.' It had started to rain again. A boy on a bike rode through a puddle, making spray that splashed on her legs. 'Oi!' she shouted after him. He called 'Sorry' over his shoulder and carried on down the street. Frances chafed at the mess on her legs as she brushed it away and they walked on as the rain came down harder. 'I knew I was wrong, but it was too late.'

They hurried along to Barkhouse Lane. The curtains had already been drawn and Jessie thought how hard it was going to be in the coming dark months with no light at all to welcome them home.

Frances pushed the front door open and they stood in the hallway, shaking off the worst of the water from their coats before they hung them on the rack. 'You should think before you speak, Jessie.'

Jessie tried to interrupt. 'But—'

Frances put her hand up to stop her, then rested it on her arm. 'I know you were being kind, but you can't solve everyone's problems for them. Sometimes you have to let them work it out for themselves.'

19

Johnny stepped out onto Cleethorpes station in the late evening and made his way to the Cliff Hotel. He stopped outside the Empire and read the posters. There was a talent show on the twenty-first and, this week, cine-variety: *Suez*, starring Tyrone Power and Loretta Young, with live entertainment from the Variety Girls featuring Jessie Delaney. Their photographs were in the display cases at the front and he leaned in close to look at Frances. What the hell was she doing here, in a small seaside theatre, when she danced like an angel? She'd had to step in for Ruby when she had her appendix removed and although he'd been concerned for Ruby, it was a dream to dance with her, to hold her so close. She was sensational, and he'd been glad that she'd been thrust full centre into the spotlight – it was what she deserved. When she didn't come to America, he'd thought it was because she'd chosen her career over him, so why was she hiding away in the provinces?

Jack was waiting at the hotel and, after checking in and arranging for his bag to be taken to his room, Johnny joined him at the bar. He liked him enormously; Bernie had said to trust his gut and he had. If he had to be partners with anyone, it would be with men like Jack and Bernie.

'What can I get you, Johnny?'

'Scotch and ice.'

Jack ordered it and Johnny pulled out a stool and sat down, leaning his elbow on the bar. The bartender placed his drink on a mat and he picked it up, sipped, the burn welcome in his throat. Johnny looked about him. The bar was busy with military personnel he recognised as coastal command. The sinking of HMS *Royal Oak* by a German submarine in the Orkneys the previous weekend was still the main topic of conversation. Over eight hundred men had been lost.

He felt uncomfortable, the only younger man not in uniform.

Jack cleared his throat. 'You said you had a proposition to put to me?'

He looked at Jack, who was smiling, putting him at his ease. He'd noticed, hadn't he? Well, it wouldn't be like that forever. 'I did, Jack.' He'd spent the entire journey working on it, in between worrying about leaving Ruby alone for forty-eight hours. He was hoping that was all he would need. Frances hadn't replied to any of his letters and he needed to know where he stood. If there was a chance—

'I'd like to make a guest appearance, tomorrow tonight. Sing, dance, a couple of numbers, a precursor to the season at the Palace. A sort of live advertisement – coming soon to the Palace, sort of thing.'

Jack's enthusiasm was evident. 'Absolutely. That would be wonderful, although it's only a three-piece in the pit – piano, double bass and drums; not what you're used to.'

'That's fine. It doesn't have to be perfect.' He paused. 'And the girls will be there?'

Jack picked up the beer mat, flipped it on its side and tapped it on the bar. 'They will. Unless you don't want them to be.'

He caught Jack's eye. He must have guessed there was more to his request.

'I don't want them to know.' Johnny rolled his glass around on its heel. 'It's complicated.'

Jack smiled, understanding. 'These things are.'

At ease with Jack, he told him a little of his relationship with Frances. 'I'd love to dance with her again. A bit of a surprise for the audience.'

'And for her.'

What could he say? How could he tell him it was about the magic? Would he understand that everything hinged on holding Frances, on dancing with her, creating that indefinable connection he felt when she was in his arms? She'd been reluctant to speak with him when they'd met and he had no idea what he'd done wrong. He'd seen the anger in her eyes. And pain. Was he the cause of it? If he knew what it was, maybe he'd be able to make it right.

'I've written to her, sent flowers—'

'We've all seen them.' Jack grinned. 'And she hasn't written back?'

Johnny shook his head.

Jack laid the beer mat down, rested his glass on it. 'Listen, Johnny, I'm willing to give it a go.'

He touched Jack's shoulder. 'Thanks, Jack. I'll make sure it's a success.'

Jack laughed. 'As if Johnny Randolph could be anything less.'

* * *

Johnny spent the day at the hotel, resting, thinking, staring out of the windows across the estuary. Ships were moving in and out;

there was a mock castle to the left, a tourist attraction. He liked the place more than he had done the last time he was here with Bernie. In the afternoon, he went downstairs and found a room with a dance floor where he could rehearse and limber up. How long was it since they had danced in front of an audience, he and Ruby? He couldn't count the night at the Café de Paris when he'd told her she was unprofessional, and yet here he was, arranging to do the same. What was worse? Ruby's drunken impromptu performance or his intended ambush of Frances? He picked up his jacket and made his way to his room to shower. Well, Frances hadn't answered his letters, or acknowledged the flowers. He had nothing to lose...

* * *

Johnny and Jack chatted in Jack's office at the theatre while the film was showing. He hadn't been this nervous before a performance in years. It was good to be fired up about performing. But would Frances go through with it? He could wing it if she walked off, win the audience over, dance one of his solos. But it wasn't the audience he wanted to win.

Jack led him through the pass door on the dress circle at the intermission before the girls went on. They remained hidden in a dressing room and Jack turned up the tannoy so they could hear the girls sing. Johnny would come on at the end of their performance; Jack would introduce him. The band had been primed during the afternoon, arriving at the hotel at Johnny's request to go through the music, the timing. At Jack's signal, he went up into the wings, stood in the shadows as the girls performed their last routine. His heart was pumping as it hadn't done in years and he leaned forward slightly, watching Frances singing the harmonies to Jessie's lead when she was more than capable of doing the same herself. Frances was a leading lady and he had no idea why she was holding herself back. None of it made sense. When the girls took a bow at the end of a song, Jack walked out onstage. The three of them were surprised and Johnny felt uncomfortable, springing this on them, but he had to know and this was the only way he could think of. She wouldn't kick up a fuss, not in front of an audience, not in front of her friends; she wasn't like Ruby, thank the Lord.

He flinched. Ruby would hate it if she knew. Hate him, but then she did already, so what difference did it make? He wondered what she was doing now, left to her own devices, and shrugged the thought away. She was an adult. He had to stop worrying about her and live his own life.

The applause died down and Jack stepped forward. 'Ladies and gentlemen, aren't these girls brilliant? Let's show our appreciation again.' Jack clapped, his hands high, leading them. The girls smiled, bowing and taking another call, then Jack quietened the audience with his hands. 'I'm delighted to announce that we have a special guest tonight.' He stretched out his hand and announced, 'Mr Johnny Randolph!'

There were gasps and cheers and the audience applauded as the male half of the famous Randolphs walked onto the stage, waving, smiling. Out the corner of his eye he could see Frances, the shock on her face, the excitement and bewilderment on those of her friends. He felt a sharp stab of shame, but he had to go through with it. It was a test, not for her, but for him.

He bowed, taking the applause. 'Thank you, ladies and gentlemen.' He put his arm out to the girls, smiling. They smiled back but beneath her smiles Johnny could see that Frances was thunderous. He walked towards her, taking her hand and bringing her forward. Jack stepped back, taking his place between Jessie and Ginny.

Johnny stood stage centre with Frances. He could feel her nails digging into his palm.

'A few years ago, I had the pleasure of dancing with this young lady, Miss Frances O'Leary, in *Lavender Lane*. You may remember it.'

There were shouts of appreciation.

'Thank you. Some of you may have seen it.' He sensed Frances's fury but he couldn't stop, wouldn't, not now. He wanted to dance with her. Longed to. He turned to Jack, gave a slight nod of his head, and Jack led Jessie and Ginny offstage. Johnny held on to Frances. He wouldn't let her go, not this time.

He turned to her and she faked a smile at him, to the audience. 'We'd like to give you a small taste of our success. Gentlemen...' he said to the boys in the band. He stepped back from the microphone and Frances tried to release her hand but he pulled her close. Her anger was obvious, her body rigid with fury and a sliver of doubt shot through him. He ignored it. 'Go with it, Frances. Do you remember the moves?' It was a ridiculous question; he knew she would, and he was suddenly excited, her anger irrelevant. The band began to play and he swept her into his arms. To his delight, she moved with him. The audience disappeared, everything and everyone melting away because, at last, it was just the two of them. She was light and fluid and he felt such joy within him, a feeling long forgotten. He put his arms to her waist, lifted her, and her body was beautiful lines, her hands expressive, sweeping out and then to his face, touching him and then away.

Johnny grasped her hand and she twirled away from him, then he pulled her back, wrapping his arms about her, and it felt so good to have her close again. The complicated knots of his life unravelled as they danced. He put his cheek to hers, feeling her skin, the smell of her hair, as she leaned against him and he wanted it to go on forever. It was nothing like dancing with Ruby. He could express movement with Frances that he couldn't with his sister. This love was different, all-consuming. The music came to an end and she was in his arms, their cheeks touching, staring out into the audience. 'Damn you, Johnny,' she whispered as they took the applause. 'Damn you.'

He held her hand and put out his other hand towards her for the audience to appreciate her. She dropped her knee to a low curtsey, smiling out to them. He let her fingers go and she rushed into the wings. He called her back and she came to the side, not to him, gave a little bob with her head, glaring at him with such pain that he felt suddenly ashamed, the joy of the moment dissipated. My God, what had he done? He could see the tears glistening in her eyes.

Jack came back on, said a few words with Johnny and announced the intermission. Johnny took the applause and rushed into the darkness of the wings, racing down to the dressing rooms to find her. He knocked on the door and Jessie opened it slightly.

'Can I see Frances? I need to talk with her.'

She kept the door tight so that he couldn't see into the room.

'Please, Jessie. It's important. I have to leave on the early train tomorrow.' The girl hesitated, stared into his eyes, then slowly opened the door and stood back. Frances was sitting, shaking, her breath coming in quick bursts.

'Jessie!' she hissed, looking away from him. Ginny turned, awkward, and he felt truly ashamed at what he had done to the three of them.

'I'm sorry, girls.'

Jessie stepped back against the wall. Frances got to her feet.

'Are you? Are you really sorry, Johnny Randolph?' She folded her arms, trembling, and he knew it was with rage, not fear. 'That was cruel. Cruel.' She was close to tears. 'But then, that's you all over. Nothing new, nothing I didn't already know.'

He tried to step into the room. 'Please, let me explain.' Oh God, this wasn't how he'd expected it to go at all. He'd thought she felt as he did, that she would know. 'I've got so little time.'

'What if I hadn't remembered the routine?'

'I knew you would. We had something special, Frances.'

She lunged at him, screaming, 'Get out! Get out!' Ginny rushed towards her, holding her back. Jessie came to the door, pushed him away.

'You'd better leave.' She wasn't angry, just sad for her friend as she gently forced him out into the corridor.

'Tell her I'm sorry. It was meant to be a surprise,' he said, as she closed the door on him. It was a feeble excuse, a lie, but words had failed him.

* * *

He waited at the stage door, chatting to George, the lovely old guy who was the stage doorman. He couldn't leave without speaking to her. His head was a mess and suddenly the pressure of the last year came into sharp focus – the realisation that he'd blanked it all out, thinking only of work, of keeping Ruby from hell-bent self-destruction. Neither of them had been able to believe it when news came of their mother's death. They were lost without her. Rudderless – and they'd had to go out onstage, night after night, smiling, singing, dancing as if they hadn't a care in the world. The after-show drinking to unwind became something more. Ruby had used it to drown her sorrows. Was she doing that now, now that she was alone and he was here? Ruby was right, dancing was all they had – but he wanted more; he wanted Frances.

He straightened up when he heard the girls' voices as they came down the corridor and started on the stairs. He brushed his collar, adjusted his tie, smoothed back his hair. George tactfully disappeared into his office, head down, shuffling papers. The three girls stopped when they saw him, Ginny and Jessie turning to look at Frances.

'Five minutes,' she told them. They nodded, and left through the pass door into the theatre. She had calmed although it was clear her anger was still raw.

'Can we talk?'

George cleared his throat, squeezed past them. 'I do believe Mr Holland wanted to see me,' he said, following Jessie and Ginny.

She adjusted her bag, the strap of her gas mask over her shoulder, folded her arms and glared at him, challenging. 'Make it quick. I'm tired.'

He wanted to take hold of her hands but he resisted, knowing he'd already far overstepped the mark with her.

'I didn't know what else to do. Did you get my flowers, my letters?'

She looked up at him, through her long dark lashes. 'I did.'

'But you didn't reply.'

She chewed at her lip. 'And you expected me to?'

He frowned. 'Of course. Why would I write, otherwise?'

She huffed. 'I wrote to you.' She looked over her shoulder, towards the pass door, perhaps willing her friends to come back.

'When? Last week.'

She gave a small laugh. 'No, let's see, when was it?' She tapped her finger on her chin. 'I think the last one was sometime around November 1936. One of many, I might add.'

He was shocked. 'I didn't get them.' It was clear she didn't believe him. 'Look, when we left for America I promised to write, Frances, and I did. I promise you I did.' He'd written to the theatre, to her rooms when the show ended but nothing ever came in reply. 'I thought you'd met someone else.'

'Oh, no, there was no one else.' She looked deep into his eyes and he caught the sadness in her voice. It gave him hope. He reached out to her, took her hand just as the two girls came back to join them. 'I'll be back in December. I have to put a show together first.' He had to work on Ruby, who was still reluctant to leave London, but he would come without her if he had to. 'But I *will* be back. Something went wrong. I have no idea what it was, but believe me, Frances, there was never anyone but you.'

She withdrew her hand as George returned and the moment was lost. 'Night, girls,' the old boy called cheerfully as they opened the stage door and stepped out into street. They waved their good-byes, closing the door behind them.

Johnny shook his hand. 'Thanks for keeping me company, George.'

'My pleasure, Johnny. I hope we get the chance to do it again.'

'Oh, we will. You can be sure of that.'

20

On Saturday, the day of the talent show, Jessie received a telegram from Bernie Blackwood. Things were moving again in theatreland and the impresario Vernon Leroy had been in contact, offering her a supporting role in a production come the new year. It wasn't the part she'd been promised, but things had changed with the outbreak of war. Investors were still nervous. He hoped she'd understand. Jessie handed it over to Grace.

'Well, darling, only you can decide whether to take it or not.' Her mum's voice was level, betraying nothing of her opinion one way or another. 'It's your life, your dreams.'

Jessie had expected her to be more helpful. 'But what about you and Eddie? I feel I've brought you here and now I'm thinking about abandoning you.'

Grace laughed gently. 'It's hardly abandoning. We're more settled than we've been in a long time.' She held out the telegram and Jessie took it, folding it in half and tucking behind a plate on the dresser. A part in a West End production – it was what she'd wanted, but everything had changed, and not only because of the war. There was Harry to consider; they had a wedding to plan, a future... but what kind of future would they have? She leaned against the dresser.

'I don't know what to do...'

Grace picked up the sock she was darning for Eddie, pushing the heel onto a wooden mushroom, easing it into place. 'You don't have to take the first thing that's offered.'

'As I did when I came here?' She watched her mum take up her needle and thread it with grey wool.

Grace looked up. 'It all worked out, didn't it? But it's a good thing to bear in mind. I think you have to concentrate on what you *really* want.'

She wanted so many things, that was the trouble. To help Grace, to be with Harry – only that was impossible, as it was for so many others – and in the meantime she could still pursue her career. 'The money will be much better.'

'The bills will be higher,' Grace offered as a word of caution.

Jessie sat down beside her. 'I'm scared.'

'What of?' Grace stilled her hand and Jessie reached out for it, clasping it, feeling her mum's firm grip that belied her frail appearance. She was much improved, her strength returning.

'Not making the right decision.' Jessie blew out her breath, letting her shoulders sag. 'I wanted to be successful so that I could bring us all together.' It wasn't the only reason but despair had made her brave enough to take a chance.

'And you've done that,' Grace said. Jessie wanted to do so much more. It was all right lodging here, with Geraldine. She'd been an absolute angel when Jessie had arrived with her mum and Eddie, her unexpected and unprepared-for lodgers. It had been under Geraldine's watchful eye that they had nursed Grace back to health. She knew Grace enjoyed the companionship of the older woman, and was certain it was reciprocated. But Jessie wanted Grace to have a house of her own, to have the lovely things she deserved.

'It's a good opportunity,' she said eventually. It wasn't the stellar trajectory she'd dreamed of, but it was the West End.

'It is.' Grace was non-committal.

'You're not helping,' Jessie said, trying not to smile. 'Coming here was one thing; London's another matter entirely. And we weren't at war then.'

Grace let go of her hand and stroked Jessie's hair. 'You know how hard it is, Jessie. Does it still make you happy?'

It was hard to know. These last few weeks had been strained, the colour that came with the summer variety show sadly missing. Vernon Leroy offering her the moon had lifted her far beyond what she'd dreamed of for herself. She should be elated, but it was as if all the stuffing had been knocked out of her.

* * *

Frances came in late from her lunchtime shift at the pub and stuck her head around the door.

'Wait for me, Jessie, if you will. We'll walk together?'

Jessie said she would and Frances thundered up the stairs, coming back down again within a few minutes. Since Johnny Randolph's surprise appearance at the Empire on the Thursday evening, Frances had kept out of everyone's way, spending longer at the pub and dropping straight into bed after their performance. It was clear that it had shaken her to the core but she'd refused to talk about it, only saying that it had caught her off guard, that she was frightened that she'd made a fool of herself. Jessie knew it was more than that, but also knew better than to push. Frances would talk in her own time. When Frances came down again, she'd unpinned her dark hair and was flicking it about her shoulders. 'Time for a wash?'

Jessie looked at the clock. 'If you're quick.' She got her gas mask and bag ready, her jacket from the hall and pulled it on while she waited for Frances, who rubbed at her face with a towel, pulled at her hair with her fingers and decided to do the rest at the theatre.

'Enjoy yourselves, girls,' Grace said.

Jessie leaned forward and kissed her cheek. 'We'll do our best.'

Grace held her gaze. 'That's all you have to do.'

* * *

There was another bouquet of roses waiting for Frances at the theatre. George looked bashful as he handed them over. 'From Johnny Randolph?'

Frances opened the card and read it. 'An apology.'

George nodded. 'Expect he's had time to dwell on the other night when he surprised you. Although the audience loved it, and you did make a lovely couple, if I dare say so.'

Frances leaned forward and kissed his cheek. 'You dare, George. You're the only one who could get away with it. Would you like to take them home for Olive?'

He pushed his glasses on top of his head. 'She wouldn't take another woman's flowers; it wouldn't be right. You'd best enjoy them for yourself.' She hadn't thought of enjoying them, beautiful as they were. She'd felt they were a bribery.

'At least he's tried to make amends,' Jessie said hesitantly.

'Yes,' Frances said quietly. But it would take more than flowers to restore her trust. He had been genuine, that was obvious. Confused too – as was she. He'd said something had gone wrong, and it had – but how and why? It would be something to do with his mother. Perhaps they would never know.

* * *

Ginny was already in the dressing room. She'd brought a couple of photos and old postcards and was pinning them around her mirror when they walked in, the two of them slinging their gas masks in the corner. She hadn't yet put on her make-up and in the glare of the white light from the bulbs she looked gaunt and hollow-cheeked.

'That's a good idea, Ginny.' Frances placed the flowers on the side; she'd get a vase for them when she had a minute. George was right, she should enjoy the beauty of them. She drew out her chair, pulled off her shoes. 'Still being sick?'

'Not so much.' Ginny leaned forward, pushing another pin into the wall. In the mirror, Frances saw her wince, tense herself. Frances opened her make-up box. 'Dolly said we've got quite a few booked for tonight.'

Jessie pulled her dress over her head and shook her hair, wrapping her dressing gown about her. 'It will be good to have a few more bums on seats. It's like pulling teeth some nights.'

'That's variety for you.' Frances spat into the small block of black eyeliner and pulled the brush over her eyebrows. There was a knock on the door and Chip, the new call boy, stuck his head around it. His grey hair tufted wildly about his ears and he was slow on his feet. He'd retired but Mike had called him in to work the tabs – pulling the curtains in and out needed a slow hand so he was well-suited to it, and as Jack was trying to run everything on a shoestring, many of them were doubling up on what needed to be done.

'This is your half-hour call, ladies.'

'Thank you, Chip, darling.' Frances winked at him and he grinned, showing his big, yellowing teeth. He moved aside to let Annie, Jack Holland's assistant, into the room and left them to it. She was holding a sheaf of index cards with the names and talents of eager participants who had already put their names forward.

'Seems to have got the locals out, girls. All the eager future stars have brought along their families, so we've sold quite a few tickets. It's the best we've had in weeks. Who's going to take charge of these?' She held the cards up and Jessie came forward and took them from her.

She flicked through them. 'I think people are getting used to the blackout and gaining more confidence.' Jessie placed the cards on the dressing table.

'Or they're getting bored,' Annie said as she left.

'This could be fantastic. Or it could be a ruddy disaster,' Frances said when they heard Annie go up the steps to the stage.

'It's going to be fun,' Jessie said. 'Don't be such a grump.'

Frances ignored her. 'I wonder what idiots we'll get up tonight, thinking they're Gracie Fields or George Formby.' She sat back in her chair, her long black hair brushed and tamed, pushed away from her face and held in place with kirby grips.

Her words irritated Jessie. 'It doesn't matter, does it? They're people with dreams. We all have dreams, all of us.'

Frances wondered what Ginny's dreams had been. Had they been similar to her own? Perhaps not. The girl had already said she was doing it for her mother. It wasn't the same as doing something for the love of it, like Jessie and she had done. But they were all doing it for someone else in the end. Frances picked up an emery board and drew it over her nails.

'All right then, Shirley Temple. Let's hope we've got something to look forward to.'

Jessie grinned and Frances found herself smiling too. The girl was forever putting her foot in it, but she was an optimist – and optimism had been in short supply lately.

'Speaking of which: have you heard from Bernie?'

'A telegram came today. Not what was planned, something else, but it's been so long that I'm not sure whether I want to go now.' She was hesitant. 'They dropped a bomb at Hoy, in the Orkneys, only a few days ago. It might be us next. It could happen tomorrow. Here. Anywhere. I'd rather be with Mum and Eddie. If we go, we go together. I can't help thinking of all those poor kids gone to strange places they've never heard of. They must be so frightened and their parents worried sick. I mean, they could be with anyone, couldn't they?'

Frances's forehead prickled with sweat. At least she knew Imogen was with kind people. How many other parents could be sure of that?

'We must be brave,' Ginny said quietly.

'They won't know the gravity of it, Ginny. Most of the ones I saw lined up the other week were oblivious, looked like they were going off on some grand adventure. And their mothers holding back the tears.' She didn't want to talk about it but felt she needed to, to speak of her fears. 'Some of those parents might be in here tonight, hoping to think happier thoughts. We need to make sure they do.'

Frances dipped her head under the table, pretending to rummage in her handbag. The metal clip snapped as she opened it and when she felt the tears that threatened had gone, she reached in for her handkerchief, discreetly dabbing at her eyes, pretending to blow her nose. It would be so much easier if she could talk to them both, be upfront about her past, her relationship with Johnny. She decided against it. Ginny might think it a way forward, and much as she loved Imogen, she wouldn't advocate her situation as being suitable for anyone else. Even after all these years she was still ashamed that she'd been so foolish. She glanced to the roses. Yes, it would take more than flowers to heal her pain.

'I think we'll have to work hard to hold it all together,' Ginny said, standing up and slipping off her robe. She took the red dress that Dolly had worked on from the hanger and put it on, turning her back and lifting her hair for Jessie to do up the zip. 'At least you don't have to play the piano.'

Frances got into her own costume. Grace was a superb seamstress and the costumes were gorgeous, with fitted bodices and skirts that flared out when they danced but otherwise draped in folds. Unfortunately for Ginny, the design accentuated their small waists, but Dolly had been able to finesse them with waistbands. She had come up with an idea to make the three of them slightly different so as time went on she could let Ginny's out without attracting too much attention.

Annie knocked on the door. 'I'm going to get the contestants to come through the pass door at prompt side. If one of you can come with me when you're ready, we'll bring them backstage and then you can have a chat, put them at their ease, find out what they're going to do. I've sorted a running order with Mike.'

'I'll do it.' Jessie looked to the other two for agreement; Frances wasn't bothered and Ginny was doing as little out front as she could get away with. She left with Annie and when Frances heard their footsteps on the stairs that led to the stage, she turned to Ginny.

'How are you feeling?'

She shrugged. 'I'm trying not to feel.'

Frances understood completely.

'I know I've got to think about what will happen afterwards.' She sank down into the easy chair, careful to smooth her skirt as she did so. 'But my head feels like it's full of wool and I'm so tired when I've finished at the laundry. The extra money for the shows is a godsend, but it's exhausting, and I don't know if I'll be able to do both. The panto will be a welcome boost for my savings but I'll have to give up my job at the laundry to do it. I don't expect that they'll have me back after the panto ends. Not that I want to go back there, but...' Her voice faltered.

Frances squatted down beside her and held her hand.

Ginny hung her head. 'Don't be nice to me. I don't want to cry.'

Frances gripped her hand. 'You're not on your own, Ginny.

There are places you can go when the time comes.' They realised that Jessie had come back in and Ginny looked up, brushed a tear from her cheek. Frances got up and Jessie wafted the cards in her hand.

'Eight hopefuls, so far. I've put them in the old band room. Ron's having a quick fag by the stage door then he'll come and talk through what they want him to play, if anything.'

Frances made one last check in the mirror. 'Welcome to the glamour of showbiz!'

* * *

The band room was crowded with eager hopefuls. Some of them had brought their own music and Ginny took it, matched it against the running order, and got it ready for Ron, the pianist.

Dolly peered into the room. She spotted Jessie and came over. 'Jack sent me down to help.' She looked about her. 'It's a good assortment. Not just singers, thank goodness. At least the audience will get a bit of variety.'

Chip called overtures and they left Dolly to chaperone the acts and went into the wings. Jessie peeped through the spyhole.

'Not a bad house, three quarters at least.'

Ginny took a turn. 'Oh, there's something about the excitement waiting for a show that makes me feel so happy!'

Jessie rested an arm on her back. 'I know what you mean. Gives me butterflies every time.'

The girls opened with 'When You're Smiling', hoping to encourage the audience into doing as instructed. They were receptive, in a good mood, and the girls went down well. Jack was waiting in the wings and applauded them when they came off.

'Wonderful, girls. All that lovely energy you've put out there. That's what we need.'

Jessie walked back out onstage to introduce the first act. They'd decided a woman they'd called Madame should go on first. She swanned onto the stage, Frances coming up at the rear with a spoonback chair on which the woman placed her generous bottom. Madame made a great drama of getting herself settled and played her accordion to accompany a dismal, dreary song. Just when they thought she'd finished, she decided there was another verse. The girls huddled in prompt corner. Mike leaned in, his face sinister in the blue light.

'We'll have to do something. She'll be on all night at this rate.'

Frances stepped in. 'Give the signal for the tabs, Mike. Jessie can walk on applauding and introduce the next contestant and when the curtains are closed, I'll get her off.'

Mike agreed. 'Fair call. Even I wouldn't argue with Frances.'

Frances raised her eyebrows at him, and he pretended to cower. She laughed. He gave the signal for Chip to close the curtains and Jessie marched out, her smile wide, clapping with her hands held high.

'Wasn't that wonderful, ladies and gentlemen? Thank you, Eglantine Powell.' Jessie continued applauding; the sounds of Madame's protests filtered through the curtain.

Jessie introduced the male baritone then watched him from the wings. He was good, which was a relief. She peered into the darkness of the wings on the far side. Chip was leaning against the proscenium arch, watching the singer, moving his head in time to the music. Ginny was standing behind him with two boys who would sing and dance, the Lister Brothers. Their hair was slicked back and they were in their best shirts and ties, their cheeks rosy. They skipped onto the stage when Jessie introduced them and went into a Flanagan and Allen routine that was a hit with the audience. They had them singing along as if they were the real thing. Frances came and stood beside her.

'There will always be a line of young hopefuls queuing up to take our place, won't there?'

'Let's hope so, for all our sakes. In a few years, if the war lasts, they'll be fighting on the front lines. Doesn't bear thinking about.' She thought of her brother. Her mum was scared too – she knew that from the way she looked at Eddie; she was trying not to show it, but it was there all the same. How could she go to London and leave her to more worry? She looked again into the wings. Ginny was bent over, holding her stomach. She wobbled and staggered into the darkness.

'Oh!' Jessie exclaimed, slapping her hand across her mouth. Frances dashed behind the backcloth and Jessie could just make her two friends out as the boys strolled along the stage. Chip looked across to her, his hands splayed. She leaned into the light so he could see her and mouthed, 'All right?' Chip gave her a thumbs up.

The boys ended their act and Jessie skipped on. She would guide them off herself and bring on the next act. As the boys took an extended bow, Frances appeared in the wings, her face flushed. Jessie smiled to the audience and Frances came onstage with an elderly man who was going to play the whalebones. Frances walked casually back to opposite prompt before disappearing into the darkness again. When the applause died down, the man went into a long introduction to the origins of the whalebones, what he was going to play, what it signified. Jessie's heart sank.

Frances returned and stood beside her. 'Ginny doesn't feel too well. I've made her lie down in the dressing room. We'll have to do the rest between us.'

'Is she all right?' The girls watched the old man rattling his bones.

'So far.' Frances leaned back to Mike. 'Looks like we've got another one. Let's get him off and the last act on.'

The girls went into action as they had done before, taking off the errant performer with winsome smiles and a flash of the legs, their skirts swirling as they spun onstage. The old man didn't stand a chance. When he was safely returned to the wings, Frances went to check on Ginny.

The last act was introduced. A barrel of a man walked on with his ventriloquist dummy, which he perched on his arm, although it looked more like he was sitting on the man's generous belly. His patter had the audience rolling in their seats with laughter.

Frances reappeared. 'Dolly's looking after Ginny. She sent her dad over the road for a hot water bottle and she's tucked Ginny up in the chair in the dressing room.'

'That doesn't sound good.'

Frances looked towards the stage, the light softening her dark features. 'What will be, will be.'

The girls worked together to finish the show. All the contestants were called back and stood beneath the spotlights. Jack came onstage to represent the judges and gave their verdict and the ten-pound note to the winners – the Lister Brothers. Frances and Jessie went back to the dressing room, but Ginny had gone.

'I'll check the lavvy.'

Frances scanned the room. 'Her bag's gone.'

Jessie ran up the steps to the small office at the stage door. 'Have you seen Ginny, George?'

'Left not five minutes since. Wanted to get off home.'

Jessie dashed back down the stairs, pulling off her costume, kicking off her shoes, Frances doing the same. Dolly came in. 'Could you hang our dresses up? Ginny's gone off on her own.'

Dolly paled. 'Is she all right?'

Jessie was forcing on her shoes. 'I don't know.'

'Let me know when you do!' Dolly called after them. They dashed down the corridor and into the dark street, thankful that the moon was half decent, and hurried through the marketplace into St

Peter's Avenue. There was no sign of Ginny. They stopped, catching their breath for a second, making their way to Bowling Lane. The street narrowed, the bricks uneven beneath their feet. As their eyes adjusted, they saw her leaning against the wall, bent over, clutching her stomach. Jessie got to her first, putting an arm about her, trying to help her upright. A man with a tin hat and an ARP band on his arm hurried towards them.

'All right, ladies. Can I be of assistance?' Ginny groaned and Frances stepped forward, blocking the man's view of Ginny.

'Food poisoning. She's already been sick once. We're quite all right. We're not far from home.'

The warden didn't seem inclined to move. 'If you're quite sure?' He stopped. 'Where are your gas masks, ladies?'

Frances took him by the shoulder. 'We've only just come out. We were going back to get them.'

He shone his torch and the narrow beam flicked over Ginny's face. 'Where do you live?'

'Kew Road.' Would he leave them alone, for God's sake?

'All of you?'

'Yes, all of us. Please, let us get her home?' Frances pleaded. 'We shouldn't have come out.'

He tilted his head. 'I'll let you off this time.' Frances took hold of Ginny's arm, hauling her upright and they began to slowly walk towards Ginny's lodgings until they heard the man's boots clip the pavement as he turned down a side street. Frances ordered Jessie to turn around.

'What?'

Ginny pointed with her hand. 'Wrong way. I'll. Be. Fine.' She drew in a long breath, pulling herself up, and they loosened their grip.

'Course you will,' Frances said smartly. 'You're coming back with us.'

'I can't.' She was speaking through gritted teeth.

Frances gripped her tightly.

'Don't talk cobblers, Ginny. You either come with us or we call an ambulance.'

Ginny cramped again and moaned. It sounded hollow and painful and Jessie just wanted to do something, anything, to relieve the girl's pain. Frances switched on her electric torch. Blood trickled down Ginny's leg and she reached down with her hand and began to cry. 'It's too early.'

'Come on, Jessie,' Frances said quietly. 'Let's get her home.'

21

Jessie fiddled about for her key, opened the door and guided Ginny into the room that led to the kitchen, where she sat her on a chair, Frances supporting her.

Grace had heard them and came into the room in her dressing gown. Ginny hung her head.

'What on earth is the matter, girls?' Grace saw the dried blood on Ginny's leg. 'Oh, sweetheart!'

Jessie bit at her lip. She was terrified for Ginny but what could she tell her mum? That Ginny was having a miscarriage? Frances saved her the trouble.

'It's complicated, Grace.' Frances held on to Ginny's arm. 'Is it okay if we take her upstairs and get her to bed?'

Blood was seeping through Ginny's skirt and Grace looked at Frances and an understanding passed between them. There was no need to say any more. 'Let me get some hot water.'

Ginny sobbed, and said, 'I'm so sorry, Mrs Delaney.'

'Hush now. No need for you to apologise.' Grace pressed a gentle hand on the girl's shoulder.

Ginny was distraught. 'I shouldn't have come.'

'Nonsense!' Grace was brisk but kind. 'Can you girls manage?'

Jessie helped Ginny to her feet. 'We can. Thanks, Mum.' It was all so awful. Frances opened the door, switched on the light and led Ginny upstairs.

'My room,' Jessie said in a loud whisper. She saw Geraldine at the top of the landing in her nightwear.

'Dear Lord, are you girls all right?' She stood back on the cramped landing, looked at Ginny's face. 'Oh.' Jessie felt Ginny's body sag again. 'Is your mother awake?'

'In the kitchen.' They steered Ginny down the small corridor to Jessie's room at the back of the house.

'I'll find some towels, old sheets,' Geraldine called as she went downstairs.

They settled Ginny on the small chair in the corner of the room and Jessie turned back the sheets, wondering what else to do now that they had got Ginny here. Frances removed Ginny's clothes, covering her with a blanket. Grace came in with a bowl of water, soap and a flannel and Jessie rushed to take it from her. 'You should have called. I would have fetched it.'

'No matter,' Grace said quietly. 'Would you like me to take over, Frances?'

Ginny seemed to fold in on herself and Frances twisted to Grace. 'We'll be fine, thank you. Jessie, would you get the enamel pail from under the sink, and bring it up for us and some old newspapers?'

Jessie pressed her lips together, tears pricking at her eyes. She felt so damn useless.

'It seems Frances has everything under control, Jessie, and I'm sure everyone is in need of a good hot drink. Come and help me, darling.'

It took Jessie all her energy to move. Thank God Frances knew what to do. She couldn't move, watching Frances, so calm, not the shivering wreck she was herself. Grace touched her shoulder, stirring her to action and she bundled up Ginny's soiled clothes. She stopped at Eddie's door. Could he hear? Her mum put her hand to her back, pushing her forward.

'Don't worry. That boy would sleep through an earthquake.'

It felt like an earthquake as Jessie made her way to the kitchen. As she helped her mum, she heard Ginny's moans filter through the floorboards. Grace handed her the kettle. 'Don't be afraid.' Jessie filled it with water and put it on the cooker as Ginny let out a blood-curdling howl. She burst into tears with the shock of it and Grace opened her arms and held her, stroking her hair.

She was never going to have children.

Never.

* * *

Frances washed Ginny as best she could, mopping her head with a cool flannel. Through the worst of it she rubbed her back, talking her through the pain, not flinching when Ginny gripped her hand so tightly that she felt the blood had stopped pumping through it. Jessie, white-faced and red-eyed, had brought up the pail and some old newspapers and stood by the door but Frances had urged her to go back downstairs. There was nothing she could do; the girl looked terrified, and Frances needed to concentrate.

'I know it's for the best. It's what I prayed for,' Ginny gasped.

Frances moved a strand of hair from her face that was red with effort and pain. 'It doesn't make it any easier, though.'

'No.' She bit down, panted through the pain as Frances had shown her to do. Frances pushed open the window. Where was Billy Lane now? Men moved on to their next conquest, leaving a trail of despair and destruction in their wake, oblivious of the agonies they left behind, but the women couldn't. She breathed in the cold air, her eyes adjusting to the darkness, the middle hours of the night holding the stillness. Ginny would forget Billy in time, but Frances had Imogen and would always be reminded of Johnny. She'd been shocked when he'd turned up at the Empire, furious when he sprang the dance on her. But when they danced, everything was so right. She hadn't wanted to look at him but couldn't look away. She tugged her cardigan tight about her.

'Close the window,' Ginny said through clenched teeth. 'I'm fine.'

'Course you are, darling.'

Throughout the next hour, Frances sat with Ginny, holding her hand, wiping her brow, rubbing her back, crooning. Ginny grunted and groaned, walking about the limited space, holding on to the wall, pressing her hands against it until she felt gravity working in her favour. Frances went to her side. 'This is the hardest bit. In a few minutes the worst of it will be over.'

* * *

Afterwards, Frances drew a cloth over the pail and crept downstairs with it. Grace was sitting at the table, her eyes closed, Geraldine reading a book by the light of the small lamp on the dresser. Jessie had dropped her head onto her arms but sat up when Frances entered the room, looked at the bucket then at Frances, fear clear upon her face.

Geraldine got up and took the pail from her. 'I'll take that.'

Blood had dried on Frances's hands and she went through to the kitchen, rubbing the bar of soap over her hands, up her arms, washing them in the cold water. She filled a pan of water and put it to boil as Geraldine came back into the room.

'How is she?' Jessie ventured, her voice croaky.

'Exhausted. I'll wash her, then she can sleep. There's nothing more we can do.'

Jessie followed Frances upstairs with a fresh bowl of warm water with which to bathe Ginny. She looked haggard and drawn, but she was peaceful, no longer in such pain. Jessie took hold of her hand. Ginny's voice was weak.

'I'm so sorry to put on your mum and Geraldine like this. What must they think of me?'

Jessie smoothed her fingers over Ginny's hand. 'They're worried about you. We all are.'

Tears ran down Ginny's cheeks and she drew her hand across her face. 'I'm not crying because I'm sad. I'm tired, that's all. Just tired.'

Frances washed her. Jessie found a clean nightdress and they laid a towel over the sheets and placed her in the bed, pulling the blankets up to her chin. Jessie bent forward and kissed her cheek. 'We'll be next door. Call out if you need us.'

While Frances dispensed of the water downstairs, Jessie collected her own nightclothes. She listened at Eddie's door as she passed but heard nothing. Eventually Frances came upstairs and the two of them got into bed.

'Will she be all right?' Jessie's voice was small.

'She'll recover.' Frances turned on her side. 'Now, go to sleep.'

Jessie fidgeted, and Frances waited, knowing what would come next.

'How did you know what to do?'

Frances stared at pale shadows slicing through the gap in the curtains. 'I knew a girl, Violet. In the same situation. There was an older woman there and I helped her, watched what she did.' She had been terrified, just as Jessie had been earlier, but she had remained at Patsy's side.

'But you were so calm.'

She turned onto her back. 'I might have looked calm, but I wasn't. We all put on a brave face, don't we?' Ginny would put on a brave face, carry on; so many girls did. If they survived.

* * *

In the morning, Frances was first out of bed. She tiptoed into Ginny's room and gently lifted the bedding. The bleeding seemed to have stopped, the towel between Ginny's legs red, but not too much. As she lowered the sheet, Ginny opened her eyes.

'Thank you.'

Frances touched her hand. 'You're welcome, darling.' She sat down on the side of the bed. 'We need to get a doctor to check you over. I think everything came away, but better safe than sorry. We don't want you getting an infection.' Ginny wept silent tears. 'I know you feel you'll never recover from this, but you will.'

'I didn't want it, Frances, but now it's gone I feel...' The tears came again. 'I thought I'd have someone to love, someone who would love me.' She rubbed her face with the back of her hand. 'Ridiculous, isn't it. I'd have had to give it away and that made me sad too, to think that a part of me was somewhere out in the world and I would never know where it was.'

There was nothing Frances could say. If it hadn't been for Patsy, she would have had to do the same.

'Can I get you a drink?'

Ginny gave her a weak smile. 'I've put you to so much trouble...'

'Not at all. No one else is awake so we'll share a nice quiet cuppa.'

'Can I share too?' Jessie put her head around the door.

Frances got up. 'You can stay with Ginny. I'll bring them up.'

After the tea, Frances changed the towel and settled Ginny back to sleep. She gathered the soiled cloths and went downstairs and out into the garden, where she unhooked the tub from the nail on the back wall and ran cold water from the outside tap, dropped in the towels, swirling them around with the wooden tongs, then refreshed the water. When the water ran less pink, she added soda that had been diluted in hot water and left them to soak. There was a sharpness in the morning air; the north wind pinched her face and her hands were raw from the water. She pushed them to her waist and leaned back, easing into the aches of her body, then hurried back into the house to warm herself by the stove. Grace was in the kitchen.

'I've lit the gas fire in my room. Come and sit down; you must be exhausted.'

She didn't argue. She went into Grace's room at the front of the house, settling herself in the small easy chair. The fire was welcome, the warmth it gave out more so. She shivered and Grace took a small blanket from the end of the bed and gently draped it about Frances's shoulders. It made Frances think of her own mother and she suddenly felt vulnerable. Her thoughts skipped to Imogen. She stared at the radiant glowing red on the gas fire, the hissing sound like air leaching from a tyre.

Grace returned carrying a tray. She passed Frances a mug then pulled out the toasting fork, fixing a thick slice of bread on it, and held it in front of the fire. Frances watched Grace checking the bread for colour before turning it over. As she buttered the first slice, Geraldine came in with cups of tea for herself and Grace and placed them on the small table between the chairs at the window. She slipped behind Frances's chair and drew back the curtains to let in the morning light.

'How is she?' Geraldine sat on a hard chair she'd brought in from the room next door while Grace took the chair opposite Frances.

'Sleeping.' It was all Frances could offer. Grace put the buttered toast in front of her and she bit into it.

'Poor child,' Grace said, passing another slice of toast to Geraldine. Jessie came in, settled at her mother's feet and took charge of the toasting fork. Grace ran her hand about Jessie's face and Frances felt a lump swell in her throat. She put down her toast, unable to eat.

'It's a sorry state to be in so young but a blessing nonetheless.' Geraldine bit down on her toast and the noise set Frances's teeth on edge. She closed her eyes and eased back into the chair, let the warmth envelop her, the sounds of the room fade away. Imogen would be awake now, and images of her sleepy little face washed before her...

'Imogen?' Frances snapped her eyes wide. Had she spoken her child's name out loud? Jessie was staring at her. 'I-I imagine,' she stammered, trying to cover her slip of words, 'that Ginny will sleep most of the day.' She forced herself to look more awake than she felt. This was not the time to say anything. Not with Ginny as she was. She drank more tea, emptying the mug, returning it to the table.

'It's a lucky escape your friend has had. She'll be able to get on with her life, sadder but wiser, I hope,' Geraldine said and picked up her cup and saucer. 'It must have been a worry for you, Grace, when Jessie left home. A young girl on her own.'

Jessie was indignant. 'That's a bit unfair.'

'Well, I was worried. A mother always worries for her child.' Grace was calm, soothing.

'It's always the girl's fault, isn't it?' Frances snapped. 'Men walk away and no one needs to know anything about *their* indiscretions.' She felt her anger swelling. Johnny had walked away and then come breezing back into her life as if nothing had happened. 'Why is it always the girls who carry the blame?'

'Because they are the ones who get pregnant,' Geraldine replied.

'It's as simple as that.'

'But it's not, is it? Simple, I mean.' She was on her feet now, tiredness cast off like an old cloak. She stopped, calmed herself. 'Ginny was seduced, enticed; she was – is – a lonely girl.'

'We're all lonely. It doesn't mean you have to give yourself to any chap that spins a yarn.'

'Speak for yourself, Geraldine. I'm not lonely at all.'

They stared at her. The gas fire hissed. How could she have been so spiteful?

Geraldine didn't deserve that; none of them did. Jessie got up and came over to her.

Frances sank down into the chair. 'Please forgive me, Geraldine.'

Geraldine rubbed her hands on her thighs, got to her feet. 'You're tired. I know you didn't mean it.' She stared into the distance. 'Even so, I am lonely.' Frances was sick to her stomach but there was nothing she could do to take back her words. 'Work to do.' Geraldine picked up the chair and left the room. Jessie sat on the arm of the chair next to Frances, who hung her head in shame. Jessie would never understand her outburst; none of them would. She was surrounded by people who thought it was Ginny's fault – and they would think it was her fault too. They were both soiled, like the sheets soaking out in the yard, with stains that would never go away...

* * *

At eight, Frances pulled on her coat and got ready to leave. She flicked her hair out of her collar and pulled on her beret, checking herself in the mirror in the narrow hallway. Jessie came out to her, closing the door, whispering, 'Where are you going?'

Frances smoothed her hair, tucked it behind her ear. 'To Patsy. It's Sunday.'

'But what about Ginny?' Jessie looked up the stairs.

'Ginny will be fine.' Tiredness hung heavy on her and it would be heaven to go back to bed, to sleep away the day, but she wanted to be with her child more than ever. She turned from the mirror. 'Remember to call the doctor.'

The fear was plain on Jessie's face. 'What do I say to him?'

'Jessie, your mother is here, as is Geraldine. And Ginny will have to speak up for herself.'

'But she's our friend,' Jessie pleaded, following her to the door. Frances sighed heavily, too tired to explain. 'Is Patsy more important?'

Frances pulled the door open. She must keep her head, keep up the façade. She gave Jessie a smile, touched her shoulder. 'I'll be back this evening. As usual.'

* * *

Imogen was waiting at the window with Patsy's boys. They waved when they saw her at the gate and Frances felt her heart swell with love, her tiredness fall away as she strode up the path. The front door was flung open and Imogen ran towards her, Colly and Bobby close behind. She threw herself into her mother's arms and Frances swooped her up, swinging her around, the child laughing as Frances planted kisses all over her face. She knew what Ginny had meant when she'd said she wanted to be loved. She nuzzled into Imogen's neck before settling her child down onto the path. Patsy welcomed them at the front door.

'You look rough,' she said, taking Frances's coat and gas mask and hanging them by door.

'Thanks!' Frances grinned and Imogen dragged her into the front room where a fire burned in the grate. Frances warmed herself by it as she recounted the events of the previous night.

Patsy was sympathetic. 'It's for the best.'

Frances closed her eyes, Ginny's pain foremost in her mind. 'It is.'

Sufficiently thawed, she settled on the sofa. Imogen disappeared briefly and came back with a book of fairy stories and handed it to her mother. Frances opened the cover, ran her hand over the page as Imogen leaned close. She put her arm about her and the child snuggled closer still. Frances planted a kiss on her head. She smelled clean and pure; it was a comfort. 'It reminded me of Violet. Do you remember?'

Patsy plumped up her cushion, sat back. 'I haven't forgotten any of those girls. Nor the ones no longer with us. Such a waste.'

Frances agreed. 'That wasn't the only drama of the past few days.' She told her of Johnny's ambush of her.

'That's a dirty trick to pull on anyone!'

It still made her stomach turn to think of it. 'It was. I was shaking for a good hour afterwards.'

'I'm not surprised. Did he explain himself?'

'Only that he couldn't think of any other way to get my attention.'

Patsy picked up her knitting. 'Well, you could have saved all that if you'd not been so stubborn. He's reaching out to you. You can't leave him dangling forever.'

* * *

Later, as they busied themselves in the kitchen preparing vegetables, the children drew pictures at the table.

'Did Colin get his call-up papers?'

'No, he's fishing.'

'Is that better or worse?'

Patsy leaned on the sink and stared out over the garden. The trees were bare now, the apples stored on racks in the shed, the soil on the vegetable patch freshly turned that morning. 'I have no idea. I'm always relieved when his ship docks.' She paused. 'But I don't think he's just fishing, not these days.'

'What else can he be doing?' Frances twisted, checked on the children.

Patsy shrugged. 'Who knows. He won't say anything but he's back and forth to Norway, I do know that.' She ran water into the pan and put it on top of the cooker. 'I reckon Colin thinks the less I know the better, but I hate being kept in the dark. I'd rather know – wouldn't you?'

Frances considered it. Would she rather her imagination run away with her? Or would she want to know the truth, however bleak? She joined the children at the table, admiring their masterpieces.

'Who's this?'

Colly pointed out his family, little round bodies and stick arms. He'd included Imogen as part of it. It should have made her happy, but she felt a flicker of regret.

'Mine, Mummy! Look at mine.' Imogen put her little finger on the figures. 'That's me. And that's Bobby. And Colly. And this is you. And this is my daddy.' She twisted to look at her mother and Frances felt her stomach lurch. 'Where is my daddy, Mummy? Is he at sea on Uncle Colin's ship?'

Frances clutched at her throat. It was the first time she'd asked. 'He's not on a ship but he's a long way away.'

Patsy came and stood beside her, studying the children's pictures, saying quietly, 'She's growing up, Frances, and the questions are just beginning. How long can you keep everyone in the dark?'

Imogen picked her crayon and started drawing a big fat sun in a cloudless sky.

22

Johnny leaned forward, shuffling the contracts spread out on the coffee table. The print was small and reading through the countless pages had made his eyes sore. It was early November; time was ticking on and Ruby was digging in her heels but he had to get her signature on them to move things forward. He eased back in the chair. It was quiet without Aunt Hetty, but she'd left her mark. The flat was more homely, made so by the plump cushions she'd purchased at Liberty's and the Aubusson rug beneath his feet that had arrived soon after she'd left. All the family photos had been unpacked and were arranged around the room so that wherever the two of them looked there were memories of shows, of meeting their idols – the Astaires – and, most importantly, of their parents. He got up and went to the mantel, took down a photo. Mother was in the centre, holding their hands, a child either side, he in his smart shorts and jacket, Ruby in a white dress, a huge white bow in her hair. He'd promised his mother he would take care of her. Getting out of London was the right thing to do, and Aunt Hetty, although doubtful, had been in full agreement in the end. He'd told her of finding Frances again, and asked her not to say anything to Ruby. Aunt Hetty had agreed, but thought he was wrong to do so.

'Don't keep it from her too long, my boy, not if you harbour any hope of her being happy again.' He hadn't been thinking of Ruby's happiness, not then.

He replaced the photo.

The doorbell rang. He shook his head. 'She's forgotten her key again, Mother. What will I do with her?' He went to the door and found Mickey Harper there. He seemed to be everywhere they went these days, sidling up to Ruby at the Savoy, bumping into them at the Lyons Corner House on the Strand. There were men like him everywhere, hoping that if they hung around long enough they would get lucky. Well, not with his sister he wouldn't. The guy gave him the creeps and he needed to do a little digging. He made a mental note to ask Bernie about him when they next met.

'Hey, Johnny, where's your sweet little sister?' He peered over his shoulder. 'Is she here?'

Johnny stood in the frame, making himself as large as he could to block his view. 'She's not, Mickey.' How the hell did he know where they lived?

'Odd.' Mickey smirked. 'She said she'd meet me. Didn't she tell you?'

'Must have slipped her mind.' Johnny held on to the door, pulling it close to his back.

Mickey jangled the change in his pocket. 'Shall I come in and wait?'

'At any other time that would be no problem,' Johnny said, hoping to stymie him, 'but I'm on my way out.' He rolled down his sleeves while Mickey leered at him. 'It's a good job you interrupted me, or I'd be late.' Johnny was about to the close the door.

Mickey leaned on the jamb. 'I'll walk with you.'

Johnny bit the inside of his cheek. Now he would have to leave. He lifted his jacket from the chair in the hall and slipped it on as they waited for the lift. Mickey looked about him. 'Smart place.'

'Yes.' Johnny willed the lift to go faster. They heard the clang of the mechanics as it arrived on their floor, the jolt as it settled. Johnny drew back the grille and they got in, both facing forwards.

'Crazy girl, Ruby. And great fun. But then, you know that.'

Johnny merely smiled. What on earth was she doing hanging about with the likes of Mickey Harper?

* * *

The room was small and dark, for little light came in from the window at the front of the shop. The fat man was bent over his desk that was cluttered with small screwdrivers, bits of broken jewellery, a calendar that hadn't been turned since the fourteenth of May.

'Take a seat,' he offered. She looked about her. A boy clattered around in a small workshop to the side and she caught him looking as he went about his business. She pulled her collar higher, hoping to hide her face.

'I can't offer any more than two hundred and fifty pounds,' the jeweller said, removing his eyepiece. He sat back in his chair, waiting for her answer, pushing his bottom lip forward.

'But I need five hundred.'

'Then take it somewhere else. I'm doing you a favour, no questions asked. I don't know where you got it, do I?'

He placed the brooch on the desk. It wasn't the most expensive piece she'd ever owned, but it was the most precious. The rest of her jewellery had gone to pay her debts and, latterly, Mickey Harper. There was nothing left to pay him off with. If only Johnny hadn't gone away those two days, he might have saved her from this.

She put her fingers on it. Her mother's brooch. The man was watching. He didn't care what it meant to her, did he? It was a business transaction. The same as Mickey Harper. Men controlled everything. She heard her mother's voice, felt the anger, the disappointment. She tossed back her head. 'I know it's worth far more than that.'

The man clasped his hands together, resting them on his belly. 'Last month, maybe, last year definitely.' The door opened, setting the bell tinkling over the door.

Ruby picked up the brooch, slid it into her bag. 'I'll think about it.'

'Up to you,' he said, looking over her shoulder at the man who had walked into the shop. 'You know where I am if you change your mind.'

* * *

Outside, she hurried down the alleyway until she was back on the main street. She was already late for Mickey and she didn't have the money. He'd threatened to tell Johnny. He had photos of her in various stages of undress: sprawled on a bed, a thin sliver of a satin sheet covering very little; another with no sheet at all. She shuddered. She vaguely remembered going into a room, in a club, somewhere off Piccadilly, drunk as she so often was. Drinking helped numb the pain. It stopped her thinking about what she had done, what she'd lost. Mickey had introduced her to one of his friends, who had seemed nice. Respectable. A photographer, Mickey said. An artist, the man had corrected. Odious little man! She'd been so damned stupid. Johnny would be livid. She knew she pushed him to the limits, but he would always be there for her; the thought comforted her. They weren't two people, they were one: the Randolphs.

People pushed by her and she slowly came to her senses, made her way down the Strand. A Nippy showed her to a table in the Lyons tea shop where she'd arranged to meet Mickey, and she sat down. People came and went and there was no sign of him. Perhaps something awful had happened to him. She hoped it had. After twenty minutes she picked up her bag and hurried home. It was all such a mess. She had resisted so far, but if the only escape was Grimsby, then so be it. They would be earning again and she could pay her way out of it, start afresh.

She was feeling more positive as she turned into the street, a plan forming in her head. She took her key from her bag, dropped it, bent to pick it up and as she did so, heard a familiar voice – one she didn't want to.

'Well, whaddya know. Ruby Randolph,' Mickey said loudly. 'I thought you'd forgotten our little meeting.'

Ruby looked up, seeing first Mickey then Johnny. Johnny was furious. He was managing to contain it, but only just, and she tried to control her tremors. Would Mickey make a scene in the street? Would he tell? He wasn't carrying the photos. Had he already given them to Johnny? A quick glance at her brother told her that no, he didn't know. Not yet. She plastered on her sweetest smile.

'No. No, I hadn't. I got held up. I was with Katie, Katie Grant.' She was agitated; why was he here? He'd said to meet at Lyons, she was sure of it.

'Have you got that thing I asked for?'

'No, Katie couldn't get hold of it.'

'Hold of what?' Johnny asked.

Ruby felt the heat rise in her neck.

'Oh, some photographs,' Mickey said. Ruby rushed forward, took hold of Johnny's arm. 'Movie stars, you know the thing. Get them in cigarette packets. Collector's items, aren't they, Ruby? Ruby said she had a friend who had a special edition.' He looked up at the flat, then to her, raising his eyebrows. So, he knew where to find her. Had he followed her home? She was so drunk sometimes she wouldn't have known if he had.

Johnny pulled her close, wrapped his hand over hers and she was glad of his strength.

'Thank heavens you came back,' he said briskly. 'We'll be late for our meeting with Bernie if we don't get a move on.' He turned to Mickey. 'Sorry to dash off, old chap.'

Johnny started walking and Mickey called after them, 'Don't forget the photographs, Ruby.'

Ruby looked over her shoulder. Mickey was standing on the pavement, grinning. She turned back, furious. Johnny was silent until they rounded the corner.

'I didn't know we had a meeting with Bernie?' She was almost running to keep up with him, his strides were so long.

'We haven't. That vile man came to the flat, looking for you. Did you tell him where we lived?'

'No, I would never do that. I don't know how he knew.' She followed him into the courtyard entrance to the Savoy.

'Mr Randolph. Miss Randolph.' The doorman bowed his head as they walked in.

'While we're here, we might as well have a drink – and you can tell me about Mickey Harper.'

Ruby linked her arm in his; people recognised them and smiled as they made their way up to the American Bar. Ruby smiled back. Here was her chance.

'Oh, let's not spoil the afternoon. We've something to celebrate.' He stopped and turned to her. 'I've changed my mind. I will come to Grimsby.' She pulled him closer, flicking at his lapel, patting at it with the flat of her hand. 'Reluctantly, of course, but I know it's the right thing to do.' Was it enough to delay talk of Mickey, if not distract him altogether? 'You're right, Johnny, we need to invest in the future. And if the future is in Grimsby, then that's where we'll go.'

23

As November drew to close, it brought with it a sense of hope and excitement. Grace was assembling the ingredients to make a plum pudding on Stir-up Sunday and Christmas cards had appeared in the shops. Frances had put a doll by for Imogen, paying off a little each week. She was certain Imogen would love it. These little things, the anticipation of her daughter's joy, made the sacrifices worthwhile.

Tickets for the panto were selling fast and it was beginning to look like *Aladdin* would be a sell-out until the end of January. It was the positive news they all needed. Ginny hadn't left Barkhouse Lane since the night of her miscarriage almost a month ago. Geraldine had insisted she stay, as long as the girls were in agreement, which they were. The doctor had pronounced her fit and well, and as they prepared to go into rehearsals she'd given up her loathsome job at the laundry and Jessie hers at the solicitor's. Frances would still do the odd shift at the Fisherman's Arms, helping Lil whenever she was free, but now their days would be taken up with rehearsals, and once the panto was up and running, their afternoons and evenings spent at the theatre.

The Randolphs were in Grimsby; the local paper had made a great deal of their arrival. Johnny wanted to meet but so far their rehearsal times had clashed. In a way, Frances felt relieved. It was all such a turnaround and she wasn't quite sure how best to go forward.

* * *

On a misty Monday morning, the cast of *Aladdin* had gathered in St Peter's Church Hall and knuckled down to work, wanting to make the most of the rehearsal time before the show opened on the eighth of December. They'd seemed nice enough and, in the first awkward days, threw themselves into getting to know each other. The festive appearance of the room had added to the atmosphere, giving them something to talk about, to break the ice with the newcomers. Paper chains were draped across the ceiling and a large tableau of the nativity ran the full length of one wall. It had been created by the Scouts and Brownies who used the hall throughout the year. A donkey with uneven legs was carrying a smiling Mary towards a small wooden shack made of sticks, a scowling Joseph leading the way. Cotton-wool sheep dotted the hillside and a gold foil star hung high above them all.

'It doesn't seem so long ago I was at school doing the same,' Jessie said, pointing out the host of angels made from paper doilies.

'And making snowflakes from newspaper, cutting out the little holes,' Ginny added.

Frances smiled. She had spent the Sunday doing exactly that with Imogen, Colly and Bobby. It had brought back happy memories of sitting at her mammy's kitchen table. It was important to remember the happy times.

During Wednesday afternoon, Ginny and Frances weren't needed and settled down on a couple of chairs watching the others rehearse in small groups. Don Roper, the dame and director, was standing with Joe Taplow, a long thin chap with sandy-coloured hair and glasses. Don was talking and gesticulating and Joe was nodding his head. He seemed a gentle sort and not at all suited for the part of Abanazar, Aladdin's wicked uncle.

They paid attention when it was Jessie's turn to rehearse with Kitty Bright. Her hair was red as rust, harsh, not like the glorious deep copper of Ginny's, nor did she have Ginny's soft features. Frances had met her type before, nose in everyone's business and eager to spread it around – along with everything else she possessed. She pitied Jessie having to play Princess to Kitty's Aladdin.

'Poor Jessie,' Ginny said. 'Kitty's very commanding, isn't she?'

'It will be good for Jessie to work with her, even though she might not think it,' Frances commented. 'I know Jessie was disappointed about not getting the title role but Kitty has more of a name and people know who she is. Jessie's not quite top-of-the-bill material yet.'

When he was satisfied with their performance, Don dismissed them and Jessie came back to her seat.

'I've a lot to learn,' she said ruefully. 'I need to be more forceful.'

'No, you don't. Then you'd be like Kitty.' Frances patted her on the shoulder. 'Be yourself. That's the key. There's no one else like you and that's as it should be.'

They were dismissed at five.

Frances opened the door to the street where they assembled in the winter darkness. A choir was rehearsing in the church over the road and they listened as they sang the last verse of 'In the Bleak Midwinter'. The moon was low with only minimal light to guide them and Frances switched on her torch.

'Come on, girls, don't shilly-shally. I need something to eat before I go back to work. I'm famished.' They decided to walk up through Sea View Street, wanting to peer in the shop windows using the light of their torches. The displays had been suitably decorated for the season and ideas for Christmas gifts given prominence: gloves and scarves, fine handkerchiefs and cosy slippers. Jessie pressed her finger to the window.

'That's not unlike the handkerchief my old boss, Miss Symonds, gave me as a parting gift when I came to Cleethorpes.' She rooted around in her pocket and pulled it out. The girls compared it.

'A lovely gift. And one you've used often, Jessie.'

Jessie ran her fingers over the initial J Miss Symonds had embroidered. 'She was a lovely old woman. I hadn't thought I would miss her as much as I do.' She put it back in her pocket. 'That whole life feels as if it belonged to someone else.'

Frances put her arm about her. 'Well, it didn't. It was part of your life that you've left behind. We all have to do it if we are to move forward.' She patted Ginny on the shoulder. 'The past is behind you too, Ginny. Leave it there. Don't let Billy win.'

Ginny bristled. 'I don't know what you mean.'

'Sure you do. I've watched you give all the men a wide berth. Even Don, and he's no threat to you at all. It's Joe who needs to keep a lookout from what I've seen.'

Jessie blushed. 'Frances!'

They walked on. 'I've been around a lot longer than you two have. You learn these things.' Frances hugged Ginny close. 'Be brave, darling. Not all men are like Billy Lane.'

'But how will I know?' Ginny's eyes glittered with moisture, but it was hard to tell whether they were tears or because of the bitter cold.

Frances linked her arm through hers. 'You have to let go of your fear, little by little, and open your heart to love someone.'

'Like you?' Jessie challenged. 'And Johnny Randolph?'

'That's different,' Frances said curtly as they headed home. 'Completely different.'

* * *

Frances pulled her coat collar up around her ears and wrapped her scarf about her mouth as she made her way to the Fisherman's Arms. A thick fog descending, the temperature had plummeted in the last hour. Lil had already opened up and Frances hurried through to the bar. Boxes of paper decorations and pine cones were stacked on one side and Lil, her arm resting on one of the pumps, was looking at Fudge, who was curled up in his usual spot.

Frances unwrapped her scarf and took off her hat. 'Where's Artie?'

'Copped it,' Lil said sadly. 'Blackout caught him out, poor old sod. Didn't see the bus coming.'

'Oh, no!' She put her hand to her mouth. 'Poor Artie. I didn't imagine...' She sighed. 'How sad.'

'Aye. It is. Them Germans haven't dropped a ruddy bomb yet and I reckon we're popping more off ourselves.'

Frances went and sat beside the dog that was resting his head on his paws. He whimpered as she ran her hand over him. 'He looks so sad, Lil.'

'Aye, he does. Do you want to take him home with ya?'

Frances glanced up, still rubbing the dog's neck. 'Isn't there a Mrs Artie?'

'Not that I know of. He was on his own, was Artie.'

The dog lifted his head and rested it on Frances's lap. 'I can't take him back with me. The house is full.' Much as she loved dogs, he was way down on the list of priorities.

Lil patted the counter. 'Guess I'll have to take him until I can find him a home. I can't have him sitting on me doorstep day and night.'

'Did you hear that, Fudge? Lil is going to look after you.' The dog wagged his tail. Frances got up, went behind the bar and washed her hands. 'He'll be company for you.'

'Not the sort of company I was hoping for.'

Lil held fort at the bar while Frances unpacked the boxes, decorating the high shelves at the back of the bar with pine cones and holly. She cleared the narrow shelf above the till and placed a small wooden stable with the nativity figures on it, tucking a sheet of cotton wool around the edges to represent snow. Would they have snow this winter? She hoped it wouldn't be too bad if it did come. It would make getting out to Waltham difficult but it would be fun making snowmen with Imogen and the boys. She watched Lil talking to Big Malc through the mirror. What was Lil doing for Christmas? She hadn't even asked.

As the regulars came in, Fudge invited comment and talk of Artie, customers chipping in bits and pieces until they built up a picture of his life.

'Well, for a quiet man we knew plenty about him after all,' Lil said. 'Just goes to show you.'

'Show you what?' Frances was at the optic, getting a double whisky. She handed it over, got the money and rang it in the till.

'How we give little bits of ourselves away, even if we don't know it.'

24

It hadn't been as bad as he'd imagined it would be. Ruby's change of heart had flummoxed him for a time – would she change her mind again? But she hadn't, and she'd been swift to pack, eager to rehearse. They had put together a show using many of the routines they'd done in America and Jack Holland's secretary, Annie, had secured them a house in Park Drive in Grimsby. For the first time in months he'd felt a glimmer of hope that Ruby would finally settle down and the sense of unease at bringing her to Grimsby abated. They spent the days developing new routines, Johnny trying to find the delicate balance of keeping Ruby busy without overworking her. It had been a huge success so far, and they were playing to packed houses almost every night, which helped. To his regret and frustration, he hadn't had time to meet up with Frances. Neither had he told Ruby about her, and Aunt Hetty's words jangled in his head, that it was wise to tell her sooner rather than later. He'd been on the verge of it numerous times but he hadn't wanted to spoil the easy peace they'd had these past few weeks as they worked on the show. Ruby had been more of her old self, still brittle, still delicate, but she was improving all the same. He would tell her tonight, once he'd had a chance to speak with Frances.

He found Ruby sitting on a bench in the rear garden, a blanket over her shoulders. The winter sun was low in the sky and the warmth from it was enough to be able to enjoy it for a while. She was drinking tea from a china cup, leaning her head back so that the sun could kiss her face. He was pleased to see that she looked less haggard of late. Mrs Frame, the housekeeper, was wonderful, a surrogate mother, and there was a sense of home, of peace about the place. He joined her on the bench, stretching out his legs, resting his hands between them.

'This is the life, eh.'

She opened one eye. 'Are you being sarcastic?'

He nudged her. 'Be truthful, Ruby. It's not as bad as you thought it would be.'

'You have no idea what I thought it would be.' She closed her eyes again. 'That godawful smell of fish makes me sick, but I've got used to it.' She opened her eyes, placed her cup down on the small table to the side of her. 'I suppose you can get used to anything – eventually.' A robin hopped about and she tossed crumbs from her plate.

'I'll take that as meeting with your approval, then.'

'Don't push it, brother.' A sudden gust set stray leaves rolling along the lawn like pennies.

'Nice to have a garden, isn't it?' It was a luxury they seldom had. America had been non-stop city to city, travelling on trains from state to state, staying in high-rise hotels and apartments with no time to enjoy the parks and open spaces. The garden at Park Drive was long with trees and mature shrubs filling the beds along the fences that separated the house from the ones on either side of it.

'It's all barren; the trees have no leaves and there are no flowers.'

'It still has colour. Can't you see it?' Had life dulled for her so much? She was quiet. He stood up, held out his hand. 'Time we got ready.'

'Do we have to go? Really?' She took his hand and he pulled her to her feet.

'Yes, we do. I promised Jack Holland we'd be there for the first half of opening night of the panto. Well, opening afternoon.' They walked up the small steps and through the French windows into the sitting room. 'Not sure whether people will come out this early, but these are not normal times. I admire Jack for even trying. But he's been successful so far.'

'Let's hope it stays that way. For our sakes.'

Johnny put an arm about her shoulder. 'Trust me, Ruby, it will. We've made a sound investment. Jack and Bernie are good partners.'

'You hardly know them.' Her voice was softer now, the fear leaking from the gaps in the brittle shell she hid behind. 'How can you tell?'

He shrugged. 'I know how many sharks there are out there.' He thought of Mickey Harper. 'You have to tread carefully. We have a reputation to protect.' She shivered and he tried to encourage her. 'I'm working on getting us cabaret at the Savoy. Things are looking more settled; people are taking a chance again.' He hadn't broached the subject of enlisting since that night at the flat with Aunt Hetty. They'd moved the National Service registration age up to men of twenty-three in October. In time, he would go. In time, he would have to.

They walked through to the hallway and Ruby went upstairs. The door to the kitchen opened and Mrs Frame came out.

'Are you to be having something before you leave, Mr Johnny? I've got some soup on the go.'

'That will be wonderful. We'll eat in the kitchen, if that's not too troublesome?' Johnny looked up the stairs to his sister.

Ruby leaned over the rail. 'Thank you, Mrs Frame. I won't be more than ten minutes.' Johnny raised his eyebrows. 'Make that thirty.'

He walked back into the sitting room and closed the doors into the garden. The house had been let fully furnished. It was decorated with heavy fabrics that kept out the cold and the sitting room had a gas fire so that it would be warm when they came in from the theatre. Thankfully, Mrs Frame had stayed on as housekeeper. He wrote to Aunt Hetty and told her of their good fortune. She had warned that Ruby might relapse into her former behaviour but so far – he tapped the wood of the easy chair – she was improving daily. He picked up the paper and tried to read the headlines but couldn't concentrate and lowered it onto his lap, closed his eyes.

* * *

Ruby slipped off her dress and threw it in the general direction of the chair. She would wear the red this afternoon. Festive, cheerful. She went to the window and looked out across the park where a scattering of children were running along the paths, weaving between the shrubs and chasing each other. It wasn't too bad here and she loved the garden – not that she would let Johnny know that. She had felt the darkness of the last few weeks dilute. London was far away – and so was Mickey Harper.

Christmas was on the horizon, the new year close behind. She gripped the windowsill, put her head against the cool glass. Maybe next year would be kinder to them... She went over to the dressing table and patted her cheeks with rouge. Johnny was right. The show was going well, and she would die rather than admit it to him, but she was enjoying every minute. She reached across and picked up the Christmas card Aunt Hetty had sent. A snow-covered scene, children pulling a sledge, their faces shining with happiness. There had been a letter too, telling her to be strong, to look to the future that would be bigger and brighter – and what their mother wanted for them. Mother. Her jewellery box was open and she took out Mother's brooch. She had almost sold it. What on earth had she been thinking of? She clutched it tightly, finding new resolve. Next year would be better; she would make it so.

* * *

They waited in the hall for the taxi. Ruby had made every effort to look the part. Her fur stole was wrapped about her and she pulled it high on her shoulders so that it accentuated her small face, her pointed chin. It was fastened with their mother's brooch, the diamonds catching the light, and she fiddled with it constantly.

He was glad when the car arrived. He tugged again at his cuffs, ran his finger around his collar.

Ruby turned to him. 'Are you nervous?'

'What makes you ask?'

She looked to his cuffs. 'You keep tugging at them. You always do that when you're nervous.'

He placed his hands in his lap and looked out of the window as they turned to travel up the hill towards the main road. He should have told her...

'Who else is in the show? Anyone we know?'

'You haven't been the slightest bit interested before. Why now?'

'Boredom.' She grinned. 'Might be someone we can have fun with.'

Where should he start? 'Bailey and North are the Chinese policemen; Kitty Bright is the title.'

'Ugh. That tart.' She put her hand on the seat in front. 'If I'd known she was in it, I'd have stayed at home.'

The car pulled up outside the theatre and he rested his hand on her arm. 'People are having a tough time, Ruby. It's our job to make life a little more bearable, help them forget their troubles.'

'I know. You don't have to remind me. I'm doing my best.'

He took her hand, squeezed it. In her own way she was doing what she could. Most nights she would spend an hour or more at the stage door after each show, chatting to the chaps in uniform who waited in the cold for her after every performance.

A doorman rushed forward and opened the taxi door. Ruby stepped out, followed by Johnny, and people gasped and nudged each other. He held back, letting her have her moment. It made her happy – and the happier she was, the better she'd behave.

* * *

She stepped into the foyer of the Empire and people stood back while she swept in, shoulders back, head held high. She could hear her mother, telling her to be professional, to be something special for people, and she wanted so much to be special. The foyer was full of families, eager children, the pitch of their excitement ringing in her ears. Oh, to be a child again, with all the magic... Her heart shrank. There was no more magic. She heard her mother again, berating her. Up went her head again. *Smile, my darling, smile.* She tugged her stole, clasped her hand over her brooch. She could do this. It was easy to pretend.

Jack Holland weaved through the crowds towards them.

'Johnny, Ruby. So glad you could come.'

Johnny put out his hand and Jack took it, shaking it vigorously. 'We won't be able to stay until the end, Jack, but we wanted to be here for the opening.'

'Glad you got here at all.' He slapped Johnny on the back and turned his attention to Ruby. She was enchanted. Jack was tall and dark and rather dashing, a little like Errol Flynn though perhaps not so naughty. Shame. He shook her hands, holding hers in both of his, and she saw what Johnny had described: an honest man, one possibly too nice for this business. A striking, haughty woman was heading their way and Ruby couldn't decide whether she was smiling or sneering as she sashayed towards them.

She held out her hand. 'Audrey Holland. I've so admired you and your brother. Like our very own Astaires; weren't they wonderful? Did you ever see them on the London stage? No?' She tilted her head, not waiting for Ruby's answer. 'Perhaps not. Far too young. Come, my dear. We have a private room upstairs. I managed to secure a bottle of champagne.'

Ruby looked over her shoulder and pulled a face at Johnny in the hope that he would rescue her. He wiggled his fingers in a small wave, listening to Jack. The bastard! She reluctantly followed Audrey upstairs, thankful for the promise of champagne to soothe the tediousness of the inevitable small talk.

* * *

Jack led Johnny into the auditorium, where the early birds were taking their seats. There was a bubble of happiness in the air as lively children wriggled along the rows, shushed by mothers and aunties. What men were among them were in some sort of uniform, mostly army but a lot of what he recognised as the Naval Reserve.

They went through the pass door at the side of the stage and Jack led Johnny downstairs, where a cluster of babes were listening to instructions from their chaperone. Johnny smiled; it brought back memories of when he and Ruby were small, getting the adrenaline rush of being onstage before the curtain went up. He still had it, to a degree, but it wasn't the same. More the pressure of not disappointing these days. He checked over his shoulder. With luck, Audrey would commandeer Ruby until curtain up.

He followed Jack down the corridor, Jack knocking on each door and briefly introducing Johnny to them – the local dancers, Bailey and North, Don Roper. Johnny wished them all the best for the performance, each time hoping behind the door he would find Frances. Jack stopped in front of a door, looked to Johnny and knocked. Jessie opened it and he could see Ginny staring at him. Frances was standing behind her and she wrapped her dressing gown over her costume, and smiled.

Jack stepped to one side to allow Johnny to walk forward. He hesitated. Someone knocked on the door behind them and they turned.

'Chip?' Jack said.

'You're wanted front of house, Mr Holland.'

Jack spread out his hands. 'Will you excuse me, girls. Johnny?'

Johnny stayed by the door. Behind him, small children hurried down the corridor, their chaperone hissing at them to 'walk'. The other two girls busied themselves getting ready, doing their best to appear as if they were not in the slightest bit interested on the scene playing out before them.

'At last,' he said as Frances stepped towards him, her dark hair loose about her shoulders. She was already in her costume, a jewelled top and diaphanous harem pants that gave only a hint of her long slender legs. He wanted nothing more than to sweep her into his arms and kiss her hard, damn hard, but he held back. He would have to wait a little longer.

'Now that the show's up and running, I thought you might be able to fix a time to meet up, for dinner, somewhere. The Royal?'

He didn't want to go back into the auditorium, not now he'd seen her. There was so much he wanted to say. He heard a commotion in the corridor. He made to move but Kitty Bright stepped out of her dressing room as Ruby came down the stairs and he tensed. The dancers tumbled out, followed by the babes, a sea of satin in red and yellow, surging down the corridor like a wave, bringing Ruby ever closer. He pressed himself against the wall, letting them pass, hoping that Ruby would wait too, but she was oblivious, forcing herself against the flow. He tried to move but couldn't, and then he didn't want to, understanding that Ruby would have to find out some time. She swept up beside him and peered into the room, smiling benignly at the girls until she registered Frances.

'Oh! You.'

No one spoke; no one moved.

'Frances O'Leary. Well, well.' Ruby turned to Johnny. 'Now I understand.'

Johnny sucked his cheek.

Frances stepped forward. Her feet were bare, her toenails painted bright red. 'Ruby! How lovely to see you again.'

Johnny put his hand on Ruby's shoulder. 'Good to meet old friends, isn't it, Ruby?'

She shrugged his hand away. 'Old friend? It was a little more than that, wasn't it?' Ruby was shaking her head from side to side. She turned to him, her jaw jutting forward. 'I should have known, shouldn't I.' She looked so hurt and he immediately knew how stupid he'd been, telling himself, telling Aunt Hetty that he was thinking of Ruby's well-being when he'd only been thinking of his own.

'Ruby. Please.' They could hear the musicians taking their places in the orchestra pit.

'The curtain's going up,' Jessie said quietly.

'Bright little thing, aren't you?' Ruby spat.

Johnny put his hand under Ruby's elbow. 'Please excuse us, ladies.'

He guided her out into the corridor and though she stumbled, he kept pressing her on, pushing their way past Kitty Bright and Don Roper. Ruby was trying to wriggle free but he drove her forward, up the stairs and out onto the street. It was raining and George stepped out, offering them an umbrella. Johnny took it, holding it over her.

'You sly, crooked bastard! You liar! You b-brought me here...' She was breathing hard and fast, clenching and unclenching her fists. He braced himself, knowing what would come next, and she rushed at him, slapping his chest with the flat of her hands, over and over again, and he stood there, letting her release the fury, the disappointment. When she stopped, he gently took hold of her with his free hand. What had he expected? That she would be happy for him?

'I'm sorry, Ruby. I should've told you Frances was here.' He should have been braver. It would have saved her this. 'I love her. I have always loved her.' She slapped him one last time with her free hand, half-hearted, her rage ebbing.

'You know Mother didn't like her!'

'Mother didn't like anyone. Not if she thought they'd come between us.'

He felt the cold rain running down the back of his neck, soaking through his jacket.

'I thought you'd come here for us, for me.' A tear ran down her cheek and she quickly pushed her finger to the corner of her eye to stem the flow. 'It was for her all along. You just wouldn't admit it to yourself.'

He couldn't argue. They could have gone anywhere in the country; they could have stayed in town. She scrutinised his face. 'I was right.' She turned on her heel and marched off.

He hurried up beside her. 'Where are you going?'

'Home. Wherever that is. London. Anywhere but here.'

He grabbed at her arm, pulled her back. 'You can't. I need you.'

She looked down at his hand, peeled it away from her sleeve. 'I thought you did. I was wrong.' Her voice quivered with emotion and he took her arm again, gentler this time.

'Come back in, Ruby. Please. We'll talk later, I promise.' The rain had stopped, and he withdrew the umbrella. Their breath clouded and intermingled. 'We can't let people down. It's not who we are.'

Rain clung to the fur on her stole. He knew she would do as he had asked; there was something in her eyes – the fire had gone from them.

Outside the Empire, Ruby powdered her nose and refreshed her lipstick while Johnny opened and closed the brolly to shake off most of the rain. It was dreary and grey, the sea churning as it crashed along the walls of the promenade. He walked to the door, held it open for her. She hesitated. He held out his hand and after a second or two she took hold of it. It was light and warm inside the theatre and he felt as if a window had opened.

25

Jessie turned up the volume on the tannoy so they wouldn't miss their cues. They would have at least ten minutes before any of them were due onstage – Jessie as the Princess, Ginny her handmaiden, and Frances as the Slave of the Ring. The overture ended and they heard a warm burst of applause.

'Oh, Frances. What on earth have you done to upset Ruby Randolph?' Jessie pushed the door shut and leaned against it.

Frances had expected Johnny to turn up at some point but hadn't bargained for Ruby. It was obvious he hadn't told her Frances was in the show. 'Breathed the wrong way? I have no idea.'

Jessie came away from the door. 'No, you're not going to get away that easily. She was fine until she saw you.'

Frances sighed. Ruby's outburst couldn't be explained away as nothing. 'I was competition and she was jealous when Johnny started spending more and more time with me. I was her understudy. During the run she had to be rushed to hospital and I went on in her place. Their mother, Alice, saw what was happening between me and Johnny and tried to come between us.' Frances was surprised how much it still rankled. 'She threatened me, told me that she could pull strings, that I'd never work again. That as soon as Ruby was back I would be in the chorus – and there I would stay.' She lowered her voice. 'Don't you dare breathe a word of this to anyone.'

'God, what a cow,' Jessie said.

Ginny nodded in agreement. 'Did you tell Johnny?'

They heard a roar of laughter as Bailey and North made their entrance as the Chinese Policemen. Patsy was out there somewhere with Colly, Bobby and Imogen. Would she enjoy the show? Jessie and Ginny were waiting for her to speak.

'No. I wasn't sure he'd believe me – it was his mother after all. And I was young.' She smiled at them. She was the age Ginny and Jessie were now, not much more. 'His mother made every effort to come between us, so we kept it quiet, met in secret. She couldn't be with him twenty-four hours a day – although she did her best. She made Ruby suspicious, made out I was trying to take her place. I heard her say it.' She took a deep breath. 'We were engaged.' The girls gasped. 'He bought me a ring and I truly thought we would be together for always. He asked me to keep it quiet until he found the right time to tell his mother and Ruby.' She gave a small laugh. 'Not that there was ever a right time. But I trusted him. Believed him.' They heard someone walk along the corridor. The tannoy system crackled, the audience laughing and applauding. 'Sounds like a good house.'

'And?' Jessie ignored her attempt to distract them. 'What happened next?'

'He put his career first, just as his mother wanted him to. The Randolphs came as a pair. It was a bond that couldn't be broken – only Alice Randolph didn't see it like that. And she poisoned Ruby so that she thought the same. We were friends to begin with, I liked her, but when she came out of hospital she changed. I could see she was afraid. She had her mother to blame for that. Ruby more or less cold-shouldered me from then on.' She sighed. 'Then they went to America and he forgot all about me.' She thought of Imogen, out there, so close to her father—

'But he loves you. You can tell, from the way he looks at you. It's as if he can't see anyone else in the room.'

'And neither could Ruby,' said Ginny, getting into her costume, urging Jessie to do the same. 'I'll bet his sister has something to do with keeping you apart.' Ginny fixed her headdress on with pins, leaning into the mirror to fiddle with the loose strands of her hair.

'She's her mother's daughter,' Frances said, shrugging. There was a knock on the door and Chip gave them their cue. 'She will always be his sister – and I can't afford to battle with her. And I have —' She was about to say she had Imogen to think of but checked herself.

'Have what?' Jessie put her foot on her chair, fastened the strap on her shoe.

Frances tried to think of something. 'Yet to meet Mr Right.'

'I think you've already met him,' Ginny said, as she walked out into the corridor. Jessie followed her, leaving the door ajar.

Frances fixed her jewelled headdress in place and went up into the wings. Jessie was onstage, falling in love with the forbidden Aladdin. Joe was waiting in the wings, dressed in black and silver, an extravagant turban on his head. His dark eyebrows had been thickened and shaped and he looked menacing, even though he'd confessed to not feeling it. They had all worked hard in rehearsals, Joe most of all, learning to be bad when it was against his nature. Frances peered through the spyhole, watching the audience. Ruby was scowling, seated between Johnny and Jack, while a few rows behind them, Imogen sat with Patsy, enchanted, her face aglow as Princess Jessie sang 'Someone to Watch Over Me'. When the song ended, she clapped her little hands in delight and Frances wished for all the world that the make-believe could last forever.

* * *

When the curtain came down at the interval, Johnny and Ruby
were led from the auditorium, Audrey walking alongside Ruby,
obviously enjoying the attention that celebrity engendered. Ruby
was playing her part. She smiled and waved, signed autographs,
blew kisses, transforming the energy of her rage into being larger
than life. It was what people expected of them: to be happy and gay
all the time – for how else could they entertain if they didn't hide
their own sadness?

Ruby's face was a tight smile as Audrey introduced her to a
rather round woman and her equally round husband. He was
sweating profusely, mopping his head with a handkerchief. Ruby
gave him a limp handshake and she flashed her eyes at Johnny, who
swept in to rescue her, taking her by the elbow. 'Sorry to steal you
away, little sis, but we need to leave for our own show. Would you
excuse us?' He beamed at the couple, said goodbye to Audrey and
Jack and hurried Ruby outside to where their car was waiting.
Johnny opened the door and Ruby slid onto the seat. He dashed
round to the other side and got in beside her. 'Thank you.'

She stared out of the window. 'What for?'

'Staying.'

* * *

When they arrived outside the Palace, they waited in the car until
the driver opened the doors. Ruby stepped out onto the pavement.
The air was full of smoke from the factories around them and the
odious stench of fish. She'd thought she'd got used to it, but now it
stank stronger than ever and at that moment she hated it. Johnny
was waiting by the stage door. Well, he could wait a little longer.
Her head was spinning, trying to make sense of it all. That after all

these years he had found Frances, here – had chosen this theatre because of her. She pulled her stole about her, held on to the brooch. How she wished Mother was here: she could tell her how frightened she was, frightened of Mickey Harper, of Frances, of losing the last person in the world who loved her. She breathed in, hating the smell, looked down at the pavement, at her shoes that glittered with diamanté. It all felt so stupid here, so false, and she was keenly aware of how ridiculous she was, how out of place. But where did she fit? Who was she without Johnny? She lifted her head and made her way to where Johnny was waiting and stood with him for a moment, understanding now, when she hadn't before. There had been something different about him and now she knew what it was. She gave a slight nod of her head and he opened the theatre door. Stepping inside, she floated past Jeff at the stage door office in a trance, her heels echoing in the emptiness.

'Miss Randolph, your mail,' Jeff said, as she opened the door to the corridor. She turned ashen. Jeff was holding a large brown envelope and a few smaller white ones. Johnny had the key to their room and reached up to take them, but Ruby moved quickly, snatching them from Jeff's hand. The handwriting on the large envelope was one she'd come to recognise. Her fingers were trembling and she couldn't breathe; her legs couldn't hold her up. Johnny swept forward, taking her by the elbow, and hurried her into their room where she collapsed onto her chair, still gripping the envelopes tightly. Johnny went to take them from her, but she managed to pull her hand away. The smaller envelopes fell to the floor and when he bent to pick them up, she slid the brown envelope face down on the dressing table.

'What happened?' He tossed the letters onto the dressing table. Her breath was coming hard and fast, and she placed her fist on her breastbone. He went to the sink on the back wall, brought her a glass of water.

'I don't know,' she lied. 'I suddenly felt faint.'

'This is all my fault. It's the shock. I should have told you about Frances, but there never seemed to be the right time and to be honest, there's nothing much to tell.' She gave him a small smile and he ran his hand over her cheek, pushed her hair back from her face. She reached up, rested her hand on his. There was never a right time for bad news, was there? 'I didn't want to hurt you, Ruby. Please believe that.'

She should tell him about the photos, the letters. Why had her mother made her save them? She'd never understood. Was she going to give them to him at some point? Is that what she was meant to do? It was too late to ask. Nausea swept over her and she leaned forward, her hand on the dressing table, saw the envelope again. She looked at Johnny through the mirror.

'I need something to eat. Would you get me something, a cracker? Something small?'

'I don't like to leave you...' He squatted beside her, gently taking hold of her hand. She bit down on her lip. 'Oh, Ruby, what are you doing to yourself?'

Ruby thought he wouldn't care so much if he knew about Mickey, about the blackmail. He would get Frances to take her place, just as her mother had warned her. Frances was a better dancer, even Ruby knew that.

'Please.' She forced herself to smile at him.

He picked up some change from the table, hesitated. 'I'll be as quick as I can.'

She waited until the door clicked shut then stood with her back to it. Her fingers trembled as she tore at the envelope. Inside were two photographs of Ruby, one where she was lying on a bed, naked, save for a sheet that was pulled across her middle. In the other photograph, she was minus the sheet. She looked in the envelope again and withdrew a note in Mickey Harper's hand. *Enjoying your time at the Palace? Coming up for a few days. Would be lovely to see more of you.*

Her hands were shaking uncontrollably as she pushed it back in, along with the photos. Johnny must never see, never know. He would hate her, loathe her for what she had done. And if he found out about the letters, what then? She'd only been doing as her mother told her but would he believe her? Now that he'd found Frances, he would leave her. And what would she do without him?

* * *

The entire company assembled onstage for the finale as the audience called and cheered their approval. Frances peered out into the auditorium. Imogen was standing up from her seat, she and Colly side by side, clapping, jumping up and down. That was what panto was all about, setting off on a magic carpet ride to a land of dreams, where good conquers all. As the curtain came down for the final time, she hurried offstage, eager to get out front to be with her before they caught the bus back to Waltham.

* * *

In the dressing room, Jessie flung herself into her chair and Ginny stepped out of her finale costume and hung it up neatly, everything slow and measured. Jessie hadn't even taken her costume off and Frances was at the door.

'You're in a rush to get to the bar.' Jessie picked up a rag and dipped it into the cream, wiping off her dark make-up, thick black and orange appearing on the cloth.

'I want to say goodbye to Patsy before she leaves.'

Patsy was waiting in the foyer as arranged and Imogen and Colly rushed forward, throwing their arms about her. She caught hold of them and ran her hand over Imogen's hair. Imogen tipped up her head and smiled, her eyes shining, and Frances yearned to leave with her, to leave everything behind and walk into another life, one in which she was always with Imogen. Patsy and Bobby stood back as people pushed past them to the exit.

'It was wonderful, Franny.' She took hold of Colly's hand. 'The kids loved it.' She leaned close, whispered. 'I saw the Randolphs.'

Frances tensed. 'Did they see you?'

'I doubt it. And he wouldn't remember me. We only met a couple of times.'

Frances held on to Imogen, the small hands warm in hers, and squatted down beside her. 'Did you have fun, my darling? I saw you singing when Widow Twankey had the big song sheet at the end. Did you like it?'

Imogen nodded excitedly, nestling close to her mother. Frances ran her hand around her child's face but Imogen looked beyond her, eyes shining, her smile growing wider. She held out her arm and pointed.

'The princess!' Frances froze then struggled back to her feet.

'Jessie!' Frances stepped towards her, hoping to hide Imogen, knowing it was already too late. Jessie stared at Imogen, then Patsy, Bobby and Colly in turn. Patsy took Imogen's hand in her own. People pushed about them and there were icy blasts as the doors were opened and closed. She tried to relax. 'This is my friend Patsy – and the children.'

'Lovely to meet you, Jessie, but we must dash or we'll miss our bus.' Patsy turned her back and was off through the door, pulling the children with her.

'Ow, Mum!' Colly called out as she jostled them through the doors, pushing past a couple of old ladies who were blocking the doorway. Imogen turned her head, smiling at Jessie with admiration. Jessie watched them as they went out into the darkness.

Frances galvanised herself. 'I'll see you later, Jessie. In the bar.'

Jessie nodded mutely, and Frances hurried through the doors, thankful to be out in the street. It was freezing and she wrapped her arms around herself, and dashed across the road to join Patsy at the bus stop.

'Oh, God, she knows!'

Patsy reached out to her. 'Is that a bad thing?' The bus was coming down the hill, the thin slits of the headlamps showing as it made its way towards them.

Frances blew out a long breath. 'I have no idea.'

* * *

Jessie walked through to the bar and pushed herself to the window, stepped through the curtains and pulled them behind her to keep out the light. Over the road, Frances had her back to her and she watched her squat down in front of the little girl, touch her face, hold her. Then she stood up, kissed the top of her head. The little boys said something and she knew from the way Frances moved her body that she was answering them, but Frances didn't kiss them. Jessie stepped back into the bar. The girl was the child in the photo in her bedroom. Imogen, the girl Frances had said was her niece. But it was a lie. It wasn't Patsy who was so important every Sunday. It was the girl.

* * *

The bar was warm and welcoming. Jack and Audrey were moving through the crowd, chatting, smiling. There was much shaking of hands and slapping of backs. Frances stood by the door, peering from side to side. Ginny waved to her and she eased her way through the crowd. Jessie handed her a glass. 'Got you a port and lemon.'

'Thanks.' Frances held her gaze. Ginny's attention was else-where. Frances and Jessie looked in the same direction. Joe Taplow was leaning against the wall, staring into his pint, gangly, awkward.

Ginny glanced at them, blushed. She picked up her drink. 'I think he'd rather be anywhere but here.'

He looked up and saw them and Frances waved him over. It was a cowardly thing to do, but it would stop Jessie asking any awkward questions for the time being. Joe pulled up a stool and sat beside Ginny. Bob Bailey had been watching and he walked over, stood next to Frances.

'Where's your partner?' Frances tried to be relaxed but knew she was overcompensating. How much longer would Imogen be a secret now?

'Giving me a wide berth.'

'Oh?'

He shrugged. 'Something we don't see eye to eye on. Nothing much. Can't be mates all the time, can we?' Joe drew another stool close and Bob sat down. Frances moved up a little. Jack came over and Bob and Joe got to their feet.

'I wonder if any of you are able to help.'

'We will if we can,' Bob offered. 'What's the problem?'

'The children's home in Grimsby have been in touch. They usually have films for the kids on a weekend but their projector's broken and can't be fixed. They've asked around, and ours is too large for them to use, but when I heard about it, I thought – well, I hoped, as it's almost Christmas – we could do something a bit special for them.'

'I'll go,' Frances said, sensing escape.

'Me too,' Jessie agreed. 'We can do something together?' Frances could hardly refuse. 'What about Ginny?' They looked over to her.

Joe was doing simple tricks with a penny, Ginny his audience, the happiest they'd seen her in weeks.

'Can't let these girls go unaccompanied, Jack,' Bob said. 'I'll go and Sid will too. I'll make sure of it.'

'That's good of you, especially at such short notice.'

'Not at all,' Jessie said. 'I count my blessings that I've got my mum and my brother. Even more so at Christmas.'

Frances looked away. 'I'm going home to get an early night. Busy day tomorrow.' She put her glass down on the nearest table and Jessie did the same, slinging her bag over her shoulder.

'I'll come with you.'

* * *

Jessie didn't say a word until they got into bed. Ginny had remained in Jessie's old room, while Frances and Jessie shared the double bed. It was cold and they layered themselves in jumpers and woolly socks over their pyjamas. Frances turned off the bedside lamp.

Grace had put a hot water bottle into the bed and they got in, feeling the warmth on their feet.

'God bless your mam,' Frances said, when her teeth had stopped chattering.

They lay in the darkness until eventually Jessie said, 'Why didn't you tell me?'

Frances shifted in the bed. 'Jessie, I...'

Jessie sat up, leaned across Frances and put the lamp back on. 'The little girl with Patsy. She's not your niece, is she?'

Frances sat up, pulling the blankets up to her chin. Her breath was a cloud.

'Imogen is my daughter.' Her voice caught with the pain of it, with the lie of it. It had been a whisper that sounded like an explosion, but Jessie hadn't flinched.

'Why did you keep her a secret? Why?' Jessie shook her head, not understanding.

'To protect her.'

There was no point in holding back any more. Jessie listened as she told her of how Johnny had gone off to America, promising to send a ticket that never came; of how she'd discovered she was pregnant, had hoped and prayed that a letter would come but nothing ever did.

'Does he know of Imogen?'

'He can't do. I told him in my letters but it's obvious to me now that he didn't get them. If he had, he would know, wouldn't he?'

'How on earth did you manage?'

'If it hadn't been for Patsy and Colin...' She stopped, finding it hard to express what they had done for her. 'I can never repay them for all they've done for me.'

Jessie clasped her hand. 'One day you will, Frances. We all get our turn.'

26

It seemed she had talked half the night and lain awake the rest of it, for when dawn broke Frances was exhausted. She watched a shaft of cold morning light filter through the gap left in the curtains. It was a habit she couldn't break, for somewhere in the darkness there had to be the hope of light. A new beginning. Her nose was cold and she hunched the blankets up about her shoulders. She'd expected to feel relieved that Jessie knew but instead she felt afraid. As if she was losing control. She sat up on her pillows, adjusted the blanket. Jessie groaned, turned away from the wall.

'Are you awake?'

'Uh-uh.' Her voice was croaky. She coughed, scratched her head, pulled herself upright, tugging the bedclothes about her. 'It's freezing.'

'We're a pair of daft beggars, aren't we? Me and you scrunched up in here and Ginny getting a bed to herself.' Jessie yawned, stretching her arms out of the blankets, she shivered, tucking them up to her chin again.

'You could swap.'

'Never.' Jessie yawned again, and Frances did the same.

'She's doing okay, isn't she?' Frances said, thinking of how Ginny seemed to be finding her way again. Grace and Geraldine had been kind, although Geraldine couldn't help voicing her disapproval in small ways. She gripped Jessie's arm. 'Please don't say anything. About Imogen.'

'I won't.' Jessie frowned. 'I promised. Although I think you're wrong. Mum and Geraldine would be more cross that you've struggled on and kept it from them. I know I am.'

Frances couldn't bear it; this was what she'd been afraid of. She threw back the blankets, wanting to move, not think... She pulled on her dressing gown.

'But there never seemed to be a right time.'

'There never is. For anything. Only time.'

'That's a bit profound this early in the morning.' Frances drew back the curtains. The sky was heavy with dark clouds and rain ran from the gutters.

Jessie slid to the side of the bed and wiggled her feet into her slippers. 'I used to think I had all the time in the world to do all the things I wanted to.' She stared towards the window. 'I'm frightened for Harry every day, every single minute. I think of all the time I've wasted already.'

Frances picked up her washbag, wrapping the cord around her fingers. 'I can't say anything to comfort you.'

Jessie got up. 'It's the hardest thing, isn't it? Having no words of comfort.'

Frances opened the door. 'Sometimes just being there for each other is enough.'

* * *

The fire was lit in the room downstairs. Eddie was sitting at the table with a mug of tea and Grace was standing at the cooker;

Ginny was washing her smalls in the kitchen sink.

Frances put her washbag on the dresser and stood in front of the fire, warming her hands. She turned her back to it, letting the warmth hit her legs. Grace placed two boiled eggs in front of Eddie and Jessie fetched the plate of toast their mother had made for him and put it on the table, taking a slice for herself. She pulled out a chair next to the fire and slumped into it.

'What time do you have to be at the children's home, you two?'

'Ten.'

The front door opened and Dolly's voice rang out: 'Coo-ee.' An icy blast accompanied her as she hurried in and closed the door. She unwrapped her scarf and pulled off her gloves, taking a note from her pocket, which she handed to Jessie.

'I didn't think you'd want to wait. Mike took a phone call at the theatre. He popped it over to Dad.'

Jessie opened it. 'Harry's got leave!' She flung her arms around Dolly then did a little dance in the room and Frances laughed. Eddie stuffed the last piece of toast in his mouth, got to his feet and took his jacket from the back of his chair.

'Do you think he'll come in his car? He might not be able to get petrol.' He took his cap from the dresser behind him and pulled it hard on his head.

Jessie read the note again. 'I don't care if he comes in his plane and lands it on the beach!'

Grace was smiling and Frances could see the love and pride shining from her face. 'I think that's a bit extreme, Jessie love.'

'I don't give a fig.' Jessie laughed. 'Just to see him again. It's the best Christmas present ever.'

Eddie leaned over to kiss Grace, and as he did so she pulled his cap over his ears. 'Scarf?'

He pulled it from his pocket, grinning, and wrapped it around his neck. He called goodbye to Ginny and waved, said the same to the other girls. They heard him whistling as he opened the front door and went out into the street.

'When is Harry's leave?' Grace got up and began clearing the table.

'This weekend. He's hoping to be here later tonight.'

* * *

Dolly walked with them to the theatre. It was hard to tell whether it was colder outside than in. The forecast had said snow was on the way. The shops along the main road had put in extra effort with their decorations, hoping to entice people to throw caution to the wind and spend on their loved ones. The three of them stopped briefly to admire a scene: a sleigh piled with gaily wrapped presents and a tailor's dummy dressed as Father Christmas. Imogen was getting excited and the boys too. They had come home from school with little gifts they'd made, pictures they'd painted.

Imogen would be ready for school soon, something else she needed to think about. There would be no more travelling for a while. Not for her, anyway. Inside the dressing room, they gathered their things together.

'Which costumes should we take?'

Dolly went through the garments on the rail.

'Take this one.' She held out a lilac full-length dress that shimmered with diamanté and sequins. 'The kids will love all the jewels. It makes you look like a proper princess.' Frances recalled Imogen's little face at the panto. It had been Jessie that she'd fallen in love with; at the bus stop she could talk of nothing else. Frances began putting her make-up into a vanity case.

'Shall we share?' Jessie came over, adding her sticks of greasepaint to Frances's. 'We might as well make it as easy as we can for ourselves.'

Dolly covered the costumes with cloth and helped Jessie fold them into a suitcase.

'This is going to be awkward,' Frances said, as the pile accumulated. 'By the time we've got our bags and gas masks we'll look like a couple of pack horses.'

'We could go in our costumes,' Jessie offered, grinning.

'Well, good luck with that. I'm not going in chiffon harem pants and bare feet. I'll get chilblains.' The three of them laughed and once their things were organised, they sat down to wait for Sid and Bob to arrive.

27

Frances pushed the bell and the four of them waited in the porch of the children's home. They'd managed to avoid the rain but would certainly meet it on the way home. At least they weren't bedraggled before the show, that was the main thing. A woman came to the door, hurrying them inside.

'I can't thank you enough for stepping in like this.' She was tall and smartly dressed, her grey hair set in curls and brushed away from a broad forehead. 'Mr Holland has been beyond generous. You all have. This is a special treat indeed. Oh, Irene Lewis.' She held out her hand and they shook it in turn. She was brisk and efficient and reminded Jessie of Miss Symonds again. She was going to come and see the pantomime with Norman and Beryl. Would Aunt Iris come too? No, definitely not. Aunt Iris thought the theatre and its people lacking in morals. What would she have thought of Ginny? And Frances…

They followed Irene into a large room with parquet flooring and a small raised platform at one end, the high walls decorated with Christmas murals the children had created. Heavy dark curtains hung at the high windows and a rosewood piano that had seen better days was pushed against the wall. Jessie walked over to it and played a few notes. She grimaced.

'I know. It's a bit flat.' Irene raised her eyebrows.

'Doesn't matter.' Jessie was cheerful. 'We'll sing louder and Bob has his ukulele. Although what Christmas carols sound like on a uke is anyone's guess!'

'You'll soon find out,' Bob said with a smile.

Sid went to the end of the room, hopped up onto the platform and jumped up and down to test the floor. He walked over to each side, taking in the space they had to work with.

Frances held up her case. 'Any chance of somewhere to change?'

'You can use my room,' Irene said and took them back to the entrance, where a typist was working in a reception office.

'Can I get you a warm drink?' Irene asked. 'It's very cold out there. Tea?'

'That would be lovely.' The girls put down their bags and removed their outdoor clothing. Jessie peered out onto the street then settled herself down on the sofa. Sid sat next to her. Bob was reading the certificates on the wall.

'This brings back some memories. None of them good ones.' Sid was looking about the walls, which were decorated with long photographs of children who were lined up outside the building, some sitting cross-legged on the floor. Above the desk hung a portrait of King George.

'Were you in an orphanage?' Jessie was curious.

'In and out.' He folded his arms. 'When my mum couldn't keep us, we went in. When things got better, we came out again. Bit like the "Hokey Cokey".' He smiled. 'Did it a few times. She did her best, bless her, but times were tough back then.' Jessie glanced at Frances. Was that something she'd had to do, with Imogen? How little she'd known about her friend.

* * *

They took it in turns to use the mirror to put on their make-up, using a lighter hand than was needed in the theatre. They heard the children lining up outside, the sound of excited chatter, someone barking at them to shush, then silence, save for the sound of shoes as the children walked on. Sid and Bob stripped off and got into their policemen costumes.

The girls called 'Break a leg' after them as they left the room and finished getting ready themselves. Out in the hall, they sat on chairs meant for visitors and waited for their turn. Sid and Bob were working the kids to a crescendo, the sounds of laughter coming in waves that got bigger and bigger.

'Nothing can beat that sound, can it?' Jessie peered through a gap in the door. The children were sitting cross-legged on the floor, boys on one side, girls the other, teachers on chairs along the sides of the room. They were all laughing, some of them wiping away the tears from their eyes. She smiled, remembering how her father always told her that entertainment lifted people away from their problems and miseries, allowed them to forget how bad things were. She put her hand to her heart. Another Christmas without him. At least she remembered him, would always remember him. And they had Mum.

'The kids are loving it.' Jessie let go of the door and sat down.

Frances was pacing up and down. 'I can hear.'

Jessie's smile disappeared. What an idiot she was. Frances was thinking of Imogen, wasn't she? Frances sat down next to her. 'Why don't you bring Imogen to Barkhouse Lane?'

'Don't, Jessie. Please.' Frances got up and resumed her pacing.

'You should be together. It would be easier.'

'Easier for who?' Frances stopped. 'I have to think about what's best for Imogen. That's my first, last and only thought.' She sat down again. Bob sounded a hooter and the children squealed with delight. 'Imogen is safe where she is. Settled. I don't know what I'm going to do after the panto.' She began wringing her hands. 'If I sign up with ENSA, it'll mean going away again and I'll have taken her away from Patsy for nothing. And she'll need to start school at some point.' She sighed. 'You wouldn't understand.'

Jessie was affronted. She folded her arms, staring at the entrance doors. The rain was coming down now, beating against the windows. 'That's a bit unfair.'

'I didn't mean to be.' She sighed again. 'But you can't possibly know how it feels.'

'Maybe not.' Jessie sat up. 'But I know what it is to miss a parent. One that you can never have back. I know I'm older, but it's still the same – we all want our parents.'

'We do.' They were silent.

Thoughts tumbled in Jessie's head and she was shocked. Surely Frances had told her parents? She turned to Frances, who was looking at her, almost as if she knew what Jessie was going to ask next.

'They don't know,' Frances said. 'I couldn't go back to Ireland. It would break their hearts.'

'But it...'

Frances was shaking her head. 'Don't, Jessie. Please don't tell me how lovely it would all be. How the roses would be around the door, the sheep gambolling in the fields. It's not like that.'

'They write to you all the time. Your brothers, your sisters – do none of them know?'

Frances looked down the long dark corridor. 'No one.'

'But...'

Frances put up her hand to silence her. 'I'm not talking about it. We need to concentrate.'

Jessie sat on her hands and stared at the floor. She couldn't bear to think of Imogen without her mum. It had been bad enough leaving her own mum in the summer – and she wasn't three years old.

* * *

It was a wonderful afternoon. The children were delightful; they listened when Jessie and Frances sang songs from the pantomime and then Jessie sat at the piano and encouraged the children to join in with Christmas carols. The sight of their happy faces as they sang 'Jingle Bells' was one Jessie would never forget.

Irene gave a lovely thank you speech at the end of the performance. She led the children in three cheers and the hoorays nearly lifted the roof off. They walked back into the office, applause ringing in their ears, and got changed. Bob sat in his vest and trousers, sweat still leaking from his chest and back, dripping down his temple.

'Beats a lie-in any day of the week.' There was no dissent.

* * *

Johnny left Ruby to sleep, asking Mrs Frame to make sure she ate something when she awoke. He took his heavy coat and hat from the stand in the hall and wrapped his plum cashmere scarf about his neck. The temperature had dropped these last few days and he pulled up his lapels, head down against the rain as he headed for Brighowgate. He'd called the theatre that morning to thank Jack for his hospitality the day before, and he'd told him of the girls' visit to the children's home. He took a shortcut through the park. It was empty, the lake still, no brightly coloured yachts, no wooden battleships patrolling today. Staying in Grimsby had made him fully aware of the battles that were already taking place. The army was heading south, but the boats and ships had already suffered losses. He didn't even want to contemplate how cold it must be in the North Atlantic. It was cold here but not as cold as New York. They had been there the Christmas after Mother had died and it should have been a triumph, but it had been bleak. Was that the start of it? He crossed the road. A Christmas tree was set up in one of the bay windows, bright and cheerful. He should get a tree for the house; it might cheer Ruby a little. He pushed his hands into his pockets; he had no idea what to do any more. The only thing that gave him any kind of hope was Frances. The sky grew darker and he heard a distant rumble of thunder and quickened his pace. He stopped in front of the children's home, the rain running off the brim of his hat. Lights were on in the office and he pulled the front door open and walked into the lobby. Kids were being led out of a hall, a long line of boys looking straight ahead. He knocked on the open door marked 'Office', and saw Frances through the door leading to another room. She saw him. Jessie leaned forward and said something to Frances he couldn't hear, and came out to him. She was fastening the buttons on her coat.

'She'll be out in a minute.' Irene came from the hall. She furrowed her brow. Johnny was used to the expression, the sudden recognition that they knew him but not from where. He held out his hand.

'Johnny Randolph. I'm a friend of the girls.'

'Of course. Would you like to sit down?'

He shook his head. 'I'll stand, if I'm not in the way.'

Jessie went back in, came out carrying cases.

'Can I help?'

She grinned. 'I wish you could.'

Bob and Sid followed, Frances lagging behind. 'Johnny.' Sid shook his hand with vigour.

'Good fun?' Johnny asked.

'It was. The kids were great.'

Jessie stepped forward. 'I'll take the bags to the bus stop. You two need to talk.'

'Here. Let me.' Bob took the case from her and the three of them made to leave.

As they opened the door, Frances called out. 'I'll catch you up.' She wound her scarf around her neck and adjusted her beret. He waited while she put on her gloves.

'I came to apologise for yesterday.'

Irene was walking towards them.

'Not here.' Frances smiled at Irene. 'Thank you, Irene. It's been a wonderful afternoon.'

Frances put the strap of her gas mask over her shoulder and Irene returned to her office. Johnny could hear her telling the secretary about the show. Frances started walking towards the door and he rushed ahead, held it open. She shivered as she stepped out into the air, pulling her scarf up about her face so that he could only see her eyes. Had she expected him to kiss her? She waited, watching the retreating backs of her friends as they headed for the bus station. The rain had steadied into drizzle and droplets fell softly; she dipped her head.

'I wondered if you'd have dinner with me?' His breath swirled about him as he waited for her to answer.

'What about Ruby? She won't like it.' There was no hint of anger in her voice and for that he was grateful.

'It's not about Ruby, Frances. It's about us.'

A bus drove past, its engine slurring as it slowed, the brakes squealing, exhaust fumes filling the air as it went by. He took hold of her gloved hand. 'Have supper with me, tonight, after the show?' She withdrew her hand, put it in her pocket, looked up into his eyes. Could she see how much he loved her?

She nodded abruptly, then turned away, walking towards the

bus stop. It felt as though his heart would burst and he hurried beside her. 'I'll call the theatre, send a car when the curtain comes down.'

'Will you?' She didn't believe him. Well, he'd prove her wrong. Something had happened, he didn't know what, but the only way to find out was to talk about it.

'The car will be there, I promise.' She waited at the kerb, looked both ways and crossed. Another bus went past, briefly obscuring her. He remained where he was as she joined the others and he watched them get on the bus, Bob and Sid taking the cases. They moved along the aisle, took seats. Frances was sitting by the window. He could make out Jessie nudging her, then she waved. He took his hand from his pocket, held it up to her, turned around and headed home.

* * *

As the bus moved off, Frances pulled the scarf from her face. It had been so hot she could hardly breathe. Jessie tugged at her arm.

'Well, what did he say?' she whispered. Bob and Sid were sitting behind them.

'He asked me to supper.'

Jessie sat back. 'Please tell me you said yes?'

'I did.'

Jessie let out a long breath. 'Well, thank the Lord for that!'

28

Ruby had slept for most of the morning. When she eventually came downstairs, Mrs Frame had hovered around like a mother hen while she ate. She cleaned her plate and regretted it. Johnny came in.

'Where have you been?'

'To the children's home.'

'For the children?' She stared at him.

He sat down opposite her. 'To see Frances. She was doing a little show there with her friend, and Bailey and North. I'm having supper with her tonight.'

Ruby was silent. Johnny was talking but she couldn't hear what he was saying. She shouldn't have eaten anything. Her stomach churned and she could feel the acid pumping into it, burning her insides.

'I need to get ready for the show.' She pushed back her chair, ran upstairs to the bathroom and locked the door. Her heart was pounding so hard that it hurt her chest and she knelt in front of the lavatory and stuck her fingers down her throat. When it was over, she sat with her back to the cold tiles. The emptiness felt good and she remained there until she felt able to move.

* * *

Despite everything, the show went well. She concentrated hard, feeling light, as if she was floating. The audience was warm and giving and the applause was a balm, soothing, nourishing, and she wished it could last forever. Johnny took the bows and they came back for three encores. He wasted no time getting changed.

'Jeff will call a car when you're ready to go home.' Ruby watched his lips moving, his reflection in the mirror, agreeing, not knowing if it was the right thing to do. He splashed himself with cologne, leaned down and kissed her cheek. She could see the excitement in his eyes and, for the briefest of moments, she hated him for being so happy. He put his hand on her shoulder, standing behind her and she reached up and took hold of it. It was warm and strong and safe and she wanted him to stay. 'I hope it goes well.'

He squeezed her hand. 'Thanks, Ruby. That means such a lot.' He adjusted his tie and reached for his coat, then he held his hat in his hands, turning it by the brim. 'Are you sure you'll be all right?'

'Of course.' She blew him a kiss as he left.

She sat for a while as other members of the cast and crew called out as they left the theatre. Reaching into her bag, she took out a half-bottle of gin and drank it back. It warmed her throat, then her stomach. She pulled a rag from the pile, taking off her face, her smile smearing against the white linen.

Someone knocked on the door and she called for them to come in. Jeff put his head around the door.

'Old friend here to see you, Miss Randolph.' He stepped back – and Mickey Harper walked in, putting out his arms.

'Ruby, darling!' He came towards her, embraced her, and she

tensed her body, trying to make it smaller. She smiled over his shoulder at Jeff, who was waiting by the door.

'Thanks, Jeff.' She pulled away from Mickey, hating the smell of him, the sight of him. 'How lovely to see you.' She gestured for him to sit down on the battered sofa. Jeff closed the door as he left and Mickey sat back, his legs spread wide. He looked about the room.

'Not your usual standard, eh, Ruby? How's it going?'

She sank into her chair, her back to the mirror, fearing her hammering heart would break her ribs.

'What are you doing here?' She struggled to keep her voice steady, as if she didn't care.

He spread his arms along the back of the sofa.

'I waited till Johnny left. I don't think he likes me.' He checked his nails, picked at his thumb.

'I wonder why?'

Mickey tilted his head, leering. 'He might not like you, either, if he knows what you've been up to.'

She twisted away from him and began putting on fresh make-up. 'He won't find out.'

Mickey leaned forward, let his hands hang between his legs. 'You've got the money, then?'

She patted powder on her nose. She mustn't let him see how scared she was.

'Almost.' She took out her lipstick, applied it. 'You'll just have to wait a little longer.' He got up and stood behind her, his hands on her shoulders and she wanted to be sick.

'I can't wait, Ruby. It's cost me to come and find you.' He laughed, baring his teeth. 'Did you think you could run away and hide?' He shook his head. 'Tut, tut, tut, poor little Ruby.' He pulled an envelope from the inside pocket of his coat. It had Johnny's name on it. 'Pity he wasn't here to collect it himself. Perhaps tomorrow?' She snatched it from him and he shrugged his shoulders.

'Plenty more where they came from. Shame you haven't got the money. You could've had the negatives.' He fastened his coat. 'I'm at the Blenheim. Sweet dreams, gal.'

When she was certain he'd gone, she stumbled to her feet, ripped off her robe and got into her dress, shaking uncontrollably. She rummaged in her bag for the gin, and emptied the bottle. Jeff would get more from the Palace Buffet next door. She sank back onto her chair. Her make-up was ruined and she reached for another cloth; there was nothing she could do but start again...

* * *

A car pulled up outside the hotel and the driver hurried round and opened the door for Frances. It was a far cry from earlier that day when they'd struggled on the bus to the children's home. She got out and walked towards the entrance. A liveried doorman opened the door and she hurried inside; he pulled the heavy curtain behind her. It was bright in the foyer and she blinked until she became accustomed to the light. On the right, a girl in uniform waited at the reception desk and Frances walked past her to the cloakroom, where she handed over her thick coat. She took a deep breath and headed for the dining room. It was fairly quiet – most of the diners would have eaten long ago and were either in bed or drinking at the bar. She gave her name to the man at the restaurant entrance and was led to a small booth. Johnny got to his feet.

'You came!' He seemed surprised. The waiter pulled out the chair and she sat down.

'You didn't think I would?' The waiter gave them a menu and she opened it, watching Johnny's face.

'I wasn't sure.'

She read the entrées. 'That I'd keep my word?'

He didn't answer, and looked at the menu. He asked Frances

what she'd like and ordered the wine. The waiter returned with it, waited for Johnny to approve, then slipped into the background. He raised his glass and she did likewise. 'To the future.'

She clinked her glass to his but didn't say anything.

He put his glass down, touched his knife and fork. 'Who knows what kind of future that will be. For any of us.'

'Indeed.'

He opened his mouth to speak, stopped, started again. Eventually he said, 'Is there anyone else?'

She took a sip of her wine, which was rich and smooth on her throat. There would always be someone else, but that was not what he was asking.

'Bob?'

She laughed. 'No. No one else.'

His shoulders softened; he gave her a gentle smile.

'And you?'

He toyed with his glass. 'There were girls. But no one special.' He paused, held her gaze. 'No one like you.'

He'd have to work harder, rolling out cheesy lines like that. She didn't want to be loved and left again; she wasn't sure she wanted to be loved at all. She'd managed on her own so far but Patsy's words niggled at her. Imogen was his daughter too.

They talked and it got easier. She enjoyed his company and she'd missed it. He asked her what she had been doing since they'd left and she told him parts, but not all. She talked fondly of Lil, of working at the Fisherman's when the theatre had closed, of her lodgings at Barkhouse Lane, how kind people had been to her. She asked of America. He told her of Ruby.

'Is that why you came back? I'd thought you'd been gallant and returned to fight for king and country.'

'Ouch!'

She was embarrassed. 'I wasn't being rude. I couldn't think what else it could be. War has been on the cards for a long time and America's safe. For now, at least, and you were successful.'

'I intend to enlist.'

He looked ashamed and she hadn't meant to make him feel small.

'You don't have to explain.'

He wiped his mouth with his napkin. 'But I do. Mother was ill and came home. Seriously ill. She didn't tell us and when we found out it was too late.' He looked away from her, stared at the painting of a trawler on the wall. 'Ruby took it badly. Very badly.' He paused. His smile was sad. It had obviously been a painful time for them both. At least she still had both her parents and she could go back – one day...

'That's why we're here. Well, one of the reasons.' He gazed into her eyes. 'I've invested with Bernie Blackwood and Jack Holland – in theatres. I needed Ruby to find a home, away from London and all its distractions... I wanted to make sure she's looked after. If anything should happen to me...'

There was so much she wanted to say to him. Where could she start?

'I waited, you know; I waited a long time.'

He nodded. 'Me too.'

'You said you'd send a ticket, that you wanted me to join you.'

'Oh, darling, please believe me. I sent a ticket. It was almost the first thing I did. I had a huge argument with my mother about it—'

The two of them looked at each other. 'And did you post it to me.'

He shook his head. 'I left it with the concierge at the hotel.'

'Ah. You didn't tip enough.'

'Or not as much as my mother.' He dropped his napkin on the table, his face darkening. Frances wanted to weep. His mother would never know of the damage she had done.

The waiter took the plates away and they ordered coffee. She thought of the picture Imogen had drawn at Patsy's.

'Does Ruby know you're here with me?'

He took out his cigarettes, offered her one and she took it. 'She does. I told her. No more secrets.' He sparked his lighter, held it to her and she leaned into the flame, then sat back.

'You're deep in thought,' he said.

She fiddled with her napkin on the table. How she wished she could turn back time! He leaned forward and took her hand. It felt so good to touch his skin, to be so close, and she knew it would be easy to let down her guard, to let love in again. He was earnest and she couldn't think of anything to say, wanting to hold on to the moment with nothing of the past to spoil it. He screwed his cigarette into the ashtray, looked beyond her. There was a disturbance in the foyer. They could hear a woman's voice. Johnny got up.

'Ruby!' He scrambled to his feet as Ruby staggered in, swaying wildly. One of the female attendants was trying to talk to her but she swung out her arms, catching the woman on her cheek. Johnny rushed forward. Ruby's fur coat was falling from her shoulders and she hunched it up, losing her footing. Johnny caught her before she fell. Frances came up beside him, unsure of what to do. The pain in his face was unbearable.

'Oh, darling, Johnny.' Ruby's words were slurred and she was dribbling. Johnny hauled her upright and Frances moved forward and took her other side. 'Ha! I knew it was you.' She wiggled her finger at Frances. 'All along, I knew. He loves you. Did you tell her you love her, Johnny? Did he?' She went limp like a rag doll, her legs collapsing. People were coming into the lobby, collecting their coats, staring at the three of them.

'Let's get you home, Ruby,' Frances whispered, coaxing her like a child. Between them they managed to get her to a leather sofa and Frances sat with her, trying to quieten Ruby's incoherent ramblings while Johnny went to organise a car. He returned, grave-faced, and sat down beside his sister. Frances got up to claim her coat, pulled on her beret, stuffing her scarf into her pocket, and went back to them. Johnny was holding Ruby's hand, talking to her in a low voice, their faces close, and she realised then that it was all hopeless, that Ruby would always come between them.

The doorman came forward. 'The car's here, Mr Randolph.'

They helped Ruby to her feet and walked her to the car, made sure she was safe inside it.

'Forgive me, Johnny.' She was reaching out for his arm. 'I didn't know. I had no idea.' Her cheeks were stained with black rivers as her mascara ran. Johnny talked to her, his voice soft, soothing, stroking her face. He leaned forward, asked the driver to wait and closed the door. Frances put on her scarf, her woollen gloves. The temperature had dropped and ice was forming on the windows. Johnny came to her, caught her arm.

'I'm so sorry, Frances. I can't let her go home alone.' It was embarrassing for him and she didn't want to make it worse.

'Ruby needs you. No need to apologise.' He took her hands in his. She looked into his eyes, his sadness evident and she was surprised how much it hurt her. 'It's been a lovely evening, Johnny. Thank you.'

'It hasn't ended the way I wanted it to.' He glanced at the car, turned back to her.

'Take her home,' Frances urged. 'Look after her.' He let out a long sigh, as if he wanted to let go of a huge burden.

'I love you, Frances. I have always loved you.' He kissed her and his kisses were light, then fierce and she gave in to him, the warmth of his body so familiar. It was as if time stopped and the years fell away in the darkness and she longed to stay there, not thinking, only feeling, never wanting it to end. Another car drew up beside them and Johnny released her, kissed her again, briefly this time, the longing clear, and she bit her lip to stop herself from wanting more. Johnny stepped back, moved towards the car and she got in. She wound down the window and he caught her hand again. 'I won't let you go. Not a second time.' He leaned in, kissed her – and for one wild moment she believed him.

* * *

The driver helped Johnny get Ruby into the house. He turned on the gas fire, pulled the easy chair close and sat Ruby in it. She was incoherent, babbling then terrified, sobbing, wailing. She'd never been as bad as this, never. When she had calmed, he laid her on the sofa and covered her with a blanket, propping her head with cushions.

'You won't let him hurt me, will you?'

He put his hand on her head. 'No one will hurt you, Ruby.'

She caught his hand. Her nails dug into him. 'I haven't got the money.'

'What money? For who?' He wanted to be angry with her, but he couldn't. It was his fault she'd got this bad. He should have bought them out of the contract, come home.

'Don't let Mickey get me. Please. Don't let him.'

He stroked her forehead; she was sweating now, her hair damp, and he sat down beside her. 'Mickey's not here. You're quite safe.' He kissed her temple. Their mother had done the same when they were small. His thoughts flicked back to Frances, then to his mother, the ticket to America, the sickening moment in the restaurant when he realised what she'd done. He could have been with Frances all along but that wouldn't have suited Alice. It would have derailed her plans for them. She had controlled their lives more than he'd ever known and look at the two of them now. Ruby was a mess.

'Oh, Johnny,' she whispered. 'I'm sorry. Truly, I am.'

At last she slept and he sat on the floor, his back against the sofa, watching the flames in the fire. Things had been going so well, Frances had been like her old self – the girl he remembered, the girl he loved. Being with her, after all the years of loneliness, made everything else seem small and insignificant. Ruby moaned and he reached up and took her hand in his. In the morning she would be sober and he would find out exactly what she was frightened of.

29

Jessie clasped Harry's hand as they walked along the promenade. He looked smart in his uniform, his dark blue overcoat belted against the wind. She hadn't seen him for ten weeks and he looked changed, older. He had four days' leave and had arrived late on Saturday night, staying with George and Olive, who had kindly offered him a bed. They'd spent the whole of Sunday together, making plans, and were up and out early on Monday to make a start on them. Neither of them had slept much – although Harry was in dire need of it. He was exhausted but he wanted to make the most of every hour that he had with her. He'd been relieved when she'd told him she wasn't going to take Bernie Blackwood's offer, not this time. He hoped she'd turn the next one down too.

They stopped and leaned on the rails. Barbed wire lay in coiled spirals along the sand and the steps were barred with wooden planks, warning signs forbidding them from going any further. The tide was out, way out, but the day was clear and they could see the lighthouse at Spurn Point on the other side of the river.

'It's a far cry from summer, isn't it?'

'A world away, darling.' She moved closer to him, making her teeth chatter with exaggeration. He nudged her and she laughed and kissed him. He was so glad she was his girl. They started walking again and he put his arm about her shoulder. She leaned into him, happy to be close and they made their way down towards the pier, taking in the long walkway that seemed to stretch over the sea. 'Remember when we danced on it, Harry?'

He nodded. 'We were supposed to be dancing in the ballroom, not on the walkway.'

'It was fun, though, wasn't it?'

'It was.' And so different from the way he spent his days now. Being in the air was exhilarating; it still took his breath away, to soar above the fields and towns, the land that he loved, the land they were fighting for. But Jessie – she was his whole world. He pulled her towards him again. Seagulls soared high above them.

'It seems such a long time ago, and it isn't. Not really.' She sounded wistful. He moved his arm, took her hand in his. All he had worried about then was Jessie – did she love him or would she fall for someone else's charms? There was far worse to worry about these days. Like staying alive. She smiled and it made him forget.

'Shall we catch the bus, then? Or keep on walking down memory lane? We've a ring to buy and I have no idea how long it will take you to make up your mind.'

The bus was full and they made their way to the back, delighted to find an empty seat. She sat by the window, pointing things out to him as they headed for Grimsby and when they reached the town hall they got off and walked along Victoria Street, looking in the windows, holding hands. They stopped outside a jeweller that had its name across every window in black and gold lettering: *A. C. Pailthorp*. He studied Jessie's reflection in the glass as she pointed to rings, her eyes shining, wanting to burn her happiness into his heart so that he could carry it with him. Sprigs of holly and ivy were placed among the display and glass baubles in bright colours sat among swathes of gold satin that wound about the trays of diamond rings.

'It looks a little like Aladdin's cave, Harry. Do you think I'll get three wishes?'

He kissed her again, laughing. 'I only want one.'

He guided her inside and she gripped his hand, her excitement palpable. He couldn't stop smiling at her delight as the cases were brought from the window and she tried on rings. She held out her hands, tilting to let the stones catch the light, asking for his opinion.

They settled for one with three diamonds. It fitted perfectly. He put it onto her finger, and she kissed him. 'Happy?'

Jessie stretched out her arm, splaying her fingers, admiring the ring. 'Deliriously.'

'You don't want to change your mind?' He took out his wallet.

She shook her head. 'About the ring?'

He grinned. 'Or me?'

She kissed him again. 'Never.'

Jessie left her gloves off, wanting to keep looking at her diamonds. He laughed. 'I'm glad I made you happy. It means everything to me. You mean everything to me.'

She linked her arm in his as they left the shop. 'I never knew just how much.'

Jessie led him down an alley between the jeweller's and the bank and stepped into a café, tucked away from the main street. A waitress showed them to a table and they sat down and removed their coats, Jessie taking every opportunity to admire her ring, then look at him. They gave their order and he took her hand in his to get her attention, covering the ring so that she looked at him.

'So, what's been happening? The show good?'

'Fun. We're playing to full houses every night. It's glorious. The kids are great and I get to act. Although I have to kiss Kitty Bright on the cheek every night and marry her.'

He laughed. 'As long as it's only pretend. It will be our turn soon. For real.' The waitress brought their order and they tucked in. She asked about his work and he told her as much as he could, as much as he dared. 'We've been night flying.'

She frowned. 'It's dangerous. I can tell from your face.'

'It's all dangerous, Jessie. You have to pay attention. Or...'

'Or what?' She gripped his hand. 'I want to know. Good and bad.'

He explained about having to rely solely on instruments, that you couldn't use the landscape for markers, that it was cold and tiring, made your eyes sore, your brain hurt. 'But I'm good at it. Don't worry, darling. All those hours cooped up in the solicitor's office at your Uncle Norman's has stood me in good stead. My powers of concentration are immense, thanks to him.' It didn't comfort her, he knew it wouldn't, but he couldn't make out it was all a bit of a lark. It was war and he'd already lost friends. Mistakes, careless mistakes, a lapse in concentration, an idle thought... He wanted to talk about something else. 'Ginny looks well. Happier. She's over Billy? And that other stuff.'

Jessie looked about her, leaned forward. 'I wasn't meant to tell.'

He leaned into her. 'Don't worry. I won't tell a soul.' He took hold of her hand. The diamonds caught the light and she grinned, then was suddenly sombre. 'What?' He was confused.

'I don't like having secrets from you, Harry. It's not right. But...' She drained her cup. 'Shall we walk back to the bus? I don't feel we can talk in here.'

He paid the bill and picked up his cap. He held the door for her and once again she linked her arm in his, this time resting her hand on his arm, wiggling her fingers. He kissed her temple and she told him about Frances. 'Please don't say I told you. No one else knows, not Mum, Geraldine – no one. It's been such a burden. I have no idea how Frances managed all these years.'

* * *

Frances was making up the fire in the bar when Johnny walked in. Two old boys were playing dominoes at their table by the window; they looked up briefly when he entered then resumed their game. She raked the coals, put another offcut of timber and a few lumps of coal on. The wood spat and crackled as the flames took hold. Fudge was sitting on his usual seat, his head towards the heat, and she ruffled his head. Johnny came towards her, sombre in his dark overcoat. She went behind the bar and rinsed her hands at the sink below the counter, dried them on a towel. He took off his hat and placed it on the bar.

'I came to apologise. Again.'

'You have nothing to apologise for.'

Lil stuck her head around the door that led to her back room. 'Are you all right, lovey?'

She turned to her. 'I am, Lil.' Lil went back in her room. The landlady had been suffering from a cold and Frances had told her to rest, saying she'd call if she needed her. 'How is Ruby?'

He blew out a breath. 'Can I have a drink first?'

'That's what I'm here for.' She got him a whisky.

'Far too early in the day, really.' He sipped at it, put the glass down and stared into it.

'That bad, eh?'

He looked up. 'Worse. Ruby is being blackmailed.' He lowered his voice and told her all he knew. 'I got the whole sorry story out of her yesterday. I was only too grateful we didn't have a show in the evening. When she sobered up, she was hysterical.'

Frances leaned in close to him. 'You haven't left her alone?'

'No, we have a housekeeper, Mrs Frame, who's old but tough – you know the type.'

Frances grinned. 'I do. She sounds like Lil. The landlady here.'

Johnny was rolling his glass around, staring into it. She watched him, understanding how lonely he must be, for all his fame and money. He was no different from Artie, God bless him, or Big Malc or any of the other men who came through the doors of the Fisherman's Arms, looking for company. She asked him what he was going to do.

'Pay him. What else can I do?'

She leaned on the counter. 'It doesn't seem right, to let him get away with it.'

Lil walked in, blew her nose, stuffed her hanky up her sleeve. 'Who's getting away with what?' She narrowed her eyes. 'Johnny Randolph?' She looked at Frances, raised her eyebrows. Frances did the same. Lil leaned on the beer pump, one hand on her hip.

'You can trust Lil,' Frances said. 'She won't tell a soul.'

'My lips are sealed,' she said and Johnny told her. 'Well, the ruddy snake.' She smacked her hand on the counter. The domino players glanced in their direction. No one liked to upset Lil. 'Franny's right. You can't let the bugger get away with it.'

The door opened and Jessie walked in with Harry. They were holding hands as they came to the bar. Jessie reached her hand over the counter and Frances took hold of it; her fingers were freezing but Frances totally understood why she'd removed her gloves. She admired the ring, then Lil took over. 'Lucky girl!'

'I'm the lucky one.' Harry put his arm about his beloved and she snuggled into him, her face beaming. He glanced around the pub. 'Drinks all round to celebrate my good fortune!' The chaps playing dominoes voiced their thanks and, as Lil poured, Harry took their drinks over to them and stayed and chatted a while. Jessie looked at Johnny, flashed him a smile and leaned across the bar to talk to Frances.

'I didn't get a chance to talk to you yesterday and we were out early this morning.' She grinned at Johnny, then back at Frances. 'It obviously went well?'

Frances pursed her lips.

'Oh.' She reddened. 'Have I put my foot in it? I saw you and Johnny and thought, well...' Her voice trailed off. 'Me and my big mouth.'

Johnny pulled up a bar stool and settled himself on it. He looked truly miserable. Defeated, Frances supposed, and she didn't think it was about the money or the photographs. It was the damage Ruby was doing to herself that was hurting him most, and learning that his mother had choreographed their life in ways he was only just discovering must have been a bitter blow.

'I'll tell you about it later,' Frances said and glanced at Johnny, 'but it's up to Johnny what else gets told.'

His tale was punctuated by Jessie's angry outbursts. 'How could anyone do that? It's wicked.'

'There are wicked people everywhere. We can't always tell them from the good guys.'

Harry had come back and stood next to Jessie, listening. 'You can't pay him,' Harry said. 'It's blackmail and that's illegal.'

'If I involve the police, it will make it a huge scandal. I'd rather pay him off and keep him quiet.' Johnny took a swig from his glass.

'And let him get away with it?' Jessie was shocked.

'To protect my sister, yes.'

The door opened and Ginny walked in followed by Joe. They made a space for them at the bar and Jessie quickly brought them up to speed with the conversation.

'Surely between us we can do something to help?' Harry said and Jessie looked at him adoringly. It made Frances smile.

Joe and Ginny got their drinks and went to sit down by the fire. Jessie and Harry joined them and when Joe moved up the banquette, Fudge growled.

Lil shouted across to them, 'You can't sit there. That's where Artie used to sit. Fudge still thinks he's gonna come back one day. He might be a little dog but his bite's sharp enough if you upset him.' She took over in the bar, urging Frances and Johnny to sit among their friends.

'But you're not well, Lil.'

She shrugged it off. 'I'm as right as ninepence. I'll only sit back there feeling sorry for meself. Get out there with your mates for half an hour.' Lil winked at Johnny, who waited until Frances had come from behind the bar then walked with her to where the others were sitting. They dragged more stools over and Jessie and Harry made room for them. Harry slapped Johnny on the shoulder.

'We're trying to find a way to help. We can't let that scum get away with it.'

'Can't you do something, Joe?' Ginny asked. 'With all your magic.'

'It's not magic. It's misdirection. It's making them look where you want them to look, see what you want them to see.'

Harry leaned in close. 'Sounds exactly what we need.'

Between them they worked out a scheme to retrieve the negatives to save Ruby any undue embarrassment and get the loathsome Mickey Harper out of their lives forever.

'It's worth a shot. We have nothing to lose; we only have to act the part.'

Johnny grinned. 'That's what we all do best.'

Frances went back behind the bar, not wanting to take advantage of Lil's generosity. It had been good to sit there, with her friends, with Johnny.

'You make a lovely couple,' Lil said. 'He clearly adores you. He's got all that worry and the only thing that keeps him going is looking at you.' Lil touched her arm. 'Life's short, lovey. You might not get another chance. He seems a nice young man. And he obviously loves his sister.'

'He does.' Frances watched him. 'That's half the trouble.' He shook hands with Harry and Joe then came back to stand with Frances.

'By, lad.' Lil sneezed and rubbed her nose. 'You look better than you did when you walked in.'

'I didn't know I had friends then.' He pulled the bar stool across and sat down. 'And I didn't have a plan. Now I do.'

He filled Lil and Frances in on the detail.

'That's everyone in agreement, then. And you're sure you don't mind us using the pub, Lil?'

She shook her head. 'I'll bat him round the lughole meself, if I get chance.'

Johnny laughed. 'Then it's all down to Ruby. Let's hope she's able to hold her nerve.'

30

Just after opening hours on Tuesday morning, Ruby sat on a stool opposite the fire, her back to the door, an unlikely addition to Lil's usual clientele. She looked incongruous in her fur coat with beautifully made-up face and perfectly coiffured hair. Harry sat on the banquette seat, his arm round Jessie, and Joe was playing dominoes with two old boys, the perfect spot from which to observe his prey. Big Malc had been recruited in case they needed a bit of muscle and he was chatting to Lil at the bar. Frances left them talking and went through the door to the back room, leaving it ajar so she could hear what was happening and for Lil to give the signal. Johnny was sitting at the small untidy table and Fudge was lying stretched out in front of Lil's gas fire.

'How's Ruby?' Johnny asked. It had been hard convincing him that they could pull it off, but Harry had said that it was worth a try. And why give in to bullies? Wasn't that what their country was fighting for?

'She looks okay,' Frances reassured him. 'I think she'll be fine. It's easier when you know you have friends.'

He cleared his throat. 'We don't deserve this, not me anyway. I barely know any of you.'

'But it's the right thing to do, Johnny. Too much thinking and not enough doing doesn't get you anywhere.'

'When did you get so wise?' he asked. It wasn't really a question, but Frances wouldn't have answered it anyway. It would have taken too long and they needed to concentrate on pulling this off. They'd had a practice run-through making sure everyone knew exactly what was expected of them. It was the oddest rehearsal she'd ever done. She heard the pub door open, then Lil coughed and spluttered, blew her nose like a raspberry.

'That's my cue. Mickey's arrived.' Frances picked up the dog lead. 'Ready for your starring role, Fudge?' she whispered as she fastened it to his collar. As she stood up, Johnny came close, kissed her on the lips, touched her hand.

'Break a leg.'

She pulled away. 'I'll do my best not to.'

* * *

Mickey Harper was wearing an expensive coat with an astrakhan collar and he slid onto the banquette seat opposite Ruby without removing it. The fire was roaring in the grate, giving out a fierce heat. Her own coat was draped over another stool, her bag underneath.

'Why, that coat makes you look almost respectable, Mickey,' she said.

He smirked. 'That's what success does for you, Ruby. And you should know. You can dress things up how you like, but underneath we're naked all the same, aren't we?' he said, a leering glint in his eye.

She didn't comment, only watched as he settled himself, and removed his hat and gloves.

'Nice little place.' He looked around. 'Going to get meself something like this back in town. A pension for me old age.'

'When you've run out of women to prey on?'

'Now, now, Ruby. It's not my fault if you like a drink or two.'

'No, but it's your fault for taking advantage.' She gritted her teeth to stop them chattering. The heat from the fire was hot on her face and she wanted to move her chair but couldn't. Joe had to have a clear view. 'How did you get those photos?'

'A friend of mine. I tip him the wink at the right time. Lots of rich little girlies know how to party so there's a room at the back of the club. We've got a nice little thing going.' She wanted to push him into the fire. 'I only have to watch and wait. Bide my time.' He sniggered. 'You're not the first. And you won't be the last.'

'Where are the negatives?' She still doubted whether he had them with him. He enjoyed the control he had over her. Would he really relinquish it? She was beginning to tremble, but she took a deep breath and steeled herself. She must carry on, must remember that she wasn't alone. Not any more. She could almost sense the kindness of the other people in the pub, protecting her, and yet she hardly knew them. Why were they helping, especially Frances? She didn't owe her anything. Quite the opposite. She mustn't let her mind wander; she must concentrate.

Mickey leaned forward. 'Have you got the money?' She reached into her bag, showed him the thick envelope. He leaned forward to take it, but she held it tight, opening the flap to show they were real notes, then replaced them inside her bag.

'You can have it when I've seen the negatives.'

He pulled an envelope from his inside pocket and she relaxed a little. Joe would have seen clearly which side it was. She held out her hand.

'I want to check they're the right ones.'

He raised his eyebrows. 'I'm impressed. Didn't have you down as being that smart.' He took out one strip of negatives and showed it to her. She held it against the light of the fire and wanted to be sick. She handed it back and he put it in the envelope with the others.

'I've learned a lot because of you, Mickey. Because it's a business transaction at the end of the day.'

He was smug. 'That's the way to look at these things. Business.' They swapped the envelopes, Ruby putting hers into her bag, he slipping his into his pocket. They were halfway home.

'Shall we have a drink on it? Isn't that what you do when you complete a deal?'

'I like your style.' He got to his feet. She had clearly surprised him, as had been her intention. 'What are you having?'

'Port and lemon.'

He went to the bar and Ruby heard Lil deliver her line perfectly. 'You're not from round here, are ya?'

'Here on a bit o' business.'

'Oh, aye? What can I get you and your good lady?' He gave his order and Lil got it for him. He returned to his seat, a drink in each hand, and was about to sit down when the front door opened and Frances walked in and let go of Fudge's lead. He bounded to Mickey Harper, barking, then biting at his ankles. Mickey's beer slopped over the glass and all over him so that his coat was covered in best bitter. Oh, the satisfaction!

'Ruddy dog! That's me new coat. Look at it!' He raised his fist. 'Why you little—'

Ruby got up, knocking over her stool and as Jessie rushed towards the bar, Lil threw her a cloth.

Harry stepped forward. 'Can I help?'

Frances fussed around, pretending to grasp for Fudge's lead, the dog jumping up and down, barking furiously. Jessie rubbed at

Mickey's coat and Joe got up and took the cloth from her, patting it harder, apologising to Mickey as he did so.

'It'll take more than a tea towel to sort this mess out, sir.' It was pandemonium and Mickey Harper had had enough. Ruby threw back her head and began to laugh. It made him furious.

'You can wipe that smile off your face, you little trollop!' It made her laugh even more; she was hysterical with the tension of it all. Big Malc turned from the bar and stood next to her.

'Is this man bothering you, miss?'

'He was.' She fought to control herself. 'But he isn't any more.' She stood as tall as she could, though her legs felt hollow. Mickey pulled his coat about him and strode towards the door, swearing under his breath. He left it open, letting the cold air rush in. Joe got up and closed it, then walked towards the fire and rubbed his hand over Fudge's back.

'Good dog. There's a very good dog.'

Johnny came from behind the bar and hugged his sister. Jessie was behind him and she picked up the stool that had fallen over and Johnny sat Ruby down on it. His hands were firm and she felt safe. She hadn't felt that way in a long time. She was trembling all over, her teeth chattering, and was suddenly cold despite the fire so close. Frances fussed over Fudge and he jumped up and sat in his place. He put his head between his paws and stared at Ruby, his little chocolate brown eyes bright, and it was all too much. Ruby burst into tears and Frances crouched down beside her.

'It's all over now, Ruby. All over.' Jessie produced a handkerchief and Ruby wiped at her eyes. Johnny took the negatives from the envelope and threw them into the fire and Ruby watched as they curled and twisted in the heat. How could so little do so much damage?

* * *

Ginny dashed over to Joe and kissed him. He was clearly taken aback and Frances hid her smile. 'The hero of the hour!' It was Joe's turn to blush. He took a brown envelope from under the table and gave it to Johnny.

Johnny pulled out the notes.

'When do you think he'll realise that he's gone home with a wad of newspaper?'

Joe put his hand in his pocket. 'Probably about the same time as he goes to look at his watch.' Joe held up a wristwatch and they all burst into laughter.

Harry got the drinks in and they waited to see if Mickey Harper would return. He didn't.

'That sent him off with a flea in his ear,' Lil said, triumphant. 'You kids did a grand job.'

Ruby stared into the flames. There was no trace of the negatives, not one shred. The boys got up and stood at the bar. Frances was chatting with Jessie and Ginny was sitting with the shy magician whose sleight of hand had made sure that they didn't lose their money. She owed them so much, especially Frances. She had wronged her all those years ago and had no idea how she would ever make it up to her. But she would try. Johnny came over, put a hand on her shoulder.

'Feeling better, Ruby?'

She touched his hand. 'I feel dreadfully tired.'

'It's the shock,' Frances said kindly. 'You'll probably be tired for a few days. But it will get better. You'll feel like the sun has come out, even if it is the middle of winter.'

Tears rolled down the girl's cheeks when she'd thought she had no tears left. Could she ever see the sunshine again? Feel its warmth?

'I don't know how to thank you, Frances. You and your friends. I don't deserve it.'

Frances took her hand, wrapping her own around it. 'It's got nothing to do with deserving things. No one should be treated that way.' She smiled. 'Look on it as an early Christmas present.'

'I was mean to you.' The words caught in her throat, but she had to say something, make a start. 'When we were in London.'

'It's in the past, Ruby. Leave it where it belongs.'

Ruby closed her eyes. If only it were that simple.

31

It was almost halfway through December and Frances, Ginny and Dolly were sitting at their usual table in the window of Joyce's café. Joyce had gone to town on the decorations and bright ropes of streamers hung across the ceiling from corner to corner and side to side. Tinsel was draped across every one of the framed photographs of stars who had appeared at the Empire and sprigs of holly and ivy had been placed along the windowsill. In the corner by the counter stood a wonky Christmas tree, overloaded with bright shiny baubles and a string of lights that flickered on and off until Joyce kicked at the plug.

The door opened and Jessie walked in, her eyes and nose red and puffy.

'He's gone?' Dolly moved up a chair so that Jessie could sit down. She nodded.

'Did you set a date?'

'It all depends on his leave.' Jessie leaned forward, admiring her ring as the diamonds caught the light. 'It's not what I'd dreamed of. I always thought I'd have a church wedding, but I don't care about the dreams any more. I just want to be Mrs Harry Newman.' Her voice faltered.

'A change of plans, that's all it is,' Frances said, hoping to comfort her. 'A change of plans.'

Joyce brought over a tray with tea and teacakes on it, which she put down on the table next to them. Ginny put her hands up to take the cups as Joyce passed them over.

'Chin up, you lasses. The lads need to see your smiling faces, not your tears.' She put her hand on Jessie's shoulder. 'I know it's hard, ducky, but you've got to be strong like they're having to be strong.'

Dolly smiled. 'You're right, Joyce. Us sitting here worrying doesn't help anything, does it?'

'No, it doesn't, lovey. We've got to make sure everything keeps ticking along, make sure they've got something worth coming home for.' She held the empty tray to her chest. 'I hear you're doing a special show for the lads and lasses in the forces on Christmas Day?'

Frances stirred the pot then poured the tea. 'We are.' She'd been looking forward to spending the day with Imogen and it had been a blow, initially. But she counted her blessings. Those boys in the audience were someone's children, someone's father, brother, all of them far away from home. Jack had been in talks with the mayor of Cleethorpes. There had been rumblings that the Ministry of Works were looking to requisition the Empire for a forces canteen. Jack had asked the cast if they would mind putting on a show on Christmas Day and everyone had been more than happy to oblige. They felt it was the very least any of them could do.

'I think it's wonderful. And I want to help. So me and me daughter are going to cook Christmas dinner for you all after the curtain comes down. We've all got to do our bit to keep up morale. And, well, that's my little bit. I know you've got your mam here,

Jessie, but I was thinking of you lasses and the rest of the cast. None of you will be able to go home till the new year.'

Jessie got up and hugged her. 'You've got a heart of gold, Joyce.' Joyce wriggled, uncomfortable with Jessie's show of affection and Frances smiled. Jessie either didn't notice or didn't care.

* * *

George was settled in his chair in his small office at the stage door, reading the paper, when they walked into the theatre. He let it drop and got up, handing them their keys and their mail. Ginny hurried downstairs to see Joe.

'It's good to see her happy again, isn't it?' Jessie said.

'It is,' Frances agreed. There was a letter from her parents, a postcard from her brother. More Christmas cards. She put them into her bag. 'It's nice to think she found some magic at last.'

In the dressing room, Frances dropped her bag on the table in front of her chair and put her hands on the radiator. It was scarcely warm enough to make much difference. Jessie sat down in front of the mirror. There was plenty of time before they needed to get ready. 'It's good of Joyce to do Christmas dinner, isn't it? I'm glad we're doing a show because Harry won't get leave. It looks like Ginny is getting close to Joe – and you'll have Johnny.'

'Nice try.' Frances took off her dress and pulled on a thick dressing gown she'd brought from home before sitting down and brushing her hair away from her face, twisting it in a knot at the back of her head. 'The Palace is doing a show for the troops as well, at six o'clock, so everything will clash. If we do see each other, it will be brief.'

Jessie hesitated, then said, 'I know you think I'm nagging, Frances.'

'That's because you are, Jessie dear.' She was irritated but didn't want to upset Jessie further. Harry's leaving was still uppermost on her mind. 'It's been so rushed; all the drama with Ruby hasn't helped. The two of them have a lot of baggage to sort out.' She'd told Jessie of their suspicions about the ticket that went astray. 'I can't bring Imogen into a life like that. It's not fair.'

'You'll run out of excuses. Best to get it over and done with. Think how wonderful Christmas will be.'

Frances thought of the picture Imogen had drawn, of her questioning where her daddy was. Did she have the right to keep her child from her father? She began applying her foundation with a sponge. Ginny opened the door but didn't come in. The girls turned to her. She looked worried.

'There's a call for you, Frances. It's Patsy. George says she sounds distressed.'

Frances flung down her greasepaint and ran down the corridor, barging past Kitty. Frances heard her shout, 'Manners!' as she pounded up the stairs to the phone. There was no time to apologise. It must be serious if Patsy had called the theatre. George held out the phone and she pressed it to her ear. Jessie came up and stood beside her.

'Patsy?' It was difficult to hear above the babble the babes were making as they made their way to the dressing rooms. Frances turned her back and stuck her finger in her ear to block out the noise.

'Oh, God, Frances.' Patsy's voice was tight. 'It's Imogen. And Colly.'

'What?' Her heart was pummelling in her ribcage. 'What's wrong, Patsy, are they ill? Have they been in an accident?' *Not Imogen, please, not Imogen...*

'Th-they're missing.' Patsy's voice fractured. 'I – I think they've come to you.' She explained that she'd found Colly's money box empty on the bed. 'I can't find their coats and outdoor clothes.'

Jessie was beside her and Ginny had come, Joe too. George moved people away. 'A neighbour saw them waiting at the bus stop.'

Frances let the phone drop.

'What is it? What's wrong?' Jessie's voice was getting higher. Why were they here in the light and the warmth? It was so cold outside. And so dark. Jessie shook her and it moved her to action.

'It's Imogen. Patsy thinks she might be coming here.'

Ginny frowned. 'Who's Imogen?' It was an innocent enough question, but it sounded damning now. She made for the door, tugged at the handle but Jessie stopped her.

'Think first, Frances. You need help. Us, your friends. There's strength in numbers – like when we all pulled together to help Ruby.' Frances let her arms fall. Jessie was right. She turned to face the people who had gathered in the lobby. Her friends. Friends she had deceived. She looked to Ginny.

'Imogen is my daughter.' She registered the shock on faces around her but this was not about her. Imogen needed her. She quickly relayed what Patsy had told her. 'Imogen and Colly, Patsy's boy, came to the panto. Imogen was obsessed with it, the princess and the jewels, the colour, the pretty lights.'

'How old are they?' Joe asked. He stood head and shoulders above them all, and Bob and Sid crowded about her, Kitty, Don Roper, with his red nose… She wanted to laugh but her heart was hammering. Dear God, let them be safe. 'Imogen is three.' Her voice broke and she balled her fists. 'Colly's almost six.'

Joe took charge. 'Ginny, go to front of house and alert them. What do they look like?'

Jessie came forward. 'Imogen looks like a small version of Frances, dark hair, dark eyes. Colly's got sand-coloured hair. They're about this tall.' She demonstrated with her hands and then Joe divided them into groups and gave them instructions.

'They won't go far,' Joe reassured her. 'They'll stick to what they know.'

Frances caught a sob in her throat.

Jessie held her hand. 'We'll find them, Frances. We will.'

Frances wished she could believe her. This was her fault. Thinking she could control everything, have it the way she wanted. This was her punishment. It was what she deserved. But not what Imogen deserved. She barged past Jessie, pulled the door open and ran out into the street. It was pitch black and she blinked to get her vision after the light inside the theatre. It was cold, icy cold, and as she turned into Market Street, she felt the full blast of the wind. It was black right down to the pier, down to the water. It would be freezing. *Stop, stop!* Imogen wouldn't go there, not to the sea. No, she wanted the princess. Colly was a good boy, a clever boy; he would keep Imogen safe. She pulled her dressing gown about her. Her hair was falling from the pins and blew about her face; she pushed it back and Jessie caught her, stopped her. They heard voices calling, 'Imogen! Colly!' over and over again. She couldn't bear it; she saw people hurrying along Alexandra Road and in the shadows she could make out one of the stage crew talking to the conductor of a bus that had pulled up at the stop across the road. The passengers were lit by the blue lights, shaking their heads, looking out into the street. Some of them got off and joined the search. A car pulled up and Patsy got out of the passenger side.

She saw Frances and ran to her, Bobby following close behind. 'Oh, Frances!' Sobs caught in her throat and they hugged each other. People were walking towards them.

'Not a sound. We should call the police. The wardens might have seen something.'

Frances was shaking with cold and fear.

Jessie caught her arm. 'Let's get you inside.'

They went into the busy foyer and Frances blinked at the

brightness of the lights. People were coming into the show and taking their seats. Dolly was in her usherette uniform and she forced the programmes into her colleague's hand and rushed over to Frances and Jessie. 'Any luck?'

Jessie shook her head, gripped Frances's hand. Frances held on as if she was holding on to life itself.

'I've had a thought.' Dolly smiled at Frances, but for once Dolly's smile wasn't the sunshine it normally was. What if it was too late? They could be lost, anywhere. In the cold. She couldn't bear it.

'What thought, Dolly?' Jessie was taking control. God bless Jessie...

'They could be inside the theatre already.'

The other usherette came to stand beside Dolly.

'We would have seen them,' the other girl said, 'two little kids on their own.'

'Not necessarily,' Dolly replied. 'We'd be looking for the parents – and when everyone comes in together you don't notice so much. We'd have thought they were coming back from the lavatory.'

Frances pulled away from Jessie, who rushed after her. She hauled the door open to the stalls, ran down, looking frantically down the rows, up into the circle. Where would they be? She saw a sea of faces staring back and she pulled her dressing gown about her. She could see Dolly walking steadily down the middle aisle, the other usherette at the far side, asking, checking. She heard a voice and hurried towards the sound. A woman was standing in the middle of the aisle, talking to small children; she couldn't see; why wouldn't the blasted woman move? Frances called out, 'Imogen!' The woman turned.

'I'm afraid they're in the wrong seats.'

Frances cried out, almost fell as she pushed herself forward. 'They're here! Oh, my God, they're safe!' Patsy ran to her side.

People were huffing and puffing at her outburst but she didn't care. Imogen was there, and Colly, sitting in the same seats as they had before, waiting for the show, waiting for the magic to start. The woman stood back and Frances swept Imogen into her arms, hugging her so tightly, kissing her head, crying, laughing. She would never let her go again.

* * *

It took a while for things to calm down, but when the curtain went up it was only a few minutes late. Seats were found for Patsy and the children and for the neighbour who had driven Patsy to the Empire. Colly seemed quite unperturbed by all the fuss, his mother's tears. The performance was a blur; Frances managed to get through it, but was glad when it was all over. The overwhelming fear followed by the exhilaration of finding Imogen safe had left her feeling wrung out and exhausted. And now she was left with the reality. Everyone knew – well, almost everyone. Jessie had been wonderful, filling Ginny in with the details. They had both been so considerate, but Frances felt Ginny deserved more of an explanation.

'I'm sorry I didn't include you before, Ginny. Jessie found out... and after all that you'd been through—'

'Poor Jessie. Piggy in the middle. It wasn't so long ago I did the same.' Ginny unpinned her hair, shook it free and began brushing it into smooth waves. 'I don't think I could have done what you've done, if things had been different, Frances. I think you're very brave.' Ginny started to get changed into her outdoor clothes. They could hear the babes being herded out of the dressing rooms, their footsteps as they raced up the stairs. 'What about her father? Does he help?'

Jessie looked at the floor. Frances paused; her secret was out and the world hadn't ended. It would all come out soon enough.

'Johnny. Johnny's her father.'

Ginny was shocked. 'Johnny Randolph? And he didn't help you?' She frowned. 'I thought he was really lovely.'

'He is. He doesn't know.'

Ginny leaned against the dressing table, her face revealing her obvious shock.

'I know,' Jessie said. 'She hasn't told him.'

'But I will,' Frances said quickly. 'Please don't say anything to anyone, Ginny. I have to tell him myself.'

'Will you?'

Frances nodded. 'It's complicated for him at the moment – and for me. There's been the messy business with Ruby, his mother's deception—'

'And yours,' Jessie added.

Frances looked down at her feet. 'For the right reasons. I've had to protect Imogen, protect myself. People can be cruel.'

Ginny reached out and pressed her hand to Frances's shoulder. 'I understand. It was what I was most afraid of myself.'

Frances hung her head. 'I've been ashamed for so long that it's hard to let go of it.'

* * *

Frances carried Imogen all the way back to Barkhouse Lane, and Ginny and Dolly walked with them. Ginny was going to stay with Dolly for the reminder of the panto – George and his wife had already aired the bedroom for her. Everyone had been wonderful. She regretted holding back as long as she had.

Jessie went inside the house and knocked on her mother's door and Grace called for her to come in. Jessie went in first, then stepped to one side to let Frances pass, Imogen asleep in her arms. Grace let the newspaper drop to the floor and got to her feet.

'Glory be! Frances, put the child on the bed.' She did so and Imogen moaned a little and turned on her side but didn't open her eyes. Grace looked at the child and then at Frances. 'No need to ask whose child she is!'

France's throat was thick with pain. There was such compassion in Grace's eyes that Frances wanted to cry, but she didn't. Tears had never helped.

'I'll get my things,' Ginny said.

'I'll put the kettle on.' Dolly followed her out of the room. Frances sat on the bed, holding Imogen's hand, watching her sleep, stroking her head, wanting more than anything to lie down beside her. Now that they were safe, she felt depleted.

Grace put her hand on Frances's shoulder. It gave her a little strength. 'Get Geraldine, Jessie,' Grace said quietly, and Frances twisted as Jessie left the room. 'You don't want to have to tell your story twice. You look exhausted.'

'I am.' Frances stood up. The room was cosy and warm, the gas fire low, the lamp soft. Safe. Imogen was safe. And she was here. It was what she'd wanted for so long.

'Oh, Grace, I'm afraid of what she'll say.'

'Say about what?' Geraldine came in, wearing her dressing gown and slippers.

Frances moved away from the bed. 'My daughter. Imogen.' The child murmured at the mention of her name, sucked at her thumb.

Geraldine gazed at the child. She peered down her nose at Frances. Frances straightened her shoulders. If she wanted them to go, Lil would have them. It didn't matter. Someone would take them in, or she could go back to Patsy.

'Your child?' Geraldine said quietly. She paused. 'I can't tell you how disappointed I am, Frances.'

Frances held firm. 'I knew you would be.'

'And offended,' she continued, 'that you thought so little of me. That I would judge you harshly, without asking questions.'

Dolly came in with a tray of hot drinks and hovered in the doorway, unsure as to whether she should stay or leave.

Geraldine turned. 'How kind, Dolly. Now, sit down beside your beautiful daughter, Frances.' She took a mug from the tray and handed one to Frances, and to Grace, then took one for herself. The two older women took a seat in the window and Frances sat down on the bed. Jessie came in and sat on the floor by the fire with Dolly. 'Right,' Geraldine said, not unkindly. 'Begin at the beginning. We are all ears.'

When she had finished, they all agreed she had indeed been brave – and silly not to trust them.

'But the day war broke out, you were quite damning about the type of girls in the theatre, Geraldine,' she said.

'A sweeping statement. Forgive me. If I'd have known the effect they'd have had, I would have bitten off my tongue.' She got up and walked over to Frances, rested a gentle hand on her shoulder and gazed down on the child. 'Quite a beauty, like her mother. I'm looking forward to getting to know the latest addition to our household when she wakes.'

It was too much for Frances. She swallowed down the hard lump that had formed in her throat. 'So it's all right if we stay?' Her voice cracked.

Geraldine gave a slight nod of her head, seemingly unable to find the words, and she looked so sad that Frances felt even worse. 'We are all being judged, Frances. And we judge in return. I was wrong. So were you.' She clasped her hand. 'Now get this child upstairs to bed and we should all do the same. We start afresh tomorrow.'

32

It was the Sunday before Christmas, a Sunday when Frances didn't have to leave the house early. She would never have to do that again, not as long as they all lived at Barkhouse Lane. The vegetables for dinner had been peeled as they always were, the dinner cooked and cleared away, and for once Frances and Imogen had been a part of it. Eddie was sitting on the floor in front of the fire in Grace's room, helping Imogen complete a puzzle. Grace was sewing in her chair by the window, lit by the sun as it dropped low in the sky, and Geraldine was reading. In the bay window, between the chairs, the girls had placed a Christmas tree and Imogen had delighted in helping to decorate it. She had settled down to their topsy turvy life, accompanying the girls to the theatre, being fussed over, falling asleep on a pile of coats in the corner while the girls came and went onstage.

Frances sat with Jessie on Grace's bed, pillows against their backs, making paper chains.

Jessie leaned close and whispered, 'When are you going to tell Johnny?'

'Oh, let me enjoy this time with her.' It gladdened her heart to see Imogen so content. She had struggled with whether to keep Imogen with her; the boys would miss their little companion and Imogen would miss them, especially Colly. Patsy had reassured her that they would all adjust quickly to their new circumstances and that the boys were looking forward to the rare treat of their father being home for Christmas. Frances and Imogen would join them on Boxing Day.

Jessie took a strip of paper and looped it, dabbing paste on the end and pressing it tight until it held. Frances passed her another strip.

'Time is slipping by, Frances.'

She knew Jessie was right, that Johnny deserved to know, but for the first time in her life she felt a sense of ease, that life was uncomplicated. 'I will tell him. But I have to do it in my time, in my way.' She moved the paper chain over her lap. 'I could face it if he left me again, but not Imogen.'

'Surely you trust him?' Jessie whispered.

It was difficult to know whether she did or not. She wanted to, but something inside her couldn't let go, a small voice that said, *Hold on*.

'I trusted him before and he let me down.'

'It was hardly his fault was it. It was his mother.' Jessie was thoughtful. 'I think you're afraid.'

'I am not!' It rankled. Jessie knew nothing of what she'd been through, they'd been through.

'That's not what I meant.' She watched Imogen put the final piece inside the jigsaw, clap her little hands. 'You're afraid of being happy.'

Frances looked about her. 'I am happy, Jessie. I have my child, good friends. The only thing I'm afraid of is that I'll have too much...'

* * *

For the first time in years, Frances was filled with hope for the future. The last performance on the Saturday before Christmas Eve had held a special magic, and she had left the theatre with Jessie, anticipating the joy that tomorrow would bring. That Christmas Eve fell on Sunday made it all the sweeter, being able to spend the whole day with her child. The excitement, the build-up, and being able to leave presents at the foot of Imogen's bed. That night, while she played Mother Christmas, the grown-ups gathered downstairs, the kitchen full of the smells of the season, pickled onions and smelly cheese, the rich scent of Christmas pudding. Afterwards, she'd lain awake, her child at her side, watching the dawn creep through the gap in the curtain, knowing she would never receive a better gift.

* * *

In the morning, they gathered in Grace's room, the fire aglow, the presents set under the tree. They had come together at Barkhouse Lane only months before but now they were as tight as any family. Eddie had been working hard, saving hard, and had delighted Jessie with the gift of a guitar.

'There isn't room for a piano, but this is the next best thing.'

Jessie was thrilled and sat on Grace's bed, strumming Christmas carols while Imogen played with the doll Frances had bought her. She'd felt extravagant, spending so much, but it was worth the celebration. Geraldine sat on the floor with Imogen, helping her to dress the doll in the woollen coat and bonnet that Grace had knitted.

Imogen put the doll's bonnet on and Geraldine tied the bow under its chin. 'Are you going to give her a name?' she asked.

'I'm going to call her Jessie, because she's a princess,' the child said, beaming, and Frances felt as if her heart would burst with the warmth she felt inside.

The clock on the mantel chimed the hour.

'Time we were leaving.' Geraldine got up, peering through the nets at the window. 'No sign of snow, Imogen. Not yet. But it will be cold, so we need to get wrapped up warm before we leave the house.' She left to get herself ready, as did the others, and they all appeared in the street in their best clothes, wrapped in newly knitted hats and scarves that had been Christmas presents from Dolly.

They called at the pub to wish Lil 'Merry Christmas!' Big Malc was in his usual place at the bar, Fudge on his seat by the fire, and a few of the lads in uniform had called in on their way to the theatre. Lil lifted the flap and came out to them. She kissed Frances and Jessie, touched Imogen's head, admired her doll.

'What a Christmas it is, eh, Franny? Bet you never thought it would turn out the way it has.'

Frances felt tears prick at her eyes. Happy tears. Lil had been so generous, in her heart and spirit. She had been there for them all, in some small way. And here was her pub, filled with friends.

'Lot of lonely people out there. All them boys away from home, their loved ones. I'm glad you're doing this show.'

'You will come to Joyce's when you've locked up?'

'I might. I'll see how I feel. Might just want to put me feet up.'

'But it's Christmas, Lil,' Jessie cried. She took her hand, squeezed it. 'Please come.'

Frances knew she wouldn't. Lil didn't need anyone. And there was always Big Malc if she did.

They walked down towards the Empire. People were wrapped up warmly against the cold, kids on their bikes, a lad walking on stilts. It all seemed so normal – and it would have been, save for the absence of all the young men, the fathers who would be over in France. At least Johnny was here. He'd said he would sign up once he knew Ruby was safe. But now she was...

The troops were already milling around the theatre, lorries and trucks parked along the road. They parted at the stage door and Geraldine, Grace and Eddie went to Joyce's while the girls and Imogen went into the theatre.

* * *

George was already in his office and he came out when he saw them.

'No need to guess what Father Christmas brought for you, Imogen.' She held up her doll and he bent down, admiring it. He brought out a parcel, wrapped in jolly paper. 'A little gift from me and the missus.'

Frances kissed his cheek. 'That's so kind of you both, George.' They skipped down to the dressing rooms, wishing everyone 'Merry Christmas!' Ginny was getting ready, Dolly seated in the easy chair. Imogen hurried towards them to show them her doll and the girls grinned when they found out her name.

'Is she a naughty dolly, or a good dolly?'

'Oh, a good dolly,' Imogen said, her face serious. 'She's a princess.'

'So she is.' The girls laughed and Jessie cradled her namesake while Frances removed Imogen's coat, hanging it up beside her own. When she turned back, Dolly was holding a length of red ribbon.

'Would you like Mummy to put this in your hair, Imogen?' She took a narrower strip. 'And one for your Jessie too, so you can be the same?'

Imogen beamed and Frances lifted her onto the chair, telling her to stand so she could see herself in the mirror. Frances threaded the ribbon through her fingers and began to brush Imogen's hair, smiling at her child's reflection as she did so. There was a knock at the door and Jessie went to open it, the doll in her other hand. The room fell silent as Ruby swept in, her arms full of gifts. Frances stopped brushing, her hand trembling. She began to brush again, trying to appear as composed as she could, as if little girls came into the dressing room every day to have their hair brushed. She could be anyone's child. Anyone's. Ruby placed the presents down on the dressing table, staring at Imogen through the mirror. Frances tried to tie the ribbon, all fingers and thumbs.

'Oh, Ruby, you really shouldn't have.' Jessie dashed forward, gabbling, trying to counter the tense atmosphere that had been created when Ruby walked in. Frances felt as if she were made of stone, didn't want to speak in case she broke the spell. Ruby was almost in a trance but she shook herself, smiling at Jessie, at them all.

'It's a thank you, for what you did for me.'

'We did it because it was the right thing to do,' Ginny said, standing up and coming closer to Frances. 'You don't need to say thank you.'

Ruby was looking at Frances and back to Imogen. Frances could almost see her brain clicking over, working it out.

'I need to say so many things.' She took a deep breath. 'And I have to start somewhere.' She handed over the boxes. Frances put down the brush and Ruby handed her a small parcel wrapped in expensive paper. Imogen was mesmerised by the sparkling diamonds in Ruby's brooch.

'Pretty,' she said.

Ruby came close, studying the child's face, then she reached out, touched her hair. 'Do you like it?'

Imogen said she did. Ruby held it closer to Imogen and as the light hit the diamonds, it sparkled brighter still. Imogen ran her fingers over it, her face alight with pleasure.

'My mummy gave it to me,' Ruby said. 'It's very precious. As you are precious to your mummy.' Imogen let go of the brooch and Ruby stepped away. She went to the door. 'I came to Grimsby thinking I would hate it.' She took a deep breath and her voice quivered as she spoke; she looked directly at Frances. 'I'm glad I came.' She wiggled her fingers at Imogen. 'Merry Christmas, girls.'

Everything was frozen for a few seconds, the girls staring at Frances, wondering what to do. Frances threw down the brush and ran after Ruby.

'Ruby!' Ruby stopped, turned. Tears glistened in her eyes and for a moment Frances hesitated. 'Please let me tell him myself?'

Ruby looked small and afraid. Beyond the make-up, Frances could see that she was weary. The last few months must have taken their toll but it was over now.

'Of course. I'm so sorry, Frances. Truly. For everything.' She left, her head down, and Frances hurried back to the dressing room. Dolly had fastened the ribbons and the girls stopped talking when Frances returned. She took Imogen down from the chair.

'Will you take her to Joyce's, Dolly?' Dolly didn't ask any questions, simply took Imogen's hand in hers and left the room.

Frances began getting herself ready, fighting to stop herself shaking. Would Ruby keep her word?

Jessie asked tentatively, 'What did she say?'

'Nothing – but she knows.'

Jessie opened her present. It was an expensive bottle of perfume. 'She didn't have to do that. It's too much.'

'That's all Ruby knows how to be.' Frances steadied her hand.

She was ready when the knock came on the door and Johnny peered around it. His plum scarf was loose about his neck, his coat dark on the shoulders with spots of rain.

When Jessie and Ginny made to leave the room, he stopped them. 'I seem to scare you two away!'

He grinned and Jessie fumbled. 'We thought you'd want the privacy.'

Frances couldn't bear it.

'Ordinarily I would,' he said. 'But we have to be back at the Palace. We're hosting a dinner there for some of the Naval Reserve chaps. Then the show and, well, like you, it will be a long day, but worth it.' He looked at the gifts on the dressing table. 'I see Ruby beat me to it. She'll never forget what you three have done for her.' He smiled. 'And neither will I.' He withdrew a square box from his coat pocket and handed it to Frances. 'Happy Christmas, Frances.'

She took it from him, her heart still pounding and managed to smile. 'Should I open it now?'

'It's up to you.' He wasn't pressing her to do anything and she relaxed a little, knowing Imogen was safe with Joyce. The girls were right: she should tell him, but not now, not this moment. She undid the paper, opened the box and found a necklace with a single teardrop diamond. She lifted it out. 'Do you like it?'

'It's – it's beautiful.' She tried to open the clasp, but her hands were trembling.

'Here,' he said. 'Let me.' She lifted her hair and he placed it about her neck, fastening the clasp. Jessie and Ginny admired it and she turned to him, aware the girls were watching. He touched her face, kissed her cheek and she longed to take his hand in hers, to lead him away and tell him everything. Would she ever find the right time? 'I must leave.' He looked to Jessie and Ginny. 'Good to see you, girls.'

'I'll come with you. Say goodbye.' She followed him down the corridor and up the stairs, out into the street. It was cold and she wrapped her arms about her for warmth.

'I didn't get you anything.' There hadn't been time, nor the money, for every spare penny had been spent on Imogen.

'I didn't want anything, Frances. I wanted you. That's all I ever wanted.' It began to snow, soft flakes that landed on her hair, on his coat collar, and she reached up to brush them away. He caught her hand, kissed her fingers, pulled her to him.

She looked up into his eyes. He was kind, generous – and she loved him. But she didn't need him... Ruby came out of the stage door.

'Oh, there you are.' She glanced at Frances and reddened, knowing she had interrupted something special. 'Sorry, Johnny. We need to leave. The car's at the front.' Ruby went back inside and, as the door closed, Johnny swept Frances into his arms and kissed her so hard that it took her breath away. She held back for a fraction and then gave herself to him, for his kisses were like life itself and she felt something awaken in her that hadn't been there before. Was it happiness? At last?

He kissed her again. Her lips, her cheeks, her forehead, and she laughed as the snowflakes fell and melted in the warmth of their breath.

'I must go.' She let go of his hands and he went inside. She remained on the pavement, watching the snowflakes swirl and fall in the quiet street as it settled on the ground. She hoped Ruby would be true to her word, but if she wasn't, there was nothing she could do about it. She could feel the chains she'd held on to so tightly begin to fall about her feet.

* * *

It was fun onstage that afternoon, a totally different experience, playing to an audience devoid of children. They had worried whether the lads would join in with the 'He's behind you!'

nonsense but it had been needless. They had joined in wholeheart-edly, and when Joe came on, shouting 'New lamps for old!', a wag in the audience shouted, 'Put that ruddy light out.' It brought the biggest laughter of the afternoon.

When the curtain came down, the cast went out front in their costumes, chatting to the lads and lasses who were out there in their uniforms. Autographs were signed, publicity photos handed out – and many of the lads left with lipstick kisses on their faces. When the last one had gone, they went back to their rooms, changed and headed over to Joyce's. The smell of roast beef greeted them when Jessie opened the door.

Grace and Geraldine were red-faced, their sleeves rolled up to their elbows. They stood with Joyce, passing plates over the counter, which Eddie and Dolly took, weaving between the tables, serving the cast and crew. Ginny took a seat next to Joe. She picked up her cracker, held it out to him. They tugged; she won. She unfurled the paper hat and placed it on his head. Jessie smiled; he deserved to be crowned. It was his idea that had made sure that Ruby had a better Christmas than she would have had. When everyone was served, Grace, Joyce and Geraldine took off their aprons and sat down to join them. Don got up, glass in hand.

'I hope you'll join me in a toast. To the wonderful Joyce and her lovely assistants. Thanks from us all, and a very merry Christmas.'

They raised their glasses. 'To Joyce and her helpers – merry Christmas!'

After the meal, Eddie and Dolly cleared the plates and Kitty led them in a singalong of carols.

It was hot and it was loud, and laughter filled the room. Frances felt so very blessed. Jessie leaned back in her seat. She turned to Frances, whispering, 'Do you think Ruby will keep her word and not tell Johnny?'

'I want to think she will.' Something told her Ruby would.

'She doesn't look well, does she? I thought she was very thin.'

Imogen came to her and she pulled her on her knee and kissed the top of her head. 'Perhaps she'll get well now that she's got Mickey Harper off her back. It must have been dreadful.' The girl had tortured herself. More so keeping it from Johnny.

As if catching her thought, Jessie said, 'Secrets aren't good for anyone, are they?'

33

As Christmas Day drew to a close, Ruby was empty but for the memories of a job well done. The audience had been pretty special, those young men who would be leaving their loved ones behind to fight for king and country. It had been good to see people so happy, to give something and want nothing in return more than smiling faces. They had finished with a sing-song, something they'd added for the occasion, and she had led them in a medley of songs, conducting them with her outstretched hands. There had been rows and rows of smiling faces, boys some of them, away from their families. It broke her heart to think what many of them would face in the days to come. Johnny had grasped her hand as they took the applause, the boys cheering and stamping their feet in appreciation. He pulled her to him, hugged her. Every time she looked at him, she saw the child, Imogen. In the end she stared past him, not being able to bear the overwhelming sense of hatred and loathing she felt for what she had been party to. It was long after midnight when they got back to the house. Johnny poured them both a drink and when Ruby stretched out on the sofa, he tucked a blanket over her legs. 'You made a lot of people happy tonight, Ruby.' She stared into the fire so that she didn't have to look at him. He put a record on the gramophone and they listened to Christmas carols until her eyelids were heavy and she fell asleep. He woke her, helped her upstairs and she lay on her bed, the curtains wide, looking at the stars in a crisp black sky. Puffy white clouds floated across. What would it be like to climb on one and float away, far, far, away?

She heard him come upstairs not long after, humming to himself. The sound of his voice was comforting. He was happy. He would be happy with Frances. And Imogen. Oh, God, what had she done? He knocked on her door.

'Goodnight, Ruby. Sweet dreams.'

She managed to call out, 'Goodnight.' Her voice felt as if it was coming from somewhere else. She lay there a long time, afraid, wondering what she could do, playing out scenarios of what Johnny would do when it all came out. He would never forgive her. Not for this. She hauled herself up, felt the rug under her bare feet, brought the letters from the wardrobe. Why had her mother done it? Why hadn't she opened them? Was it too late now, to put things right? They didn't belong to her; they belonged to Frances. She found some paper, wrote a letter, wrapped everything with Christmas paper. Somehow, she would make it right.

* * *

The day after Boxing Day, Frances went into the theatre to discover a gift on the dressing table. Jessie hung up her coat, peered at it. 'Lucky you.'

Frances checked the label. 'It's not from Johnny. Not his hand.' She undid the string and peeled the paper away to find a battered shoebox. She removed the lid; inside was an envelope with her name and, underneath, more envelopes. Her letters to Johnny, others with her name on, so obviously from him. She sank down into the chair. Jessie rested a hand on her shoulder.

'What?'

Ginny hurried to her side. 'My letters! Our letters.' She looked through them again. 'And a ticket for America – in my name. My ticket...'

Jessie gripped her shoulder. Frances had the white envelope in her hand.

'Ruby?' Jessie said. Frances nodded. Jessie pulled her chair close, sat down beside her, pressing her hand on Frances's arm. 'Aren't you going to open it?'

Frances swallowed. She didn't know if she dared. It was all too much. She felt waves of anger and rage sweep over her, followed by a surge of happiness and hope. Yes, it was hope, because Johnny was the man she'd thought he was all those years ago. Tears fell and she put her hand to her mouth, her body racked with sobs she'd tried so hard to hold in. Jessie pulled her hand away, hugged her, held her like a child.

'Let it all out, Frances. Let it go.'

Free at last, Frances did.

* * *

Frances handed the letter to Jessie. The handwriting was erratic, loopy, parts of it incoherent. It took them a while to decipher the words. Ruby explained that her mother had thought Frances was after Johnny's money, his fame. She'd convinced Ruby that Frances wouldn't settle for just that, once she got her claws into Johnny. She would want to take Ruby's place too. Not only in his life, but in their act. And what would Ruby have left then? How would she manage? She had been terrified, had done exactly as her mother had asked. She'd made sure she was always at the theatre first to get the post, always offered to take the mail. Johnny hadn't suspected a thing. He had trusted her.

'Will you tell Johnny?' Jessie gave the letter back to Frances.

'It's not my tale to tell.' Her eyes were red, sore. 'Ruby has respected my wishes. She obviously hasn't said anything to Johnny.'

'And you still haven't told him?' Ginny raised her eyebrows.

'I couldn't find the right time. Or the courage. We're having dinner on Sunday. I'll tell him then. It has to be right.'

Jessie was not convinced. 'Delaying hasn't worked for anyone. Not for Ruby. Not for you. Sunday is New Year's Eve.'

'A fresh start,' Frances said. 'It's the right time.'

* * *

It was New Year's Eve. Five days since Ruby had sent the letters. Five days and nights when Ruby had waited for Johnny's anger, his rage. She was prepared for that but not this silence, and keeping the knowledge of his child from him was unbearable, but she mustn't say anything. She'd promised Frances and she owed it to her. Ruby hung her dress in the wardrobe. What had Aunt Hetty said about tidying? That it would help her tidy her thoughts. She gazed about the room. It was all neat. Everything where it should be. She ran her fingers over her silver-backed brush and mirror, sat in front of her dressing table, brushed her hair. Everything felt lighter; she felt as if she could float away on a cloud.

Johnny knocked and came into her room.

'Are you sure you don't want to come with me? It's not too late to change your mind, you know. A woman's prerogative. Especially tonight.'

'Quite sure.'

He stood behind her, kissed the top of her head. 'Make sure you get something to eat.' She reached up for his hand and he clasped it in both of his. Tears brimmed in her eyes.

'I wish you'd let it all go, Ruby,' he said, 'leave it in the past where it belongs.' She flinched. Frances had said the same. Would she still think it now? There had been no word from her...

'I love you, Johnny, you know that, don't you?'

He squatted down beside her. 'Of course I do, silly girl. I love you too.'

Her heart felt as if it had crumbled to pieces. When she heard the front door open and close, she went to the window, watched until he disappeared out of sight. Tomorrow it would be a new year, a new beginning. Would she be on her own? Without Johnny? Snow was starting to fall again and she felt like she was in a dream. She could see small lights on the other side of the park, the moon reflecting on the lake. She slipped out of the house, leaving the door open. She wouldn't be long; she just wanted to be where the light was.

* * *

Johnny turned the corner. He shouldn't have left Ruby on her own, not on New Year's Eve. He should take her with him; Jessie would be glad of the company, and Ginny. It would be better if she was with people. He checked his watch, wiping away the snowflakes that fell on its face. He would only be a few minutes late and Frances would understand; the weather was slowing everything down. He pictured her waiting for him at the Dolphin Hotel across the road from the Empire. They had met there before and it had been her choice. He patted his pocket. The ring was still there. He hesitated then turned back, hurrying through the snow. A woman was crossing the road over to the park; astonishingly, she wasn't wearing a coat. He peered, the snow coming faster now, and realised it was Ruby.

He shouted, 'Ruby!' but she didn't stop, moving trancelike along the path, and he ran, his feet slipping in the slush, his heart pounding, calling her name, the snow catching in his mouth. 'Stop! Stop!' Could she hear him? She must stop, she must. He ran through the park gates. His brain didn't want to register what his eyes were seeing as she walked into the water. He ran faster, slipping, stumbling. She fell and he lunged forward, grasped at her arm, held on, fell onto his knees in the water. It wasn't deep but it was cold and he gasped at the shock of it, pulling her up, dragging her to the edge, crying her name. 'Ruby! Oh, my God, Ruby.'

Her eyes were closed, her face white. A couple ran towards them and the man tore off his coat and put it over her, helped Johnny take her in his arms.

'Over there.' He indicated with his head. The light was shining out from the hall and the man helped him carry her across the park and into the house, his wife following, closing the door behind them to secure the blackout. Johnny settled Ruby on the sofa, then eased off her clothes and covered her with a blanket as the man turned up the fire.

The woman came to him. 'Let me get help.' He managed to garble Mrs Frame's address and the pair of them left the room. He was talking to Ruby, shaking her gently, rubbing warmth into her body. God, if anything happened to her, he'd never forgive himself.

* * *

It was busy in the dining room of the Dolphin Hotel. The staff were milling around, preparing for the evening's entertainment. The cutlery and wine glasses glittered in the light of the chandeliers. It looked gay and inviting and she almost wished she would be seeing in the new year here, with Johnny, and not bother going on to the Empire. She checked her watch. Was it fast? Yes, it was a little.

Musicians came in and started setting up their instruments. The drummer placed the cymbals on stands, the sound of them ringing out as he fixed them in position. The sense of anticipation was all around her. She checked her watch again. Imogen would be at the Empire now, with Grace and Geraldine, because Jack was throwing a party for the cast. Lil and some of the customers had been invited and Joyce and her family would be there. She could picture them gathering, walking up the stairs to the top of the building, just as she could picture Johnny meeting his child for the first time. This was the best time to tell him, the cusp of the year and a sense of new beginnings.

* * *

Ruby opened her eyes.

'Thank God!' She reached up, touched his face. He caught hold of her hand.

'I'm so sorry, Johnny.' Her body was trembling and she tried to will it to stop but she couldn't; it made her tired.

She saw faces, strangers. Who were they? Then a woman, older; she tried to focus. Mummy? Her heart shrank with the disappointment.

'Oh, Ruby, what a thing to do.' Mrs Frame squeezed Johnny on the shoulder. 'Get out of those wet things, Mr Johnny. You'll catch your death.'

'You silly, silly girl.' He kissed her hand, kissed her forehead, and sat back, stroking her hair. She took her hand away from his cheek.

'Frances knows.'

'Knows what, darling girl?'

Tears began to fall; she didn't think she had any left but still they came. Big fat tears that were warm on her face.

'I gave her the letters.'

'What letters?' He felt chilled as Ruby told him of their mother's deception, of her own part in it. He was angry, but not with Ruby. The full extent of their mother's ambition for them was exposed and Ruby was the embodiment of the damage she had wreaked on them both. At that moment, he hated his mother for what she had done.

Mrs Frame tugged at his arm. 'Go and get changed, my boy, or you'll be ill yourself.'

He got up. The clock chimed seven. 'Oh, Lord, I was meant to be with Frances! Will you wait while I see her, Mrs Frame? I won't be long, but I can't let her down. She'll never forgive me. Not this time.'

'My old man will come here to see the new year in. Off you go. I'll take care of Ruby.'

Johnny dashed upstairs to change.

The doctor came into the hall as he gave his thanks to the couple who had helped so much, then called for a taxi. 'I've given her a sedative, but I'd advise you to seek specialist help as soon as you possibly can if you want your sister to get well.'

* * *

The taxi made its way slowly into Cleethorpes. The snow was coming in drifts now and the car kept sliding across the road. In the end it was quicker to get out and walk. He strode up Isaac's Hill, pulled his scarf up about his face, and held on to his hat. He hurried straight into the dining room, hoping she would still be there, but the room was empty save for the staff and a few musicians warming up. He walked away, desolate, but then he saw her by the side entrance, putting on her coat.

'I almost missed you.' She didn't smile as he'd thought she would. 'Forgive me, Frances. Please let me explain.'

He looked haggard, his eyes so sad. It had to be Ruby. Had she told him? He ordered a large whisky and a waiter showed them to a table in a quiet corner. Johnny told her what had happened.

'Is she all right? Is she safe?'

'She is. She will be. Mrs Frame is with her. The doctor checked her over, gave her something to help her sleep.' She reached out for his hand. 'I thought I was doing the right thing,' he said miserably, 'getting her away from London, the partying, the drink. I knew nothing of Mickey Harper.' He squeezed her hand, and stared into her eyes. 'And I was selfish. I saw you that day when I came with Bernie Blackwood and I thought there might be a chance. I wasn't thinking of Ruby then, at all.' He kissed her hand. 'She told me.'

Frances held her breath.

'About the letters. I had no idea. She offered to post them. And my mother too. I didn't think anything of it, just handed them over. She preyed on Ruby's insecurities—'

She could only imagine what it had felt like to receive such news. That his mother had controlled their life to such an extent, with not a care for their happiness, only their outward success. And what an empty success it was. He shook his head, still disbelieving, the agony of the night clear on his face.

'When she saw you, it must have brought all Mother's manipulation to the fore, that you would take her place. I think she thought it was the end. There was nothing left for her.'

'She was afraid,' Frances said. 'We all make mistakes when we allow fear to take over.' He would understand that that was what she had done, let fear colour her judgement. She and Ruby were the same.

'She's not strong, like you, Frances.' Frances hadn't been strong at all, but she'd had to find it within her, for Imogen. She hoped that Ruby would find hers. He kissed her hand, let it go. 'We'll have to close the show. I'll be taking Ruby to stay with Aunt Hetty – I should have done that in the first place. Then I'll get her the best help money can buy.' He paused. 'I thought work would help her. It helped me, when I thought I'd lost you.'

'Don't hold it against her, Johnny. What she did, she did because she loves you. We all do what we think is right at the time.'

'I had a ring.' He patted at his pockets. 'It's in my other suit.' He laughed, a sad laugh.

'They all say that.' She smiled, hoping to lift him somehow. She knew now how much he loved her. In his sadness, it shone through.

He took her hand again. 'This is not what I wanted it to be like.'

'Not everything goes the way we want it to. But we get there in the end.'

He touched her fingers to his mouth, his breath warm on them, then he leaned across and kissed her and she closed her eyes; a pool of sadness filled her, for him, for Ruby, for all the lost time.

She got up. 'My friends are waiting for me and you need to go back to Ruby.'

He walked her to the theatre and they stood on the steps, the world white, snow illuminating the dark night. He took her in his arms and kissed her. 'I'll be back as soon as I've got Ruby safe. Do you believe me?' He held her around her waist.

'I do.' How could she be so happy, and so desperately sad?

'If only I had that ring.'

She laughed. Snowflakes fell on her lips and he pulled her to him and kissed them away and she didn't feel the cold or see the darkness any more.

A taxi was waiting by the front of the theatre. He stood by it and she held on to his hand. Could she bear to let him go again? She pulled him away, towards the theatre, up the steps and into the foyer. He was laughing, his sad eyes sparkling, and she stood close, put her hands either side of his face, kissed him. They'd both waited too long – now it was Ruby's turn to wait, and, knowing his sister was safe with Mrs Frame, she led him up the stairs, past the dress circle and onto a small landing.

'Wait.'

He waited, bemused.

* * *

The room at the top of the Empire was cosy, the fireplaces at either end burning bright with logs. She moved through the crowd to where Grace was sitting with Geraldine; Imogen was asleep, her dark curls falling onto Grace's lap.

Jessie came over. 'Where's Johnny?'

'On the landing.' She scooped Imogen into her arms, woke her gently with kisses. Imogen blinked at the light, smiling sleepily. Jessie went ahead, making a path for her, clearing the way. Frances was talking to Imogen, whispering, watching the child's eyes as they widened with delight and anticipation. Jessie opened the door and Frances stepped out into the darkness of the hall, down to the landing. Johnny looked up, stepped forward. She let Imogen down gently, holding on to her shoulders as she faced her father. Time seemed suspended as he looked to the child. Their child.

'I couldn't tell you before.' The struggle was over, at least for her. She didn't have to think about Ruby. Not tonight. The night belonged to the three of them, a family at last. Johnny squatted down and she managed to find her voice, the lump in her throat so big, so wide. 'Imogen, this is your daddy.'

He was shocked, disbelieving, looking to her then to Imogen, the realisation that this was his child slowly registering. He bent forward, making himself smaller, eye to eye with Imogen, and opened his arms, and Imogen left her mother's side and went to him. He swept her into his arms, standing, laughing, kissing, and laughing again. He held her for a long time, burying his face in her small body, bewildered. He put out his arm to Frances and she went to him, and he wrapped it about her shoulder, pulling her close. She placed her hand on his chest, feeling his heart beating, so strong. He kissed her head and she looked into his eyes.

'How? Why?'

She placed her finger on his lips. 'Not now. There'll be time enough later. But it's New Year's Eve and our friends are upstairs. Will you stay?'

He brought her to him, kissing her face. Imogen giggled and Frances smiled, Johnny too. 'How could I leave?'

* * *

The room was a sea of happy faces when the three of them walked back in. Lil was dancing with Big Malc, Fudge lying so close to the fire he might melt. Don Roper was entertaining the stage crew with stories from his repartee and George and Olive waved as they passed, their faces rosy from the heat. Geraldine got up, making a place for Johnny to sit down with Imogen. He held her on his lap, talking to her. Imogen showed him her dolly and Frances went to get drinks. Bob was topping up Audrey's glass and flirting with her. Her trilling laughter could be heard in all four corners of the room and she was sweet and gracious to everyone gathered there, regardless of their position.

'Make the most of it,' Bob said to Jack out the side of his mouth. 'She'll have one hell of a head on her tomorrow.' He slapped Jack on the back, and he laughed so hard it set him off in a coughing fit. They were surrounded by friends, seeing out the old. Soon it would be time for the new.

At five minutes to midnight, Jack tapped on his glass with a spoon. He waited for the noise to die down before he spoke.

'I'm glad you could make it tonight, friends – or should I say family?' A cheer went up. Audrey was smiling, red-faced, and Jessie giggled. Frances nudged her. Dolly and Ginny came close. Over in the corner she could see Imogen fast asleep, Johnny holding her tight. Jack continued, 'There's no such thing as the good old days. The best day we have is now. Let's enjoy it while we can.'

Johnny laid Imogen down on the chairs and came to Frances and together they joined the circle, their arms crossed, hands held, and as the clock chimed the hour they sang 'Auld Lang Syne'. As it ended, Johnny broke free, drew Frances to him and kissed her lips, her cheeks, her hair. She pulled away, laughing, and they were swept into a joyous round of hugging and kissing to welcome the year.

When the celebrations died down, Johnny went back to Imogen and took her onto his lap. Frances left him, just for a moment. There was so much catching up to do, so many lost moments, but there would be new ones to grasp hold of from now on. She joined with Jessie, Ginny and Dolly and they took their drinks and went downstairs to the dress circle, opened the balcony doors and stepped out. The moon was bright, leaving a silver path along the water, ships silhouetted on the horizon. The snow had stopped and a blanket of white covered the road, the pavements. Out on the street, people called out the new year. There was a sense of promise in the air.

'It's a different kind of looking forward, isn't it?' Jessie said. 'Now that we're at war. Who knows what the year will bring? For any of us.'

Frances linked her arm in Jessie's, held out her elbow for Dolly and Ginny to do the same.

'Whatever it does, we'll be ready for it.' Frances pulled them close. 'We're the lucky ones. We have each other.'

She thought of Ruby, of how she must feel, alone on this of all nights. She could forgive her and Johnny would too. But for the moment she wanted to celebrate. She had friends, good friends, she had Johnny and Imogen – and at last she knew what happiness was.

ACKNOWLEDGMENTS

All the places in my story exist – the Empire, the Dolphin, the Fisherman's Arms and so on – but the interiors and characters are fully imagined. And as always, any mistakes are my own.

So many people helped me get the Seaside Girls in the spotlight and I'd especially like to thank Vivien Green, who has guided, directed and encouraged me the whole way. My magical editor, Caroline Ridding, and all at Team Boldwood who breathed new energy into the Seaside Girls and let them live again.

Once again, my everlasting thanks to the superlative Margaret Graham. I am one lucky woman to have her in my life.

Helen Baggott for Mondays and all the days in between.
It goes without saying that I owe so much to my mum and dad, Tom and Joan Lee, who loved me and my sisters, Dianne and Taryn, beyond measure. We really were the richest kids in town. Family was first, last and everything in the middle – it always will be, no matter what that family is made up of.

To my children – all six of them – because we don't do in-laws. I love them dearly. They are my greatest happiness, my grandchil-dren my greatest joy. I feel so very blessed to have them.

And I had to leave the top of the bill until last. To Neil, who left me alone to write even though he was bursting to interrupt; for all the teas placed quietly on my desk, and for a million other things, for the endless laughter – I always get 100% entertainment value – whether I like it or not! It's never been a dull moment even though many times I have longed for a quieter life – but the everyday tumble of life is where the stories are.

ABOUT THE AUTHOR

Tracy Baines is the bestselling saga writer of *The Seaside Girls* series. She was born and brought up in Cleethorpes and spent her early years in the theatre world which inspired her writing.

Sign up to Tracy Baines's mailing list for news, competitions and updates on future books.

Follow Tracy on social media:

twitter.com/tracyfbaines
facebook.com/tracybainesauthor
instagram.com/tracyfbaines

ALSO BY TRACY BAINES

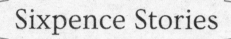

Sixpence Stories

Introducing Sixpence Stories!

Discover page-turning
historical novels from your
favourite authors, meet new
friends and be transported
back in time.

Join our book club
Facebook group

https://bit.ly/SixpenceGroup

Sign up to our
newsletter

https://bit.ly/SixpenceNews

Boldwood

Boldwood Books is an award-winning fiction publishing company seeking out the best stories from around the world.

Find out more at
www.boldwoodbooks.com

Join our reader community
for brilliant books,
competitions and offers!

Follow us
#BoldBookClub